DONALD SMITH is the author of two previous historical novels, *The English Spy* and *Between Ourselves*. He is also internationally respected for his role in the renaissance of traditional arts, Director of the Scottish Storytelling Centre and an experienced playwright and theatre producer. His non-fiction includes *Storytelling Scotland: A Nation in Narrative*, *God, the Poet and the Devil: Robert Burns and Religion* and most recently *Arthur's Seat: Journeys and Evocations*, co-authored with Stuart McHardy. A selection of Donald Smith's narrative and dramatic poetry, *A Long Stride Shortens the Road*, was published in 2004 to mark the opening of the new Scottish Parliament at Holyrood, and his book on the Scottish independence debate, *Freedom and Faith: A Question of Scottish Identity* is also published this year. Born in Glasgow to an Irish mother, Donald Smith was a postgraduate student at Edinburgh University's School of Scottish Studies, where the combined influence of Naomi Mitchison and Hamish Henderson diverted him from academe to the arts. Donald Smith led the final successful campaign for a National Theatre of Scotland, of which he was a founding Director. He has five children and one grandson.

Praise for Donald Smith's previous work:

The English Spy

Donald Smith is master of the spying game. THE SCOTSMAN

Smith does a thoroughly good job of conjuring up the Edinburgh of 1706 and the wheeling, dealing and politicking that went on to get the Union through the Scottish Parliament... Anyone interested in the months that saw the birth of modern Britain should enjoy this book. THE SUNDAY HERALD

Excellent... a vivid sense of time and place. THE HERALD

The English Spy *shows us how this story, like all important stories, is all, and always, in the making.* SCOTTISH REVIEW OF BOOKS

Compelling from the opening sentence to the last word. LIFE AND WORK

Between Ourselves

The evocation of atmosphere is superb. THE TABLET

The raciness of the prose Smith gives to Burns strikes the same tone as Byron... a convincing picture of the Edinburgh of the late eighteenth century. THE SCOTSMAN

Few of us would try to capture a great artist's voice in prose, but Burns' voice here is a convincing one. THE HERALD

Smith can certainly carry a tale – and who is to say his interpretation does not go close to the heart of a great love story. THE DAILY MAIL

God, the Poet and the Devil

As Donald Smith points out in his superb new book, Burns' belief in God is strong, though at times he is overwhelmed by the mystery of God and the difficulty of finding language to speak of the divine. THE HERALD

Donald Smith is a superb guide through this territory. LIFE AND WORK

Beautifully and clearly written I read it at one sitting with joy. RICHARD HOLLOWAY

Arthur's Seat: Journeys and Evocations, with Stuart McHardy

In walking the paths, we somehow write our own meaning and value into the stones themselves, so that they touch us personally. THE SCOTSMAN

The remarkable guide to Edinburgh's famous landmark… hidden secrets and long forgotten fables. EDINBURGH EVENING NEWS

Ballad of the Five Marys

DONALD SMITH

Luath Press Limited

EDINBURGH

www.luath.co.uk

First published 2013

ISBN: 978-1-908373-89-2

The author's right to be identified as author of this book
under the Copyright, Designs and Patents Act 1988 has been asserted.

The paper used in this book is recyclable. It is made from low chlorine pulps produced
in a low energy, low emissions manner from renewable forests.

Printed and bound by Bell & Bain Ltd, Glasgow

Typeset in 11 point Sabon

For my mother

Author's Note

THOUGH THIS BOOK enjoys the freedom of fiction, my purpose is to evoke a real person in her time. Who was Mary Queen of Scots? That question has perplexed me since childhood, and I am not alone. So I ask forgiveness if I have unwittingly trod on anyone else's holy ground.

However, through researching and writing, I have come to distrust the conventional readings of Mary as either a deceitful adulteress or a pious martyr. Both are based on propaganda and deliberate distortions which have remained insidiously influential for centuries.

I acknowledge my debt to many historians and biographers while exculpating each and all from my end result. Of the older books T.F. Henderson's *Mary Queen of Scots: Her Environment and Tragedy* is exemplary in its commitment to primary sources, though I do not follow his judgements. Antonia Fraser's biography, *Mary Queen of Scots* remains a good psychological guide. More recently John Guy's *My Heart is My Own: The Life of Mary Queen of Scots* returns to the sources, particularly the English ones, to shed valuable new light on the evidence against Mary. Rosalind Marshall is one of the few biographers to take a serious look at the four Marys in her *Mary Queen of Scots and her Women*.

I also owe a debt in formative years to Fionn MacColla's historical fiction. MacColla's work is sadly an unfinished and still largely unrecognised project. To Robert Crawford, I owe an apology for quoting from his fine translations of George Buchanan's Latin poetry and misattributing them to the Marys. I hope he will take that as a roundabout compliment. The full translation of George Buchanan's 'Epithalamium' can be read in *Apollos of the North* (Edinburgh: Polygon, 2006) edited by Robert Crawford. To Stewart Conn, I owe a huge thank you for much patient listening and acute observation.

I could not have tackled this work without my wife Alison's generosity. I apologise for organising a trip to modern day Reims before discovering that that the Abbey of St Pierre, along with Marie de Guise's tomb, had been destroyed during the French Revolution. History goes on happening.

Stewart Succession to the English Throne

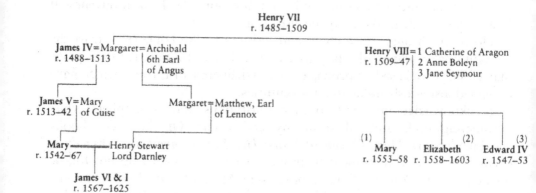

Henry VII
r. 1485–1509

James IV=Margaret=Archibald
r. 1488–1513 | 6th Earl
of Angus

Henry VIII=1 Catherine of Aragon
r. 1509–47 | 2 Anne Boleyn
3 Jane Seymour

James V=Mary
r. 1513–42 | of Guise

Margaret=Matthew, Earl
of Lennox

Mary———Henry Stewart
r. 1542–67 | Lord Darnley

(1)
Mary
r. 1553–58

Elizabeth
r. 1558–1603

(2)

Edward IV
r. 1547–53

(3)

James VI & I
r. 1567–1625

Principal Characters

James Maitland, son of Mary Fleming and William Maitland

Sir William Maitland, Secretary of State for Scotland

Sir Richard Maitland (James' grandfather)

Mary Stewart, Queen of Scotland, and, for a time, of France

Marie de Guise, Mary's mother and Queen Regent of Scotland

Mary Fleming, principal lady-in-waiting

Mary Livingston, lady-in-waiting

Mary Beaton, lady-in-waiting

Mary Seton, lady-in-waiting

James Stewart, Earl of Moray, half-brother to Mary Stewart

Henry Stewart, Lord Darnley, Mary Stewart's second husband

James Hepburn, succeeding his father Patrick as Earl of Bothwell, and Mary Stewart's third husband

Elizabeth (Beth) Hepburn, Cellarer of Haddington Convent

John Knox, Protestant Reformer, previously a priest

Sir William Kirkcaldy, knight and soldier

Margaret Kirkcaldy, his wife

Sir James Kirkcaldy, his father, formerly Court Treasurer

Sir James Balfour, courtier and politician

Sir David Lindsay, courtier and dramatist

George Buchanan, scholar and poet

Sir James Melville, courtier and diplomat

The Last Mary
Rheims, 1597

James Maitland

ON THE SECOND day the weather continued fine. The road was dry and on each side flat ground stretched as far as the eye could see. There were few travellers but courteous greetings were exchanged as each passerby turned their attention once more to navigating the noonday heat. What did they see in my lonely figure? A gentleman about his own business, French judging by his dress and Picardy accent. No one saw the Scots exile, a Maitland of Lethington loyal to the traditions of his family and kingdom.

I had gone from Paris to Rheims before and criss-crossed the plains of northern France to Louvain, Flanders and the Dutch cities many times. My business was with Scottish and English exiles, exchanging information, and planning for restoration. Now that cause seemed lost, the hope extinguished. James Stewart was clearly poised to succeed Elizabeth Tudor on the throne of England, uniting the two kingdoms under one Protestant monarch. Mary of Scots had been our last flickering light.

Why had my ancient country denied the faith of our ancestors and of the civilised world? The nobility of Scotland had bought the Church at the lowest price and sold our nation to the highest bidder. And my own father accepted one part of this bargain, before refusing the other.

Villages drifted by on both sides but I pressed on, keen to reach Rheims by evening. In Lothian the air is never windless, white cloud drifts even on a summer's day, and two hours of sun bring one of rain. With a sudden stab of longing, I saw Haddington clustering round the Tyne fords with St Mary's Lamp rising squarely from the valley floor as if planted there by some giant hand. Beyond the church tower the Lammermuirs are wearing a white shawl of snow. To see Lethington again, even once, and hear the raucous cries of rooks wheeling above the castle gardens to roost in the ash and oak trees planted by my father. He did not live to see them grow through my childhood years.

I wanted to understand his thoughts and actions. Suddenly that seemed more important than ineffectual pamphlets and secret letters going to and fro between men afraid to speak their mind for fear of arrest and torture. I cannot turn the tide of what now is, but perhaps I could tell the truth of what was and end the lies. Does truth still have power to convict?

Today I will meet Lady Margaret Kirkcaldy at the Abbey St Pierre in Rheims. Having sought refuge there after her husband's execution, she is now the Abbess, distinguished by charity and gracious rule. She knew my father and mother, and Queen Mary when she reigned in Scotland. Also living in quiet seclusion at St Pierre is one of my mother's dearest friends, Mary Seton. She was the last of the four Marys to leave the Queen.

· Through my interviews at the Abbey I hope to complete my enquiries, and then publish an account of those troubled times in Scotland. My first aim was to explain my father's actions but this has been a harder task than I realised at the outset: other voices demand to be heard as the story has so many tellers. Soon I became aware that, though her name is on every lip, Queen Mary's own story remains untold. Between hateful propaganda and slanted piety her true feelings and motives have been hidden or distorted.

By late afternoon the Cathedral of Rheims was rising on the horizon like a Spanish galleon above the waves. Coming into the town, I stopped in the market square to gaze in admiration at the towers which reach to heaven. I led my horse by the bridle past the Cathedral, turned up the Rue St Pierre, and approached the Abbey precincts, grateful for the cooling shade between the high narrow houses.

Lady Margaret herself greeted me in the guest chambers and ordered refreshment to be brought. She seemed unbowed by age or suffering, fine in skin and feature, and with a steady eye that combined mature beauty with authority in equal measure. I was moved to find myself in the presence of someone who experienced at first hand events that shaped my life, driving my father to his early death and his son into exile.

When we had exchanged the normal courtesies, I asked her about the news from Scotland.

'I am not closely informed of what is happening at home,' she responded cautiously.

'King James now rules in alliance with England,' I probed, aware that her husband had made this alliance his life's work and then turned against it at the cost of his own life.

'Indeed,' was her non-committal reply.

'The Earl of Morton was tried and condemned for his part in Darnley's murder.' Whether Morton was responsible for the brutal assassination of Mary's consort or not, he was certainly answerable for the judicial execution of my father and Sir William Kirkcaldy. 'He denied his guilt to the last.'

'The mills of God, Master Maitland, are slow but sure. Earl Morton showed no mercy to others and has received none. Yet I forgive him and pray for his soul along with all the rest.'

'His principal accuser was Sir James Balfour,' I prompted, 'the arch-deceiver became the final instrument of vengeance.'

'It is a sign of our troubled times that such a man should engineer the destruction of many, and yet survive all his victims.'

It was frustrating to question someone so reluctant to divulge her undoubted knowledge, or even her feelings. I made a last attempt.

'Word has come from England that William Cecil has died in prosperous old age.'

'The ways of God are strange.'

Lady Margaret was not to be provoked even by the fate of the man who contrived Queen Mary's end.

'We are enduring a wicked age,' I replied in similar vein.

'In just such a time our Saviour lived.'

I resigned myself to failure and changed tack.

'Reverend Mother. I wonder, might I ask you...'

'Yes?'

I felt her eyes on my face as I struggled to express myself.

'Forgive my curious spirit.'

'You are a historian, I believe,' she countered with something like amusement in her quizzical look.

'I am trying to write a history. My question is how you, a Protestant, have found peace in this Catholic sanctuary?'

Lady Margaret smiled for the first time.

'You must understand, Master Maitland, that the Abbey of St Pierre is a community of women, devoted to the service of Christ and living in harmony with one another.'

'Yes.'

'You do not grasp my meaning. We live in obedience to the Holy Gospel, and not to kings, or preachers, or even popes.'

'Do you not acknowledge the authority of the Pope?' I asked, genuinely surprised.

'Of course I recognise the Holy Father. But the Bishop of Rome has never troubled me in this place, or I him. Now, shall I call Sister Mary?'

'I would be very grateful. Thank you for your help in allowing me to visit,' I acknowledged.

'I thought long before agreeing. Not least for your mother and father's sakes. But I must warn you that Sister Mary does not keep well. Her mind sometimes wanders.'

'She is a good age, Reverend Mother.'

'It is not age that troubles her. Sister Mary is haunted by regret and guilt that she was not with the Queen when she was executed.'

'My mother told me she was sent away for the sake of her own health.'

'Mary Seton was the last of the Marys to remain with the Queen. She feels therefore that she should have been there, even sometimes that she was there. I shall fetch the sister and you will see for yourself how she is today.'

I was left in the wood-panelled room remembering that Mary Stewart had spent her last days in France within these chambers, and that her mother lay buried in the Abbey Church. The evening shadows gathered outside the narrow windows.

The door opened and Lady Margaret led in a bent, withered dame. I was taken aback to see Mary Seton so decrepit, having in my mind a portrait of her exquisite features framed by smooth raven hair. But as the old woman shuffled forward, I noticed that her white locks were neatly dressed and pinned inside her cowl.

'This is Master James, Sister, William Maitland's son, James.'

She turned a vague rheumy eye in my direction.

Lady Margaret tried again. 'Mary Fleming's son, James – he is writing a history of his father's life and of Queen Mary's reign.'

The eye shifted into focus.

'Her Majesty remained calm and undisturbed. When we burst into lamentations she said, "Weep not for me but rejoice, for today you will see Mary Stewart relieved from all her sorrows."'

The wavering voice trailed off, but the air around us had become charged with tension. The slight stooped figure seemed to grow in stature and authority.

'Sister, please take some refreshment.' Lady Margaret poured a few drops of red wine into a glass and added water. 'Tell James, Sister, about when you last saw Her Majesty, and how you cared for her through her long imprisonment.'

Mary Seton put down the glass having barely wet her lips.

'It was only with difficulty that we were allowed to attend Her Majesty on the scaffold. A block and a chair were placed there covered by a black cloth.'

I tried to interrupt. 'Please, Sister Mary, I don't need to hear such upsetting details.'

'Be quiet, young man. When she was seated in the chair the warrants were read. She refused the Dean's prayers and implored the mercy of Heaven. Holy Mary, Mother of God, pray for us sinners now, and at the hour of our death.'

Lady Margaret and I crossed ourselves but refrained from adding Amen.

'Refusing help, she took off such parts of her attire as might obstruct the deadly blow. Then commanding us to be silent, she laid her head on the block.'

'Please, Sister.' But Mary Seton's voice was getting stronger.

'It took three blows to sever the head from her neck. Then the executioner held up her head and the Dean cried, "So perish Queen Elizabeth's foes." But none could say Amen.'

She looked at us reproachfully.

'The head fell to the ground, leaving Her Majesty's best wig in the executioner's grasp.' She paused. 'Is that what you need to know?'

'Yes, thank you, Sister Mary, I am moved by your testimony. You have been of great assistance to me. I am truly obliged.'

There was nothing new to be gleaned from Mary Seton. She was trapped in the past.

'You want to tell the truth?' Two dark blue eyes were now fixed on mine. 'And end all the lies?'

The sister's head lowered, and she appeared to struggle with the folds of her habit.

'Let me help you, Sister,' the Abbess said, moving towards her. But Mary Seton waved her away, and with another tug she pulled out a cloth bundle, bound in soiled ribbon. She lifted the package onto the table.

'Take this.' She fell back in the chair exhausted.

Lady Margaret stared at the bundle in surprise.

'What is it?' I asked. But her eyes had clouded over once again. Without further delay, Reverend Mother raised the old woman bodily in her arms and half carried her out of the room.

Returning a few minutes later, she told me that the sister was sleeping quietly. She appeared to have suffered no ill effects. Mary Seton seemed more at peace, free from the anxieties that often troubled her rest.

'I shall leave you to your studies, Master Maitland.' Lady Margaret made no direct reference to the bundle which still lay between us, untouched. 'Please give my warmest regards to your mother when you next write, and give her our news.'

I assured her that I would. She started to leave, then hesitated for a moment.

'Fleming was first among the Marys. I admired her greatly. Please tell your mother she is always in my prayers and in my heart.'

Then she was gone.

As soon as I was shown to my room, I unwrapped the bundle with unsteady fingers, and laid out its contents on the table. There were letters, and a series of small bound volumes like journals or day books. Everything had been tightly packed. At a glance I could see four or five different hands and some headings that had been written by children. I could not bring myself to begin reading.

My mother had been Queen Mary's chief lady-in-waiting, but as I grew up she was reluctant to speak about the tragedies that marred her life. My father died before I could speak or listen. But as I looked at these papers, I felt on the verge of a lost world, which in some strange sense, was a part of me that remained hidden, unexplored.

I drew my chair nearer to the fire, picked up each volume in turn, and gently teased open pages that had been tightly pressed for so long. With the table on my right hand and a basket of logs on my left, a long night's vigil commenced.

Before leaving Rheims the next morning, I made a reverence at the tomb of Queen Mary's mother in the Abbey Church. As I lit a candle to the blessed memory of Marie de Guise, I pledged to publish her daughter's story, however incomplete, however shocking or intimate the matter, so that her true self might at last stand clear for all to see. In God's mercy, Queen Mary's own mortal relics may yet come to rest here in Rheims beside her mother, reunited in this holy place of peace.

The Guest Mistress bade me farewell at the Abbey gates, I turned back towards Paris with my precious burden.

Learning to Dance
France, 1548–1559

James Maitland

THE READER HAS a right to know something of his guide and author. I left Scotland as a young man, because of my Catholic faith, and went into exile in Europe. While my family, the Maitlands of Lethington, were conforming to a new political order, something in my nature stubbornly identified with an older family tradition. Queen Mary had recently been executed in England and my mother had remarried. I was dissatisfied with the condition of my native land.

I conceived the idea of telling the story of my father's life by writing a chronicle of those times. I had not known him when I was a child which made me more curious. Though Protestant by conviction, William Maitland urged tolerance, upheld royal government, and remained loyal to Queen Mary.

To aid me in my task, I had my father's state and private papers, which he smuggled out of Edinburgh Castle before his death. With these were the fragmented memoirs of his comrade Sir William Kirkcaldy, which seem to belong to that gallant soldier's last months. I have the testimony of my own mother, Mary Fleming, who was chief lady-in-waiting to the Queen throughout her reign, and the strange account of Elizabeth Hepburn which was recorded in Haddington Convent.

Travelling in Europe, I have gathered a narrative supposedly dictated by the Earl of Bothwell before he succumbed to madness and disease in prison, and a manuscript of John Knox's 'History', edited by his Secretary Bannatyne, which is in open circulation. Subsequently I have obtained, from a most reliable source, fresh documents, some in the Queen's own hand and some the private diaries of her ladies, the four Marys.

I confess, however, that this endeavour has not progressed according to my first plan. My father's purpose and actions have proved harder to discern than I had expected, for in his own writings he conceals as much as he reveals. I have found that we are divided by religion, even in death. Nevertheless, I believe that these pages will vindicate his cause.

What began as a hard task, cutting a straight path through the maze, appeared at points almost impossible. Sometimes as I read, these documents spoke directly to my heart: I was caught up in the emotion of the moment and enjoyed a poet's freedom. In other parts my mind questioned what was before my eyes, wishing to qualify or correct. Truth comes in many forms so I have decided to lay them all out, that everyone may judge for themselves.

Like so many others, William Maitland lived in the shadow cast by Mary Stewart. She is the true north to which every lodestone points. No one is unaffected by her life, yet the Queen's testimony remains hidden. Only the stubborn loyalty of Mary Seton, the Queen's last Mary, has enabled her voice to be finally heard.

In pursuing this work, however imperfect, I have found my own vocation after many wandering years in exile. For unveiling truths inconvenient to those who fashion worldly histories in their own image, I expect no praise or reward. But I can be patient since what we have seen darkly in a mirror will eventually be known face to face. For now our sight is imperfect and I must retrace my steps from the conclusion of the story to its beginning, for all the Marys.

Day Book of the Marys

He may be God, with a big beard. Long and grey in a white robe. His eyes smile.

Father Gardener. And this is our garden. He planted little bushes for our wall.

To make it safe. But we plant the flowers.

Ring a ring a roses
A pouchie fou o posies
Atishoo! Atishoo!
We all fall doun.

You must fall down. No, no. I won't fall. For I am the Queen.

Everyone is quiet. We were wondering.

Yes, this is my island. I am Queen here and my boat will come for us. They will row across for us again. I don't know when. We may live here for evermore. Don't cry, because we shall all still be friends. You be mother, Fleming, and give us bread to sop our broth.

Then we must be good and do our lessons.

Clever maids letters learn, foolish girls careless turn.

The Marys are my ladies. Beaton is clever, but Livingston loyal. Fleming, my cousin, must be first always. Seton, well Seton may bring my rosary, since she knows so many prayers from home.

But this is home now, just for a time as we are safe here.

Who must we be safe from? Our old enemy.

I do hope *Maman* will come to see me.

The sun is shining later so we go to see our flowers instead. Rosemary and Marigold, tall Lupin and blue Lavender. All in rows like our soldiers. Here comes Father Gardener with his nodding head. Run, quick, to the trees and grasses. We can hide. Find daisies, buttercups and Bride's gold dandelion for our hair.

Mary, Mary, quite contrary
How does your garden grow?
With bluebells and tortoise shells
With red rosehips and fairy lips
With honey sips and buttercups
With hairy thistles and maids' kisses

No, I won't, I won't. You be it. You won't, you won't.

But Fleming will decide. Fleming is fair, Fleming is just, Fleming is old, her birthday comes first. You be mother, Fleming. Mary.

We kneel in a row to say Hail Mary, Our Father, our Mothers. I see her bending down to kiss me. Lovely lady, come low to touch me, as you are so high. Your face soft on my fingers. Breath on my lips. I was a baby in her arms like Jesu.

Her picture is in the great church.

Sweet little boy, but we little girls have no mothers here.

Hands clasped, head bowed. No wriggle or giggle. I must show them how. Monks and servants.

One, two, three
Holy Trinity
God the Father, Spirit, Son
Holy Mary, prayers be done

I am not what they think. Messengers come, whisper and open letters, look at me. We are not frightened, though we are alone, on my island. I will not be theirs.

The boat comes. And my mother sails with her. She is here with me, and all my Marys. We are joyful, as she is a grown up Queen with lovely dresses. And I am a pretending Queen. Now we Queens play together, not apart.

We are going to my castle at Dumbarton where a great ship will come and carry us over the ocean

Big ship, tall ship, Galleon fine
Over the seas, with gold and wine

Are you coming with us, *Maman*? Will I go with you?

Never beg or plead, little Marie, for it is not proper. *Propre*, mine own.

We are all going to my castle, where the big boat will come.

Winds blow and rains fall, so we will chance all. But we are not on our own, since all the mothers have come. All the Marys' mothers, fine ladies four, and Marie five, bees come to their hive.

They take us to the walls to look out onto the river running, and the green banks flowing, and the rain falling, and the wind blowing. They take us to the boat with white sails flying.

This is not our lovely lake, but a little boat in big waves. Salt sea on my lips. Blow wind blow. For we will not leave ourselves behind.

White handkerchiefs waving on the shore.

Au revoir, Scotland.

She will come to visit soon.

Below decks on the big ship we stay. Darkness rolls, and heaves. The old enemy may come so we must learn our lessons and be good girls, playing quiet games.

Sea-sick, sea-sick,
Jelly legs, and dizzy heads.
Babies below, ladies above,
Roll the waves, in search of your love.

Fleming

Dear Mother, we are going safely to France. The boat is very big. I tuck Her Majesty up in bed. When the Marys are all in bed, I blow out the light and think about you, and about Papa who has gone away. I miss my brother very much. I am pleased that you are coming to France in the other ship. But I will look after all the little ones until you come. I love you very much, Mary Fleming.

Beaton

Dear Mother, we are going to France. The waves are very big so I curl up small in bed. I have read all my primer and know French very well. In France I will be able to speak in my French. But I expect we will learn Latin too. When I see Uncle Cardinal I will give him your love. I hope you and Papa and all my sisters are well too. I think about you every night, your loving daughter, Mary Beaton.

Livingston

Dear Mother, we are going brave to France. The boat is very big and sea wild. I sleep beside Marie every night to keep her safe. English may come but no harm. The waves are rolling. She goes up on deck and I would like to go with her. But I have to sick. I love you and Papa very much, but I do not cry in bed. I am your big girl now, Mary Livingston.

Seton

Dear Mother, we are going over the sea to France. Please do not be afraid. I pray every night for my Queen and all the Marys. I remember what you told me about our Holy Mother. Marie is sometimes naughty but we forgive her. Please remember me in your prayers. God bless you and Papa, with all my love, Mary Seton.

Mary

Dear *Maman*, we are very tired since there is not enough to do in the big ship. I like the wind and big waves. I get cross sometimes when I cannot go up on the deck. I still do my lessons. I hope it will be better in France, for we need our garden again to play. Please tell God to visit me in France, and come soon, as I do not wish to be alone. I and all the Marys send their love. *La Reine Marie.*

* * *

Beaton

A book of games, plays and notices, written at the Court by four ladies in waiting and their Queen.

Mary

It is a Folio, which is a Queen's book. Grannie Bourbon has her household book, and I have a household now.

Fleming

But this is different. It belongs to the children. No adult will ever be allowed to read this book. By Mary's command.

Livingston

Only those we allow will read this folio, or write in it. They are Francis, Elizabeth, the four Marys, Claude, and little Louis if he is not sick.

Mary

Only those I permit will read this book. They are Francis, Elizabeth, Charles, little Louis, Fleming, Livingston, Beaton and Seton. I shall sign this, Mary of Scots, for though Francis will be a king he is not one yet.

Beaton

All others are forbidden. It is secret to us.

Seton

Livingston has shoulder length chestnut hair. I bind this into tresses and wind it into a crown when we are at court, to sit under her linen veil. Often she likes the tresses to fly free, especially when riding, and hunting when she is permitted. Beaton is blond and very curly by nature. I trim and crop her curls which never lie down.

Fleming is brunette and her hair falls in delicate waves round her warm colour. I tie her hair with ribbons to train it back round her ears and neck. I love Fleming because she is so kind. My own hair is dark and quite dull so I cut it short and tuck it under my bonnet. I admit that this bonnet has river pearls sewn into its hem, which makes my dark hair look better.

Mary Stewart's hair is thick and auburn, almost red like a Highlander. When she lets it fall down over her shoulders she seems a grown woman, not a girl, but that is only in her bedchamber. I plait the tresses into coils which I wind round her high brow. Mary is beautiful, and she likes to look in the mirror as I pile up her abundant hair. Sometimes she leaves off her headdress and puts a diamond tiara on top of her auburn crown, in the bedchamber.

Mary

A Queen must confess more than a commoner or even a courtier. Grannie Bourbon takes me every day to the priest. We receive Holy Communion. But I like it best when we kneel together, Grannie Annette and I, before the Virgin. She knows how hard it is when your mother is far away. We pray for *Maman* far away in Scotland, and Uncle Francis and Uncle Charles and all the Guise. I cannot remember much about Scotland except for flowers in my garden. Then Grannie prays for lots of people I do not know. Many of them are in Heaven like Grandpa Guise, or like King James my father, whom I do not know except in a picture. He has red hair too. Last of all we say our rosary. Holy Mary, pray for us sinners now and at the hour of our death, Amen.

Beaton

Amo, amas, amat, amamus, amatis, amant. We are all learning French but also Latin. The teacher says that if we do well at Latin then we can begin Italian. This is France but everyone wants to be Italian in clothes and houses and drawing pictures. The Pope is Italian. I am not sure if the Holy Father is in fashion here or not. Queen Catherine Medici is the Pope's niece, as the Medici are in charge of everything in Italy. I like poetry and speeches but not histories even when they are in Latin. French poems are very good and Queen Mary has her own poet Monsieur Ronsard. Everyone thinks I am very clever but not, of course, as clever as the Queen of Scots. She is very fast at lessons and scolds all the children when they are slow. Especially Francis and little Louis, before he became ill and died. Boys are supposed to be more clever than girls so clever girls should pretend. Mary does not like pretending. She is to give a speech to the King and all the Court.

My uncle was Cardinal and Lord Chancellor of Scotland till the rebels killed him. I think he was a bishop in France too. Is that why I have to live here? Queen Mary's uncle is a cardinal as well, so that makes us good friends of the Church. Seton prays for us all every day. Mary Stewart, our Queen, says that in Scripture there are only three Marys but she has four.

Mary

I cannot write in our book today because I am too sad writing to *Maman* in Scotland. It is very far away. They say it is cold in Scotland but sometimes it is cold in France as well.

Livingston

Château means castle but in Scotland *châteaux* are smaller. Here the castles in which we stay are palaces. Except for Fontainebleau which is my favourite place to stay. We have many horses there and are allowed to go riding and sometimes hunting in the forest. At Callendar when I was wee, you could ride out of the castle and up onto the moors and forests. It was called Slamannan which is a Scots word. I am writing it down here so that I always remember names from my home. Beaton is a good rider as well as me, but Mary Stewart is best. On a horse she has no fear and would gallop ahead through the trees if the men did not hold her reins. When we are on horseback we are free, but when we are inside our palaces there are rules for everything we do, unless we hide.

Mary

Livingston is right. Fontainebleau is the best for riding because it is a royal hunting lodge. One day we will go hunting and not be held back. I will teach Francis not to be afraid for Kings should not ever be afraid. My favourite *château* is Anet, because it has the best gardens for walking and playing. Also it is Lady Diane's favourite. I think that King Henri has given it to her, because she is so beautiful. She is very kind to all the Marys but especially to me because my mother is in Scotland. Her skin is smooth like cream and she lets me touch her and try her oils and perfumes. There is something fragrant about Lady Diane and the King likes nice smells. I would like to be beautiful like her but I think my skin is too white. Lady Diane says I shall be beautiful and told the King and Queen Catherine. She is best friends with the Queen. I have no best friends but love all the Marys, Elizabeth, Claude and little Francis. Perhaps he is my best friend, but I like Diane most of all. The King wants me to be kind to Francis and to love Diane.

This bit was rude and was written by Elizabeth, but it has been scored out by Fleming.

Livingston

I love Lord James because he is the best rider and hunter. He is Mary Stewart's brother but is a bastard. I don't care as he is a royal bastard.
> Livingston must be more careful, even if our book is secret. Fleming.
> Unless we tell our secrets this book will be dull. Beaton.
> We should not quarrel but be like sisters to one another. Seton.
> Don't be so holy, Seton. We are five Marys and not three.

Beaton

Lady Diane has arranged dancing lessons for all the children. She watches while the musicians play and the dancing master puts us through the beat with a cane. I think he likes to whack the girls' behinds. We have to dance with each other, but Mary partners with Francis, even though she is taller. We would laugh but the Poitiers is unbending. The Queen steers him round keeping time, with a solemn expression.

Fleming

Her Majesty has had an audience with the King. She and Francis talk with *Le Roi Henri*. He is the Dauphin of France and she Queen of Scots and 'a special daughter of France'. They play with each other every day but converse like strangers. 'I am very honoured to meet His Majesty the Dauphin. I bring him the greetings of my Scottish kingdom, and of my mother Queen Marie de Guise.' I am her chaperone. 'We hope very much that your mother will come soon to visit us here in France', Francis stutters. 'Indeed, nothing would give our sacred person greater joy.' She plays her part guiding young Francis through the performance, like a game of toy soldiers.

The King looks on with dark eyes and his hawk nose, drinking it all in. He is master of the masque, and knew my mother. She came with us from Scotland but I have become more grown up since she left us to go back. Because of that man and his dark eyes. Sometimes I am afraid that everything that may happen has already been decreed. What does he intend for the Marys? Shall he send us away as well? I shall not leave the side of my Queen, as this is my sacred duty.

Mary

The King and I talked together. He called me his own daughter and asked me what I thought of Lady Diane. I said I loved her best of all which pleased him very much. Then he spoke about Francis as if he were a stranger. But I spoke fondly of Francis as my dear playmate and brother monarch. I said we would be bound together by ties of duty and affection. The King said that I was wise beyond my years – an old head on young shoulders – and that he had more profit in talking to me than with one hundred of his courtiers. Fleming was not present. We were private together.

Beaton

Mary presented her oration to the Court. I stood behind her, notes in hand, but she was word perfect. She declares that women should be educated because they are intelligent governors of the realm and of their own natures, if given equal learning. She was applauded, especially by the King. Yet what she says is denied by almost everyone. I saw Queen Catherine look closely at my mistress as if seeing her for the first time. Mary's brow was shining and her colour high. I never loved her so much as today, because she said what was inside me too.

Mary

Maman is coming to France at last. I hardly see her face at night any more. She will be here within weeks, or even days. My whole life so far has been for this moment. Now I shall not be left on my own again.

Beaton

We shall be going to Rouen as Marie de Guise will arrive from Scotland. Our Mary is excited but very tense, wound tight within herself. It is too much to hope, fatal to expect. Before we leave Paris there is a court ball. The great hall is cleared, the music poised for a pavane. Will the King himself lead a lady to the dance? All wait with respect. But young Francis comes to the floor accompanied by four pages. We bring Mary forward and she curtsies. He bows, and they turn into the dance, hand in hand. Everyone watches as she steps and glides like a Queen, hiding all her partner's awkward stumbles. The music swelled with applause; pair by pair the company takes to the floor in golden silks and crimson satins. We stand to one side and watch our Mary, slender in royal blue, our Grace dancing into the future.

Maitland of Lethington

William Maitland of Lethington

This is my father's own hand. He has left no record of his early years, other than these adult journals. They are full of his thoughts on the condition of the realm. He is very politic and questioning in the modern way.

Lethington is only a house. A valuable estate which one day should be mine. The house of my ancestors, a noble name. None stands higher. I will restore the gardens which I love, like terraces on the Loire. But I must prove myself first. I shall do this by always treating my name and my work with the utmost seriousness, but never my own self. I regard that with quizzical detachment and sometimes derision.

When everything dear to the house of Maitland is at risk, I am removed to safety. I was in France before and there is security in what is known. My father, too, was put to the schools in France. There he got law, and poetry. Good Sir Richard – courtier, diplomat and poet – and in his own way an enigma. Is he also detached, but unable to confess?

Our girl Queen lives in belle France, and is pledged to marry the Dauphin, so France is a safe harbour for loyal Scots gentlemen. And profitable, if I can fathom French designs. I am not sure if that is what my father intends.

Lethington Tower has been burned and our estate is a camp for Haddington's besiegers, Scots and French. This is what France has cost our nation. The English would make Lothian an Irish Pale, a fortified state from which the natives may be subdued or at least resisted. Are we heathen savages?

Which is why Scotland turns to France. Better an unequal ally than a conquered province. The English have a strangely blinkered view of their nearest neighbor, and we must be careful to live up to their prejudices. They expect bloody resistance with at least a dash of barbarism

But in France I shall see more closely what alliance means. Are we a province or a nation? We are destined to join England or France. Yet can we be our own still? He who discovers an answer to that riddle will stand behind the throne. It is a game of hazard.

The English invade at great cost to their purse and to Scottish lives. Yet French coffers too are emptied in the attempt to win Scotland back. Have we gained or lost? It lies in our Queen's marriage, as she may be Queen to four kingdoms, if Ireland counts.

The next stage of this drama will be played in France. That is what Sir Richard realised.

Puzzles are passed down through the generations. My grandfather could be inscrutable. I remember him well for he lived into a ripe old age, long after his son, my father. When his sight failed it was the task of my aunts to record his poems and other writings. But of his own life he would only say, 'The world is very strange and I have seen many changes.' A sphinx could be more confidential.

My father acquired a more ambitious creed, but no less upright. The clues are in these meticulous densely covered pages. Was anyone other than himself ever supposed to read them? I am in his labyrinth searching for my thread.

William Maitland will get learning, but in a style Sir Richard may not approve. My wits were whetted in the schools at Paris but I am no longer an idle student. A new world has been discovered but it is in our own minds as well as the Americas. I am a citizen of this new age, but derive amusement from the death pangs of the old.

The view from one side of the river is different from the other. Left bank and right bank. In truth you can hardly see the river for houses stacked drunkenly together, mists, and piles of barely floating rubbish. Then, every so often, floods cleanse the soul of Paris. The city closes round you, peopled by fantastic creatures of the day and night. All life is here.

In St Andrews you can always smell, and usually see, salt ocean. Edinburgh turns its back on the sea to live in open market squares, and lurk in secret courts or closes, but the hills and rivers are never far from your eyes. Even the gentle slopes, woods and pastures of Lethington are nearby – I can call them to my view when I am melancholy or disturbed. The streets of Haddington rest peacefully below the Lammermuirs, but Paris is a world unto itself, apart from nature. Man is remade here as the creature of the city, not of the country, or even the nation. Here is France and Europe, Babylon and Rome. Scots College and College de France. University and Palace. The old world and the new.

In the Scots College as a boy, I slept on straw and fed on gruel. But now I lodge south of Seine in rooms furnished with a bed that does not fold away, carved settles with arms on which to rest a book or glass, and Persian rugs before an ample fireplace. True comfort for one no longer forced to memorise a lesson. My present orbit is not the schools but Court. A Scots gentleman attends on royal France, courtesy of Sir Richard's guineas.

Though I read still in texts as well as faces. Like a physician who takes his patient's pulse while scanning a book of cures.

The young Queen, Mary of Scots, was received here as a child with royal honours. Her entry to Angers is remembered, because she was attended by four pretty little maids. A doll Queen, the lass held herself with solemn dignity. Prisoners were graciously released at her command.

All becomes slowly clearer for my father. News from everywhere arrives in Paris. Boulogne had been recaptured from the English. In Scotland, Haddington had been abandoned by its starving garrison, and one by one England's forts were dismantled. So in due season Marie de Guise came to France to share Scotland's triumph with her allies, and to see her growing girl, our young Queen of Scots. This was my father's chance to show his mettle and he takes it with his usual discretion. He seems more at home with French subtlety than Scots gusto.

At Rouen the Scots arrive, a straggling troupe of earls, courtiers, knights, wrestling with too much baggage, giving precedence to no one, fighting for place and lodging. My vain, proud, calamitous countrymen, bragging to all and sundry how they had defeated the English. They are a band of strolling players ready to play farce or melodrama alike. The French look on bemused and yet indulgent to les Écossais très fiers.

Amidst the drinking and squabbling, I make myself useful, advising here, cajoling there, administering my little store of experience. For the first time I meet Lord James, the Queen's brother. A sober youth, he holds himself aloof and canny. There is matter here to be probed.

As a Guise, Marie herself is taken to the bosom of the Court, enfolded in the royal embrace. With King Henri, Queen Catherine – the Medici – and Mary of Scots, she sits in state beneath a golden canopy to watch a grand entry across the Seine Bridge to Rouen. From where I watch beyond the stand tiers of godly beings seem to rise midst waving silks and banners towards the skies. And at their summit the monarchs sit like Jupiter and his heavenly council, clothed in light.

Drums and trumpets. The great cavalcade begins processing towards the bridge, at each end of which a towering triumphal arch has been erected. The arches proclaim an Age of Gold, religion restored with culture, learning, music and martial might.

First comes a panoply of flags and heralds all emblazoned with three crescent moons. Their motto resounds –'three crescent moons will fill the earth'. So Henri, King of France, of England and now of Scotland will command the globe. Yet gossip has it that the full moon is Poitiers his mistress, with her glowing form rising on the King. Henri likes to flaunt every kind of triumph.

Now come all the dignities of Rouen – nobles, merchants, councillors, guild masters, crossbowmen, mace bearers and notaries. I saw Henri lean down to Mary to pet his little favourite – ma propre fille. Did his consort look for a moment hard and sharp? A Medici look. The crowd roars as Rouen's soldiers march past followed by eighteen Roman gladiators whirling in close combat as they move along. All are swept into the city gates, and everyone turns to eat and drink until the next wave arrives.

If all Scotland came together to fashion a parade, we might equal the spectacle so far, with some tumblers and masquers added for satiric zest, rollicking up the High Street. But what comes next belongs only to a France, or the Empire. Even England might not attempt it, except in Henry Tudor's time. Gaze on imperial might; submit; obey: those are the lessons to be scanned.

The first float is drawn by four winged horses. Its charioteer is the mighty angel Fame, also winged and enthroned, with a trumpet to his lips and round his feet scenes of bloody conquest. Next comes the capture of Boulogne modelled like some war game on another float. This scene is accompanied by swordsmen, pikesmen, musketeers, and cannon hauled by plumed horses, caparisoned in silver. After them prisoners taken in the siege are dragged along, followed by more gladiators. And at the centre of the column, garlanded with fanfares, drowned by cheers, six mighty elephants – creatures of the Indies with flapping ears and a long snaking trunk instead of a nose. So Hannibal, so Henri. The rabble are completely taken in by papier mâché. I salute this art of painting and design: we do not have its like at home.

Scotland though is not forgotten. A troop of Roman warriors preceded by drum and trumpet, bear a line of banners. Dundee, Broughty Craig, Edinburgh, Eyemouth, Inchkeith, Haddington. Each one a conquest, repulsing the English claim to occupy and rule. They might be cities for all anyone knows. We Scots look on from the royal pavilion, in the lower tiers.

Henri himself, followed by Queen Catherine, our Mary with the other royal children, and Marie de Guise, descend to lead the last procession into Rouen. Mounted on a white charger Henri heads a pageant of court officers towards the bridge. Then all comes to a halt, for on a specially constructed island, two naked tribes appear, men and women. They hunt, cook, trade and then begin fiercely trading blows. Here is fabled Brazil to which France also lays her claim. The uncovering of nature, even in its secret parts, delights the multitude.

At the city gate the King is met by two children carrying a coiled snake eating its own tail in flame and smoke. 'Here is Time' was the motto. Suddenly the stage becomes a giant globe lapping at the fires. Rent asunder the globe reveals a mighty Triton mounted on winged Pegasus. Last of all the globe re-forms bearing an image of the King at whose feet this final scene is laid. The spectacle has reached its apt conclusion. Then all dissolves, as people fight to gain the Cathedral for a Victory Te Deum and solemn Mass.

I withdraw to read the royal proclamation issued that day to the Sultan at Constantinople and proclaimed at the Mercat Cross of Rouen: 'I have pacified the Kingdom of Scotland, which I possess with such authority and obedience as I do in France. To which two kingdoms I am joining another, England, which by a perpetual union and confederation, is now under my control as if it were my own self. The King, his subjects and his powers unite in such a way that the three kingdoms together can now be considered one monarchy'.

To this claim I must reply at tonight's feasting, flattering without ceding anything from the negotiations to come. For which Scot will guard his tongue in drink? I shall be prudent, yet eloquent. Here my usefulness begins: my presence on the stage will be noticed.

'How happy is Scotland to be favoured, fed and maintained like an infant on the breast of the most magnanimous King of France, the greatest Lord of all the Earth, and the future monarch of that round machine. For without him you would have been laid in ashes, your country wasted and ruined by the English, utterly accursed of God.'

When is he ironic and when sincere? Does this sow the seeds of dissent or display staunch loyalty? It can be read in two opposite ways, even by its author. Perhaps a letter was dispatched home to make his feelings clear, but has not survived. More likely William Maitland declined to commit his thoughts into anyone else's keeping.

I am beginning to discern the father whom I never knew. He has been accused of treachery, double dealing and deceit, a serpent of guile. Meikle Wily, they called him, the Machiavelli of his age, bent only on advancement. But his thoughts are politic, his words always in season, guiding and guarding the Scottish nation. My father plays a long hand.

To see them together is delightful and instructive. We are in the gardens, surrounded by nymphs and fountains. Music plays somewhere from a maze. The young Queen is aglow with charm. Her high brow gleams, auburn hair swept up and back. She is tall beyond her years and sex, but knows how to hold herself without stooping shyness, and to be gracious and courteous, while light dances in her eyes. She is still a girl for all the formality, full of fun and mischief though not without a dash of self-will, the natural hauteur of her station. Like me she chuckles at the world in secret.

Beside Mary her mother seems poised as a statue. Yet the Guise too has charm and beauty with eloquent features and the stature to command. Her figure is fuller and more mature, most gratifying to the eye and always clothed in a way that draws admiration. But there is a reserve, as though life has tried her and taught caution. The beautiful eyes appraise you. Are they green or almond or even grey? She inclines her head a fraction and listens with care, considering how to respond.

I am not the only one to be heard attentively. I have watched her manner with my compatriots, and with French courtiers. She is at home in both languages but only it seems truly at ease with her family. Yet they will send her back to rule Scotland, alone, and the mother and daughter so lately reunited will be divided once more. That is the Guise ambition – to rule through the royal houses of Scotland and of France. Their influence reaches everywhere, and the talk is all of Marie de Guise becoming Regent of Scotland.

James Stewart has been at court again to see his sister. For one so young he is close and silent as the tomb. Prior of St Andrews he may be by royal convenience, but he is no churchman. Nor does his religion look to Rome. I detect ambition rigidly concealed.

We converse at length about the Regency. He understands the game of power and hints that his own contacts in England, and those in exile, want a Protestant Scotland and eventual union of the crowns. He was trying to gauge my intent, but I managed to be confiding and indefinite. The Scottish lords will as ever bide their time to choose the most advantageous loyalty. Stewart the Bastard may be made of sterner metal than their type.

Twice he mentioned William Kirkcaldy of Grange, as if his stay in France had special significance. I have marked Kirkcaldy here at Court as a handsome hothead. It seems that John Knox too is still wandering somewhere in Germany in exile. He is the kind of zealot any nation should avoid. The Protestants offer reason and conscience in place of blind obedience, but Knox wants to endow his own doctrines with divine authority. Yet the Bastard remains in correspondence with this preacher,

whose reputation is high amongst the godly sort. Is Knox a principle for
him or a tool?
  Stewart is returning to Scotland ahead of the Guise.

Are our lives guided by providence or by fate? The men who will join a
Scottish ring around our Queen are already linking hands. William Maitland
meets all those who will mould events in Scotland. The threads were spun in
France, for good and ill.

The Court moves back to Paris. Kirkcaldy is also in town having obtained
a royal commission for service in the army. We agree to meet in a tavern,
The Golden Cockerel on the Île de la Cité, but when I arrive Grange
is ensconced with young Bothwell, Earl Patrick's puppy, who has just
arrived at the Scots College. My family knows the reiving ways of these
Hepburns who covet their neighbours' acres. Bothwell's cold gaze shows
that he knows that too, but disdains to care.
  But Bothwell is an amusing young blade scarcely into britches and
swaggering with self-conceit. He and Kirkcaldy make a striking pair.
Grange red haired, fair, locks and beard neatly trimmed, curled close in the
court fashion. Hepburn is dark complexioned with flowing black hair and
a youthful beard. The eyes are black too, though piercing and intense when
his concentration is aroused. He sports an earring and a broken nose as if
some vagabond was his mother; but then maybe she was.
  They are two military men discussing tactics in their cups. I am left to
one side as a duller, bookish gentleman. Young Hepburn is no sluggard
when it comes to the history of war. He argues a point about light cavalry
which Grange concedes. They move beakers and flagons around the table
like Hannibal amongst his elephants.
  We order wine with olives, then beef, and more wine. Bothwell waxes
in his cups, describing the whores he has enjoyed in Paris. First he will
take her foremost and then by the arse and then again. I see the disgust
in Kirkcaldy's eyes. His father, the old Treasurer, schooled him Protestant
Bible in hand. But Hepburn was educated by his uncle the Bishop, who
has eleven bastards at the last count. Yet the dissolute prelate of Moray
founded the Scots College in Paris. The ways of God defy any reason.
  I take my leave unnoticed while Kirkcaldy is holding Bothwell by his
flowing locks and banging his head on the table to wake him up. I cannot
question Grange tonight. What I have to ask cannot be tried within
another's hearing, even when unconscious. Walls have ears in whispering
Paris. Even the tables.
  It is a relief the next day at court to be flocked by Mary's attendants
flapping silken banners for some game or dance. Sunlight dispels the
gloom of Paris taverns, and a fresh breeze blows away night vapours. I can
shed grave time, and be innocent once more, playing amidst the trees at

Lethington, harvesting fallen apple blossoms under my mother's careful eye.

What a troupe of young beauty the Queen commands: Beaton with her ringed yellow curls, Livingston lithe and tall, and Seton with her wan face framed by raven hair. Fleming's body swells with all the promise of female fullness. Yet they are merely planets attendant on Mary's shining globe.

Kirkcaldy arrives resplendent in court dress, surmounted by a cap plumed in blue and gold. He is the centre of attention, the gallant soldier, mobbed by female devotees. Only Mary holds aloof knowing she is made to be the object, and not a source, of admiration. But her eyes betray envy, not of Grange but her more carefree playmates. These girls are no longer children in an orchard.

As the troupe is led away to lessons, I walk along a tree-lined avenue consulting with Kirkcaldy. In the open air we can be discreet. He came with a commission from the English Government to spy upon the French Court, where Scots have such easy access. But now that Mary Tudor reigns in London, English money has run dry, so he has joined the French army. Nonetheless his loyalty is unchanged and his message is that friends of England wish to count the Maitlands among their allies.

I do not declare myself, pleading Sir Richard's years and his devotion to the Crown. Yet I hint at sympathy, and a desire to live in amity with our southern neighbour. I am not against reforming Mother Church. All things in moderation.

We agree to keep in touch, condemn Bothwell as a callow roué, and part friends.

I walk back towards the château, hoping to see the Marys and their Queen, without the radiance cast by Kirkcaldy's sun. But everyone has withdrawn to their chamber for a midday siesta, so I go to mine and take up Machiavelli's treatise. All teachers hitherto are bairns compared to this man's probing of the human heart. Sophistries and calculations are laid bare like bones exposed beneath the surgeon's knife. Subtle Italian, your land gives us more than all the Popes of Rome. Speak it not in Paris where truth dare not be uttered except in the dark.

Day Book of the Marys

We have sworn that from now on this book will be for our eyes alone. We shall write down what we want each other to read, but no one else. Seton, Beaton, Livingston, Fleming and Mary R. Our words against the world.

Beaton
I am surprised that anyone should resist the Queen. But some here at Court say that girls should not be educated in languages, history and philosophy, since their work lies in the nursery and in their husband's bed. Mary's oration praised the education of women, and the need for women rulers to be schooled in statecraft. They say this is an Italian fashion which leads to depravity, and effeminacy in government, because our sinful lusts sway the judgment of men who should be sober minded and led by reason. Eve should be neither counsellor nor ruler in the realm. That is all very well in books, but if the Adams we know are anything to go by, Eve should be accounted paragon.

Fleming
Beaton writes what she hears in the court and reads in books we are not supposed to study.

Beaton
The library is open for all to see – are we blind or unable to parse a Latin verb? Caveat lector. Anyway, Catherine the Medici will not allow such slanders to be spoken against her. Is she not a ruler in all but name? May she also smile on Mary Stewart.

Mary
Why should woman bear alone the burden of Eden's sin? Is she not redeemed by Christ as much as man, and called to nurture, educate and govern where it is her appointed right? I summon Thomas More to my side; the wisest man in Christendom is my authority for female wisdom. Besides the King himself smiled his approval of my speech. Why be bound by old ideas?

Fleming
We have been reading in Plutarch's Lives. Cleopatra was a queen who let her heart be ruled by passion. That is the lesson to be learned.

Livingston
She took Caesar and Mark Antony to her bed.

Seton
I do not think we should debate things we do not know.

Beaton
Why else do we read but to understand what we do not yet know?

Mary
But was that passion or policy? I mean Cleopatra.

Livingston
Surely love conquers all?

Beaton
Whose philosophy is that?

Seton
We should obey Mother Church and all her teachings.

Fleming
Love is dangerous.

Mary
That is why we must educate our minds and learn to guide the human heart. Not least our own.

Mary
I shall write to *Maman*, since she is still travelling home. Where is Scotland? It is lost to my mind, but I can draw it from Ptolemy's map. It is far north from here, and flat in its lower part though mountainous above. It takes a long time to sail there especially if English ships attack. I could not go home with *Maman*, but must stay at Court in France. It is not fair to leave me behind. I want to be beside my mother so we can be queens together in my father's kingdom. I want to go there. What use is being Queen if I cannot command?

Fleming
Mary is very poorly with racking pains. When the pain recedes she lies without moving or speaking. Some say it is her mother's going and some that she has a fever which will not be calmed. When my mother left I had to be obedient and serve the Queen as before. It is a great responsibility looking after all the Marys.

Seton

I pray for our Mary to God's Mother, so that her sickness may be healed. Mother of Sorrows, by the sorrowful wounds of Jesus your Son, have pity on us all parentless and far from home. Amen.

Livingston

I have had enough of sickrooms, and will go riding with Sir William Kirkcaldy. He is a true Scottish knight.

Our Queen must have entertainment to recover, not solemn little Francis coming silently to hold her hand, or Seton always counting rosary beads. I think I know the game she needs. Have fun and forget.

Fleming

There is new colour in Mary's face, and she asks for fruit to eat. Praise be for we could not bear another loss. Her life is precious but fragile. It is our task to nurture and protect Mary since she is destined to play her own part in all this history we are supposed to read.

The Queen has the same lessons as Dauphin Francis. He is heir to the throne of France but she is already the ruler of Scotland. William Maitland explained it to me. Because Mary has come of age her mother can be Regent rather than the Hamiltons. They are very proud even in France.

Livingston

Hamilton's son, the Earl of Arran, called on us at Court. He rolls his eyes like a madman and drools in his food. There is something wrong with that boy and I pity anyone who has to marry him. He is a dribbler.

Beaton

Marrying is not the question. Government is. Mary learns the duties of Princes. Together she and I have read Cicero on public conduct. That was when she scolded Francis for not attending. He always wants to go and play like a child, and his Latin is hopeless.

Mary

I love the poets best – Du Bellay and my own special Ronsard. I try to translate him into Latin, Scots, English and Italian, but he sounds best in French – *mon coeur pensif, mes yeux, chargés de pleurs.* Why should I be sad? Is it that sweet poison that flows into the deeps of my heart? Who has stolen into my heart? You must guess of whom I speak.

Seton

The Latin poets are best for philosophy and learning. Such as George Buchanan, the Scot who writes in Latin. The French poets are light and frivolous. Most of the Scots poets are rude.

Livingston
Seton is a prude.

Fleming
No one should be called names in this book.

William Kirkcaldy came again today to the Louvre, and stayed with us in the gardens. After a while he walked along the flowering borders with Her Majesty, taking her by the hand and listening courteously to all her remarks. He is very handsome and a true gentleman admired by all, but I kept them in my sight as a chief lady-in-waiting should.

Beaton
We make too much of these Scots gallants. Have they nothing to do in Scotland?

Fleming
Beaton is shrewish, and was very rude to William Maitland.

Seton
He may be a Protestant.

Fleming
Perhaps, but he is very clever and will be Her Majesty's servant in Scotland.

Livingston
So he says. I do not like the way Maitland stoops over you and purrs like a cat.

Beaton
Let them all come to Court. Mary is Queen of all the Scots.

Fleming
We made marmalade today, as Mary is not receiving visitors. We tied on our aprons, and sliced quinces into a jelly pan. We smear each other's cheeks with sticky juices. Seton is the best jam maker of us all. We shall preserve our fruits in jars layered with sugar.

After our cooking we sang. Mary accompanies her lute like an angel changing her tone in harmony with the room or her mood. She is the best musician among us.

Mary
My little dog Francie is sick and cannot play. I hope that he will be better soon as I love him very much.

Beaton
James Stewart came to see Her Majesty. He was dressed all in black,
with a black beard and eyes. He wants Mary to make him Earl of Moray
instead of Prior of St Andrews as he does not want to be a priest. It was
more telling than asking, because he says he is closer to her in blood than
anyone else. He spoke about their father James when he was young. She
drank in every word and called him brother. But he seems very gloomy and
something about him scares me. He has a dark complexion and a black
shadow beneath his smoothly shaven cheeks. His big nose is crooked and
his eyes are too small. He is going back to Scotland anyway and I am glad.
Everyone there calls him the Bastard.

Livingston
I agree with Beaton. I did not enjoy his Lordship's visit either. James
Hepburn is much more amusing. His curly dark hair tosses and tumbles
when he shakes his head and bows close towards you, or kisses your hand
very slowly. Does he have thick lips? Or is that just an effect of his earring?
I think he is most gallant.

Beaton
Popinjay with his gold earring. A gilded boy with a bashed nose. His lips
make me shudder.

Livingston
At least he rides and likes dogs, which is more than you can say for
Maitland or Lord James.

Seton
William Maitland always takes me to feed my pony, as he is my cousin.

Mary
William Kirkcaldy is the perfect knight.

Livingston
Today we shall embroider, and then dance. Let us put books aside, and
trace patterns on the canvas.
    Join hands in a ring, then break and change and turn again into the
circle.
    When we dance with Mary we are stars and constellations moving in the
sky. We shine. But we are only circling round to receive her light.

Mary
I cannot shine without my Marys. Let us remain forever partners in the
dance.

Beaton

As long as Mary is in our circle she will be protected. Until we cannot bear the brightness.

Livingston

The herald has come to announce a royal festival. At last something is happening. I thought we might die of boredom.

* * *

Fleming

Queen of Scots and of France. What she has always desired is finally decided. To wed dear Francis and reign in France. God be praised.

Beaton

For Francis it is nothing more than a holiday or a new suit of clothes. He will have his playmate, his sister, beside him. As he was brought up to expect.

Livingston

Mary to marry. The whole Court is looking on with envy. Queen Catherine, Poitiers, the King himself gives place. Our Mary is the love of every eye. I love weddings and this one will be very special.

Seton

What will become of the Marys? Are we still to be closest in Her Majesty's household? I pray that it may be so. I want always to be with her.

Beaton

The Marys must all grow up. This marriage secures Scotland for France and for the true Catholic religion. Marie de Guise will continue to rule Scotland. It is the Queen's right and the Scots commissioners will have to acknowledge her. The Guise are triumphant behind the throne.

Fleming

The commissioners have arrived. Two earls and Lord James Stewart, broody as ever, and Beaton's cousin James the archbishop, the Laird of Dun, and my own dear brother John, Lord Fleming. When I see and touch John suddenly I long to be home. Will we ever be allowed to return? I do not feel that France is my home.

Livingston

Dreary commissioners are not interested in feasting and hunting. While our Mary is radiant in a whirl of parties and outings. Everyone attends on her joyfully, but old Erskine of Dun goes round with a Bible in his tunic. We are missing Kirkcaldy since he went home. Lord John is nice but married. Kirkcaldy is a proper man. Even Jamie Hepburn was entertaining, with his squashed nose. What kind of place is Scotland? I am not sure I want to return there.

Beaton

Livingston is bored and flirtatious. Why does she not court some French attention if Scots are not to her taste?

Livingston

So Beaton has her eye on Monsieur? Why not name names in our book? Fleming has a new correspondent. William Maitland has written a letter from Scotland.

Fleming

Maitland is made Secretary of State in Scotland. He is clever and kind and better than all the knights or gallants.

Beaton

Fleming loves Maitland. Livingston loves Kirkcaldy.

Mary

Now that I am to be married, I shall not write more in this book. Though I will still read it sometimes.

Seton

Maister Buchanan came today to make poems with us. He is very clever and becoming famous.

Beaton

Only because he was imprisoned by the Inquisition.

Seton

He was innocent of any heresy and freed. And when in prison he prepared his Psalms of David.

Beaton

Mary prefers the French poets.

Livingston
Only because they flatter her more.

Beaton
Does Buchanan not charm?

Livingston
He is too old, and smells musty.

Seton
His learning brings honour to Scotland. And his piety.

Beaton
I think he may be a heretic. Seton herself will become corrupted.

Livingston
Don't bully Seton. Must he always write in Latin though?

Beaton
He speaks it like a native.

Livingston
I thought he was Scottish not Roman.

Seton
We shall record our poems as they are completed.

> *Sacred Sisters by Mary Seton*
> Moments ago the poet's laurel was withered,
> The lyre was mute, I lost all hope.
> But now Apollo throws his shrine's doors wide,
> Delphi's in action and the sacred sisters
> Leap with fresh laurels from its glorious cave.

Livingston
Diane de Poitiers says Seton has written well. It is a very correct poem.

> *Epithalamium by Mary Beaton*
> Go, then, and blaze the way with wedding torches
> And laughter linking all your peoples' hopes,
> Prayers, good wishes. Francis, you go first,
> Sure in royal birth, a Prince of Hector's line,
> Clinch in your heart your lawful wedded wife,
> Your natural co-equal whom her sex

Gives you as one obedient to her wish,
Whose own free choice has made her now your spouse.
Beauty's finesse, high forehead, dimpled cheek,
The gentle light that's laughing in her eyes -
All show she fuses wisdom with her youth,
Effortlessly majestic, subtly lovely.
Nor does her cleverness, preoccupied
With all Athene's work, yield to her beauty,
But, educated by the nimble Muses,
Her wisdom nourishes profound content.

Seton

Everyone agrees that Beaton's poem is very fine. Poitiers says that we should all recite before the King but I could not read aloud in public. Let Beaton do it; she has the best voice, apart from Her Majesty.

To Francis

Your patience wins a prize which, had the ancients
Won it, would have meant that Menelaus
Never would have wept for kidnapped Helen
Whose beauty Paris knew he had to steal
Across the surging sea; whose beauty Greeks
Joined forces to win back. Yet in your case
Pale Venus would have given Priam's son
The lovely Helen with no need for war.
Francis, you're brave as any Greek or Trojan,
And you would fight to keep your young wife safe,
But Venus smiled on you and so did Cupid,
In giving you a princess close to home.
From infancy you grew up loving her.
The flame of longing made you a strong boy
And nourished the deep tenderness of passion.

Fleming

This poem is anonymous and is not for reading aloud. The author is a true poet.

The Auld Alliance by Mary Livingston

Scotland alone has lineage that holds
Two thousand years' of royal marriages,
Her people attacked by hostile neighbours
Yet always free of foreign domination.
If what you long for is a generous dowry
Then the Scottish fighting spirit is that gift.

When war ravaged all the world, and nowhere
Maintained its freedom in the face
Of Roman rule, one ancient people prized
In Scotland here unbeaten independence.
When the barbarians broke the power of Rome
Scotland alone was refuge for the Muses.
From Scotland Charlemagne brought to the French
Culdees to teach a rising generation.
Your wife brings you the dowry of a nation
Faithful to France for many centuries,
Linked to your people in a strong alliance,
Always an emblem of the winning side.

Beaton

Though Livingston wrote this she admits that Mister Buchanan helped her
with the history. Livingston does not know a lot of history. But she is a
proud Scot and so is Buchanan. He knows how to speak in Scots, English,
Irish, French, Spanish and Italian as well as Latin.

Marriage by Mary Fleming

But you, Nymph, worthy of a splendid marriage,
Though Juno and belligerent Minerva,
Venus and the fair, gift-giving Graces
Make you as beautiful as you could wish,
And though the chosen heir to France's throne
Should yield a sceptre to you and declare you
Tenderly his equal, you acknowledge
Your place as woman, and so learn to do
His word, setting your own authority
Aside in marriage, but, placing your husband
In charge, learn still to win out through your love.
Rigour is sweetened by obedience
And by obedience love is got and held.

Beaton

Fleming is trying to teach a lesson with sugared words. Will Mary start
suddenly to do what Francis tells her? Will Francis tell her?

Livingston

She will wear white. But it shows off her fair skin and red-gold hair. Can
it be lucky to wear white, the colour of mourning? No one could be more
fortunate, the happiest girl in the world. The dress is long and flowing
glinting with diamonds and jewelled embroidery. Her crown is golden,

studded with sapphires, emeralds, rubies. The court has gone crazy with talk of dresses, jewels, crowns, honours, gifts, titles. This is the wedding to end all weddings. A union made in heaven. And everyone must have their place, and their costume.

Beaton
The commissioners signed an agreement today, preserving the ancient rights and liberties of Scotland. Her sovereignty will remain intact, according to the Scots.

We are to walk in the bridal procession, but must not wear white. By order of Queen Catherine. I knew we should not be excluded. Where shall we be placed?

Don't be ungrateful and suspicious – Fleming chides us like an anxious mother hen. Fools, everything at Court is political. There are other papers being signed, out of the sight of our dull commissioners. If Mary dies her throne will pass to Francis. Till every debt to France is paid the kingdom will be governed from Paris.

Fleming
Her Majesty will not sign such papers. Beaton must not speak out of turn. We must decide the best arrangement of our hair. And our jewellery. In France we are among friends and family as much as if we were in Scotland. This is our home now.

Livingston
It's alright for Fleming. Who can I marry if we do not return?

Seton
We are sworn to Her Majesty's service.

Livingston
Mary comes to us late at night, laughing and crying like when we were girls. If Granny Bourbon finds out she will beat us.

Beaton
Beaton cannot be beaten now because she is a grown-up woman.

Mary
Tonight I stayed up very late to write to my mother. This is my last. All I can tell you is that I account myself one of the happiest women in the world.

Beaton
As we came out of the archbishop's palace a roaring wave of sound

engulfed us. Every window and gallery was packed. People hung from the roofs waving and cheering. Banners waved with *fleurs-de-lis*, and a few rampant lions red on gold.

We formed up on a walkway leading into an arched gallery. It was all open to view. Trumpets and drums. Then the Duc de Guise, a hundred gentlemen of the household, bishops and abbots, the royal brothers and uncles in shimmering court array. More musicians, the Swiss Guards marching in emblazoned tunics. I could not keep track in the swirl and clamour. Colours swam before my eyes. I was determined not to sway or stumble. But all eyes were for her, waving in white, red flowing hair beneath a sparkling crown. Francis walked beside her squat, dark, dumpy. Hats rise into the air all around. The roar was deafening. And we came on behind, far behind in the display.

We wound out onto an open stage raised before Notre Dame. Tiers rose on both sides lined with ambassadors and emissaries. Above a silken canopy of azure blue sprinkled with golden flowers. As Mary and Francis went into the Cathedral to hear Mass, the Duc de Guise stepped forward and cleared the stage so that everyone could see. Then on a signal the heralds hurled showers of golden coins into the crowd.

We went after them into the dimness of the church and the glimmer of a thousand candles. As my sight adjusted I moved forward to kneel, as Mary and Francis knelt before the altar. Time stands still: pure voices rose into the gloom. I wondered if we were in Heaven. Go in peace, the Mass is ended. Back into the light filled fanfares. More showers of gold and shouts of joy.

At the banquet I saw Mary's face wince, contort, as she sat at the top table. It was her headache. She turned towards King Henri. He signed a gentleman to lift the heavy studded crown free from her temples and hold it high above her head.

Soon her face was wreathed in smiles. She took the floor on Henri's arm. Then the revels began – jugglers, masquers dance. A mechanical ship, masted and gilded, came sliding in so Jason and the Argonauts could find the Golden Fleece. Shall we ever see such a day again?

No sooner was the feasting over than Mary Tudor died in England, her womb swollen not with child but with disease. The English are unlucky with their birthing. Her sister Elizabeth is Protestant and a bastard.

Mary has become the Golden Fleece, a prize which unites four kingdoms. She will join the crowns of England, France, Scotland and Ireland in one, crushing Spanish pride. Hers is the blood line – Tudor, Stewart and now joined to Valois. Proclamation is made in Paris and her royal arms are combined with those of England.

Mary Stewart has risen far above us. She is destined to reign in power and glory. What will become of the other Marys now?

Maitland of Lethington

From this time my father's journal turns to affairs in Scotland, where he has become Secretary to the Privy Council. It is as if the act of writing clarified his thoughts and helped him define things for decision.

He knows that every member of the Council calculated their advantage. But much of his own consideration remained undeclared. It is not fitting, he implies, or beneficial that everything be exposed to the scrutiny of lordly men. Or worse, to public gaze.

William Maitland has become a man of government. He is astute and analytical, in the Italian manner. He made his first incision in France. Now like a surgeon he cuts beneath the skin to expose flesh and bone. The symptoms of Scotland's condition were clear but contradictory. Maitland argued for legitimate succession and an English alliance. How can these be reconciled except in his devising?

I am in awe of my father's powers, young, untried, but far ahead of all his Scottish peers. Yet it is like observing the mechanism of some cunningly contrived clock move, without hearing it tick or chime. What is the impulse behind the motion?

Then the death of kings, or queens, changes everything. He has surveyed all the pieces on the board, when one essential figure topples, and every other must be rearranged. So it was with Mary Tudor and so it was again in France. Jousting, a lance pierced the King's eye, and Henri was no more. Francis and Mary were rulers of France now as well as Scotland. The fatal blow was struck by the hand of a Scots knight in sport. From such casual ill chance many consequences flow.

Mary and Francis should have come to Scotland as monarchs of a client kingdom. It would have been their nursery, their exercise ground. But now they were thrust upon a greater throne, leaving Marie de Guise to contend with England.

The wheel has turned again; the more Maitland reflects the faster events spun on.

We must act urgently, decisively.

The Privy Council will take direct control of our peace talks on the Borders. Kirkcaldy will be dispatched to secure an English alliance. Bothwell must be replaced in the negotiations. Brilliant horseman he may be, but this is a task for statesmen.

We may yet slip the French leash without war. But that depends on James Stewart and his zealous allies. Faction I know and understand, but Knox and the godly band have a kind of power that is more to be feared than respected. Are they pawns or players in their own right?

Fomenting everything, England turns Protestant again under Elizabeth, while Marie de Guise defends all Catholics in the French interest. Have we not enough to cope with in this divided kingdom without religious strife?

It is my resolve to steer the ship of state into stable anchorage, though the course be neither simple nor straight. The art is in the navigation. Events have called me to this moment and I shall not refuse my part.

This was no longer a game. My father was facing his first crisis, and things were about to get worse, much worse for Scotland, this small kingdom in a troubled world.

Mary

Dear *Maman*,

I hope you are well.

I was sad not to receive another letter from you, and fear a letter may have been lost due to the present troubles, for which I am sorry.

I wish you could come and visit me in France, and see how our lives here have changed. It is a long time since we were able to talk together. As you know I cannot come to Scotland because I have become the Queen of France.

I have my own household with a company of ladies and chamber maids, a dressmaker and jeweller, a wigmaker who tends my hair, and many other servants. I meet my steward each day to arrange household matters but it is the King's chamberlain who makes all the decisions.

My best time is picking which jewels to wear from the royal collection. They bring me so many pieces to choose from that I never wear the same items. But I have my favourites and the rope of pearls you gave me is the most precious of all.

Francis does not always keep as well as he should. I am not able to look after him myself since he is surrounded by the Court. Only sometimes at night are we able to be alone together as when we were children. We did not play at being kings and queens for long.

Please do not think any ill of me. I understand my duty and that this is what I was born to be. From my birth you have trained and guided my steps, and educated me to become a queen. It was for this I came to France leaving you in Scotland.

But, *Maman*, I sorely miss the Marys. You sent them to be my companions and my solace. They have been sent away to be schooled in French manners, according to the King's mother Queen Catherine. But the aim is to separate me from Scots company. I am to forget my native land and be wholly France. I am a slave to my duties.

Without Fleming, Beaton, Livingston and Seton round me, I am left alone. Can a queen be lonely in the middle of her household? I am certainly sad sometimes and miss my dearest friends. Please come and see me or at least write to ask for restoration of my Marys. The Medici may take notice then.

Yet if you come you will see for yourself how things are managed. My uncles are still at Court, but they have little influence. The Dowager Queen Catherine steers all. Francis must undertake what she instructs, and I am compelled to follow on like his shadow. I am watched over like a child. Diane de Poitiers has been denied the Court and I am left friendless.

I do not think the Medici likes me. I am sorry to write frankly. But I never had such looks and frowns from her before. She was usually friendly if sometimes indifferent. Now she addresses me coldly, fixes me with a hostile gaze when I venture an opinion, and commands my obedience in all things, directly or by subtle shifts and contradictions. She must have her way in everything without demur.

I am sending this with Uncle Charles' messenger, for I believe that even my letters are spied upon.

Please do not be concerned. I am strong within myself, and determined to make my own way as Queen. I shall master the art of government, since what you have always wished for me is to be a ruler.

I am very sorry for all the trouble in Scotland. Uncle Charles says that some of our subjects have risen up against us, incited by false preachers who despise the Church. Would they overturn God's order and depose their anointed Queen? I would like to come to Scotland and meet John Knox, till he answers for his doctrines. Grannie and I have you always in our prayers.

There are wars also in France, where religion is made the cause for bloodshed. Is this the Peace that Christ commanded? Francis and I do not care for violence.

Can you not come and visit me? Do not leave it so long that we become strangers to one another. I want always to have and hold you, mother, nearest to my heart. Your ever dearest and most loving daughter,

Mary, Queen of Scots

Children of Flodden
Scotland, 1543–1560

James Maitland

SO MANY ROADS lead to France. But that cannot be my resting place. I must go further back to find the start. France is the lure and distraction; my first quarry lies in Scotland.

In this regard my father contradicts himself. He sounds remote from Scotland, unconcerned with its history and intent on moving in a larger sphere. Only Lethington commands his affections. But his whole adult life was spent serving our nation. My mind returns constantly to the fate of Scotland, though my adult years have been lived in exile. William Maitland seems the exception, for my grandfather's writing is also devoted to Scotland. Yet I have met many Scots who wish to deny their patrimony and claim citizenship of a wider world.

We are all children of Flodden, that terrible slaughter, when the new century was still young. The flower of Scotland was hacked down by English billhooks and trampled in the glaur – earls and bishops, lairds and chiefs. But worst of all a nation's government expired on that Northumbrian hillside. The first William Maitland, my great-grandfather, fell there near his King, James IV. Often I heard old Sir Richard rue the day. Some were haunted by the ghosts who straggled home, others by those who never returned.

Our families, parents and grandparents, determine our fate. Or was my father right when he made power the force that drives the world? I try to put my trust in a higher destiny than human contriving. And so did she. Her portrait is beside me – Queen of Scots. Tapering fingers; auburn hair curving behind her white veil; the crucifix on her breast. She was shaping my existence when I was still in the womb. By the time I was fully aware, she was dead. Her life too was moulded from birth by family and power.

Once again after Flodden, Scotland had a child king, and all the factions sprang into life, like dogs gnawing at one single juicy bone. The fifth James, still a fledgling boy, had a mother to protect him, but she married the Earl of Douglas, leaving her infant son to the mercy of his guardians and their violent squabbles. This marriage was to have its own consequences much later, twining anew the thistle and the rose in Queen Margaret's grandson, Henry Darnley. He too was a child of Flodden.

But who can form or even guide a king? Many have tried. Lindsay the Lyon Herald was the nearest James came to a father. The wise old courtier tried to shelter his Prince's innocence, but our natures are curiously fashioned and so it was with James. He became wary and secretive, possessing all the craft and pride of the Stewarts without their open-handedness or winning charm. James assessed those around him with constraint and calculation. They in turn bargained for control, and enticed the bairn with adult favours.

Like all the Stewarts, James followed the chase from an early age, bringing down deer, wild cattle, wolves, boar and badger. It had been his father's passion and so it became his. James IV had also been a courtly lover, wooing the most beautiful of noble ladies to sire royal bastards. The son was corrupted too early by amorous pleasure. As soon as he won his freedom from rival factions, James turned vagabond to go out among the people disguised as some guidman yokel or licensed beggar. In this way he threw off the boredom of court manners to pursue sexual adventure wherever it could be found.

This was not the example expected by churchmen from their monarch. As he grew to manhood the new King James observed forms and habits of religion without conviction. He toyed with the beliefs of reformers, while steadily plundering the Church for his own ends. 'If you don't behave yourselves,' he would jeer at the bishops, 'then I'll give you some of Uncle Henry's English medicine'.

In one way, James was wholly his father's son. He sought recognition as a Prince of Christendom, not merely King of Scots. Such pride drew him steadily towards France and the Pope, for what lustre rested in taking second place to Henry the heretic? So James sought a French marriage and continental power. When his first frail flower, the Princess Madeleine, withered in our northern climes, he sent his rising statesman Cardinal Beaton to woo a second French dowry.

Marie de Guise proved tougher stock than poor Madeleine. She settled into her new homeland, holding Stirling Castle as her personal fiefdom, and gradually she won the respect, if not the love, of her moody husband.

But conflict with England again crept closer. Unable to back down, James led an unpopular and disorderly campaign into the Borders, where he was humiliated on Solway Moss. At Flodden the Scots fought a disciplined battle and stubbornly stayed to die on the front line around a king resolved on hand-to-hand combat. Solway Moss brought little loss of life, except for James. Catching an infection in the baggage train, the bedraggled king retreated north. Arriving in his beloved Fife he had to stop frequently at friendly houses, until at last he reached the royal hunting lodge of Falkland where he took to his bed.

Within days news came that his second Queen had given birth to a healthy baby girl at Linlithgow. Taking this in the Scots way as a final omen, James turned his face to the wall and died. Mary's reign as Queen of Scots had begun, even as her first cries subsided at the nipple of her wet nurse.

Sister Beth

I'VE NO MIND of my own to write this but sister, and I will call her sister, Francesca Clare keeps on at me, licking her lips like a pet cat about to swallow a robin.

'Think what you've lived through.'

'Aye indeed. Once is enough, thank you kindly.'

I pull the shawl, woven from good Lammermuir wool, more tightly round my sagging shoulders. Another log onto the blazing hearth.

'Be a dear now, Francesca, and fetch us a warming glass of claret.'

Masses cease, except the priests are hidden in holes, but the nuns of Haddington will have their winter fuel, and their rights to French wine. Thank God for his comfort. Did not the French lay our poor town waste, and the English as well? But custom and law endure. For my lifetime at least.

It was the nuns learned me my letters when I came here barely more than a lass. I can read a breviary with the best but writing comes hard now my fingers are clawed by age. So Francesca bustles round with quill and ink, and stares at me like a dog waiting its bone.

'I can write down what you remember.'

Plump lips moisten as if she were about to nuzzle some young fellow. All that can be had now for the asking. Only she's fat and I'm an old hag. But I wasn't born to ugliness, not at all, which was the trouble that brought me here in the first.

Alright, I'll try, from the beginning if it can ever be found, for there's always something that starts what began before it started.

A good sup warms the gums, whatever you chew.

My mother was a skinner's daughter from Haddington who married well to a cousin of the Hepburns, the Lords of Hailes and then Earls of Bothwell. You see she had my bosom and a silken face to go with her swelling paps. And we grew up neighbours to the Sinclairs of Morham, cousins anyway, which was important after, as Marion their daughter, who often watched me when I was little, married William Knox who was a follower of Bothwell's in Haddington, which caused me later to meet her son John, but God knows I will have the whole tale a bourach. Smudge that bit out for it comes later.

It's the Hepburns that matter the most here – and still matter if truth be told – and Earl Adam died on Flodden field fighting for the King. So young Earl Patrick came into his own even as a child, just like the new King. And he was in the hands of the churchmen, his Uncle the bastard who became Bishop of Moray, but there was little religion to show for the whole clanjamfrie, only money and lands and court office when it could be had.

The young Earl was born to trouble for like all his kin he was always raiding on the Border in Berwick and down to Liddesdale, one time pretending the King's justice, then another allying with England if there was more to be gleaned from that airt. The first Earl Bothwell gained lands and title by helping James IV have his father killed. The old king called for a priest in the cottage where he fled to shrive him, but instead got a blade in his vitals. Peace be on him.

Anyway, Earl Patrick is the one to be dealt with, by me onyroads. He was a long lanky fellow, pasty white in the flesh but very proud with it. He slid his eye past you and then back up from behind. He was a boy with the freedoms of a man and he soon picked on me, coming to my father's farm offering release from rent or service. And the eyes slid round.

Fool of a girl, more flattered than afraid, I thought me something special running to the woods to meet the young earl. And he took me in hand till by one shift or another we were lovers before I was ever virgin.

So then my belly began to swell and we seemed happy, till glowers began at home. And I was still full of health, asking him when I would be wed and carried off to live in Castle Hails where it towers above the river – not rogered in the woods around.

Aye let a tear drop slow, for never was trusting innocence so abused. Hepburn I was by flesh but of low degree. Lanky Pat was pleased to see his manhood proven but not to marry the mother. Everything was arranged without my knowing. Wealth and degree governs all, Francesca, and so it will be till the end of time, whatever John Knox had to say on the matter.

They took my bairn girl from me. Even where I lay in bloody sheets holding my own scrap of life to a sore stiffened nipple. And carried her off to Hailes where I never saw her again, even when I went there later. What happened to the lass? She comes later as well, God preserve us. Did even Mother Mary see such sorrow, before the end that is, but there was no end for me not even a beginning. Put that down, sister, for in this man's world it is woman's lot to suffer, till she shifts for herself, and then she's pilloried for a daughter of Eve, if she cannot be secret. That has been my bane throughout, the having to be secret, to my own cost, as you shall hear. Fill the glass for this next is hard to tell.

They came by night with a cart, and muffled my howling in a sack, like I was for jail or the stocks. But then I was brought to convent – not here, goose, but to the proper buildings we had then, other side of Tyne. The richest convent in all Scotland, though little I cared as the metal grilles clanged shut on young flesh. How I grat and ached, but that was a beginning too. Beth Hepburn cellarer and guest mistress – she was what came of it all. The Prioress was Hepburn, too, but highborn. They had it all in hand, the earls, though she was kindly and let me settle down in my own way.

Little did she know. Ten paternosters before another word is spilt. We're holy sisters yet, not blaspheming Protestants. One glass for comfort, two for joy. Three for digestion.

Do I think much of Pat? Not at all, and very little then. A slimy fish that could wrap his tail round you if he had a mind. So bit by bit I settled down and forgot my troubles. Word comes that the young Earl is to wed Agnes

Sinclair, Lady of Morham. Good luck to her thinks I, she'll be needing some, and so it turned out. But I was less bothered than interested since Agnes was a high up cousin of Marion, who was already married in the town to one of the Earl's men – did I tell that before? William Knox. And she had two fine healthy boys.

Sometimes Marion came to visit, for she was like a young auntie to me, and saddened by what I had suffered. Folk came and went freely then in the convent, which is hard to think on now when it is all destroyed. There was a gate and court, a great square yard round which each sister had her apartments. Aye, Francesca, rooms, not squeezed into this small house, since most were well-born, and even I was a Hepburn despite all.

There was a chamber for receiving visitors that opened into a great dining hall for feast days, though sisters would eat in their own rooms at ordinary times. Behind the hall were kitchens, stores and other offices, administering the farms and rents. There was money and lands aplenty then. Where did all that go, Francesca? To filthy Protestants like Maitland of Lethington, and even, God forgive him, Earl James. Never mind that for now. I was happy enough, and Prioress trained me up to manage the stores and kitchens. So I always fed well which was a comfort.

The chapel was at another corner of the square, set back from the public road, and they kept the Hours there, those who were able, and a priest came each day to say Mass. Beyond the main buildings, near to the town as you know, the Church of St Martin was ours as well. Crimson robes, gilded carvings, silver cups, incense and music. All roofless now. What a wreck came on mother Church. Protestant English and French cannon by turn. Honest townsfolk put to wrack and ruin whether they loved the old ways or the new, though most preferred the old.

Trim your quill now, Francesca, for this is what you need to hear. Someone will make use of this beyond our town, aye and poor Scotland. Yet I would be loath to abuse him were he not dead. For the dead can't be hurt, no more than they already suffer in Purgatory for their sins. And surely he resides there, though if Protestants don't hold with it maybe they go straight to hell. But not Master John, for he was religious in his soul, though driven by fleshly desires, as all young men are and should be, else how would humankind survive? Don't leer so, lassie, it's not becoming for a Sister of Christ.

Thank you, Francesca, I shall. It's a comfort in such times, not to be denied.

My dear Marion, and her husband William, died of the plague. May she rest in Paradise for there was not a single bad thought in her soul, whatever buboes pustuled her body. The love she lavished on her children, especially gentle earnest little John, for he was her favourite, wins merit in Heaven. Maybe she felt she had married beneath her so she would nurture such a special child that all would come right for Sinclair and Knox. I can't remember what year, but the convent was sealed up from the town for six months till the pest cleared. The two boys though were fine enough for their loss, and went to their Aunt Elizabeth at Samuelston, where she was married on the Laird.

With the bit of money left them, those lads, John and William, received the best of education. But it was John who stood out, as Marion always said he should. From grammar school he went to university and was ordained the youngest ever priest in Scotland.

Haddington was proud, but then came a reverse. There was no preferment for Father John. By rights he should have gone to Europe, which he later did in other sort than ever Pope intended, but money seemed lacking. Besides, some said Samuelston was overfond of Luther's teaching, which was treason. So John came home to attend as priest at St Nicholas Chapel, which was in the Laird's gift, but a down coming for the brilliant boy.

From there the young priest came in turn to serve Mass. I thought to go and see his mother's son. What a small pretty man, with big shining eyes, long nose, fresh-face beard to fill out his backward chin, and dainty hands. And his voice rich and deep beyond this slight, neat frame, with something feeling for Christ's pain and Holy Mother Mary. Had he himself not suffered loss? From that time convent chapel always filled for Father John, and he was made favourite for Mass priest.

I spoke to him about his mother and told him to come after Mass for sustenance. And so he did by habit, coming to my quarters by the kitchens to enjoy a hearty feed before riding back to Samuelston.

I own my fault, Francesca, in letting such a habit grow into friendship. It was not his thought or my intention. Yet he was young and sometimes melancholy as if there was a loss in his affection and a need for comfort. I was fuller now in body but well-formed and my flesh was apt for love. Aye, you may stare, but nature speaks beyond these robes and vows, and I was not meant for chaste denial. I had not sworn to such an oath, and my desire was thwarted.

Don't gape – just write down the story now you have me bothered into telling it. You know the power of wanting as much as I do. God knows I've heard you moaning in your bed so you may give over preening and simpering like a holy idiot.

He knew little but learned fast my John, attentive to a woman's body as if it were his holy mother. Out of tunic he was fine boned, lean, and muscled, a pretty man. He loved the naked, pressing on my skin, touching, stroking like a pet lamb. From youthful fumblings we came to play in earnest, not once or twice but every week and sometimes more if it might be contrived. His hair was brown but auburn at the breast creeping down to red tangled roots around the member. Don't write that, goose.

For more than a year we were bound, sated. Yet in our coupling was little joy. I felt my womb scarred and barren. The more I knew it hopeless love, the more I demanded. He seemed brooding, even in despair. Why was he discarded, unknown, left prey to secret sin? Aye, I'm sure he thought it sin, which is only nature's way with all her children. This was not enough: he wanted more, to have his specialness made known. But he knew not which way to turn.

Each day he came to serve the Mass his slender hands touched God; I felt it on my flesh – this is my body. But he was careless, unseeing what he handled. I was unable to confess, or be shriven. What could I have told? They would have run witless to expel me.

I am not sorry stealing that pleasure to myself; I am glad, for my love was already stolen, broken. Listen to me now, Francesca, there may be one love then years of solitude. See, lass, let's cry together. Feel these old arms round you for Mary Mother holds us safe. Let the devil do his worst elsewhere. There, there, that's enough blubbering.

I went to stay three nights at Nunraw Grange. There was farm business for sorting, and he came to see me there. He could lie in my chamber without let or hindrance. That was the best, out of sight or hearing, I fed him dainties, tended every need, and made my body serve his passions. But on the third day he rose and began to shut himself away from me. I saw his countenance close, even as desire sank. He was strangely quiet, was Father John, as if expecting some inner visitation. Did he have a foreknowing gift, even then?

That evening he took horse for home and I knew he would not come again. Something else was stirring; his time of waiting was nearly over. The days of destruction were upon us. His time for me had ended.

Was that love or a devilish passion, I know not? He went on to the Devil's work, but it was my time, Francesca Clare, not his. For all it was or could ever be, there was no other. Strange fruit. I never had another man that moved me like him. Sometimes, I think everything else has been a dream. Or was I dreaming then?

Dear God, for Christ your Son and all the Saints, let's have a cheerful supper and forget such sorrows. Old sins are long since paid, while we are still alive and breathing. What enters in by the mouth cannot defile, thanks be to Him.

Kirkcaldy of Grange

RIDING INTO ST ANDREWS behind my old master, the horse's breath froze on grey air, hooves on North Street cobbles. Lindsay's back swayed with the horse, straight as a staff, the way he teaches all young knights to hold themselves at ring and ball and joust.

Was this my becoming Protestant? Or was it before? Father had Gospels in the English tongue, and was always reading, quoting how the Church of Rome was Antichrist, but especially the cardinals and archbishops who prise the King's ear from his loyal servants.

And then the King, defeated on the Solway Moss, was dead. Horses clattering into the yard, I came out knowing my father was away on the campaign. War brings trouble even at home. I faced this on my own, no longer a boy. Mounted valets on each side – they're holding him up, tied to the girths, and leaning on the horse's neck. White, ghastly white, streaked with vomit.

'Kirkcaldy, Kirkcaldy! A couch for the King.'

Unstrapped, he slumps into their arms. I lead the way calling for cloths, a blanket, and warm water. He retches in the passage. Is my father safe? The King's army? I dare not ask. The women come running. As we lower him onto a bed the stench is overpowering. This is the smell of defeat, disaster. My King rotting in his own foul fluids. Dissolution of our nation and all carefree ended.

Good choleric Sir James, the old Treasurer, retired to Hallyards and stared at the logs burning. My father was suddenly worn and feeble. But I returned to Court and continued apprentice to Sir David Lindsay – proud Lyon Herald, stern in speech, until his players opened their mouths and spoke free thoughts.

Crouching in the minstrels' gallery, I would catch every word. The King was still in his high throne then surrounded by churchmen and earls and knights, aye and ladies of the realm. He had his eagle eyes on them. The feast was sated with jugs of wine going all ways, when the fool scampers cap and bells to cry an interlude.

> My great *grandpère* was Finn McCool
> Who dang the devil, and made him yowl
> He had a wife, of giant size
> Who in the stews with him lies
> And spits Loch Lomond from her lips
> Fire and thunder from her hips
> And when she rifts, the heavens lift,
> So do we mark this holy day
> Come and listen to our play.

No one notices or even listens. The players wander in – courtiers, bishops, townsfolk, and then a king. Chatter falls away. A poor man, Jack Commonweal comes, asking for the king, and they point out the player. This is not the King, says he, and suddenly everyone is listening. No, no, the King is the one who hanged Johnny Armstrong the outlaw. Only he forgot to bring justice to the poor. Because the churchmen and barons are taking their wives and daughters, and harrying them for taxes.

Next a ragged widow enters, lamenting and denouncing the priest for demanding her last cow before he would bury her husband.

Silence deepens.

Wise experience comes to back up the complaints and the player King vindicates their plea. No one attends the final dance and caper; all eyes are on the monarch. Can he have sanctioned such license? By his own Lyon Herald

James seemed sunk in his seat, eyes veiled, a countenance turned away to his own thoughts. The narrow features ringed by brows and beard. No one dares applaud and the players stand at a loss.

'Archbishop,' he snarls abruptly. 'If you don't mend your ways, I'll send six of you to England to learn better.' He signals the interlude away, and music commences. Lindsay stands behind the throne, gaunt, unbending. Is he a Protestant?

We turn into a courtyard. That King is dead, streaked with vomit. Only the Player King survives.

I climb down to hold my master's reins, and the old courtier dismounts stiffly. A servant comes to guide Sir David Lindsay up the steep outside stair. 'Follow up, William', he says. 'You might learn something.'

Through a lobby he goes, with that careful step of the elderly, and an inner door swings open. The figure by the fire seems shrivelled, ancient by comparison. Shrewd sharp features tucked under a warm woollen cap. Veined skeletal figures reach out towards the heat.

'Lindsay, come in and rest your legs.'

'It's a cauld sough.'

'You mean the weather, or the universe breathed on by God's Holy Spirit?'

Old eyes gleam with wit.

'You're too sharp for me, Doctor.'

John Mair chuckles drily, or clears his throat. An almost translucent hand gestures towards the other side of a roaring fire. 'Who's that?' I was in the doorway.

'William Kirkcaldy, the Treasurer's son. He is in my care at court.'

'Go to the kitchen, lad, and they'll feed you.'

I step back into the lobby and draw the door nearly closed. I want to hear.

'I remember when I was sent first sent to Court service.' It's my master's voice. 'He's a ready youngster, though his father's been broken by events.'

'Things are broken, Lindsay, and we must depend on the next generation to make and mend. Pour a glass for us, Herald, we don't stand on court ceremony here, poor scholars as we are. A few years back I taught a brilliant boy from Haddington, John Knox. He was first in all studies, granted papal license as the youngest priest in Scotland. Where is he now? No place, no patronage, all his promise sunk in obscurity and resentment. A nation that eats its own young makes an ill diet.'

Behind the door, I felt sympathy for a youngster cast adrift in this hostile world, like me. It was the first time I heard his name.

'The Church needs reform. The money meant for priests provides luxury to prelates.'

'Or to the King's bastards, Lindsay. I hear you've written a play.'

'More folk hear about my Interlude than listen to what it says.' From my spying angle, I saw Lindsay draw a roll of parchment from his jerkin and lay it on a reading stand propped against the philosopher's chair.'

'Is this a philosopher's study – clerks' plays and vain mysteries?' Mair chided.

'They are the people's scripture, since the Church gives them no other,' my master retorted.

'Are you turned Lutheran now?'

'No, for God requires our good works as well as our faith.'

'Without goodness there is no truth, no divinity.'

'But the Church cannot dispense goodness like two-penny candles. We need God's grace.'

'And our own free will.'

'Aye, if we can win such freedom.'

'Only Christ's sacrifice can give us freedom.'

'The Mass is a sacrifice.'

'To deny that is blasphemy. You know there must be ceremony, ritual and worship if our souls are to be nurtured. This is the miracle of grace, God made flesh, the creation restored, renewed.' The old man's face was suffused with clarity.

'The Church's ceremonies are sold like worldly goods, Doctor, to feed the avarice of popes and cardinals.'

'You are right. The Church must be reformed by its bishops in council and not governed by worldly tyranny. That is what I fear, Lindsay, that the snares of power will bind the body of Christ till all is broken, torn down, beyond repair. The spiritual life will be extinguished; the work of God's Saints in Scotland overthrown.'

'Or find a new form.'

'You will turn Protestant.'

'No, an old dog cannot learn new tricks. Yet since His Majesty's death I have drunk deep in Scripture.'

'The English Testament.'

'How else are the people to be taught? I turn again and again in its pages to the last things. I am afraid that the end of the age is coming on us like an elemental darkness.'

'Faith, hope and charity, Lindsay. Perfect love casts out fear.'

'You do not believe in history, the wheel of time?' quizzed the Herald.

'I believe in God's goodness and his omnipotence.'

'But what of his judgment – we have brought this evil on ourselves.' My master's voice was heavy with conviction.

'The sacrifice of Christ is sufficient to redeem. Do not fall into disbelief.'

'And how is Scotland to be saved?'

'By alliance with England, as you know well. Have we learned nothing from Flodden? Or Solway Moss? The infant Queen must be wedded to an English cousin, so the thistle can unite again with the rose, but this time for good.'

The scholar's mask had slipped revealing a statesman's wisdom.

'You were a Doctor of France, the most learned in Paris,' reproved Lindsay.

'Perhaps, but I had enough native wit to see the difference between kingly vainglory and the security of our borders.'

'King James hanged Johnny Armstong for our security.'

'Aye, and traipsed to France for a bride.'

'The Pope approved.'

'Quod erat demonstrandum.'

The old man leaned back in his chair, as if drained. Expecting theology, I was apprenticed to statecraft. Lindsay leaned forward close to the reclining figure. 'And what of the cardinal...' The voices lowered and mixed till nothing could be distinguished. Suddenly chilled, I turned away to seek a kitchen fire and some food for my rumbling belly.

Sister Beth

THAT WAS JUST the beginning of trouble and not its end, for though hard used, my sufferings were nothing to what came on us after. There were rumblings at first when Beaton the fat cardinal was raw sliced in St Andrews by Protestant rogues, his corpse hung on the ramparts. One wag undid his britches to piss on the great man's head. What a stramash. Fifers like young Kirkcaldy got the credit, such as it was.

Then Father John ran off there to find his vocation. Of course preacher Wishart was already burnt, which was a shame, for he was a tall slender man with dark colouring, though very learned with it. He preached here in Haddington on our sins, but got small audience. Earl Patrick had him carried off to Hailes and then sold him to Beaton for roasting. What religion's in that? Killing and burning? Mary, Mother of God, save us from the fires.

He was on the royal make then was Pat, all the old quarrels with James forgotten, now he was dead. First Pat fought with the Scots, and then with the English, all for keeping Liddesdale as his own domain. Then off to Venice he runs, some watery place, to waste his lands on wine and whores. Now he was back, supporting the bairn Queen, resisting the Protestants, and sooking up to the widow Guise. Bothwells are always kindly to widowed queens.

He fancied his chances, did lanky Pat, and put away his own good wife, Agnes of Morham, the mother of his children, on the excuse she was a cousin in blood and too close to wed. It's a crying shame and who does it remind you of, Francesca? Aye exactly, only Pat wasn't fat and stinking, just thin and oily. She was better without him.

Now Earl Pat hies to Court in the best doublet and hose, studded with jewels and handing out gold guineas as if they grew in his own kailyard. Quite the gallant, pox or no pox. His face was marked. I suppose the jewels were pawned.

But she had his measure, the French Marie, and soon Pat was in the sulks, sent packing with a tail between his legs, and an empty purse. So he'd given George Wishart to the burning and gained nothing for his pain. What can the bold Earl do now? Off to the English who pay him to lie low at Hermitage and keep out of the fight that's coming. No one guessed till the Castle at St Andrews fell down, and there was Pat's name on an English payroll. So much for his religion. Pat's son turned Protestant but that's another story.

I think my girl, our daughter, was kept all this time at Hermitage till use could be found for her. It's a cold stark place almost in England. Did she see her father and have her cheek petted, her hair ruffed? Did he even throw her a look, while he hunted and drank, plotting what he could get next? A skivvy doubtless, till she had a use for the son Hepburn, whose name curdles on my tongue like vinegar in cream. Faithless, cold hearted Pat – nothing dear but himself, not even his own boy Jamie, Agnes Sinclair's laddie. And he casts the mother off without respect or mercy, the good lady mother. Aye, and I was a mother too.

What's the use of brooding? Confess your sins to Mother Mary and leave them behind you. There was no time to spare besides, for the English were on us. While Pat was safe in his darksome castle, the manhood of Scotland was felled at Pinkie. All because they wouldn't send the babbie Queen to England to be wed. For three days the Esk ran red with blood. We took in wounded and dying like a plague season. Black Saturday. Then down they came to Haddington, Hertford's wild southern beasts, and wrecked the town, carrying off everything they could on legs, hooves, wheels. It was plain robbery. We barred the convent gates and escaped the worst for a time. Our time was coming, though.

Put down your quill, woman, for Jesu's sake, and listen to me. I'm ashamed, but I'm speaking plain and true, so hear me out. For most folk war was waste and trouble. But the war made me what I am, Francesca, it gave me chances. I thickened at the waist but my purse fattened with my belly.

You see I was in charge of all the supplies. Lady Prioress was failing and not suited anyhow to dealing with soldiery. So I bargained with the English army – and later with the French. All these rough men needed fed, and their horses wanted fodder. We had food enough snug in the convent, since the well-born sisters had made off in carts and litters to their castled kin. Up in the Lammermuirs I had stores aplenty hidden. The army had money which was easier for them to pay than risk foraging in enemy country. Some supplies I saved for the sisters, but much more was lost for a price. I became a woman of means, and why not after all I suffered? Aye, put that down if you will. When it's said and done I was able to plough, and put my hand to the furrow. Without me, Francesca, the convent would have been ruined entire, and you and I sent out with beggars' badges.

The next spring they were back, another army. Grey was commander now. This time the Prioress gave them up the nunnery and withdrew to Dunbar. She could take no more. The English began building walls and ramparts round the town, sending out to garrison Yester, Nunraw and Hailes. But I bargained again to keep our lands and manor, in return for livestock and crops when the season came.

Yet the best was still to be. A hosting of Highlanders and Scots was marching south. Grey lacks men to hold all his places and wants to give up Hailes to someone other than the enemy. Earl Patrick's lying low at Hermitage, so I offer to manage the Castle, and keep a supply route open. The servants creep back to Hailes to find me in charge – in my habit for respect. Then as soon as the Scots arrive I offer to supply them too. Prices are high in times when so much is wasted or driven off by one side or the other. Who can question a holy sister on the weight of beef?

Haddington's flat-bottomed, which was never said of me. So the English must be hollowing out a massive ditch and raising huge turf walls, one behind another. But they cannot take in all the town, so St Mary's Church is left beyond the wall, though they try to ding it down, only managing to hole the roof. This was mistaken as proved, when Scots occupy the church and build a scaffold for their guns. What a cannonade from dawn to dusk. It sounded round the country and the hens at Hailes stopped laying. And all that soldiery wanting provender for empty bellies. It's hungry work the soldiering, aye in more ways than one. Keep your eyes down on those papers, my girl, and spare your blushes.

How am I so learned in the wars? Well, thereby hangs a tale. Every cloud has a silver lining, as they say. The French arrived, armoured troops with guns and money for supplies, unlike the naked Highland savage with his skirts and empty sporran. And with the French, Italian fortifiers. It's war now for holy Europe but fought in our wee kingdom to defend the widowed Marie and her little Queen.

Leaving Sir Wilford in command, Grey went back to England burning as he goes. But at Dunbar, while the town burnt, he could not touch the castle for its strength. God preserve our Lady Prioress. And as he watches, white sails come up the river past Bass Rock. It's the French, as I told you, carrying Signor Ubaldino the master builder.

What a proper man he was, well made but gentle with it, all neatly shorn and bearded with trimmed nails and perfumed hair bound back. A courteous, cunning man without a wife to handle, here at least. He soon made Dunbar Castle impossible to take. Some said this won the war, for how could Haddington be supplied with Dunbar commanding land and sea?

Next Ubaldino started to wall in Haddington with earthworks and counter bastions. He explained it all each night when he returned to lodge with me at Hailes. I accommodated the better sort of soldier there in special comfort. It was a blessed time, always up and doing when not abed. The English were shut in now, though ever ready for some foray or supply if it could be contrived. Yet their case looked grave. The Scots camped first at Lethington, but then took the convent for their comfort, leaving me the French and Italian sort of men, who were better payers anyway.

Soon a whole Scots Parliament assembles to negotiate with the French, for what I know not. So all must needs be fed and watered to a high degree. Only Beth Hepburn has the keys, and knows the oldest wines buried in the vaults. So back to the Nunnery I go to ply my latest trade. How strange, Francesca, to see the genteel rooms of holy sisters given up to lords with all their knights and retinue crammed like goslings in a coop. To and fro the Parliament went with meetings and eatings. I hustled in all the old servants, and those from Hailes besides, but guests bred like rats. It was no concern of mine except they must be fed.

The widowed Queen, Marie de Guise, came one day riding into the convent court with all her train about her. A souple sapling she was as well, swinging from the saddle to stand taller than lanky Pat himself. Lovely reddish hair, fair skin, and grey eyes – a beauty in her prime – I say so myself. And all the heralds, banner bearers and courtiers of the day, Scots and French, clustered round her as bees to honey. She was ushered into the refectory where clerks and nobles were spreading seals, papers, quills. The baby Queen must go to France, no longer bound to Edward Tudor. In return King Henri will defend us from the English and steer the Scottish government. Hamilton will be made a duke in France. That seems the nub for all the long orations. Then more wine and food is called for and everyone mightily content.

I returned to Hailes, relieved to see them all away if truth be told, but merriness was gone from the business. Too many died, which is a waste, Francesca, of sweet flesh. First our Scots and the French thought to overwhelm the ramparts, but Wilford fought them back, an English lion. When the garrison tried to sally out, they were surrounded and lost half their number. Provisions were become scarce and I could no longer play procuress without risk.

Next, an English fleet arrived in the Forth, so reinforcements and supplies reached the famished town. But strange to say this weakened resistance, since none had volunteered to starve, and many slipped through the blockade to desert. God knows, any poor wretch would do the same before die upright on an earthwork, or stretched out like a sewer rat. Hand to hand and desperate, they killed and maimed each other without mercy. Pretty bodies ruined.

Ubaldino brooded in his room at Hailes. This was not war as it should be waged by soldiers, but the death throes of animals. He left for winter quarters and was never seen again at Haddington. What a proper man he was. And I was left to winter on my own.

Then, Francesca, came the worst, without remede or succour. A wet raw season gnawed at the vitals on all sides. Plague broke out inside the town; bodies lay unburied in the glaur. Brave Wilford took a fatal wound and was let go to die in England. Outside the town was little better, for men crouched behind their siegeworks frozen cold, soaked to their skins, exhausted, starving. I tried to offer entertainment at the castle but with poor provision. The serving lasses gave what comfort they could to hungry men, but I kept clean quarters and insisted on payment down. War grinds all grain coarse, and gives a death to feeling. The heart lies waste and silent. Will it never end? God pray, dear sister, we do not see that like again. They say the English turned to eating rats, but sure the rats were already starving.

Then of a sudden, all hope gone, there was an end. Another English army trudging through the Borders. But not to fight – they had no further stomach. Instead they gathered up the remnants and burned the rags of Haddington. They marched their survivors home shrouded in close column, or in carts, or on canvas litters. An evil work, they say, for what our town cost them, foul island in a sea of enemies. And our besiegers let them go, watching sullenly yet without fight, since they had no more stomach for it either.

Every stone standing in the town was torn down. Last of all the English stopped south of the river and razed our nunnery to the ground, as if the French Treaty they had come to wreck might be blotted out by powder and by fire. Of course the stores were long since gone, but all those pretty chambers, and the chapel where young Master John supped holy blood from our silver chalice. To see them lost forever made dry eyes weep. Even today. Look at these smudged cheeks. Aye, pass a napkin. And a sup of wine.

How time revolves. The wheel of fortune turns, Francesca. I was left at Hailes, a castle to my charge, but no convent to receive me back. I was unsure what might come, though girdled round with gold. Till Earl Patrick comes riding back from Hermitage to make his peace at Court. Somehow Pat was on the winning side again, if winning is what you call the ruin of a country. Anything he had left in Lothian was saved by me, for all the thanks I got. He died unwept soon after.

Enough for one night and maybe many more. Let's say our rosary, sister, and go to sleep, for this old body slows and unwinds. I'll take a cordial with me and trust on better dreams. God grant peace and quiet rest.

Bothwell

GO ON, FEEL IT. Hard as the sword it holds. Where I put my trust.

Aye. To win what is mine by right. With a strong arm. What did my father leave me? A name and my blood. Little else to show.

I'm not used to wielding the pen, but as God is my witness, the truth will be set down to their damnation.

But the name is Hepburn, fourth Earl Bothwell, Lord High Admiral of Scotland, Baillie of Lauderdale, Lord of Hailes and Crichton, Sheriff of Berwick, Haddington and Edinburgh. Aye, and Warden of the Marches if blood runs true. My name must be my fortune, embellished with noble insignia. Two lions pull at the rose. On the crest a horse's head, bitted and bridled. Keep Faith, the motto. And I will defend Scotland's borders for her rightful Queen.

'Your Majesty, I do not make religion an excuse for disloyalty, unlike some. I am your devoted servant. Every lance is at your command.'

'That is very reassuring. How did you find France, Lord James?'

'All the more beautiful for the sun which shines from the brow of our young Queen. Your daughter is truly a reflection of her bountiful mother.'

'You studied military affairs, I understand, as well as courtly flattery.'

'It is my belief that Scotland should have its own army and not be dependent on French soldiers.'

'Yet French women are still fair game.'

'Your Majesty must not believe idle gossip. My main exercise at Court was to train with Kirkcaldy of Grange, and to hunt wild game with King Henri.'

'The gallant Sir William. He has also returned home, but by way of England. Will you emulate his accomplishments? '

'His deeds of war and knighthood, in the service of France, are the envy of every honourable soldier.' I avoided her question and its implication.

'It is my pleasure, Lord James, to make you Keeper of Hermitage Castle, and Lieutenant of the Borders, with immediate effect. Such honour for one so young.'

'I shall give proof against all your enemies of my courage and good counsel, despite my tender years. I am obliged to Your Majesty for succeeding my father in the Marches and at Hermitage.'

'Arise, good Lieutenant. And may your motto always be your guide, unlike the late Earl Patrick.'

She gambles on me, the lovely Guise, because Scottish nobles and French commanders fall out and fail. Keep Faith. This command presents the first chance and I do not miss my mark. Regulars for the set piece; Borders horsemen for sortie or ambush. The surest weapon in all warfare is surprise. For that you must have mobility and speed, operating on known terrain.

Two days after Christmas, a hard frost retreats leaving surfaces soft but the ground firm beneath. A scattering of thin snow mantles the tops. So I cross the Tweed and catch Northumberland napping.

As the howe of the night deepens conditions smile on us. The air is raw but not freezing while low lying mist shrouds the valleys. Hooves muffled, we approach the river at Ladykirk, not at the Glendale ford. A slender column snakes across screened by the island from Norham Castle. Each man is wrapped in a dark cloak with only steel bonnets to reflect the starless sky and murky currents. But the river runs quiet, neither high nor low, and everyone is over without alarm.

No gathering or waiting on the far side, but moving on in the same formation. The breath of horses merges into the mist. Creak of saddles and brush on branches but no clash of weapons, sheathed against leather jacks, or chink of stirrups, bound with cloth. Man and beast together step with steady footprint. Unwatched we go on, skirting villages and farms, the danger-point passed over.

By now the warning message has gone from Glendale to Wooler. Cursing, Harry Percy pulls on his boots, shouting for word to go on to Alnwick where the merry Earl his brother slumbers deep from Yule feasting. The Scots are over the border. Come quickly since Percy rides north to meet the old enemy. A Hotspur to stir Northumberland awake from winter sleep.

Following the course of the Till, racing first between rocky banks but then widening and slowing. We are near the place now. A steep slope of oak and beech climbs above the watershed, flanked below by a bog of swampy turf, dwarf sedge and willow. I chose well scouting with French Paris. The infantry spreads out quietly through the wood taking cover behind leafless trees. The moss troopers wait below, drawn back from the river.

And it works. On they clatter as fast as night allows. When they pass by on the west side a forward detail fires the hayricks at Fenton, blazing up in the dark sky. It stops them in their tracks. Where are these foxes now, with torches in their tails? Percy thinks fast, and turns their heads around. Back, shouting and untangling, to Milford where they can cross and block the path to Wooler.

He's within half a mile now of the place. The troopers at the ricks show themselves and Percy gives chase. By God it is working. Clattering and crashing along the bank they come straight into the snare.

I let them past the swamp to the wood. Now. The slope explodes like a firework. A wave of sound crashes into the valley side and roars back at us. Guns flash, horses scream, riders fall. The horsemen charge into the mass emptying saddles, slashing reins and bridles, turning them back onto themselves and into the river. Gradually they win free from panic, and those behind gallop on past crumpled bodies. We pursue on horse. The infantry reform and go at the double to block the crossing at Ford. Percy's front column is over before them, but the stragglers are caught between pursuit and a hedge of pikes, and surrender.

We chase Percy further but as a grey dawn creeps into the east another column can be seen coming north. The merry Earl comes late but in force. I pull the cavalry back, form up with prisoners in train and head swiftly down to Ladykirk. Still quiet at Norham as we gain the north side of Tweed. It is a night for Scots annals. Northumberland is left to wonder what devils ravaged their Christmas cheer.

My first command is my first victory. Pity they ended the English war soon after. But no one ever called me boy again. And if you've got anything to say for yourself, you can speak it to my face now.

Sister Beth

SO BACK HE comes, quite the Lord and Master, though all those years, remembered only as a wild boy. And in his shadow that sleekit Frenchman, Paris, glued to him like a double. His personal attendant if you please, and he does look to please that one, however he may. The new Earl is a Hepburn to the fingertips, as I ought to know, with that bold slightly sneering eye that looks you over to see if you're worth the having.

Not as pretty as Pat but more manly and something dangerous in his eye. Like the old Earl he knows what's due to the Hepburn name and honour, but with Earl James there's a hard streak of 'I'll get it by fair means or foul.' Aye, a story was there ready in the making. The natures of folk are cast in a mould and there's no understanding it or undoing. Preserve us from ill – lead us not into temptation. Tell your beads, lass, but first fetch a piece of that ham, with some pickles and sweetmeats. There's no purpose in telling a tale with our bellies rumbling and farting.

The convent was patched up by now, bits of it anyway, and we're back in business but with far fewer sisters. I have my old duties too and Mother Abbess gives me free range, so I'm to and fro from Hailes, keeping in touch with the household and buying in supplies. He of course takes no notice, and if truth be told I was too much of an eyeful now for the younger sort.

Funny how blooming flesh turns creeshie without you noticing. Be warned, Francesca, for though you might be scraggy now, venial sins can glutton you. God knows I had few pleasures in those years when the English War was ended and my flesh gave up its youth to my belly.

Where was I? Yes the young Earl James. He soon found out his cupboard was bare. Then someone told him I had managed things through the siege, so he called me in for some talk of household accounts. I took him through the books, and he was quick to see the way it worked. No sluggard when gold glimmers. Within days he had the notaries disinherit his own kith and kin, so he could recover land and increase rents. This was before he got back Hermiston as well – by favour of the Guise and the strength of his arm. He was always flexing those muscles, but he knew how to swing a sword which was a form of learning much needed in the Border Marches. Lady Abbess kept any young nuns out of sight – she knew her own kin too well.

Shame for my years, since I was beginning to like the young Earl, in a motherly way. And I was related somehow, though my daughter was nearer, alas for her. For himself there was little family to speak of apart from his own respected mother at Morham, and his full sister Janet, whom he loved. With all others he was cold or casual, for what else had the child known but strangers? Maybe that was why his eye was always roving, greedy for possession. It became a curse on him, even then.

The thing is French King Henri was pierced in the throat, or was it his eye, with a lance. So our own Mary was become Queen in France and not sent home to us with her boy king. And that leaves her poor mother to deal with these Scots Protestants. And they saw their chance to wrest us away from the French, and into the arms of the English and their heretic queen. In spite of all the blood already spilled to put the English out.

But Earl James was broken into the ways of women and he had the Queen Regent charmed now too, for she was failing in health and wanted a man, not in the bodily way I suppose, though she still had her looks I can warrant. It was for the weakness of her rule and the lack of nobles to hold her cause upright.

A Bothwell for a queen, as if history turns in wheels. And he was ready and bold, though he professed Protestant. Why was that? I know not, unless he wanted the Church put aside for her lands, like the rest. Or there was a darkness in his soul that craved Calvin's cure. He was a close one, hard to fathom. He lived for deeds not prayers. God knows, he lives yet in misery.

What's your hurry, lass? Get on with the story? Alright, I suppose it's just a story to you but I had to suffer it. Pass the flagon, there's a good girl.

Anyway, word comes of secret subsidy from England to the rebel lords so they might cast off Marie de Guise in favour of I know not what – a Hamilton again, or the Bastard, but Protestant whatever. It had to be secret, for Elizabeth had no truck with godly rebels. God commands us, Mother Abbess was never tired of saying, to obey Princes. Elizabeth was a queen and so was Mary, whatever Master John had to say on the matter. So her wily counsellors had their subsidy all counted out in French crowns and sent over the Border, with promises of gunpowder to come, in Ormiston's saddlebags.

What a stroke for the young Earl, and in his own country. He never could resist the bold ploy, if it made his name resound; let the consequence look to itself. Yet he was cunning too. It was Hallowe'en and deep dark. He waits till Ormiston with seven men is near Hailes, where the road twists narrow and the trees close in around. You know the place, Francesca, for we go that way sometimes and keep sharp lookout for any landless rogues.

He closes there, riding up behind the Laird douce as you please to untie the saddlebags. Of course Ormiston flares up, but our James strikes him hard over the face with the flat of a blade and down he goes. The rest scatter for their lives unsure if they're ambushed by men or devils. He bypasses Hailes since it's too public, and rides instead, as fast as the weight allows, for Crichton Castle. Sure he knows every inch of the moor since a lad. Not even a falcon could catch him.

But word is out faster and farther than he could have wished. They're raging at him, and the Bastard, along with young Arran, raise a column to storm Crichton and get back the gold. Our man comes to, ten minutes to spare, and flees bareback with the guineas towards Haddington. But the weight drags him down so he leaves the horse and wades along Tyne to cover the scent. The wild man is still a nose ahead. Into Sandybed's he goes, aye the farmer who has his lands of the convent, the old skinflint.

But they have nowhere to hide him so they turn to us. You would have burst laughing so you would, but we had him dressed as a dairymaid and finally as a sister, with the saddlebags under his habit. And Arran's troopers everywhere sticking in their nebs. I chased them about and clattered their ears with guid Scots. They couldn't take a Hepburn in Haddington, not with Sister Beth in charge.

Mother Superior was mad with worry, while he was bored, and handling a pretty little novice like unbaked pastry before we got him away. She was the last before you came, Francesca, and then you were last of all; God spare our holy order. We smuggled him out to Borthwick Tower where he had to stand on the ramparts to watch them burn Crichton Castle's plenishings, and carry his charters off to Edinburgh. That hit him where it hurts. In the pouch.

What a power of enemies he made then, Protestant though he claimed to be. Maybe he never knew which side to choose for the best. To gamble all on one stake was his way. Whatever, he was Marie de Guise's general now, for all her French following. And the name on every Scottish tongue, aye and English ones forbye. James Hepburn, Earl of Bothwell, and let no one forget it.

Well he made sure of that in due course, did our Jamie, none surer. God forgive him where he lies, for I never shall, foul sinner. As I know better than any woman alive. But he paid, Francesca, and he's still paying so they say. Tied to a post in some darksome prison in foreign lands.

Let's say a prayer to Our Lady of Sorrows. And then we'll have some supper with another flagon of wine. I'll be the better for that and maybe able to speak some more, if it amuses you. I've seen too much, and I should be praying more and talking less. But my knees are stiff. Aye, I have my rosary here. You begin and I'll follow. There's a good girl. If she'd lived my lass would have her own bairns now.

Bothwell

THIS STRONG ARM was Scotland's defence. Aye, mother and daughter both. They can't depose a queen for all their pious cant, godly assemblies and the rest. The English arrived to take advantage of our disputes. Though I cut their supplies, and harried their lines, it was too good an opportunity for the old enemy to miss.

Then Maitland deserted us. The Secretary slipped out through a postern by dark to join the rebel lords. His reason I know not, but I shall bring it home to him when next we meet – I swore it on this sword. Immediately the Bastard sent him to England for his voice was judged more pleasing there than Knox's doom laden croak. His intelligence was our loss, I openly acknowledge. Perhaps though his kin will lose some lands by that betrayal.

Kirkcaldy and Lord James knew their business. Grange was a Hercules of France's wars, and should have stayed there. As for the rest, they were in pantaloons, ragtag recruits. The Regent's French regulars built our defences well, and my Borderers provided a gambler's throw. Mustard to meat.

The guns blasted away on both sides for days till ears were ringing. Their men got careless, some wandering off to taverns, or other diversions. So with fifty horse I galloped out to spike the guns. Then I saw Grey de Wilton hurrying over to protect them. Had he not seen enough at Haddington? I pulled round and launched at him. He half turned and got his shield up before I smashed in, mount and man going down. I swung back hard to pierce him on the ground but struck with only half my strength. Glancing up I saw my troopers falling away, so I drove the horse over his body with churning hooves, and broke back towards the walls calling retreat.

In front of both armies, Earl Bothwell felled the commander single handed, like Bruce before Bannockburn. Struck down by this arm. I took my chance. So they attacked Leith in a fury of revenge – a direct assault but launched too early. The ladders were thrown back. The few who got inside were cut down by gunners. Even the whores ran to the walls with stones and fiery coals to empty on their heads. Then they ran like scalded cats.

Then nothing did but that John Knox climbed the pulpit of St Giles to mend their spirits. He preached that God exposes his chosen to mockery and shame, so that they may know their weakness. But God chastises his children for a purpose. Let a blind world crow, for in the moment of defeat God will give strength and victory to the godly remnant.

In Knox's creed even a reverse is gain, yet there may be a shadow of truth in his rantings. We act in the moment but can never calculate every consequence. There is a tide that steers our ends, beyond our ken. But a man must act boldly and not brood. Otherwise we are slaves.

Things fell quiet so I went to see Her Majesty the Guise, cooped up in the Castle. She looked dreadful, swollen yet bloodless. But she sat upright in her chair, chalk white, with braided hair tied back and a bonnet on her head.

'Your Majesty.'

'You have rendered me good service, Earl Bothwell. You are a brave man.'

'I shall never desert you, not like Maitland.'

'You know what I want you to do.'

'I have been ready these last four or five days, only waiting on your word.'

'The English are closing their grip.' A spasm of pain quivers through her flesh. 'I need more soldiers from France, or help from elsewhere.'

'I will return with an army, and drive the rebels into the sea.'

'You will not delay?'

'I will always be in the place where my service is needed.' I felt an overwhelming urge to convince her, old and ugly as she was.

'These are my letters to Her Majesty my daughter. They are secret dispatches.'

'Secure in my trust.'

'If the channel is blockaded you are to go from Paris to Copenhagen, as lord High Admiral to the King of Denmark who has many ships.'

'Your Majesty, have no fear.'

'My days have stretched, James, beyond fear. Be kind to Mary and loyal. She will reward you as I am no longer able.'

Her eyes begin to glaze. Laudanum. So I bent down low and pressed my lips to her pudgy hand. I was sad to leave her but relieved to escape that room. It smelt of the grave.

Cold seas and prevailing easterlies, but finally I reached Denmark. We nosed into the harbour at Copenhagen. There were enough ships there to transport twenty armies. I received a royal welcome. This is how the Lord High Admiral should be treated. I belong to wider spheres, though I slipped out of Scotland like a reiver.

Frederick had cold eyes and a long nose. The veins mottled on his cheeks for one so young. The King was calculating but beside him lolloped a great German hound. His body and his Court were swathed in furs. God knows the winds were cold. He drank and hunted like a true Scotsman, so we were brothers in his flagons. He was like a boar that charges in the field, and put in his snout to empty the trough at one snort. But his eyes were cold.

He knew more than I did, and his German allies may have been willing to send troops if Denmark provided ships. But the English had spies everywhere there, and pressed their case to be a Protestant ally in place of Catholic France. It made my head ache after a long night. Why could we not have action – a fleet at sea for Scotland – before the good Queen Regent was overwhelmed? Instead another day of feasting. Tomorrow another forest, and another chase. Fortunately there was some other diversion.

Danish women are generally pasty in the flesh and stocky. They twist lots of blond hair round their heads in braids, but don't show breast or shoulder except on rare state occasions. The tone is sober, unless everyone is in their cups. Matrons seem to rule at Court and keep the young beauties carefully screened, especially from the drinking bouts. French manners are out of fashion and the whores smell of fish.

My lodgings were in town close by the castle with Admiral Thorondsen. He was a Norwegian settled there and married into a rich merchant family. They had one son and seven daughters, two of whom were grown up and married to Scots merchants. Next in line came Anna.

'You are the Admiral of Schottland.'

'I am.'

'Do you have many of ships?'

'Hundreds.'

She was dark haired and lustrous, like a Spaniard, but very young.

'Shall I call on your quarters?'

'That would be very nice, but you must ask your mother first.'

'Mother knows nothing of what we do.'

I found her to my liking, innocent and keen to please. She had her eye on me but I had to proceed with caution at this foreign Court with its northern customs. She was barely sixteen.

The Admiral seemed complaisant. It is not easy to marry off seven daughters. Perhaps he was fishing for a noble husband, in which case I would not become his catch.

One day, returning early from the Court, I found Anna and the Admiral at business in their public chamber. She was preparing bills of lading, duties and commissions, and counting out the reckoning for each merchant captain. They waited their turn and came in to meet the Admiral exchanging news and pleasantries with guttural tones. She kept in the background, severely dressed with hair bound back, but had her eye on every coin. I smiled as I pass on to my rooms. This was a different Anna from the giddy girl, and more appealing.

Two nights later I arrived home in the dark after sitting late with Frederick and Adolph. Perhaps I was clattering or cursing, but someone came behind me with a torch and followed me into the room.

'Shall I light your lamps, Admiral?'

'Thank you, Anna.'

'Will you take a glass of wine warm?'

'I think not, thank you.'

She lingered at the door, loose gowned, with long black hair down on her shoulders. Her eyes were glinting. I should not have, but beckoned with my hand which runs beneath the linen on a shoulder smooth as glass.

'You must not do this, Anna. You are a noble match.'

'I want a nobleman's bed.'

So she helped me undress. I don't remember much, but suppose I took her virginity that night. It was the first of many pleasurable beddings as she learned from me the arts of love. Her flesh was flawless to touch or view.

Even the mole below her shoulder blade was an ornament not a blemish. She was the handsomest woman I had lain with till then, though not the hottest in her passions. She passed the time and I became quite fond.

The Admiral and his lady seemed to avert their gaze for a while. Then the expectant looks started, conversations broken off, half spoken hints. A reckoning approached but as it did she became bolder, visiting each night and lingering longer in my bed, as if she were mistress and I a guest.

Fredrick was ready now to send me on to the German Rhinegrave. All seemed full of promise for my cause. He proposed that he and his brother Adolph should escort me to their frontiers with a train of knights and gentlemen. An expedition would divert him. We could be merry together on the road.

This was not the time for scandal, so I approached the Admiral to ask his daughter's hand. Only it would not be convenient to wed till I could return to Scotland. In the meantime she would accompany me. He expressed satisfaction with my proposal and mentioned the substantial dowry that it would not be convenient to pay until the marriage. Nonetheless Anna already had money of her own to cover any expenses she might incur.

No suggestion from him of holding Anna a hostage at home. He knew that citadel was breached. Instead the gold would be retained, while Anna would go with me – betrothed though yet unwed. This was her wish too, so I agreed to travel with her in my baggage. What choice had I? It was a convenient arrangement. Her lovemaking became fiercer and more possessive as if by digging in her claws she would stay attached.

Frederick was amused, and Adolph uproarious. Backslapping and more wine. Would they have been so affable had I left without Anna in train? I thought I caught those cold eyes appraising me between quaffs. Those eyes are still before me now. Will I ever escape them?

So off we went, a jovial band, with Anna flirting and entertaining like a courtier born. The brothers seemed to revel in the license so I held my tongue. Bothwell can be patient, biding his moment. We parted at the border lifelong friends.

I lapsed into a brooding silence till we reached the Rhinegrave's palace. Here she would be discreet, or share a servant's bed. Nothing should blot my triumph at this new Court. A German army would march at my back to board a Danish fleet. The English driven back into the sea. I would receive the tribute of a grateful Queen. Aye, the daughter bow before me, in her own royal chamber.

'What is the matter with you, my Admiral? Are you sad?'

'I must win the Rhinegrave's favour.'

'Shall I dress you?'

'In these old rags?'

'Then let us buy rich robes.'

'We have not yet received our subsidies from the Queen in Scotland.'

'What does it matter? I have gold to buy – look.'

'You are a clever girl. But keep to these rooms till I am received by the Rhinegrave.'

'Do I shame you before the Germans?'

'Hold your mouth and do what you're told. I'm not your father'

'Are you angry with me?'

'Leave it be.'

'Will you beat me, with your sword or with your belt? '

The kitten showed claws, and she diverted the weary hours. At courts the largest part was waiting on the great, but the Rhine grave received me well, spluttering gracious words and promises in broken English. The Danes had done their business. He did not mention Anna. I spoke for Scotland; I looked and felt like a King.

That night we celebrated the success of our embassy – Anna and I in my apartments. She sent out for food and wine. She knows the way to let go and please. Deep, drunken sated sleep. I woke to a hammering at the door. Anna startled in her shift. Messengers from France to say Marie de Guise is dead.

A Bothwell for ill luck. Her limbs bloated she expired. What a moment she chose to die. Now the English and French were treating for peace over Scotland's head. My command? Three empty saddlebags and a Danish mistress hell bent on marriage.

The Rhinegrave keeps smiling and spluttering. Damn their diplomatics. I must away to Paris and try another throw there. Would Mary still consider Scotland? Or remember my service to her mother? Our lassie Queen, mated to a weakly boy, and all the wealth of France at her command. Farewell Denmark, goodbye Germany; I might never see you at close quarters again. If I had known. Thank God we still had Anna's golden gelders to tide us over.

The best thing about Scottish inns is that they cheat you in your own language. Here they bamboozle and rob you all at once. Unending tracks and hovels, with ne'er a hill in sight is our daily lot.

Finally I left her in Flanders, where Anna had cousins. We could have sailed for Scotland where the corpse is being picked over, but Paris must be tried first, without a mistress in the baggage. After tears and embraces, I departed supplied for my journey.

Two places in the world I am content. In the Borders with a river running, a stallion between my legs, and the wind about my ears. Or in Paris. I took lodgings by the Louvre – no student's garret – and let the town renew acquaintance. The inns are good, the weather fine, and if needs must I know where the best whores can be had.

Distractions were required as I waited upon another Court seeking audience. The Queen is indisposed; she is in mourning still; the King is unwell; she must attend on His Majesty; it is a Saint's Day; the Duc de Guise would like to meet with you first, and so forth. I took to gaming which was foolish, and drinking with Scots soldiers, which was instructive. The mood was bad. The Guise faction had made peace behind Mary's back, and renounced her claim to England, all to keep their power in France. The Protestants had to be suppressed here first. Only Henri's death, they said, saved the Guise from ruin, so they delayed reinforcing Scotland till it was too late, leaving their good sister to die besieged and friendless.

When it really mattered Scotland was a bauble to their crown. And so it will be always – a plaything of England, France, the Empire, and the Pope in Rome – until we raise up a standing army and defend our own. That is what I told the late Queen, aye and now the daughter. And lay my own sword at her feet.

Her Majesty was pale and distraught. Where had all the lustre gone? She seemed strained, worn not slender. My heart went out to her for wasted beauty. I consoled her on her mother's loss and the tears sprang to her eyes. So I recounted the trials and battles of recent months, my audiences with the Regent, the words we spoke together, my deeds, my loyalty and devotion. She drank it in with shining eyes.

Were we not formed alike – a mother rarely seen, a father wholly lost. I found myself unable to pursue my suit. I held her hand, bowed, and pressed my lips to soft flesh. For a moment we were held together. Then I left to return again before too long, her mournful voice ringing in my ears, I took a horse and rode out into the forest, goading, spurring the beast beyond endurance. Then back to town from inn to tavern till the dark hours brought release. With every appetite slaked, I was brought more to myself, but still wakeful in the early hours. Am I made for womanish emotion or resolution? I cannot retrieve my early losses: let them be buried. I shall go forward unfettered, a Bothwell for hazard.

I must write to Flanders for more money.

The next time I rode to Fontainebleau. Francis, Duc de Guise, indulged me with an interview to discuss affairs at home. Their tactic was for the Bastard to rule as his sister's Regent. Did they not know he would be King? What a dour country that would be. Guise gave me to believe they still aimed at the English crown, describing how Mary had refused to ratify their Protestant treaty with the Royal Seal of Scotland.

Why should she give up her claim to England with nothing to show for it? Even in grief that woman had spirit. She will surprise the world yet, as much as she has so far delighted. I found her more reserved and grave. The pallor was still there but her stance was firmer, more upright. I made formal obeisance.

'Are all your former games gone to heaviness?'

My boldness won a wan smile.

'His Majesty has been poorly and much plagued by headaches.'

'He is young and will recover all his strength as the season improves.'

'Indeed. Shall we walk in the garden?'

She led me out with her gaggle of Marys behind, none too silent. I stared in their direction without acknowledgement.

'Are you enjoying Paris, Lord James?'

'It is my favourite town, Madam.'

'Really, then you have sampled all its pleasures?'

A touch of the old raillery.

'Your Majesty is pleased to mock me. I am more sober than my reputation, and hard pressed by the necessities of these embassies.' Is that too broad a hint?

'You shall not find us ungrateful, Lord James. Your loyalty to my late mother I know, and your continuing service is highly valued by myself. What is your news of our unhappy country?'

'Any Regent must have a Council, Madam, and it must be composed of your loyal subjects. Athol, Huntly, Argyll, who is a true Scotsman though not of your faith. The Hamiltons cannot be left out. Nor Morton for the Douglas interest. Mar, Erskine are all good men. I myself would be honoured to serve.'

'But of course, I depend on you. Duty alone will be my test, not religion. I will oppress none, so that all may practice their belief in peace.'

'That is wise and gracious, Madam.'

'Will you return to Scotland and uphold my cause?'

'That is my intention.'

'And you will also serve in amity my brother, James Stewart, as Regent?'

Had someone told her of bad blood between us?

'If that is your will.'

'My will is that all should agree to live in harmony.'

'What of England?'

I was keen to know what she intended in my own backyard.

'An honourable peace must be sought with my loving cousin, Elizabeth.'

'You have not ratified their treaty?'

'I shall study that further, and Francis and I will meet with the English ambassadors.'

'England should have no more sway than France. This strong arm will keep your southern border secure.'

I could be no clearer.

'You are a brave man,' she complimented, 'but more warrior than diplomat I believe.'

I went down on one knee, humbly repentant.

'Excuse my rough ways. I learned to live off the land and defend it against all comers, even when a boy.'

She looked away as if offended, but it was a signal for an equerry in the background.

'Please accept this token of my gratitude and esteem. Mary Stewart does not forget her friends.' I stoop in acknowledgement, gauging as I bend three bags held in the servant's arms. 'Also it is His Majesty's pleasure to make you a gentleman of the bedchamber.'

'I am humbled and deeply honoured by His Majesty's notice, and will wait upon him in his chambers.'

'When he is...'

'When he has regained his full vigour.'

'Indeed. I hope you will come to see us again soon.'

'I am not sure how long I may be detained in Paris. My affairs in Scotland demand attention.'

'How will you return?'

'By Flanders. The Channel ports are still watched by English ships, and they do not love Earl Bothwell.'

'May they have good cause.'

'Your Majesty is not all for peace and harmony.'

'Only on good terms.'

'I salute you, Madam. I thought to go by Rheims to inspect the tomb in which your mother's honoured remains will rest.'

'That is most considerate. Please greet my Aunt, the Lady Renée, and assure her of my prayers at this sad season.'

She gave me her hand and then slowly turned away followed by her ladies. Only the Equerry stayed to go with me to the stables. Three bags neatly bound at the neck. And each one contained a hundred golden guineas.

Arriving back in Paris I took the town by storm. Rising late next morning I opened two messages from Anna. In the first she was ill and begged me to return. In the second, growing with child, feverish, and fit to die.

Flanders and Scotland beckoned, though I paid my respects to the Abbess Renée, and lit a papish candle for the Guises' soul. Those French women seemed to be my guardian angels.

James Maitland

MANY ACCUSED MY father of deserting Marie de Guise in her hour of need. But they were wrong. His course was unchanged through those months of strife. When, led by France, she began to persecute the Scottish Protestants a balance shifted. The change was hers, not William Maitland's.

That is the truth revealed by these papers. The French had deserted Scotland and a new political settlement was required. There was a strong Protestant interest among the nobles, without whom the country could not hold together. Argyll, Morton who led the Douglas clan, young Lindsay, James Stewart himself, and many of the lairds were Protestant, by reason of conviction, or of hunger for the Church's wealth.

But at this same moment expediency was rotting the roots of our nation's character and civilisation. Both the Crown and the Church were weak and unable to guide events. Compromise became the watchword, and my father was a connoisseur of compromise.

The Maitland aim throughout was unity and peaceful alliance with our neighbour England. Every eye was on Elizabeth as Parliament convened in London. Which direction would she take? The correspondence shows my father was kept informed by Secretary Cecil of every move in England. Both knew their advantage lay with a parallel settlement in Scotland – a Protestant Kirk owing allegiance to the monarch alone. Everything in good order; the realm governed and directed. What matter if Catholic ways continued by custom and private conscience?

Consider then my father's anger and disgust when the mob rose up in Perth, inflamed by Knox's preaching. His letters urged the nobility to put down riots and protect the Kirks. Looting of friaries and the destruction of the monasteries was no part of his proceedings. Against his advice, the Queen Regent had inflamed opinion by summoning the preachers to trial. Now forces had been unleashed that would be hard to rein back.

To the last my father was affectionate and dutiful to Marie de Guise, going to Edinburgh Castle to pay his respects on her deathbed. She was a woman abandoned, but not by the Secretary who laboured so long in her service. She parted this mortal life reconciled with William Maitland. Let others examine their own conscience.

When turbulent factions tried to supplant Mary Stewart with her half-brother James, or with a Hamilton, he refused support, reminding all of Scotland's allegiance to her legitimate succession. He understood the nation's mood. Though the assembly that deposed the Regent commanded his support, the Secretary insisted that only a Parliament of the Three Estates could settle religion and the succession. He steered the ship through troubled waters.

So the old order was adapted in a new guise. Scotland would not change rulers, though God's Word demanded them in Knox's rubric. The kingdom of this earth was not to be shaken; the Church must look to heaven for succour. George Buchanan was summoned home to guide the ministers with humane learning, and protect the universities from their barbarities.

This was my father's most influential, if not his finest hour. With intelligence, diplomacy and skill he navigated round the rocks, letting others stand upon the pulpit or blow their trumpets in the market place. While managing Parliament, he kept the nobility from further blows, removed foreign armies from Scotland's soil, sent embassies to France and England, and reformed the Church by legal form.

It was ever his delight to exercise power without claiming any for himself. To influence and direct in secret was his art and cunning. It must have seemed that every ambition was achieved even amidst strife and faction. Only uniting the sister kingdoms remained undone, but with both rulers young, time and succession were on his side.

Then in one cruel and sudden blow all again was changed. Leafing through his papers I can sense the shock. So many gaps, mere notes in place of memoranda; at points even his meticulous hand falters.

Orléans on an autumn day. The royal consorts are departing for Chenonceau where they had spent their honeymoon, rather than view an execution. They had no taste for bloodshed. The chests and beds and tapestries and books were all packed. The barge was rocking on the Loire awaiting its passengers when orders were changed. King Francis had a pain in his right ear and must lie down amidst the empty rooms.

Doctors were summoned, a canopy erected. The ear began to suppurate and discharge. His fever rose. Mary remained at the bedside. Dispatches hastened to every corner of the kingdom, and the ambassadors took up their pens.

He was purged and vomited. His body was loose and wasting fast. When the discharge from his ear subsided, teeth and jaws began to throb. An inflammation like a quince swelled behind the ear. He endured headaches, fevers, and sickness for two weeks.

Over the last few days he was delirious. The Court was sealed to all except his mother, and Mary his wife. Death came as a merciful release, and Europe was left to reel in shock.

As France moves to crown another boy king, Mary is given over to pity and lament for her dear lost Francis. But the Medici, spider at the centre of the web, reduces the newly widowed household and takes the royal jewels into her keeping. The unmerciful mother-in-law forecloses to protect the interest of her own blood, flagrant, reclaiming her power.

No one considers Scotland except the Scots. Everything for which I have wrought is put at risk. All is calculated on Mary's European crown. If she comes home to rule, the Scots will have a queen without a party, a husband or religion to support her. This newly Protestant kingdom with a Catholic queen, who knows little of her native land or its factious politics. Will she

trace her poor late mother's path of sorrows? God spare our lovely Mary,
and this poor realm of Scotland, from such a fate.

My father's correspondence begins anew across the continent. If another
dynastic marriage could be made, with Spain, or Germany or even Denmark,
then danger might be averted. Mary Stewart might not return.

Yet in the strangeness of providence, if Mary had not come back to reign,
my father and mother would not have been united. He would have lost the
greatest joy of his earthly existence. He would have lacked sons to follow in
his steps, or understand his ways and worth.

Did William Maitland still believe in providence, or in the throw of
fortune? A Stoic to endure and die may have been his final faith. Holy Spirit,
guard my thoughts and pen.

This much is sure. Before the close of summer Mary Stewart came back to
Scotland, and everything was altered, for her and for my father. I was not yet
born. But the future was being fashioned in a crucible of warring elements.

Queen of Scots
Scotland, 1561–1565

Mary

IT IS NOT fitting for a Queen to share her private thoughts except with her equals. Not even with my Marys, who share everything with each other, while I have grown apart. If I speak only to myself, you will still listen. I do not wish ever to be alone again. I hold my pen to write, the paper smoothed out before me, its texture like a fine brocade. The touch comforts my hand. In words there is a world that I can make my own, when I am left to myself.

Francis became ill at Orléans. I was still grieving for you, *Maman*, and for our lost kingdom of Scotland. We wished to leave before the execution of the noble Condé was carried out. I do not like such loss of life. Why must all these disgraces and defeats end in butchery? I hope that Scotland is less cruel than France, yet fear that men everywhere hunger for revenge.

We were going to Chenonceau where Francis and I were betrothed. We spent our first weeks there also playing at being married. We were packed up and ready to embark on the royal barge, when Francis felt sick and giddy. Then a piercing pain began in his ear.

We went back to his bedchamber which was now empty and stripped down to bare boards and walls. Cushions were brought and he was laid down twisting in agony. I sat by him trying to hold his hand. Sometimes he clutched at me furiously but in other moments he was entirely lost to me.

The doctors came like disturbed rooks, pecking and croaking. Inflammation of the ear seemed their best description and they began with mustard plasters, salves and poultices. A mattress was unloaded from the boats, and four men raised his body and lifted it over. His dark hair was matted and tangled, his face white and smeared with ointment. A canopy was rigged to veil His Majesty, and a stool was carried in so that I could sit low beside him, or kneel to pray.

By evening the pain seemed to ease, and a fever began with flux and sweating. They came to and fro with cloths and pots, hanging the canopy with fragrant herbs to try and suppress the stench. I sat on all night, retiring only to wash and change. My head nodded with sleep but I remained conscious throughout of my dear one's restless tossing frame. Every so often he would moan or mutter but he did not look at me or speak. Was this how my own father died of a fever? Near dawn the ear began to discharge noxious fluids. I thought of the plague and how I might be next to sicken and die. But I reached out and took his sweaty hand in mine, to dare God, for I did not feel that I could die. Were we not too young?

By midday the flow had ceased, and it seemed as if the fever might abate. I went to wash, ate some bread dipped in wine, and lay on a couch in the antechamber till evening. When I returned to my station, a swelling like a pear had formed on the side of Francis' head and he was very hot. As darkness fell the fever climbed again. I insisted on holding the cool water and cloths myself, and bathing his brow.

When we were children I used to mop his smeary face. Little Francis, who grew to be a King. He stopped being a child to become a boy. This is like when he had measles or the sweating sickness, and I played at being nurse. Wife.

This creature in the bed, dissolving before me, had limbs and a soft white belly; black hairs were sprouting on his chest, like seedlings in the garden. His eyes were soft and dark like a dog fearing rejection or the casual blow. Francis, my puppy, we were happy and loving in our own chamber.

Was that what Grannie meant by conjugal relations? Cuddling, rolling and rubbing beneath our canopy. All the time we were coming closer. He was getting stronger and manlier. The seeding again, of new life, spilled warmly, to grow damp and cold on my flesh. Then I could get up to wipe it off and wash.

Is this my little warrior, my sweet Francis? Stinking in his vomit, and worse. All the wiping in the world will not make him clean. Can the herbalists not do better for a King, to control the stink? Their purges and enemas make it worse.

Queen Catherine arrives and tries to take charge. I will not let his mother have my place. She did not care for him when Francis was at her knee, so why should she usurp me at his sickbed? I see the judgment of death in her eyes, as she instructs more physicians. And I too am condemned in that gaze: a Guise. Now she will have control of this Court. I cannot think beyond this bedside; the rest is of no account to me.

The doctors plan to bore into his head to relieve the pressure. They assemble their instruments of pain, but the swelling subsides. Hope surges up. Then suddenly fever mounts again. I am taken off to sleep. I return. My little Francis is wasted, diminished flesh on gaunt bones. All that puppy fat has burned away.

By morning he is gone. Thank God he can be at rest. I cannot weep. Must not be other than I am, numb, insensate; this is a kind of death in which my unfamiliar person still responds slow and sluggish to a disembodied me. Is that what it feels like to die? I remember that once long ago I was joined to that Mary in the flesh. Shall I ever be married to myself again?

Sitting in darkness, calm and still, veiled in mourning. I cannot be touched.

If only there had been a child. I thought there was; to call my own, heart.

Francis was my child. You remember when we had to dance before the King, his father, and I had to steer every step and make conversation for two of us. Beaton was going to giggle so Fleming had to pinch her hard. I was Queen beside my consort, a fellow monarch, not a child.

Everything was written in our book, even what Poitiers said about perfumes and complexion, or how we chattered about young men like Kirkcaldy or James Hepburn. Poor Poitiers will never regain Court favour. The Medici will see to that. I used to stroke Diane's skin so smooth beneath my palm. She was fully formed, abundant in her own flesh, replete. Not like my awkward bony frame.

I think William Kirkcaldy very handsome, even if he is a Protestant. Could I have chosen a young gallant, like Livingston does, I would have chosen him to be at my side. He is on a white horse and I on a grey, galloping through green leaved branches. Are we in Scotland, in this dream, *Maman*?

My Marys are coming back to join me, now that my household is reduced. I have my own estates to sustain me. In France, with my Marys, we can go on.

What was it like when you went to Scotland as a Queen? Was my father strange or brooding? You did not speak about him much. You had babies born and die. You had a castle, a palace of your own, and your household around you, at Stirling. I must pronounce it with the 'r' extended, as you taught me, Stirrrling. Did you cry for home at night, missing Grannie Bourbon? You were a widow and a mother already in France.

France is my home. Though I come from Scotland, I was educated in France, and am Queen by my blood of Scotland, France and England. I am granddaughter of Henry VII; that cannot be annulled. Queen Dowager of France. Girl queen no longer. Queen Consort no longer.

What is my place in this puzzle?

The uncles have betrayed us, *Maman*. They sold my birthright to retain their power in France. They left you at the mercy of Scots Protestants, and signed a treaty to give up my claim to England.

I shall not sign their treaty. What is written in the blood cannot be set aside so lightly. My cousin Elizabeth will understand that without the claim of birth our royal estate is worthless. Some would have it so, lacking order or degree. They do not desire God's peace but unending conflict. They claim the people's cause and make their lives a misery.

I have sent Elizabeth my portrait and trust that she will send me hers. We are two queens cast on a world which men would direct. I want her friendship and she will not deny me hers. Is she tall or short, fair skinned, red haired? What colour are her eyes? How would we stand one beside another? Royal cousins: sisters left to ourselves we agree on all things, religion excepting, but we can learn to accept our differences as long as our kingdoms live at peace. Will she marry too?

The Uncles consider offers for my hand, from Austria, Denmark, German Princedoms, behind my back. They want to sell me to Spain, but the Medici will not allow me to be great at her expense. I have lost my family, not just my husband.

I cannot weep because my eyes were already dry.

Rheims is the best place. Aunt Renée reminds of you. She keeps her youth and dignity. The high chambers and silent vaulted corridors breathe our faith. When I was a little girl, Grannie Bourbon and I knelt together at this altar where I kneel to pray for you.

Your belongings are spread out in Renée's apartments. I had to make the inventory. Your dresses are all black, your cloaks lined with wool worn bare. I touch the ragged fibres with my fingertips. I cannot smell your scent.

Did your splendid beauty come finally to this – a faded tapestry, one cape of violet velvet? So sparse; jewels gone to pawn for guns and powder, a woman without adornment or display. I remember your gorgeous colours, the lustre of your pearls and flesh. The perfume of your majesty. My bounteous fragrant mother.

The coffin is dull grey lead. Inside your body is embalmed, veiled beneath a pall emblazoned with a white cross. I cannot see into this tomb but cover you with woven silk, emerald and golden yellow. Colours of the spirit overcome fleshly decay.

They would not bury you at Holyrood beside my ancestors the kings, your king, my father. They laid you on trestles in the Castle but now you are come home, to Aunt Renée and to me. And we will lay you here in the Abbey's blessed peace; and light perpetual will shine upon you. I thank God for the comfort of our religion, the true Catholic faith.

The lights on the altar, before the Blessed Virgin, are your requiem. Broken for us, tended by you, Mother of Christ, I have you in my mouth for life eternal. We are not separated by mortal death but eat together, united at the feast of Heaven. This do in remembrance of me. You are my body and my blood forever.

I should stay here in the convent and make my home with you.

Mary

MY BROTHER JAMES has arrived from Scotland and lodges in the town. The Uncles are at Rheims to pay respects to their beloved sister. Why did they not go to Scotland and rescue us? I am no longer Guise, not in my heart. Are hearts not ours to dispose of as we please?

The ambassadors came in with solemn faces, and hinted about another marriage. If only the Marys were here they would take them off one by one. Beaton and Livingstone do their voices, while Fleming tries to maintain decorum and a straight face. Elizabeth has still not sent me her portrait, yet we are supposed to be like sisters. I do not think that Secretary Cecil favours my correspondence. He is not my friend.

But my Marys are coming next week. Shall we all go home to Scotland, as once we sailed to France, when you waved us off, all the mothers together? Apart from Fleming's mother who came with us for a time. We didn't understand why she had to return and Fleming wept salt tears. We thought it was because she had to be like the rest of us, motherless. They say Lady Fleming was surprised by the Medici in Henri's bedchamber. Court scandal; I mistrust such gossip. What are the palaces like in Scotland?

We have spoken together for three days without pause, brother and sister. We walk and talk and walk again, inside and out. The cloisters are worn by our steps; it is a private place, and we are safe here within the Abbey's sanctuary. As you are safe here, now, forever.

Lord James has grown even more serious than he was when a boy. He looks at me through grey unblinking eyes, with something in them of the cold sea. They seem to judge me as one on whom everything has been freely lavished, while he has had to make his own way, establishing himself by unstinting effort. Is that his idea of justice? We have both lost a father, but I am bereft also of my mother. He does not understand the struggles of this Court, or how I have had to please everyone since my childhood. I never knew my father who took him hunting. Always the son is favoured, even when bastard-born.

Still he is my own half-brother, flesh of my flesh. I am familiar with him since my youngest days in France. There is comfort in his presence. He sits close by me, strong and compact in his body. He has an arm of steel which has already proved its worth in battle. But is his soul also adamant, his heart unfeeling? He does not touch me or embrace when we meet.

He says he did not betray you, *Maman*, but that as the kingdom had turned Protestant new policy was needed. If I return to Scotland he will support and advise me as rightful ruler of the nation, and as his own good sister, near in blood and kindness. He pays you his dutiful respect, in death.

Is that of any comfort?

Of course, in the absence of a king, he already has a ruling Council established by the nobles without my authority, in which he wields most influence. He offers me his protection, but in return he would be Earl of Moray and confirmed Regent till I return. Does he really want me to marry elsewhere and leave him to reign in Scotland? Are my Scottish nobles also searching Europe for a match that will keep me away? I wonder about Scotland and would like to see it for myself.

Yet he sits by me as a brother. He shares my thoughts and feelings. We are both without parents, and raised amongst strangers.

Lord James has a scent on his beard, like rose water. I think this an odd choice for his closely cropped chin, strong nose, full mouth with narrow lips. He has no woman to advise and guide him. What kind of Court will I find in Scotland? What kind of men will seek to govern me? I can, I think, depend on him, but shall not confirm him Earl or Regent yet.

Today we speak of religion. He says Scotland must align with England so that we may achieve unity between the realms, and peace on the island of Britain. He is testing me to see if I shall make faith a stumbling block, but I do not oblige.

Instead I ask why the Scottish lords have given up my claim to the crown of England. Is my right not the surest way by which the realms may be united?

But not as Catholic nations he counters, trying again, to flush me out.

I keep my counsel on that matter, but press my right to the succession if Elizabeth bears no children. We are both grandchildren of Henry VII, she by the son and I by the daughter. She is unmarried. He concedes my argument, without referring to their wretched treaty. If Elizabeth grants my rightful place in the succession, then the spirit of their treaty will be fulfilled, and my claim is satisfied without offence.

Because of things Lord James does not say, I feel he knows more of my refusal to approve their English terms than he is revealing. His informant is surely William Cecil in London or the English ambassador here. Nonetheless we are agreed on how we should proceed.

Of course I cannot give up my faith, since it is the true religion of Christ. Yet I would not impose on any, if they will in turn respect my freedom. He draws breath before commenting. I watch his mind turning and his eyes assess my sincerity. The face is as blank and unexpressive as his solid frame. Is he sincere?

Why turn Protestant. Is it money and lands? They say our father might have plundered the Church by reform, but he already had its wealth at his disposal. This brother James claims to be Prior of St Andrews, yet our great Cathedral was looted by the mob at John Knox's urging and he did nothing to stop it. My brother craves the security of power. I sense it from his every pore, stronger than desire or mental delight. Yet there is something earnest in his convictions. His mind is Calvinist, if not his morals. Is that the Protestant way – to believe the worst of every human will, to expect betrayal, violence and low cunning? If so I have no part in such philosophy, which can only fulfill the bleakness it foreshadows.

It might be, he insinuates, that a queen could practice private devotion in her royal chapel while the religion of the realm is unaffected. What a Protestant idea, but I will not demur. You and I, *Maman*, are *politique* in public, while wedded to the faith of our mothers. I would reign over a united kingdom, or kingdoms, by right of blood, not presumption of religion. But can such tolerance satisfy the zealots, or even Cecil's hatred of the Catholic pretender?

Lord James and I understand each other, not just as Stewarts, but as civilised creatures. His French is excellent for one who was not brought up here as I have been. We are both political. On that at least we can agree.

On this last day we rose early. Uncle Claude provided an escort to the forest where the royal hunt was waiting for us. James assures me I will never lack for sport in Scotland. Why did you not learn to hunt? I know that Grannie Bourbon disapproves, yet you were a Queen of Scots.

This is the call of life, to feel the rush of wind on your face, the whip of branches, the crack of twigs and cones beneath the hooves. The hounds lope ahead like supple, never tiring wolves, until with a blast of horns, the quarry sighted, chase begins in earnest.

This sport unites us, and I match his pace mile for mile. I do not fear the boar at bay or the royal stag who lowers his many-pointed crown to charge. At the finish I can wield a knife as well as any man. French courtiers look in askance but James knows our family passion, and for once seems carefree, exultant in the hunt and at the kill. This brings us close as kin, who rule a country rich in game. I long to see those wild lands and forests. James promises that when I return we will make a progress and hunt together at Glen Finglas. Did I hear that name when I was small? Strange on the tongue yet somehow familiar.

Back at the Abbey we eat rich food and talk long and deep over wine in my chamber. We name each of Scotland's great and weigh their worth, their place in our new situation. Without the earls and lords, he swears, Scotland cannot be governed, yet many of them are so proud themselves in nature as to be ungovernable.

The Douglas following is like the Guise in France, led now by Morton. He has written to me defending his part in this Reformation and asserting his alliance with Lord James. But he is greedy, whatever James avers in his support, and pleads his right to the estates of young Earl Douglas, whom he has in ward. Morton is not to be trusted but cannot be ignored. I will refuse his request since the young Earl is connected to me through the marriage of my grandmother Margaret Tudor to the Douglas. I shall not have my will presumed or forced. I am not some callow girl but a sovereign queen. James falls silent on Morton's merits and his religion.

The Hamiltons are next to us in blood, so the old Duke has most claim to the title of Regent. His son, Earl Arran, was proposed as Elizabeth's suitor. This spurned, the Hamilton interest offers me Arran's hand so he may climb next the throne. But once there Hamiltons would presume to rule. James tells me he is strange and may be mad. I recall he slavers in his food. We did not know what to make of Arran in France so he must be fended off in Scotland, though without offence. Hamiltons hold more of Scotland in their grasp than even Morton.

William Maitland Lord James commends as my most able statesmen. It was not his fault he had to leave my mother's service in her hour of need. Maitland too has written me a letter, offering his devoted service. Like mother, so daughter? I need his skills as Secretary and emissary to Elizabeth. The catch is that he favours English friendship and is allied most closely to Lord James. The Maitlands are true courtiers, and I will write in cordial terms since his loyalty will be crucial to my government. But might young Maitland prove false to me as he did to you?

Athol, Crawford, Caithness, and Huntly, above all Huntly, are the Catholic faction with great following in the north. I did not tell Lord James that their messenger is already here in France asking me to support a rising against his Council. He may or may not know, but is vehement the Catholic lords are unable to unite or to defend the realm, particularly against a Protestant England determined to subdue a hostile neighbour. We both have suffered the consequences of that power.

Then Bothwell too is of their party. James looks closely at me to trace my feelings about this rash young nobleman who was so recently in France. I defend him as a promising soldier, if no statesman. My brother grunts and says he would do anything for gain since Patrick the father left his cupboard bare. I am not willing to condemn Earl Bothwell who is loyal and will be useful. He is the man to hold our borders. I can see jealousy, or is it hate, in these normally blank grey eyes. How will my realm be ordered without strife and violence? It is not easy to rule such men, yet I have studied this art here in France.

That leaves Argyll, Lindsay, Glencairn, Erskine, Kirkcaldy, Ruthven and other Protestants who must be appeased by equal favour. Many though are gentleman and may be civil. Except John Knox for he will not suffer any cause for silence. We have the measure of such zealots here in France. I look forward to bearding Master Knox and hearing his theology, poor as it is. He may be more pleasing in the flesh than on the page. James seems torn between commending Knox and warning me against him, so refrains from speech. My brother is well practiced in the cult of silence.

By the end of this conversation it is clear that I am coming home, and that his Council remains in force till I return to order government with James Stewart as guide and mainstay. He will not be called Governor or Regent as I shall reign in my own right. I will write later to let him know my decision.

I do not want anything to spoil this time together, or my dear mother's sacred obsequies. He is returning home before the requiem mass, to avoid contamination.

The Marys arrive. We hold apart for an instant, but then burst into one uncontrollable flood like rivers in spate. We cannot restrain ourselves because we are united once again. They stood together in hesitation, heads lowered, but then Beaton broke ranks, next Seton and Livingston till finally Fleming abandoned decorum. We hug and weep and crush our mourning silks, and almost dance for tearful joy.

Since my marriage to Francis the Marys have been on the edge of the household, a Scottish island in the French ocean. But we shall return home together united as we came. I cannot express how I feel, so full of grief, yet happy. We are a family, equally divided from our own flesh.

They look well, except perhaps for Seton whose pallor has become perpetual, a veil of self-denial. Pious sacrifice will become her way of life. Livingston is fuller in the body, a Diana made for love and admiration. Beaton is sharp and bright as ever, vigorous in mind and body – Venus and Minerva all in one. She should be a queen as well as I – a duchess at least. I may make her one after we go to Scotland.

Fleming is the surprise. Always the elder sister, now she seems stronger and more composed than ever, Juno incarnate. She reassumes her place as chief lady without apology or fuss. She steers and chides the others, and will be my mainstay, my touchstone, the measure of conduct and of my conscience. She will manage the personal household; this is her natural part and she will perform it to the full. She fills the place left empty by mother, husband, uncles, aunt.

How did I ever cope without Fleming? Her return is like the coming of the seasons, expected yet doubly welcome. She seems more serious but her laugh is warm, and her smile always ready for the dutiful soul or the repentant prodigal alike. Dear Fleming, how could I ever survive without your companionship?

Now I can depart from you, *Maman*, just as we said goodbye so long ago, yet we never left each other's hearts. You are here at home in peace, for it is I who must go away to Scotland. But I have my family with me, as I had before. We sisters of Mary shall not be parted while breath remains in our bodies.

Pray for me now, and at the hour of my death. I keep you ever in remembrance till we meet again- here in earthly form and in heaven. I keep the thorn of Christ King Henri gave me in your honour, swathed in pearls and glass. You will be beside me always.

Goodbye, dear *Maman*. Goodbye, Aunt Renée. She has you in her kindly guarding. This lovely Abbey of St Pierre holds part of me as well. Let me return here at the end.

I am excited to be going back to Scotland. There I can reign without Medici or the Uncles always at my elbow. I shall be truly Queen at last, Queen of myself. Let fair winds fill the sails.

Le voyage commence.

Mary

OUR FINAL SCENE with Ambassador Throckmorton, is played on the quay.

'Madam, my mistress Queen Elizabeth earnestly desires that you might ratify the treaty.'

Poor Throckmorton bows repeatedly due to his discomfort. But I have my answer prepared.

'I cannot, sir, undertake such a step without the advice of my Lords in Council, since at present I am without counsel.'

'But, Majesty, it was those same lords who drafted and approved the Treaty.'

'Indeed, but I was not present in my Kingdom of Scotland at that time. Circumstances, Sir Nicholas, may change.'

'But not solemn assurances.'

This is abrupt for an ambassador.

'Pray your mistress, my royal cousin, be patient, as I am about to embark for Scotland. Have you brought your sovereign's safe-conduct for my passage?'

I know the reply to this question already.

'I regret, Majesty, it has not yet arrived.'

'So many delays. How vexing the slow conduct of affairs can be for us all.' I hear Beaton coughing back her giggles. 'Nonetheless, we shall embark come what may, as loyal subjects await my arrival.'

'Your Highness.'

We replay the whole scene aboard, with Beaton as Ambassador trying to keep her voice subdued, but getting redder in the face with every second. Fleming makes a staider me, but very proper – graceful, if a little plumper.

But we are away. Adieu, dear France, we may never see you more. We are Scotland bound.

The cargo ships are left to plough their heavy furrow. A whole household is packed in ten ships. I hope the horses will be calm. Our two fast galleys break away, cutting through the waves. We must speed past England without Elizabeth's safe conduct. I love to stand on deck and feel the wind on my face. I am without fear or sickness, facing north into the future. Everything is possible if I believe in myself, if I keep strong.

Livingston comes up with me on deck. She has the sea legs and does not take cold. Beaton has begun to retch, she says. Groans and basins below.

It was like this when we came to France as little girls, according to Fleming, and I teased them all the way without mercy. What a wild child I must have been before the Court took me in hand. A wild proud mountain Scot, I could take off this bonnet and shake my hair free, streaming in the breeze, like some storm maiden or an avenging fury. How Fleming would scold me for my dignity. There's no one here to see me apart from sailors. I could stay on deck all night and sleep tomorrow.

Is this what ancient writers call freedom?

The Admiral assures me we are entering my kingdom from the northern sea. Firth of Forth, I remember from my schoolroom maps. But all is blanketed in thick mist. The Scots call it haar like Hollanders or Germans. There are islands here, he says, and rocks, but everything is cold and shrouded. Yet this is summer. The Marys shiver below, but I am wrapped in my cloak and hood staring upriver. Is that a hill or harbour? Berwick Law, they say. What strange names everything has here. I must become more familiar with their style of speech.

The sails hang empty so the oars are lowered and we beat slowly through sluggish waters, casting lines and calling every looming shadow another sail. My escort straggles up on deck as we discern the shores, and eventually the Marys are all around me, arms linked, gazing into the mirk. What future does this place of home hold for us? We cling together in fear and in hope. Scotland is strange to us, and yet our own.

'Port of Leith to shore. Ship oars. Drop anchor.'

Cries echo between the ships, hollowed by the eerie fog. There is no sign from land, no sound. 'Fire'. A salute of guns from our galleys roars out and rolls against the sands with a dull thud. The Queen of Scots has come home, to a world asleep. Else everyone has died of plague. We descend below to await events.

Later, we go ashore in a few small boats. Some onlookers line the quay, but they are like sleepwalkers in the mist. These are my people, of the common sort, who seem ragged but friendly. They understand my Scots speech I believe, though stare at me open-mouthed when I talk to them. We are ushered into a house near the harbour front where a fire attempts to cheer bare boards. Messengers have been sent to my Council and to the Provost, but we seem to have arrived ahead of time and expectation.

As my horses have not come, we are brought Scots ponies on which to ride. The mist has begun to break up and I am very curious to see Edinburgh and my Palace of Holyrood. The horses are small beasts but spirited and we trot up the path with an escort from the Provost, who is not properly dressed to receive a queen. They do not stand on much ceremony here it would appear. He seems disconcerted, as if I was some marvel washed up from a realm beneath the waves.

Great dark shapes rear suddenly from the clouds. This is the mountain of Arthur's Seat; that the Hill of Calton. I had thought Arthur was a prince of England but it seems he reigned here as well. Over the rise is the Abbey and Palace. My mother made a beautiful garden there which I long to see. We are tired and want to come home, yet we are excited. Even though we are trying to be strict, as we top the rise we break into a gallop. I admit I broke away first, but then the others followed after with cries and shouts. And finally at the tail our escort thinking the horses had bolted. With a hurrah we clatter under the palace gatehouse. The Queen has come home like an ensign with her troop. Servants come running and my feet touch this sacred ground of Holyrood for the first time.

I must walk here on my own, though they follow behind at a distance. This is your place. The tower rooms are still furnished, barely, but the audience chambers beyond are empty, boarded and echoing. I long for rugs and hangings. Grey light washes in tall windows lending small illumination. Here you paced, leaving no footprints, but I am your familiar, your ghost.

The garden court is more welcoming, though weeds force their way through the paths, and variegate once strictly ordered beds. These are in the French fashion, and open beyond into wider gardens stretching into shrubberies and orchards as far as we can see on every side. What harmony of beauty and design, spreads out below Arthur's Hill, while partaking of this sanctuary the Abbey bounds are bathed in peaceful quiet. I like this place, our place.

We turn at last into the Abbey Church. Everything seems stark and gloomy. Where are its altars, its candles, its banners? Chapels abandoned; prayers and masses silenced; light of the sacred host extinguished. Is this what Master Knox calls holiness?

Yet the dead are here also, my Stewart ancestors. King James my royal father, secluded in his ornate tomb. Does he countenance such Protestant emptiness? And my mother's absence, his beloved Guise. Fragile Madeleine lies here, but not his true consort. She is at rest in France, while these walls whisper her name. Marie, Mary. Come back. I have come. So cold without a living flame.

Our quarters are in my father's Tower. *Son château fort et agréable.* Deserted now, but who resides in the Courts beyond, one after the other receding into the spacious gardens? Monks dwelled here once, but now there is endless accommodation for servants, nobles, royal officers. A palace as royal and commodious as any in France. Do not malign the Scots for parsimony, my Marys, salute their pride and honour. We shall earn their just esteem.

When will my ships berth so that these chambers and yards may again be our living, breathing place, the beating heart of our kingdom? Let poetry, dance and pageant reign. Let masses be said and wise decrees scribed. This is my beginning, my inheritance, and we shall make it proud and joyful. Though I must wear black mourning, and not give way to gaudy show.

'Where will the King's apartments be?' asks Beaton.

'What King? I have lost my husband,' I reply in reserved dignity.

'He will have space to choose from,' quips Livingston.

How they babble. Must the Queen have a consort who should be King? Perhaps Elizabeth will never wed. And why should I? Is once widowed not enough? Bearing no fruit.

The kingdom wants an heir, young and full of promise. I shall give birth to a manling. And you, my companions, will be wed each one to a nobleman and loyal counsellor of his Queen. We shall generate new followings and kin.

'I will never leave you, not by my choice, in life or death,' says Seton.

'No more melancholy, dear ones, no diffident looks. Turn out those trunks till we furnish ourselves with some comfort. Bring wine and cake to refresh our bodies, and may this weather lighten to tune our souls. In such echoing emptiness we will make a court together.'

I do not feel strange here. We have come home and will bring life and warmth to deserted places, a hearth for the kingdom and hope for my people. At Holyrood the Queen of Scots has come to dwell with her own. But the Queen's belly is toom; let the poor lass and her ladies be fed, lest like her father she might go begging in disguise and learn the secrets of her subjects.

Please rest and be calm. There are long days ahead of us. So Fleming.

What prudent foresight for one so young and blithe. Has Scotland made her grave before her time? We have only just landed. Our Court will mend all heaviness, and make this Kingdom light once more.

Truckle beds are spread out in the Tower apartments. I shall make my private rooms here, as my father did, because it can be sealed off from the palace chambers and offices, secure within its bounds. We are safe here, eating from our laps, sipping wine from wooden beakers. Girls again, playing at picnics.

But the mist swirls round and grey shapes mass around the palace grounds. Will they roll and break over us in drowning waves? No, the people, my people, serenade their queen with holy psalms. The Marys block their ears as pipes screech and viols scrape, out of key with untutored voices. No, dear Marys, sincerity brings harmony. Wave at the open window. Protestants should not be blamed; they mean well. Come again tomorrow, good friends, but for now let us retire to sleep. We have travelled far on unfriendly seas.

Late abed; restless night. Between wakeful moments I see an island. And on it a garden where we wander free. Hollyhocks and roses, beds of waving lavender, golden daisies with white ruffs. We put out to sea on foaming oceans and all the mothers are in our boat waving silver handkerchiefs, but I cannot hear what they are saying, mouths opening and closing as they are swallowed up by fog. I am being left behind; stone walls rear up to close me in. The dark tower stifles, smothers, and I am awake fighting for breath, panic rising.

Fleming has her arm round my shoulders and wine at my lips. I am alright; I am back at Holyrood in Scotland. My mother and my father were so near. Our Marys have become the mothers and all is well. All shall be well. God is merciful now and at the hour of our death. The sign of Holy Cross protects against our deepest fears. I thank God for my religion, when all else fails. This has been left to me for hope and courage. The morning will bring better comfort.

Fleming's breast is warm and soft like goose down in a cotton bolster. I can sleep again in safety sleep, like a daughter.

Mary

THE SHIPS HAVE arrived. Everything is here except the horses, which were diverted to England, before Elizabeth's safe-conduct was announced. My beautiful mounts will come soon, in time for our ceremonial entry to Edinburgh. Carts and mules ferry everything up with endless unpacking, decorating and storing.

These yards are a maze of chambers and cellars with room for all the household. What will it be like when Court gathers? My tapestries hang well in these fine audience rooms, and the great gallery will be magnificent for music and dancing. The Lady and Unicorn weaves will go there. There is a finely carved stone unicorn at the palace gate beside his Lion mate. I must have those marvellous creatures regilded.

My chapel is dressed, the altar gleaming with Grannie Bourbon's silks. The lamp of the Blessed Sacrament is lit, a comfort to set against the desecrated Abbey Church. It was dedicate to Holy Cross, St Mary Virgin and All Saints, in memory of my blessed ancestor St Margaret of Scotland. We pray for better times.

Beaton says Holyrood is *Chambord en Écosse*, and I see what she means in our ornate façade. But the gardens are larger here, and the setting much grander. My master gardener wastes no time as the men come back to work and everything is quickly restored to order. They are fine gardeners in Scotland, I can see, but we must have more flowers and fragrant herbs to complete Amman's design. The summer is shorter so we must work harder for the beauty and the art. Yet sun has chased away the fogs and everything is so green and bright, not blanched or faded as in Loire heat.

At last the entry. On the eve we ride by Holyrood, with Arthur's Seat rising on our left, to dine at Cardinal Beaton's mansion. This seems a strange choice to my Beaton, but it is convenient for so large a party and is a fine house in the French style. Many gentlemen of old families are there to greet me and pay homage. There is food in plenty with fine music and all are glad and merry. A few, I am told, have stayed away at Master Knox's bidding since he disapproves of courtly life. Let him repent at his own leisure but not disturb my people's happiness at their Queen's return.

Our procession began at the Castle. We rode up from the north side and in the great Port or Gate. This is a fortress, ringed by walls of rock and surmounted by towers. It stares down at the houses far below but also looks out over land, hill, island, sea. It has the nature of my kingdom in its gaze.

After stirrup cups in the yard, we assemble on open ground before the gate. Fifty Moors go before. 'Their costumes have seen better days,' says Beaton in my ear. No matter, this day is joyous. My party forms beneath a waving canopy, while behind knights and burgesses provide my escort, brightly attired and armed, flags and banners held from their saddles.

Then down into the town, hooves on cobbles, horns and trumpets sound and cheers from the gathered folk. The Castle guns roar a noisy salute and the horses start. No psalms today. In the wide Lawnmarket we pause before a wooden arch, gaily painted. This is my point of entry since there is no gate on the castle side. A choir of children sings sweetly from its battlements and, as I pass beneath, a golden globe descends and opens to reveal a bonny angel who presents me with the keys and a velvet Bible. I cannot hear his words of welcome, as I pass the books to Erskine, Captain of my Guard, but I remain passive and unmoved. Erskine is most stern and handsome.

Waving to the crowd, I move on towards St Giles where the way narrows. Here the Virtues are on dumb display as costumed virgins. Many of the nobility wait beyond the Kirk, finely arrayed and mounted to show their estate. I acknowledge all graciously and go on towards the Cross.

The common sort have massed here to see the fountains run with wine, but many were already drunk, raising unruly bottles and fondling women of the town. My guards closed up to steer me past. Livingston and Beaton were in stitches at the antics but I was composed for the present. At the Salt Tron three effigies were burning; Huntly told me later they had been priests till he arrived and turned them into disobedient Israelites. At Netherbow Gate there were more fires as a dragon was set ablaze to sacred music. Do they anticipate an apocalypse? So much paint and timber put to waste. The Council of Edinburgh seems over fond of burnings.

Beyond the gate, the nobility gathers round to accompany me to the Palace. We can relax there as the pageant is complete. People line the Canongate to wave and cheer. They are warm people in this country, who do not stand on needless ceremony or restrain their feelings. I am glad of it. But at Holyrood one last Protestant anthem is recited, as a cartload of children have been rehearsed to chant against the Mass. I thank them for their voices and retire.

I will hear no more for now about feastings. Does my Council not convene tomorrow for its first day of formal meeting? So tonight we supper in my rooms, alone with wine and dainties, and tease out every moment of this never-ending day, to reenact and criticise and praise. It has been my day for, despite all their efforts at defiance, the Calvinists could not sour it. Laugh or sing or play, since politics will have its say. But today the advantage is mine. I have been seen by my people, in royal state. They like what they see.

The palace has a different mood this morning. Many of the lords have rooms by ancestral right in this warren of chambers and dark passages. Many also have houses in the Canongate but come and go in company with those lodging here, from first light until curfew. I hear comings and goings, challenges and greetings as I drift from sleep to wakefulness. We are a Court now, not just a palace. When the nobles are in residence only this Tower is our sanctuary. The rambling ranges hum like some hive of never resting bees.

They occupy two sides of a long table, bearded and bonneted. My Lords in Council. As they arrive each comes to greet me in person. I feel Bothwell's eyes looking into mine as if to sense my inmost thoughts. Argyll, Glencairn: this is the first time I have met the western lords since they were in France. Morton – what small pig eyes he has. Hamilton and his strange son, Arran, are in attendance but silent, as if to say they reserve their position on my government. I can see there is no love lost between them and James Stewart. Bothwell seems able to antagonise all parties equally, but he discomforts my brother most of all. Why should that be?

Good Huntly is Chancellor, yet for all his bulk he directs little, since James and Maitland have everything in hand. Formal business is dispatched without discussion and they disband within an hour. As he goes Bothwell mutters that I must not let them send him to the Borders as he is my only true friend in Scotland. What a hungry young man he is, never satisfied. His face is swarthy and mottled these days, as well as broken at the nose, but his black eyes gleam with pride and desire. I like James Hepburn, and their jealousy will not deny me his loyal service or strong arm.

They retire to drink and talk in twos and threes. It seems everything important happens outside the meetings. I keep genial Athol and Lord John Stewart, my other charming half-brother, near me to make friends. Thank God I have some genial relations and my Marys. Otherwise this Court would be heavy weather.

Yet in Scotland even Calvinists can dance. When the day advances all are pleased to drink the best French wine and eat royal game. My table will be generous and my musicians naturally excel. Some nobles have their wives at Court, and they come out to view the fashions and display their native finery. Others cluster round my ladies – Livingston, Beaton, Fleming and the rest. I catch Morton leering at my wardrobe mistress with his narrow eyes. I would have all pleasance but I shall not permit immorality or license in my household. Let the godly take note and for once be satisfied.

Two days go by in conversation and recreation. This kingdom has been without a Court and now its life is being reborn. Everyone except the preachers cannot but be agreeable. Yet on Sunday, passing into Mass, I hear oaths and curses. I turn back towards the door as three or four armed men come running, abusing the priests and denouncing idolatry. Lord Lindsay is one, Arran another. Would they do violence in my own chapel? I want to confront them but Erskine draws me back behind the altar. Suddenly Lord James is there blocking the way, denying them entrance, I see the black cloth of his broad shoulders and a drawn blade.

'Stand away, you have no business here.'

His tone is calm and even.

'Cleansing papist stews is our business.'

'This service has been allowed. You have no right and if you do not give way then you will suffer for it.'

The threat is clear and they edge back under protest.

'You're treating with the Devil.'

'Nonetheless I gave my word and stand by it. So give way.'

Violence rises in his tone, straining like a hunting dog at scent. I had not seen him like this before. They went off grumbling, still with weapons in their hands, while my brother stood outside the door until Mass was done. Behind his gravity there is blunt strength.

Naked blades drawn in anger. I have never known such a thing before. My presence, it seems, is no protection.

Maitland and Lord James are in conference about the embassy to London. And again they are discussing my marriage. As if yesterday's events had not taken place, or were situated in some foreign country, not my private quarters in the palace. I approve the embassy, for my dearest wish is to be friends with Elizabeth. I shall write to her in my own terms. As for another husband, I am indifferent to such an outcome. I shall remain in mourning, as befits a widowed Queen.

Mary

I WANT TO meet John Knox. James and Maitland look askance but I must hear the dog bark from his own mouth. What is this thing I have to reckon with? Will they kill the priests and confessors before my eyes? So Maitland sends for the Minister of St Giles, who comes promptly, under my brother's watchful eye. I take Master Knox into my garden, which is filling up with new blooms by the day.

'What shall we talk about, Maister Knox?' I am careful to use the Scots address, as more friendly and familiar.

'Whatever your Majesty pleases.'

He is surprising in the flesh, smaller and somehow delicate, fine boned. The eyes are liquid, brown and melting, intense. Knox appears a man of emotion as well as reason.

'I think I shall scold you.'

'That is the prerogative of your sex, madam.'

Was that a twinkle?

'I have been told that you have raised some of my subjects against me.'

'Whoever said that has done you no service.'

'In a book, Maister Knox, written by you against the "unnatural" rule of women. You are the author of this work?'

'Indeed, madam.'

'It is not a good book, and I have set some learned men to answering it.'

'I shall abide their questions.'

He seems unwilling to take offence, yet is wholly unmoved by his Sovereign's disapproval. Has he no experience of Court manners?

'Do you hate women, Maister Knox?'

'Indeed no, your Majesty, I do not. My faults are all on the fond side.'

There is a smile in those luminous eyes. The face is slender, musing and melancholy.

'Yet you stand accused of disobedience and sedition. I can hardly believe it of such a douce and modest man. But where there is smoke, Maister, there is usually fire.'

I think there was a sigh and a drawing up of his shoulders as he stepped away from my side and drew himself up to address me at some length. His only aim is to teach simple truth according to God's Word – how we should worship and live godly lives. If that offends the vanity of papistical religion and the false authority of the Roman Anti-Christ, so be it. But it is always right to obey the commands of just and godly Princes.

'Yet you deny my authority.' I bring him to a halt.

'All through the ages, madam, learned men have had liberty to express their opinions, while living peaceably and doing nothing to disturb the peace. I have communicated my views but if the realm finds no inconvenience in a woman's rule then I shall not oppose it, except in my private conscience, unless you yourself oppress the saints of God.' He has the decency to blush and look away at this sophistry. 'The truth is, Madam, I wrote that book against the Jezebel, Mary Tudor of England. You were never in my thoughts.'

'That's as may be, but the book is about women in general.'

'Very true, but I think you have the wit to distinguish between philosophy and sedition. If I wanted to disturb your estate because you are a woman I could have chosen a better time than when your own gracious presence is in the kingdom.'

'Beautifully phrased, Maister Knox. I see you are a courtier after all. But you have taught my people to receive a different faith from what their Princes allow. How can that doctrine be of God, when God commands subjects to obey their Princes?'

'Right religion comes from God alone and not from worldly Princes. Where would you and I be if the Apostles had obeyed the Emperor of Rome?'

'They did not raise their swords against him.'

I hear my voice raised in the heat of argument. He remains controlled but emphatic.

'But they disobeyed. To disobey commands is to resist.'

'The sword, man, they did not rebel by the sword.'

'God did not grant them the means.'

'So if they have the means then they can violently resist?'

'If the Prince exceeds his bounds.'

There he is evidently wrong, and I take him to task.

'If they dislike the Prince's actions, then they can take up their swords and strike. Where then is the solemn command of scripture – to obey? Why are rulers distinguished from subjects if they are denied authority?'

With another sigh, as at a recalcitrant pupil, Knox showed his true colours.

'Madam, if my father is mad or drunk then he must be seized and bound till the madness is past. What if he attacks my brothers or sisters? He must be restrained from murder and it is no different with Princes. This is not rebellion but true obedience.'

'Well then, Maister Knox, I see how it is. My subjects will obey you and not me. They will do what they like, not what I command, and I shall be subject to them, not them to me. What kingdom could survive such government?' I demand.

His response was more conciliatory, and self-deprecating.

'God forbid that anyone should obey me or do what they please. My argument is that both rulers and subjects should obey God. And that, in return for their authority, Princes should nurture the Church. If that be subjection it will carry them to everlasting glory.'

'There I agree, but it is not your Kirk that I will nurture, but the faith in which I was born, since I believe it to be the true Church of God,'

Now he is openly provoked, and abrupt.

'Your will, Madam, is no reason. Nor does your thinking it make that harlot the immaculate spouse of Christ.'

'Remember to whom you speak, sir.'

'The Church of the Jews, which crucified Christ, was no more astray from the purity of religion than the Church of Rome.'

'My conscience does not agree.'

'Conscience, madam, requires knowledge, and I fear you have none.'

Who is he to deny my learning?

'Knowledge? Since I could read as a child I have studied religion.'

'So had the Jews. They read the Law and the Prophets but according to the teaching of the Pharisees. Have you read anything apart from what the Pope and cardinals allowed?'

'You interpret Scripture in one way, and they in another. Who is to judge?'

'God speaks plainly in his Word and his Spirit guides us into all truth. Where for example does Scripture command the Mass? It is an invention of man; let those that teach it show where it is laid down and I will grant their plea. Otherwise it is no solemn sacrifice but an abomination, like the idolatry of the Virgin Mother and all the Saints.'

'You are too harsh, sir, and better than I can answer you.'

'Would that the most learned papist in Europe were here to carry the argument.'

'You might be answered sooner than you think.'

'I would answer with my life if need be.'

'That will not be necessary. We shall live in better times, Maister Knox, and by other manners.'

'I pray God that it may be so, Madam.'

His shoulders drooped as if the fight were over. I have certainly heard enough.

'I see from the impatience of my ladies that their dinner is getting cold on the table.'

'Thank you for your patience in hearing me, Majesty. I pray that you may be as blessed within the Commonwealth of Scotland as ever Deborah was in Israel.'

He manages to incline his head without bending his stiff neck. *Sacré Dieu*, was ever a monarch so lectured?

I remained standing till he withdrew, showing no impatience or annoyance. I shall hear Mass when and where I wish, despite his preachings.

I saw Maitland studying me closely. They did not expect such an audience, and I held my own. If I take relief in tears, what is that to him or any other man?

Fleming, oh Fleming, now I feel what my mother bore. By herself.

Mary

I WANT TO spell out everything I see and rehearse it, because these sights bring me closer to you. I thought that France was what we shared and that taking you home to Rheims was the nearest we could still be to each other. But now I know that Scotland is where you belonged, and I want to share that, since I am your successor. This is our country, *Maman*.

We set out with only a small train – the personal guard, my Marys, James Stewart, and the immediate household – so we can travel quickly rather than depend on mules or carts. It is refreshing to canter away from Edinburgh on a bright breezy day, passing by woods and rigs, farm towns, and kirks in the sunshine.

We cross Cramond Brig and, coming up over the ridge, we see the wide river spread beneath us and all of Fife beyond. What big skies there are in Scotland with clouds sailing over seas of blue. I break into a gallop startling the peasants who labour in their fields. The others come on after me like a hunt in full chase. I shake the Court loose from my hair.

After a couple of hours of steady riding, we come down towards the river and the Castle of Blackness rears up ahead guarding the estuary. I send a messenger to pay our respects to the Governor but press on inland towards Linlithgow.

Niddrie Castle, a house of the Setons, is on our left, and the family ride out to greet us and press us to visit. This is some ploy of dear Seton's to introduce me to her sisters and brothers, so there is much embracing and crying on the road. I will not be moved to turn aside from our route, but everyone is happy with the warmth of this meeting. I invite them all to come on later to Linlithgow so that we can dine together.

Clattering through the West Port we come into the High Street lined with fine houses. Onlookers come running and bonnets are waved as word spreads that their queen has come. Linlithgow is a loyal town and our château rises above the houses. Coming up the Wynd, where the galleries of the merchants' residences nearly meet over our heads, we go through the Palace archway. It is handsomely ornamented with my father's chivalric arms. I stop at St Michael's Church and go in to pray before entering the palace. The altars here have not been cast down.

I touch the great font in which I was baptised, having been born on the Feast of the Immaculate Conception of St Mary the Virgin. You gave thanks to God for my safe delivery, but the kingdom did not rejoice in the birth of a girl. Yet had I not been born, within days of the King my father's death, Scotland would have fallen into the hands of Henry Tudor and of his heirs. Two Queens, two Marys, kept this nation free and independent, as she has been since ancient times. It came with a lass – I think my father was ower sair on the lassies.

I feel your presence strongly in this palace where I was birthed. It is a true royal residence and we must restore it all, chambers and audience rooms. Let water flow once more from the fountain and we shall feast in the great hall and hear minstrels in the gallery. From the galleries we look down on a fine lake.

Tonight we must be simple and *en famille* with each other. In time we will keep Easter at Linlithgow, or Yule, as royal Stewarts did before. It is good that my brother is here with us. Together we can bring the good times back, as they were before our grandfather went to war and the flower of Scotland was cut down. It was here at the gate an old man came to Margaret Tudor as she passed from the Church, warning that her husband should not go to England. And a chill passed through her heart. She did not hold his body in her arms again, alive or dead. Yet it is through her that my claim to England comes.

Morning arrives cloudy from the west with spits of showers, but I think the day will blow clear again. We cross the Avon and climb out of the valley to find the River Forth spread below us on the right once more, but with a solid massif of hills on the other side. These it seems are the Ochils, a word as strong and squat in the mouth as their appearance to the eye.

We keep on the higher ground, heading towards Falkirk, as we plan to visit Callander Castle. This is Livingston's home, bounded by woods and hunting parks while commanding the slopes on the western side of the valley. We gallop through the gates beneath waving trees. And when we arrive the Flemings are here as well, gathered in welcome. They have ridden over from Cumbernauld to see their beloved daughter. Tears and hugs over again, and I am introduced all round. For them our youth is a chapter of lost years. But these families are loyal, the fabric of this Kingdom, and it is through them that we shall restore our nation's prosperity and good name.

We are well entertained, and pressed to stay, but drag ourselves away to take advantage of the long light evening and reach Stirling. The skies are clear but tinged by crimson in the west, as we top a hill and see Stirling Castle rising from its plain like a ship on the ocean. Before us is the field of Bannockburn, and beyond the citadel to west and north, steep Alpine ranges, ridged and pinnacled, are bathed in sunset, like battlements in an apocalypse. These are the never ending Highlands, wave after mighty wave, all in this kingdom, larger than we had imagined from schoolroom maps. We pause to take in the panorama before breaking into a canter, determined now to reach a goal so near and the safety of its walls before darkness falls.

The town is lit to welcome us with torches and braziers. People are waving on the streets, accompanied by pipes and drums. Acrobats and jugglers come tumbling down the broad market square, where in front of their Tolbooth the Provost and Baillies are assembled in official welcome. Toasts are pledged and quaffed to repeated cheers as new barrels are broached for distribution to the commons.

Horsemen wait to accompany us up and onwards through the town. On each side we pass the mansions of the earls, rich in carvings and hung with banners. Each household stands at their gate with arms at salute and flags flying. As we cross open ground towards the portcullis the last red light throws the fortress and its ring of mountains into black relief. Finally we enter your castle and home. We are exhausted and fall into our beds without ceremony or delay.

We are up early to walk the ramparts and gardens. A theatre of nature is laid out around us. I summon Maister Buchanan, who is lodged here, to point out the scenes. We have never seen him so moved, almost passionate. He is my Scots Poet now.

'This is my calf country, Madam', he tells us. 'See there – Menteith, where your lady mother took you as a child to shelter on the Isle of Inchmahone.' I peer out into the cloudy distance where my island lies hidden. We were all there together. 'And beyond stretches the Lennox – that is Ben Lomond above the clouds.' Perhaps now, he hints, the Earl of Lennox will return home from England with his fine son, Darnley. In Scotland it seems even the scholars have some clan to which they are loyal.

Moving round we are looking down at the river and the hills are much closer. 'That is Dumyat, Madam – the Dun or fortress of the Maetae. They were a lost people with their own language who reigned here in ancient times. That bridge below is where William Wallace defeated the English army when he enticed them over to the marsh beyond and fell on them fiercely. Through the pass of Allan there is Dunblane where the Saint of Bute founded his cathedral.'

'Is that not where Margaret Drummond and her sisters lie buried? She was my grandfather's love but the nobles poisoned her so he would marry Margaret Tudor.'

'So gossips and rumour-mongers say, but history is something other.'

'You despise the storytellers? I seem to have known such stories from childhood.'

'Indeed, most of Scotland's histories are story, lies, and fable. They wrote in Latin with no understanding of the ancient tongues spoken here.'

'I read the Latin ones in Paris, but it appears that you must write your own history, sir.'

'I shall, Madam, if I am spared to serve this kingdom.'

'What models will you take?'

'Livy and Tacitus will shape my style, but the matter will be Scots.'

'You must come, Maister Buchanan, when we are at Holyrood, to read Livy with me. And you must write a masque for our Court. What is a palace without poets? And you are reputed to be Europe's finest.'

'As Your Grace pleases.'

He is well satisfied but reluctant to show it. There is something of the curmudgeon in Buchanan, yet he has the Muse's gift.

We return inside to eat and prepare for Mass. The chapel choir is summoned to sing once more. It is famous for its music but has fallen into disuse due to the absence of my mother.

We proceed from our apartments across the inner courtyard accompanied by two Chaplains, with the solemn chants sounding from the Chapel's open doors. Then it erupts. Argyll, still pulling on his doublet, comes running through the arch shouting in Irish. Followers appear with drawn swords. Cries for the guard. Lord James appears already armed. Does he watch every movement close at hand? He argues with Argyll, who seems beside himself with rage. Then James comes towards us and commands me to turn back. I stand my ground, and see Argyll's troopers go inside the Chapel. Screams and shouts. What outrage is this?

'It is not agreed. Only the private Mass at Holyrood. Now please go before any lives are lost. Argyll has authority here.'

'My priests?'

'Cracked heads will mend. Now go before we see worse.'

We are shepherded away by guards as if we might be assaulted next. Do I command here only for show? They are scattering vessels, shredding the music books like madmen.

This time is spoiled. We remain indoors all day. That night I topple a lamp in sleep and nearly burn myself to death. I must not show fear. Whatever happens, I must not let them see I am afraid.

The morning is wet as we form up in column, and huddled in our cloaks, trot out of almost deserted streets. Crossing the Forth by Wallace's bridge we follow the causeway towards Dumyat and then turn towards Dunblane. The Cathedral Tower appears to nestle above the village. We go out by a steep street of cottages onto higher ground and immediately meet the wind. An empty moor stretches to the west but we set course northwards, and are on the hills all day, with occasional castles and settlements on each side. Gradually the weather lightens and more distant Highland mountains emerge. I begin to stir back to life yet still cannot bring myself to speak to my brother. He seems not to notice, plodding on with his normal taciturn aspect. I start to believe his spirit is in tune with Scotland's soul; that he would be fitter than I to rule this moody land.

The afternoon is brighter as we come down into the Earn valley and follow the river towards Perth. The ground is rich, and when we climb up again it is only to look down into the even greater sweep of the Tay and its fertile plains. This river stretches back into the hills, but just before it widens to meet the sparkling Earn, the towers and steeples of the town are gathered tight within their walls.

Again the people have assembled to welcome their queen. The guildsmen perform an ancient sword dance, musicians play, and every archway is garlanded with greenery and flowers. The Provost greets me warmly, wine flows, and a golden heart weighed with coins is borne on angel wings into my ladies' hands. Our mood is lifted by this gay scene and even a Calvinist dumb show in the background, posturing against the Mass, cannot subdue the people's merriness.

A great banquet is held in the Trades Hall to celebrate our coming. Even in France I did not witness such abundance; geese and swans, duck, capons, haunches of venison, sweetmeats and pasties follow each other on huge trenchers, with copious wines and ales. It is a prosperous town, and the entertainment continues until late.

When the minstrels fall silent players come bustling in with one interlude after another. These are farces with thieves swopping sheep for babies in the cradle to escape detection, and a peasant who sends his wife to plough while he stays to keep house and wreak havoc. The Scots do not laugh quietly. Calls and jests accompany the performance, while they respond in kind and weave boisterous spectators into their action. I see Maister Buchanan's brows darken at such lapses, but these dramas do not aspire to be of Aristotle's school.

All seems well until next day when we ride the burgh bounds before departing Perth. Blackfriars, Whitefriars, Franciscans and the Charterhouse: this town was rich in sacred orders. But every window gapes, doors hang ajar, debris is strewn in the yards. Each has been sacked and pillaged. 'What has happened to the holy fathers,' I ask but none can answer. It seems they had accumulated wealth, and a Beggars Summons was nailed to their gates, threatening destruction if their worldly means were not given to the poor. Surely alms were distributed? Then John Knox came stirring the fury of the mob. All has been despoiled by those who greeted me yesterday with such joy. The crowd who cried 'Hosanna' turned to 'Crucify' before Passion Week had ended.

I was affected by these sights, and felt unable to continue with our journey. I thought they would carry me into Charterhouse, where the first King James, my ancestor, was murdered by his nobles. I sobbed till they laid me on a pallet and brought soothing cordials. I was lifted onto a litter and borne between two horses away from that loyal burgh.

I do not remember much of royal Scone, fertile Strathtay, or of bonny Dundee, though I saw its steeple rising above the glittering estuary as we were ferried across to Fife. Beaton's family came to Scone to welcome her and urge her to return home with them to Angus, where the cardinal's widow and all his kin were waiting to receive her. But Beaton would not leave me in my time of need. Besides we were set for famed St Andrews, which Beaton had never seen.

What a strange light hovers on Tay waters where they ripple to the sea, eerie yet bright and hard, so different from the soft moist colours of Stirling and Perthshire. Mine is a rainbow kingdom, and not the grey mountain realm I imagined in France, or that the Calvinists conceive.

When we touched Fife shore, I regained my strength and remounted. Now we were like pilgrims approaching the great shrine of Andrew. We wound along the shore where the monks of Balmerino came out to offer refreshment and a blessing. They at least are undisturbed. Then by Leuchars and the Guardbridge, we traced the pilgrim way looking towards the Town before us wreathed in evening light.

The official welcomes over, we rode past the Colleges and into the Cathedral precinct. The massive building loomed above us in the gathering dark as we took up our apartments in the Prior's residence, Lord James' home. It was strange to be in my brother's household for the first time, when he had been a guest in mine so often. We were hospitably but soberly entertained. After supper I sat with him a while beside a comfortable fire, though he has no small talk. He reminded me bluntly of his request to be made Earl of Moray, as this would allow him to make a suitable marriage. I promised to consider this fully when Court resumes at Holyrood. Marriages are something I can devise for others.

Beaton was up first and urging us into outdoor clothes. A keen wind was chasing clouds and sun over the sky. What a wild sea-girt place this is. We went first to view the rugged castle on its cliffs. Unspoken in our minds was the cardinal's brutal death, when his bloodied corpse hung over these walls. And at this spot George Wishart burned before the gates. Beaton is more excited than distressed, but I cross myself and pray that henceforth not one more soul will die for their religion in my kingdom. Dear Seton says a rosary.

Then we walk along the cliff, churning waves to one side and the towering cathedral walls on the other. The chapel of St Mary by this path marks where the first seafaring monks came to a lonely promontory to seek a place of prayer. We turn into the monastery by the sea gate and, passing St Rule's Tower, we enter the Cathedral from the east end. And come to sudden halt.

What harmonious majesty and beauty soars above us, reaching to the heavens with waves of northern light flowing through its wide proportions. Yet what wreckage strewn on every side, as if a ferocious gale had seized this stately ocean-going ship and shaken it almost to destruction. Broken glass lies underfoot in many colours, statues shattered, cloths and fabrics torn. As we step gingerly down, we pass altars smashed at every pillar, aisle chapels wrecked. Doors hang open and the birds of the air fly through as if it were an empty barn.

How my brother keeps his cathedral. Is this what they mean by pure religion, idolatry cleansed, swept away? But by St Andrew's sacred relics, unless we can see the saints, how will people know holiness? The Mass according to the image breakers is idolatry, but at the altar we touch and see and taste the sacrifice of Christ. What does this destruction leave our souls? Bare stone; hollow tombs echoing death. This takes heaven from us, and penitential hope, leaving hell to fill empty unhallowed minds. I am trembling with anger, not with fear.

Can they not see where this will end? A religion of fear and despair, worldly pride which acknowledges no restraints. When the house is swept bare the devil enters in to make a hell in heaven's despite. They honour nothing and no one beyond themselves. All else must be dragged down and trampled beneath their senseless feet.

I was half-carried, half-hurried, shaking and sobbing back to the house to lie down. But I cannot rest here any longer. We will go on to Falkland. I command it now and without delay. No, I will not see the University with Maister Buchanan. Let James follow if and when he will.

So our small party canters out with the personal guard. Let winds blow and rain lash till we purge St Andrews from our souls and senses. Till I saw that place, I did not truly realise what has happened here and all that it means. I must be strong and cunning if Scotland is to be restored. But for now we must gallop. I shall find refuge and collect myself away from spying eyes and gossip tongues.

We go over the hill, resting our horses on the ascent, then down into the Howe of Fife. The land is kindly here with woods and fields and farms. We thread our way deeper into the country, starting game and wild birds at every turn. Soon we come into my father's hunting parks and Falkland is in our sights, surrounded by its wooded hills and streams. The château rises through the trees in all its towered strength. The household runs to greet us with hugs and kisses, all ceremony set aside. The horses are led away and we are drawn into the palace where every room is furnished, warm, unchanged since former times.

Amidst friends and loyal servants I can rest. I will ride, hunt, eat and pray as I please. The Marys are themselves again. This place is peaceful, secure and hidden, the loveliest of all our houses. I feel you close here, *Maman*. Now I can sleep deep and long nights without dreams or terrors. Good night, dear ones.

Matthew, Mark, Luke and John, bless the bed that I lie on.

Day Book of the Marys

Beaton

I have unpacked this dusty book and opened its pages again. Now we are
together, I would like everyone to write what is dearest to them so that it
shall not be lost to each other. Mary need not read this unless she wishes,
and even then she can pick and choose. But we should speak from our
hearts, for nothing else truly serves us in this age of mirrors.

Seton

We are in our precious days, and we must mark them as if with God's
hourglass. I believe we shall all look back on these times as our happiest.

Livingston

Dear Seton, you are a sober guide when I am still a giddy girl. What a time
we have had since arriving back in Scotland. But is it really the golden time
returned? Everything is new for us and bright with unaccustomed colours.
I have not felt so full of life since I know not when. Every day I go riding
for at least two, or even three, hours. Sometimes we are hunting with the
courtiers, sometimes hawking by ourselves, and other times galloping off on
our own. She is a reckless rider when the mood comes on her, commanding
me to follow. And we let fly through the royal park, or along the sands
of Leith, or out onto the Lammermuirs in all weathers. We were never so
free in France. At Falkland we escape all watching eyes, and roam through
woods and fields, hair flowing like Diana's maidens. Or is it maenads –
Beaton knows better than I. I am so happy to be at home in Scotland. Am I
too licentious, Seton? Surely not for this release is the most important thing.
We have left sadness behind for a new beginning in our own country. So I
pray every night for each and all.

Beaton

The Court at Holyrood is the best place I have ever danced. Every night
with feasting done the carpets are rolled back and Mary leads us out
to viol, lute and pipe. The royal gallery is perfect for display. How the
Scottish nobles gawp, but in no time they too are on the floor at their
Queen's command, stepping out with the best. There is something fine and
open in these men when they cast sour politics aside and join the dance.
They are Scots in their fervour. Even Maister Buchanan is persuaded to
shake his stiffened limbs. See the garments too. Even a black stocking can
fit close and show the shapely leg to advantage. The Scottish ladies parade
their finery, but every eye is on our lovely Mary. White veil thrown back,
her red golden hair stands out against her mourning. And above black
velvet, a circlet of silver pearls heightens her tall slender neck. As for her
coiffure – there Seton has no match.

But we too are stars in the constellation. I cannot stop myself dancing on till after midnight. I cannot leave the floor as one set of partners yields in their turn, while the musicians play on, and Mary beats and claps and spins like a fire whose flames will not be doused. You will say I am extravagant. Maister Knox says we dance the Devil's hornpipe. My blood denies his calumny and claims its birthright – for this I was made. Why should we be deprived? After all Mary is our queen.

Livingston

I would like to write which men at Court I admire and which I dislike – or is it detest? Beaton is the detester, not I. Yet that is what we all did as children and I know Fleming expects us to be discreet, even here in our own book. We will have to guess each other's favourites or just drop hints. I love a guessing game, when concealment is expected. Court manners are stricter here than in France, but beneath the surface things may be different. We have never had such times before.

Beaton

What we miss here is theatre, compared with France. They seem averse to drama, as if it were an art accursed. But I have broached this matter with Buchanan who is Master of revels as well as poetry. Of course Mary cannot perform any longer in a play since she is queen, but we can while she presides. We shall become a court of interludes and masques with music, dance and elegant speeches in the classic modes. We shall appear as nymphs or muses in tribute to our queen, while the players provide farce and satire. This will please our Mary, and banish dullness from the court. Whatever else we suffer let us not be dismal, dreich as they say.

Yet be warned, we are not defended against chaos or folly in this town. In France we were confined within the Court, but here walls have crumbling gaps. I write for our instruction, as I have heard different tales. Even Her Majesty may be protected from the truth, in error. This is Beaton's skill, to listen and enquire; use it whoever wills.

Bothwell and Arran quarrelled about some woman of the town. John Knox played peacemaker – his family has some old connection with the Hepburns. So off they go to the old Duke to feast together and seal this newfound amity. But the next day Arran comes pell-mell back, whipping his horse into a lather. To Knox he goes again, this time to accuse Bothwell of plotting the Queen's abduction. So they may rule in her place, slaughtering Lord James, Maitland and any others who have misguided Her Majesty. It is like Odysseus' return to massacre the suitors. Would we maids escape execution?

Even Knox, who sees hellish sin in every peccadillo, finds this farfetched and advises him to say no more. But Arran writes immediately to Mary and Lord James repeating his tale. No sooner is this wild missive read, than a messenger arrives from the Duke to warn them that Arran is deranged and not to be believed.

The father confines his errant son under lock and key, but he leaps half-naked from his chamber to throw himself on the mercy of William Kirkcaldy in Fife. We miss that gentleman, and I speak for all the Marys without exception. Brave Kirkcaldy is barely recovered from his wounds in the late wars. We look forward to his return, since he is a courtier of merit. What a pity he married before our return. They say that his wife is a true gentlewoman and devout Protestant much occupied in giving birth to young Kirkcaldys.

Livingston

I agree, we need Kirkcaldy to bring a flavor of French gallantry. But please, Beaton, can we have the whole tale straight?

Beaton

Now poor Arran raves, dreaming himself in the Queen's bed, and hated by all. He is drowning in fantasies that feed his madness to the danger of himself and of others. He and Bothwell are examined before the Council, where Arran charges his erstwhile friend with high treason. He is wild yet vivid, naming Dumbarton as the fortress to which a kidnapped Mary would be taken. The young Earl is given up as a lunatic into James Stewart's keeping, where he remains in Edinburgh Castle caged like an animal. I have heard him shriek and howl in the tower.

Would anyone mourn his passing, apart from the Duke, his father? When someone near the throne is removed, his place will be filled by someone else. Is this not how they think in every court in Europe?

Yet Bothwell too is tainted. Was this actually a plan to destroy the Hamiltons? Or did he hint to Arran at secret ambitions of his own. He demands to clear his name in single combat – with feeble Arran – or at court of law. But Arran is royal by blood and will not be put to open trial. So Bothwell also is left in the castle to repent at private leisure. This is the man on whom Her Majesty believed she could rely. Is he traduced, though loyal at heart? Or is he as uncontrollable as he seems?

Others are pleased to see Hepburn fall away from Mary's side. Who might they be? I do not hazard. In France the Court is ringed about with royal power. Here we are exposed to faction and dispute. Only the loyalty of Scottish Lords stands between us and their own violent inclinations. I write long but to the point. Mark well and inwardly digest; a Beaton knows what flows in these Scottish veins.

Fleming

I also write seriously. Forgive me if this is too grave, or unfamiliar from my lips. My concern is above all for Her Majesty, though her wellbeing affects

us all. I feel my responsibility as chief lady to her and to us all together.
More than ever before I am in earnest. The joys of these first months must
soon subside.

The marriage question must be settled. Mary will say she is not ready
while she mourns for Francis. But her strength and welfare depend on a
husband who can share her throne and protect her interests.

I have talked about this with Maitland, whose mind is set on Her
Majesty's welfare and the kingdom's. He is definite there will be no
harmony until the succession is resolved. That means of course the English
succession, since our Mary must not wed without Elizabeth's approval.
Then her heirs will bring England and Scotland together. If Mary recognises
Elizabeth as rightful Queen, then Elizabeth will name Mary her successor.
In this way disputes are avoided and we can live in peace.

Beaton

Fleming has become political, and now she is an ambassador as well.
Under whose influence I shall not say, but I hear Maitland's persuasive
tones. Yet I dispute his line of wisdom. Elizabeth is queen in her own right.
She toys with suitors while exercising her government without authority
of man. Why does our Mary need a consort to rule as queen? I believe she
will take control and marry whom and when she wishes. That is her nature
and I am glad it should be so. Elizabeth may never name her successor for
fear of setting up a rival in the people's love or in religion. Does Maitland
argue that England will welcome a Catholic queen again?

Forgive me, Fleming, if I am acerbic, but Beatons are raised in a hard
school. I do not believe that women, once educated, are weaker governors
than men. Who has read more in history than our Mary, excepting
Buchanan himself? Secretary Maitland is a counsellor, as Fleming knows,
yet one steeped in worldly philosophies. Meikle Wily is our Machiavelli.
I say no more in case the chief lady slaps me for being insolent again. It
is very difficult to make a full confession here, even in our book, without
attracting insults. So I must not be tiresome and magnify human weakness.
I am ending.

Livingston

Beaton will soon pick up her pen to write more pages. Livingston will
wager on that if anyone dares. All this talk of marrying unsettles me. It is
too soon to marry when the fun has only just started.

Seton

We should be careful in our thoughts and in our writing, as we shall answer
to God as well as to one another. I do not understand why no one has
written of the ruined abbeys, friaries destroyed, and holy altars laid bare.
What kind of fury has broken out in Scotland? And it is still at work as men

with drawn swords try to prevent Her Majesty's own attendance at Mass.

Our Holy Father has written to the Queen. Now that she is going north to the Earl of Huntly's lands we may see a restoration of true religion in this realm. This country is larger than anyone in France conceived. I shall remain at Holyrood to look after the personal household in Fleming's absence. I am retiring and not fitted for such responsibility, but I am obedient to my duty, and my faith.

Beaton

The outcome of our travels, dear Seton, was contrary to your hopes. I am sorry for that, as piety always does you credit; however the expedition was not to restore religion but to curb Earl Huntly's power.

In the face of wild Scotland even my pen fell into arrears. We were at war for the first time, and we must hope the last. However what I write proves our Mary's womanly strength. She was always in the saddle even under threat of ambush or violent abduction. The Queen appeared in a new light, and we should remember that in days to come.

But there is a further question. Who profits by the great Earl's fall? Having been made Earl of Mar, a title belonging to his Erskine cousins, James Stewart still preferred the Moray earldom, which Huntly had appropriated to his own vast acres. Follow the acres.

After the battle, they disembowelled Huntly's giant corpse, and embalmed him to stand trial before the Council, where he received the doom of 'traitor' in person. Presumably his concern was already with a higher tribunal. We had to watch his son John Gordon hanged, beheaded and bloodily quartered, in case anyone imagine the new Earl of Moray acted without his sister's consent. Mary abhors executions but this was the result for all to see of Huntly's downfall. It was horrible, but restored royal authority in a way these lawless regions comprehend.

So from this petty war the erstwhile Mar, once Lord James, claims a new earldom, and the Earl Marischal's daughter with her ample dowry. I know we are not allowed to call him 'the Bastard', but everyone here does. He is making up fast for any disadvantages.

Fleming

Beaton, you are not discreet, and it is improper for the Queen's ladies to speak, or imply, ill of her esteemed brother. He is the mainstay of her government and principal support. I will not permit such license, even in these pages. It is unseemly.

Beaton

And could be dangerous? I am of course obedient to Fleming, as is my duty.

Seton

I am sorry to express my opinion, Fleming, but I hope you will allow me to speak of my disappointment and sadness at the loss of such a defender of the faith as Lord Huntly. Since our return from France we have seen nothing but desecrated altars and ruined churches. This cannot be for Scotland's good or Her Majesty's pleasure, since the Queen herself wrote she would rather die than be disobedient to her Faith and to the Holy Father. I know she cannot yet command religion in this realm as she might wish, but I also know that she has seen His Holiness' emissary in private when the rest of the Court had gone to sermon.

Livingston

I am bored with politics. Why does no one write now about fun or pleasure? We have become old maids overnight.

Fleming

Seton, Her Majesty cannot address matters of religion until she has come to a single mind with her cousin Elizabeth on the government of these realms, and her place in the English succession. Her devotion is constant, and heard in Heaven, but she is a queen above all else. And you are her servant.

Seton

I try to be a faithful servant, Fleming, to Her Majesty and to the Queen of Heaven. These are my God-given duties. What am I to think when the English ambassador comes to announce Elizabeth of England's crusade against the Catholics of France – her own people and kin?

Fleming

Her Majesty was restrained and dignified, Seton, refusing to quarrel, and sending her cousin good wishes on her recovery from smallpox.

Beaton

You are correct, Fleming, but when Elizabeth lay like to die did her Council approve our Mary as successor? Even the Catholic lords put Lady Lennox before her. What does Maitland say to that?

Fleming

What should he say? Elizabeth is not dead. Or married.

Livingston

Mary is a queen but also woman with flesh and blood like our own. I want to know when she will marry. And shall we be permitted to marry, Fleming? All in good time I hear you say. But I love weddings and so does our Mary.

Beaton

If Maister Knox had his way there would be no weddings only solemn
vows. Did you hear him railing in the Queen's presence against profane
dancing. Such merriment stinks in God's nostrils, in his way of it. Knox is
an earthy man with blunt speech. I think there is fire beneath that gounie
as weill as in his mou. He has his ain way with the ladies. I hae the Scots
leid an aa, lassie.

Mary replied that a scholar, far less a minister, could not be always at
his books, and that he would be welcome to a private audience whenever
convenient. That took the wind out of his sails, and she turned her back on
him before he could hoist new canvas. But even John Knox could not spoil
James Stewart's wedding with Agnes Keith. Such splendour has not been
seen in Scotland since the thistle wed the rose. The bride was beautiful and
richly arrayed, but our Mary was resplendent with cloaks of gold and silver
falling from her shoulders. Above her black velvet, three strings of pearls
were at her neck from which a golden crucifix lay between her breasts. The
goddesses of love and learning presided, while Her Majesty's fools ran riot
amidst the groaning feast. Pheasants baked and refeathered, roasted swans
with spreading wings, boar, deer, salmon, and abundant flowing wine.
Mary glowed as Queen of the banquet, her nation restored to ceremony
and plenty. This is how Court life should be conducted.

Livingston

Lord James' was not the best wedding, Beaton. That took place at
Crichton when Lord John Stewart married Janet Hepburn. Bothwell was
in favour then and transformed his castle into a palace of honour and
delight for his sister. Hunting, feasting, dancing, games followed one upon
another. The musicians were never silent from French choristers to Border
balladeers. James Hepburn can be gallant: he has bold extravagance in his
blood and will not stint if he has the chance to shine, especially in Mary's
orbit.

Beaton

Bothwell is not all he seems, Livingston, or is more than he seems. In those
days at Crichton when courtiers and servants crowded into pavilions,
corridors and galleries gossip was rife. They say he has a Danish woman,
very beautiful, secluded in a house near Morham but she was denied the
castle for fear of offending the Queen. And at Hermitage Castle, too, he
has a well-bred serving wench, young and comely, imprisoned to satisfy his
every pleasure. He is a man who likes to command womanly submission.

Some say that Bothwell's mother was a mistress of King James, and that
Hepburn is another half-brother for Mary – and Moray. Is that why those
two hate each other so much? It is because of Moray that Bothwell has
slipped prison and fled to England?

I know which woman Bothwell would like most to command. James Hepburn is like the rest – Arran, Gordon, Lennox maybe. They desire to rule Scotland by possessing the Queen's body.

Fleming

That is scandalous and irreverent, Beaton. Her Majesty is in command of her own person at all times. You cannot credit a groat of all the rumours about Bothwell. According to some he is bewitched and the Devil incarnate.

God preserve the Queen in happiness and good fortune.

Seton

Amen, and God bless this realm of Scotland. I fear the golden age may pass before we mark its fading.

Mary

SHE HAS RED hair like me. We are sisters. Her hair though is straighter then mine, which would curl more were it not tied back like Elizabeth's. I wonder who dresses her hair. The face is thinner, more austere than mine – a ruler's face – but her eyes are withdrawn and reserved.

This portrait means that she has given me her trust and friendship, in return for mine. Maitland has done well.

'Who then should your cousin of Scotland marry, Majesty?'

'Robert Dudley is the handsomest and finest of my nobles.'

She jokes, but Maitland has quick wits.

'Truly, a proper man, should you not scoop him up yourself?'

I am widowed and she unmarried, so our counsellors would have us both wed. No mere woman can govern without a consort, or give birth to an heir, which is nearer the mark. Elizabeth is strong and will not bend her will to their importuning. She and I should be allies, sister queens.

But I cannot wait on England forever. Despite all Moray and Maitland's efforts, neither the English Council nor Parliament will recognise my right. They hate Scotland, fear a Catholic alliance, and will do anything to blacken my name. It is Cecil's doing, Cecil and his henchman Walsingham, who are always in correspondence with Knox and the godly.

I have spoken privately with Maitland to engage him as my chief adviser in all matters, not least the marriage. He is close to me now, and has eyes only for Fleming. She loves him in turn but knows her duty and is discreet.

Lord James, Moray as we must learn to call him, will no longer provide sole direction of my Council. I am appointing Morton as Chancellor in Huntly's stead, and Athol will have his place. None more faithful, as a loyal Stewart and son of the Church. Athol has given good service in the recent troubles in the north.

Maitland has my instructions to negotiate an English alliance, while formally protesting if Parliament in London denies my place in their succession. At the same time we will approach the Spanish ambassador about a match with Don Carlos. It is time to cast our net wider. Uncle Charles will consult the Holy Father about my marriage and that private meeting will be reported to every court in Europe. If Elizabeth will not befriend my right, then I must press claim on England by other means. I shall be politic in all things, as I was taught, and learn the craft of government.

Above all I will not be dependent on the Scottish lords alone, or captive to their favour. I remember how they dealt with my mother. Though I love Scotland as my own country, it will not become my prison. Let Huntly's fall be a lesson to the rest.

Why should I require a husband when I have my Marys? This Court revolves around our pleasures. Together we lead the dance and when we tire of music, poetry, and plays, we take to hills and woods in pursuit of other game. Diana and her huntress band; this is our prime. I can shoot a barb a straight as any man, and ride as fast, and fly a hawk as true, or better, for the falcon knows my intent even as it quivers blindfolded on my glove.

If our mood constrains we can withdraw to private chambers and eat by ourselves, reading and writing, warming our bodies with fond embraces. Or, in a giddy turn, we slip out disguised as gallants in pursuit of harmless mischief. Another time like merchants' wives we keep house and bake or sew. I roll up my sleeves and stir preserves.

It is this joyous life my people love. Their lives are hard and they are oppressed sometimes by those who should be their succour. They want their Queen to exhibit prosperity and display the plenty of the land for all to see, dispensing justice and good cheer to weak and strong alike.

I am learning how to be Queen of Scots, and we shall ride out again in progress soon, visiting the west this time, so they may see for themselves that Scotland is not ruled by Knox and the preachers. I give them back their monarch and one day perhaps I can give them their religion.

If I marry who will I wed? They say that Don Carlos is weak-minded like Arran, and confined to a palace lest his foolishness is betrayed. Yet he is heir to Spain and to its Empire, which is strength sufficient for any cause. To encourage the Spanish, Maitland dangles the prospect of a new French marriage before them. The Medici will not have me Queen of France again, but she fears a Spanish match. So France proposes that young Charles marry Elizabeth, while I wed his even younger brother Claude, children both. I was married to a boy once before.

Some favour the Archduke Charles of Austria, Catholic yet not fanatic, to be a husband for me or Elizabeth. But he does not have the power to strengthen my claim to England. Had Elizabeth been born a man I could have married her, which would satisfy all sides of the question.

Am I melancholy? Then let us seek diversion. No more reading, we will ride out to the Forth and feel the sea on our faces.

My Uncle Francis is dead in France. He was assassinated more than three weeks ago but word came today. Strong, comely Uncle Francis shot, fatally wounded, in hate. After King Henri he was my image of a gentleman, my touchstone of what nobility in bearing, governance and kindness means. The Guise have lost their head. What family does this leave me?

I am alone in Scotland and none can reach out to help me. Uncle Charles advises, directs from afar, but has no strong arm to save. I cannot continue with this life, these duties, my charade. I weep and am crying and weep again, withdrawn in my chambers, taken to my bed. Like a distraught child. The old pain flares up in my side.

My flesh is burning. Too much to bear.

Please, take it away.

Feverish dreams. Cup to my lips. Broken sleep.

Fleming is mother now. Seton kneels by me. Infusions soothe and give some relief.

I will not see anyone. It is impossible to go on.

Calmer this morning. Beginning to recollect myself. Side easier, head light and fuzzed but not aching. I can begin in my own mind to consider what has happened. I am coming to myself.

Violence and hatred will be the undoing between countrymen and Christians. John Gordon's young body broken and bleeding. They pulled out his inner parts like some pudding. Uncle Francis shot and stabbed. I fear such violence as it tears, destroys without distinction. Once loosed it cannot be restrained except by more violence. And so it feeds, redoubles on itself, till all is wasted – everything good and precious is lost.

I feel it simmering here below the surface, unacknowledged, unaddressed, as if those recent outbursts of destruction were a passing storm, some freak of nature. These lords of mine are so hardened they barely notice cruelty lurking, and scarcely bother to repress brutality's sudden outbursts.

But in France the hatred has become outright war, fought not just on battlefields but in homes and streets and churches. Men, women, children, massacred in bitter unheeding. God preserve my beautiful country. The finest of its flowers are cut down without pity or remorse.

And cousin Elizabeth stirs this strife, sending money and troops, just as she would disrupt Scotland's peace by sending Lennox home to re-ignite old divisions. But she will not get her way. France will unite to drive the English out. Cecil's plotting and devising will backfire. I know. She does not understand France, seeing everything through English eyes.

Yet she has sent me a beautiful letter, consoling me on my Uncle's death. Elizabeth knows how much the Duc de Guise meant to me and she is tender-hearted in my loss. She too has lived midst loss and violence. If only she could feel my heart going out towards her. We could reach towards each other's loneliness like lovers do when separated. We were both orphaned and keep our hearts our own. What comfort we could share.

The storm is receding, leaving me drained, mournful in its wake.

I cannot escape Knox and his like, though I must learn better how to contain their influence. I thought that he had gone so far beyond obedience that the nobility might disown him, but I had miscalculated. Maitland was right and I should heed his warnings. There are some lords for whom Protestant beliefs are a principle higher than the law; some who do not want confrontation with the preachers, and even more whose advantage lies in piecemeal Reformation, holding the lands they have while aiming to annex more.

Do not stir a hornets' nest. I must heed this advice. They that thole shall overcome. That is another proverb I might live by, since it seems I maun thole Maister Knox. Was ever a monarch so deaved by a disobedient priest? But he is no Thomas Becket, this St John, and I should not make a martyr of him, even if I could. He is a more crafty man than divine Saint. There is flesh beneath his gown.

Though it appears I cannot suppress Knox, I have not given way to his defiant boastings. Their Reformation Parliament, as they call it, lacked my royal approval. It was illegal and could be reversed. This year's Parliament made no new settlement of religion. Between trying Huntly's waxen corpse and confirming Moray in his earldom, there was no time to debate religion. My promise not to upset the realm is kept to the letter.

The preachers rant because they want their faith established beyond dispute before any marriage, especially a Catholic one. But there they overreach themselves, pretending their godly assemblies can overrule Parliament. Knox turns his fire on the Protestant lords and is routed, since most are more lord than Protestant. Even Moray has fallen out with his favoured prophet, and their secret communings are at an end. Knox is, as they say, in the huff, but my dear brother will outdo him by far in resentful pride and disdain.

Why should I abide such contumely from a mere subject? The preacher's seditious writings are openly handed round and make a mockery of my rule. 'Such stinking pride of women as was seen at that Parliament was never seen before in Scotland. Three days the Queen rode to the Tolbooth.' His style is unmistakable, as is his contempt for my queenly authority. Of the loyal crowds cheering and waving he makes no mention.

In his preaching Knox upbraids the nobility for their desertion of his pure cause. He is John the Baptist cast into Herod's power. 'If the Queen will not agree with you in the Word of God,' he taunts, 'you are not bound to agree with her in the Devil.' A cunning trope, but devious falsehood. Yet Moray, Lindsay, and fanatic Ruthven argue that he meddles only in religion, which is his divinely appointed province. But Knox has overstepped the mark, and I will have his retraction.

'To put an end to all, I hear of the Queen's marriage.' This is his satiric vein. 'Dukes, brothers to Emperors, and Kings all strive for the best game. But whenever the Nobility of Scotland consent that an infidel, for all Papists are infidels, shall be head to your sovereign, you banish Christ Jesus from this realm. You bring God's vengeance on the country, a plague on yourselves, and maybe small comfort to your Sovereign.'

What has that man to do with my marriage?

Next it is England's turn to play ambassador. Thomas Randolph is the new emissary with his instructions from Elizabeth, as amended no doubt by Secretary Cecil. This is their reply to Maitland's official embassy, but also to his secret negotiations with France and Spain about my marriage. Clearly the news will be unwelcome as courteous Randolph takes forever to convey his message. According to Maitland, since English ambitions in Europe disappoint they are obsessed with making Scotland secure.

So it appears I must have their approval for any matrimonial alliance, which should naturally be English, and if that is forthcoming then they will establish an enquiry to examine my claim to their succession. Shall I, a sovereign queen, be subject to inquisition by the parliament of a foreign power?

They are insulting but I will not be bullied. Henry the Tudor Bully is no more. I remain impassive and say that I will consider my reply after consultation with my Council. We give Randolph no more to chew on, and he has to leave immediately, without satisfaction for his royal mistress.

When he is next at Court we bait him unmercifully.

'Randolph wants me to marry in England.'

'Has the Queen of England become a man?' So Beaton.

'Pray tell me, what Englishman should the Queen of Scots marry?' teases Maitland.

'Whomsoever she chooses,' fences Randolph weakly. 'If she can find one sufficiently noble.'

Our Shrovetide banquet is an allegory of Charity and Time. A radiant girl represents love and beauty. As long as time endures there should be amity between Mary and Elizabeth, Scotland and England. Buchanan scripted and Beaton directed with her usual panache. It was a display for Randolph and his master Cecil to ponder.

I press Randolph to honestly share his queen's true opinion, as I am at heart sincere. The word of a prince, he agrees, is worth more than the promises of inconstant counsellors. I desire Elizabeth's friendship and will be faithful. Should we not form mutual sympathy as our bond? Would it not be better if we could meet together and dispel misunderstandings forever?

They have little choice now but to express a preference. Elizabeth finally names Lord Robert Dudley. Dudley whom she has pampered in her bedchamber. Dudley, whose dear wife conveniently tumbled down a stair while he dallied with his queen. Am I to wed England's leavings?

She is not serious, and puts Dudley forward as an obscure contrivance to ensure he stays by her side. She will not marry him and will not actually let me marry him. I am not so innocent that I do not sense the mazes of a woman's desiring. Yet this surpasses all. Elizabeth does not want a husband, or an heir, so I too must remain bereft of both.

'Do you think it stands with my honour, Ambassador, to marry my sister's subject, a mere lord?'

'Surely there is nothing more honourable than to marry a nobleman, by means of which marriage you might inherit a kingdom such as England,' temporises Randolph.

'I do not look for the kingdom, as my sister Elizabeth is likely to marry and live longer than myself. I must consider my own position, and the honour of my friends and country, rather than abase my state so far. If however this is truly my sister's wish, then I and my Council will give it the consideration it merits.'

Poor Randolph. He has a hard and trying mistress at home and has to broach the Queen of Scots abroad. My brother Moray is blunter than I, as is his wont.

'Why not persuade your own queen to marry rather than trouble my sister, who has no more mind to marriage than she has to her next dinner when hungry?'

I have heard enough of this embassy. I do not decline it, or deign to reply. But I do accept Elizabeth's earlier offer to send the Earl of Lennox back to Scotland under safe conduct. She cannot have forgotten that Lennox and his Lady Margaret unite in marriage their claims on the crowns of both our countries. And they have a son, who would be a better match than Dudley if my marriage must be English. Sometimes it seems as if my sister Elizabeth is contrary at her own expense.

My summer thoughts are on another progress, through the Highlands, so that my subjects may see their sovereign and the chiefs renew their fealty to the Scottish crown. I must also pursue reform of justice to show that my Christian Majesty is more potent in the peoples' cause than all the preachers and their Protestant lordships combined.

In the north I assume Highland costume, which flows with natural colours and is most becoming to male and female forms alike. I listen to pipes, clarsach, odes and laments. I join the ancient step dance. But most of all I hunt.

Scores of men spread out along the upper slopes with numerous great dogs, lurchers and deerhounds. The gillies drive running herds of deer down through the trees, leaping and breaking like a wave. There are stags and hinds of the red deer and the smaller roe in abundance. And they do not see their danger. For out of their immediate sight they are being herded into an avenue of wooden hurdles, and are charging towards a hail of spears and arrows. It is like a battle with cries and yells, trumpets, horns and the smell of blood.

There is something too cruel in this massacre for sport. Boar and wolf prove a rarer prize which only long distance mountain tracking can win. I insist on being taken into the mountains to follow the spoor.

Everywhere I am royally entertained and feasted according to Highland custom. Better some young chief for my consort than all the suitors England has to offer. Yet if I cannot have Spain, and it seems that the Medici has colluded with Uncle Charles to prevent it; if I will not have Austria and the Empire; then England it must be.

A queen without power and connection is a mere plaything here. I might be abducted to the Isles and forced to marry some MacDonald Chief with an endless genealogy. At least he will have cousins sufficient to husband all my Marys as well. We should remain here and live the free life of nature, as the Gaels do, and learn their musical tongue which was spoken, the poets say, in Paradise.

It is my turn now in this interminable game. Lennox has returned to Scotland and proffers his devotion. What a charming cultured man, showing all the signs of once handsome youth. The barbers wait on him twice each day and he is bathed in scent. If only my Scottish lords might learn from his example. He brings new distinction to our Court, and attends at Mass and preachings with equal tact.

At his and Maitland's prompting I send James Melville as my ambassador to London to negotiate directly with Elizabeth. He may also secure permission for Lord Darnley, Lennox's son, to pay a visit to his long lost native land.

How I would like to attend at the English Court. To speak with my friends there and acquaint myself with the latest fashions, that would be heaven on earth. Then I could see with my own eyes whether Elizabeth will release Lord Dudley from her sight. However, Melville can be my eyes and ears. While conversing with voluble abandon Melville proceeds by indirections. He is frank, curious and garrulous in equal measure.

If he writes as he speaks our Ambassador's dispatches will become bedtime reading, and all of the Marys will be hungry for the next episode. But never fear, dear Melville will not stint in the telling.

James Melville

YOUR MAJESTY MAY graciously recall my long acquaintance, I believe I can safely account it friendship, with Sir Nicholas Throckmorton, formerly ambassador for Queen Elizabeth to your Highness in France. I met with him on my first evening in London and he conveyed to me the warm interest of those many friends of Your Majesty in England who wish nothing so dearly as to see your place in the succession of this kingdom secure. He also brought greetings from the Lady Lennox who wishes to see me privately, notwithstanding that nothing can be done without Master Cecil and My Lord Dudley, as we knew before. I delivered my letters tonight from Lord Moray to Robert Dudley and from Secretary Maitland to Cecil. I have also paid my compliments to the Spanish Ambassador.

The next morning Master Randolph, lately Ambassador from England to Your Majesty, came to my lodging early to convoy me to Her Highness, who they said was already in the garden. With him came a servant of Lord Dudley's leading a horse and footmantle of velvet laced with gold for me to ride upon. This servant waited on me all the time I was with Her Majesty, which was most courteous and typical of the kindness shown to me by that noble gentleman.

I found Queen Elizabeth walking in an alley. After I had kissed her hand and presented my letter of commission I told her my purpose and. sometimes being interrupted by her demands, I answered as best I could. She enquired if Your Majesty had made any answer to the proposal of marriage made by Sir Thomas Randolph. I answered, as instructed, that you had not given it due consideration as yet, since the meeting of commissioners on the border would confer and deal with all matters tending to the peace of both kingdoms, and to the contentment of both Your Majesties. And that you would send your most trusty and familiar counsellors, the Earl of Moray, and Secretary Maitland, hoping that she might send the Earl of Bedford and Lord Robert Dudley.

'It appears,' answers she, 'you make small account of my Lord Robert, since you name Bedford before him. But before long I shall make him a far greater Earl, and you will see it done before you return home. For I esteem him as a brother or best friend, whom I would have married, had I myself ever been minded to take a husband. But since I am determined to finish this earthly life virgin, my wish is that Mary my sister should marry him as most fit of all for the second person in my realm. Being matched with him would remove from my mind all suspicion of being usurped before my death, for my Lord Robert is so loving and trusty that he would never consent to such a thing while there is breath in my body.'

On the next morning, shortly before noon, I was required to attend on Her Majesty Queen Elizabeth at Westminster. And so that Your Majesty might think more of him, I saw Lord Robert made Earl of Leicester with great solemnity before the nobles of the realm in full array. Queen Elizabeth herself put on his ceremonial robe as he knelt before her, keeping a very grave demeanour. But the Queen could not refrain from putting her hand on his neck, and tickling him with a smile, in full view of myself and the Ambassador of France.

Then she asked me how I liked her Earl of Leicester, and I replied that as he was worthy so he would be happy in having a Queen so ready to reward his service. 'Yet,' says she, 'you like that long lad better,' pointing at Lord Darnley who, as a prince of the blood, had borne the Sword of State before her in procession.

I thought swiftly of Your Majesty's discretion, and your desire to keep your charge to me secret, so I replied that no woman of spirit could prefer such a man, who though very lusty, was more like a woman than a man, beardless and lady-faced.

This seemed to satisfy her humour, while giving no hint of our desire for him to be given liberty to go to Scotland and return with the Earl his father.

Today, without preface, Her Majesty announces she has appointed the best lawyers in England to search out who has the best right to the succession and she hopes it may be Your Majesty.

She said she had no intent to marry, unless forced to it by the hard behaviour of Your Majesty acting against her advice.

'You need not tell me that, Your Majesty,' says I immediately. 'I know your stately stomach. You think that married you would be Queen of England only, whereas now you are both King and Queen. You cannot endure a commander.' She enjoys such raillery if cautiously applied.

That evening the Queen appeared so affectionate to Your Majesty, and so eager to see you, that she invited me to her bedchamber to see your picture, which she delights to view since your meeting is delayed.

She opened a little desk where there was a heap of miniature portraits wrapped in paper, with the name written on each paper in her own handwriting. The first one she picked up was labelled 'My Lord's Picture'. I held the candle closer and pressed to see the image. She was loath to let me, but finally I prevailed and discovered Leicester's portrait. I asked to have it to carry home to Your Majesty but she refused, saying it was her only picture. 'But, Madam,' says I, 'you have the original,' pointing over to where the Earl was speaking to Secretary Cecil in the farthest part of the chamber.

Then Queen Elizabeth took out Your Majesty's picture, unwrapped it, and put her lips to your image. I kissed her hand for the great love I saw she bore you. Then she showed me a lustrous ruby, the size of a tennis ball. I said she should send that or else the Earl of Leicester's portrait to Scotland. She replied that Your Majesty should have both in good time, if you followed her guiding, but that for now she would send a diamond ring. Finally she appointed me to meet with her the next morning at eight o'clock when she was accustomed to walk in the garden.

I have almost lost track of our conversations there were so many and so various. But Your Majesty instructed me to use pleasantries sometimes that I might test your cousin's natural temper. Now every day she had different garments, now French, now Italian, next German, as if to prove her mistress of every fashion, wherever I had travelled. 'Now,' says she finally. 'Which suits me best?' I said Italian which pleased her mightily, since she loves to show her golden hair tied up behind in a caul and bonnet. Her hair is more red than yellow and curls naturally. As does Your Majesty's own lustrous locks.

So next, she wonders which kind of hair is esteemed the most, and whether her own or Your Majesty's were best. And which of you could be considered fairest. I said that fairness was not the worst fault of either Queen. But then she was determined to have my answer – which is fairest?

'Your Majesty is fairest in England, and Her Highness of Scotland fairest in that kingdom.'

'Do not dissemble, sir.' She was peremptory as is her way.

'Your Majesties are the brightest ornament of your Courts, but while you are lighter in colour, my Queen is very lovely.'

Elizabeth paints her face to a smooth whiteness like alabaster.

'Which of us is taller?'

'Her Majesty of Scotland.'

'Then she must be very tall, for I am neither too high nor too low.'

I felt it politic not to comment on the subject of Your Majesty's height, which as everyone knows is very pleasing.

'What leisure does she take?'

'As I left Her Majesty had just returned from hunting in the Highlands, which she loves with hawking, archery, and riding. She reads many books as well, especially the histories of nations, and poetry which she composes well. And she plays sometimes on the lute and virginals.'

'Does she play well?'

'Pretty well, for a queen.'

I had requested to be dispatched, so she chided me for wearying of her company, but I said it was time to return to Scotland.

Nonetheless she kept me two days longer so that I might see her dance. Which queen danced the best? There was little contest, so I said Your Majesty did not dance in the same high manner as she did. Then she sighed, desiring to meet Your Majesty at some convenient place. I said I should take her secretly to Scotland disguised as a page, just as James Fifth went to see who was to be his wife in France.

'I would be missed here.'

'Your chamber could be closed as if you were sick, so that only the ladies in waiting and the groom would know.'

'If only I could.'

I saw how much she thinks of Your Majesty and how dearly she wants your friendship and love.

At last she gave me my answers privately by ear at Hampton Court where she had gone, and Secretary Cecil delivered the letters in London.

'Pray,' she says, 'that my sister might wed with Robert Dudley and come to live with me, so that we might be one family together, two sisters and a brother.'

This was a new departure so I applied my customary caution.

'It is expensive to live in London.'

'Do not speak of expenses; my Exchequer would cover all.'

'And who would rule Her Majesty's own kingdom?'

'Why, Her Majesty of course, but through some noble governor such as my Lord of Moray.'

The next day my Lord of Leicester asked me to sail in his barge down the Thames to London, which is ten miles distance. He entered into homely conversation with me talking about his acquaintance with Moray and Maitland. He said he was so familiar, knowing me well by repute, as to ask what the Queen my mistress thought of him and of the marriage proposed by Randolph.

I answered coldly, as you had instructed. At which he disowned any pretence to marry a queen so great, being unworthy to wipe your shoes. He put the blame on Cecil whom he named his secret enemy. 'For if,' he says, 'I appear desirous of this marriage, I lose the favour of both their Majesties.' He prayed me to excuse himself to Your Highness, begging you would not impute such a clumsy fault to him, but to the malice of his foes.

After dinner I took leave of the French and Spanish ambassadors from whom I carry correspondence. I also received a letter from my Lord of Leicester to Moray, urging him to disavow the proposed marriage to Your Majesty. Secretary Cecil conveyed me to the outer gate of the palace after he had put a golden chain round my neck. He gave me my dispatch and a fuller account of Her Majesty's guidance, along with a letter to Secretary Maitland. These will follow soon with my person.

My Lady Lennox has also sent many good advices for your ear alone, along with a marvellous fair jewel for Your Majesty. She is still in good hope that her son Lord Darnley will make better speed to Scotland than the Earl of Leicester, and win Your Majesty's favour. She is a wise and discreet matron to whom many in England are kindly disposed at this time, for reasons of family and of religion.

Day Book of the Marys

Seton

Everything is out of sorts today. I feel I must write in our book. A letter came from Secretary Cecil following the commissioners' meeting on the Borders. The Earl of Moray and William Maitland were summoned by Her Majesty to an angry audience.

I know that I am unskilled in political affairs but something is awry. Mary is not being guided and supported as she ought. She should not be traded for an English marriage regardless of her true feelings and of her faith.

Beaton may say I am naïve, but love that surrenders to another's welfare is the most important thing. Everything else should be measured against that, as Christ taught us.

Forgive me, if today I seem anxious or melancholy. I understand that it is our Mary's vocation to rule, but that should not require the sacrifice of her happiness. If that is lost then we shall all be undone. What holds us together is what matters most. To care for Mary is my vocation.

Fleming

It must be understood, Seton, that the Scottish commissioners performed their duty. They offered Mary's hand in marriage to the Earl of Leicester, if in return Elizabeth would name her as successor. That was what had been agreed by the Council. We must act according to our duty, as Mary does.

Beaton

They persuaded Mary that she should marry Dudley, and that this would be accepted by the English. Fleming cannot deny that, however partial she has become. Perhaps the Queen should listen more to garrulous Melville, since he shows honestly what is in Elizabeth's mind.

Livingston

Beaton cannot be serious. Melville is a sweetie wife of a man. When I see him coming into the garden I run and hide. And I know I am not the only one.

Fleming

Seton is right, things are awry. Maitland and Moray were surprised and angry at the English letter of refusal. I have never seen Mary so furious. She said she had trusted their advice against her own judgment. Dudley was not worthy of her, being without royal blood, and, worse, the son of a traitor. Cecil's letter was a humiliation, withdrawing all the previous concessions and again threatening Mary with a legal trial of her right. As if she were a mere English subject. How could they have subjected their own queen to such insult? Was she plotting to steal her cousin's lover? Would they do anything to humiliate Scotland as long as their precious religion is

protected? She bitterly upbraided Moray as her brother and a Stewart of
the royal house. He of all men should know better. Why had they urged
her on this path?

The source of these troubles though is in England, not here amongst us
in Scotland. I too am worried for our Mary. Her marriage must be the main
hope of happiness.

Beaton
Elizabeth cannot bear to part with Dudley. That is the only explanation.

Seton
No, she is too afraid to name anyone second person in the kingdom.
Remember her mother's trial, and the suspicion she lived under as a child.
She will never set up a rival to her throne. That is all she has to live for.
She is a Queen.

Livingston
Seton is wiser than she lets on to others. She watches and sees things while
others chatter, and stores her harvest for a later day.

There will be a collapse tomorrow, and we will have to guard her chamber
against all comers. Our Mary is not able to cope with such adversity and
anger on her own. She is not made for cold reason or iron will.

Beaton
Mary rises to a crisis. I think she will surprise us with her determination.

Fleming
As long as she does not act without her counsellors' agreement. Why has
life become so grave?

Livingston
There are still some diversions, and this is a day of news. John Knox is
marrying Margaret Stewart, the daughter of Lord Ochiltree.

Beaton
The Queen's own cousin betrothed to lie in a preacher's bed? This will not
mend Mary's temper. He will need her permission. It is a shame the pious
English wife could not endure Scotland's rigours. She could have taken
him back to Geneva and everyone would have been better off. How old is
Margaret Stewart?

Livingston
Seventeen years; younger than all of us, but older than Mary when she was
first married.

Maister Knox's bed. Is he fiery there too? There is something... desirous about him. He eats you with his eyes.

Beaton
Exactly, disgusting. He will make her read Scripture before lying down to his ministrations.

Mary has told Randolph she intends to marry.

Livingston
How does Beaton always receive the English Ambassador's intelligence before anyone else?

Beaton
The same reason Fleming knows the Secretary's mind, and that you, Livingston, know what the loyal Catholic gentlemen are thinking, like he I shall not mention. Only I am not shamed to own my liaison.

Should we write of such things? If Mary marries we shall be writing of little else. According to Randolph, she says her Scottish subjects expect this of her. Though she would have much preferred to be in concord with Elizabeth, she could not indefinitely postpone her duty to Scotland. Did she know already what was in Randolph's dispatch? Who does she intend to marry? Is it another Stewart? We should remember that our Mary was raised to be political.

Fleming
Beaton has become a courtier, not a lady-in-waiting. Why have people begun to pen this book in riddles? Let us be plain. Elizabeth now says she will not name her successor until she herself has married or decided definitely not to marry. Maitland and Moray could not be expected to accommodate such changes of mind.

Beaton
Which means Elizabeth will never marry. She will be the Virgin Queen to her dying day. Unless... I have stroked out those words, and even the thought.

Anyway, Mary says it is a tragedy that they might harm rather than help each other – two sister queens in the same island. Randolph is begging her not to be hasty.

Livingston
In doing what? Is Mary going to marry in haste? Where is the groom?

Beaton
Lord Darnley has been granted the passport to visit his father. The

question is, has Elizabeth allowed Darnley to come because he might marry Mary instead of Dudley, or because she can instruct him not to marry Mary since he is an English courtier? Anything rather than a royal husband for the Scottish Queen. What is it that women truly want? I despair.

Seton

I sense uncertainty and danger. We must all pray for Mary to be guided through the hazards.

Livingston

Was ever such a snow and ice seen before in Scotland? Mary cannot stay inside; she is fired up and always wanting to be out hunting, visiting, riding through the drifts. We are making a progress through Fife which is surely the most frozen shire in the Kingdom, blasted by icy winds from the sea.

At Wemyss Castle the Queen's cousin from England arrives to pay his respects. Before even seeing his father or his mother's Douglas kin. He has his passport from Elizabeth to visit his father, but brings greetings to Mary from the English Court and from Lady Lennox his mother. We all attend despite the cold.

Lord Darnley is very tall and very slender. His head seems small but finely proportioned like the rest of him. Fair haired and smooth skinned. He has the manners of the Court and of a well practiced gallant. She was welcoming to him, but formal.

There are very few men who can match her height. He looks well beside her. Very handsome, though in a boyish, beardless fashion.

Beaton

Mary was taken with his person. There is no one here like him in stature or poise. She will play with this long lad for her own pleasure.

Seton

He is very confident of his station. Proud and ambitious. We do not yet know his nature.

Fleming

Mary is resolved now to make her own free choice in marriage. Her tutelage is over.

Livingston

Lord Darnley has gone to see his father the Earl, but has made an assignation to cross the Forth with the Queen in two days' time. If he makes such a pace through the country in this winter season, then he is an excellent horseman. Or an ardent wooer.

Beaton
Mary's chamber Secretary is dispatched and then arrested at Leith; his papers are seized. Has he betrayed the Queen's ciphers? Rumours swarm.

Fleming
There is no scandal. He has been released; only his papers are detained.

Beaton
Why should the private secretary be under suspicion? Is this Moray's doing, because Raulet is a Guise retainer? But he has been copying Mary's letters. For whom I cannot say, but my information is reliable. For someone in France most likely.

Fleming
I shall not write on this page or about this matter. We should not speculate, even in our private book. David Rizzio, the Italian musician, will have Raulet's place. He is already appointed.

Livingston
A singer?

Beaton
He has French as well as Latin and Italian. Clever and charming, you must admit. He will be Mary's own man and not the creature of her uncle, or of Moray, or even William Maitland.

Livingston
What if he has been sent by the Pope? He is an Italian.

Fleming
How can any one of us say or write such a thing?

Seton
Why should we not have an emissary from the Holy Father?

Beaton
Not an emissary, Seton, a spy. Anyway, he has not been sent by the Pope, but appointed because he is not another Raulet, but an intimate and trustworthy servant.

Seton
Mary will always be able to rely on us in every particular. Rizzio is a commoner.

Livingston

She has much need of our loyalty, for she has few friends in Scotland for all their show. Often she takes consolation in her own company. I hear her talking and praying alone.

Seton

No, she is talking with her mother as if she were still living on the other side of the sea. That will change if she marries. Pray God it will be so. No one deserves happiness more. Mary was made to shine. And we are her mirrors. May good fortune shine on us as well.

Fleming

Only if we avoid foolishness and loose talk. The book should be sealed and kept in the locked desk, with the key in a place which we alone know.

Beaton

We hold court at Stirling, in the French manner. Mary is always lighter and freer here in her mother's palace. It seems like a return to former days. But we are girls no longer and every day brings new consequences.

Lord Darnley dances well. He sings and plays at the viol. He fences and rides at the ring. He plays at billiards, at cards and at tennis. He joins in the masque and writes poetry. Darnley is a perfect gentleman and his eyes are always on Mary. The other lords begin to be jealous since he flaunts himself as suitor. They are jealous of his father's wealth, now that Lennox has recovered his estates in Scotland. At table yesterday Darnley said that Moray's holdings have grown too great. Does he not understand the trouble careless talk can cause? Is he so confident of his position, though newly arrived? He dines though with Moray and Randolph, and attends Maister Knox's sermons, to increase acceptance beyond the Court. Moray seems slow to detect his purpose, while Randolph believes he may be recalled by Elizabeth at any time. I did not contradict him since he may be right. I wonder though if Darnley is already beyond England's reach?

His father Lennox has instructed him how to act, but a child cannot always be obedient. He has hazel eyes that bewitch. His mouth is full but sometimes he purses up his lips and makes it small. Is he petulant?

Mary likes him. She is attracted by his type, so different from the Scots lords. I do not like him. His eyes measure you as if one were a length of damask. And naked underneath. Alright, I am blotting it out.

Fleming

She has not made up her mind about Darnley.

Maitland has been sent on embassy to France, but goes to London first. He may seek consent in France for Mary's marriage, from her family and perhaps the Medici.

Beaton

That is what we are supposed to think. But William Maitland is carrying an ultimatum for Elizabeth. Things are in the balance, and Mary is ready to act for herself. I know this for certain. Would she make Darnley King? Everything hangs in the scales.

Fleming

Let us be discreet, above all else.

Livingston

Lord Darnley is taken ill, sweating and in a fever. Mary orders him removed from Lennox's lodging and housed in private apartments in the castle. He is under her special protection.

As the fever breaks his skin erupts with a thick rash. It is pustulous and fouler than the normal measles. He is afflicted with sharp pangs in the head and belly. Mary has him bathed and anointed every day, though always with Lennox's body servants present.

He is in the room directly below her bedchamber and she slips up and down at all hours to make sure he is comfortable. There is an inner stair between the apartments.

Is this like Francis' last illness, when she would not leave the bedside? Does she think that Darnley will die as well?

Beaton

He has become the child of her compassion, the object of her love. No one else has free access to his apartment. He is hers to dote upon, cocooned in weakness and indulgence.

Maitland is back from England where he announced the Queen's intention to marry Darnley. He is closely followed north by Throckmorton, Elizabeth's latest emissary on the marriage. Arriving in Stirling, the castle gates were shut in this new ambassador's face, and he had to take up residence in the town. Melville has come posthaste from Fife to cluck like a diplomatic hen stirred from her eggs.

Livingston

Darnley is gaining strength as the scabs dry out and begin to peel. They laugh and joke together like lifelong friends. He loves her undivided attention. He does not want her to leave him alone. Mary has outlet for her frozen affections.

I understand her feelings. We are grown women and should be able to give our hearts in love. I am not ashamed to write that mine is pledged and that when Mary marries I shall ask her permission to do the same. This is not because I love her or you any less, but because I have found a different love, the Master of Sempill. See I have written his name for all to read.

Beaton

Are only men suitable to be objects of affection? Forgive me, I tease.
Livingston has chosen well, or been chosen. I only wish my heart could be
so freely given. My affections are as tangled as the Court's affairs.

Fleming

Beaton is playing with fire. Her affections are engaged with someone
whom she cannot wed.

Beaton

This is a game of fire. You cannot play without sometimes being burned.

Seton

I do not believe all that is written here is true. Such make believe is dangerous
even amongst ourselves. If we are grown then let us behave like adults in a
world of sober truth.

Fleming

I fear the world is full of lies and deceit. We did not make it so but should
not become embroiled. Let our hearts and our loves be open for all to see.

Beaton

Fleming declares her own heart. But the crooked world runs on. Events
declare themselves. Moray has realized too late what is afoot. And that
Maitland has bypassed him. Did he not see the signs? Mary has surprised
her own brother, but we have witnessed everything at first hand. The
Marys are first to see and hear and know.

Fleming

Moray was called today to the sickroom and instructed to sign a pledge
in support of the marriage. He was dismayed by Mary's assurance, when
he is used to being asked for guidance. His normal mask failed him and
he blustered angrily, refusing to sign, calling this alliance hasty and ill-
considered. He questions whether Darnley is a friend of true religion, since
he was raised Catholic and has never renounced that allegiance.

   Mary heard him without interruption, but would not allow Darnley
to reply. Then calmly she commanded Moray to leave her Court, until he
would be more inclined towards his Sovereign's will.

Beaton

Shock was written on the Earl's brow, but he turned without another word
and left within the hour. Perhaps he fears for his safety in a Court that has
become Mary's to govern?

   What differences one short year can bring. Moray's reign has ended;

Mary's has begun. This had to happen, since she is strong in her own will and desires authority.

Livingston

Mary is smitten by her love for Lord Darnley. They hold hands and she gazes at him from a stool at the bedside. She indulges her feelings as never before. She hangs on his every word and urges his recovery by force of will daily, hourly. There is something excessive in this devotion, as if her heart pretends to direct her head. Is this love or toying with love?

Seton

What will happen to us when she marries? Will we be sent away again?

Fleming

This time Mary is Queen in her own right and will keep her own household.

Beaton

Even if Darnley hates us?

Throckmorton has spoken with Mary. 'Do I not behave honourably?' she quizzes, 'marrying an English nobleman as Elizabeth requested, and her own kinsman? Have I not notified her of my decision immediately as my mind was resolved? Do I not seek the blessing of the cousin whose advice I value closest to that of my own dear, departed mother?'

Throckmorton was silenced, so Melville mumbled about good counsel and conciliation between such noble Queens, as if pouring cherry cordial on a gaping wound. It was Mary at her most assured, but when the ambassador left to write his report, Maitland urged delay till Elizabeth's reaction was known. And she accepted his advice. Is she really so confident?

Seton

Mary knows to depend on someone who is loyal and wise.

Livingston

What difference can it make now? Darnley is ennobled as Earl of Ross and will be Duke of Albany within the week. He has fourteen new knights to support his station. His recently putrid flesh is adorned with gold, silks and furs, as if he were already King.

Beaton

The Dukedom is postponed till Elizabeth's reply. Many a slip between cup and lip. Darnley drew his dagger on the messenger and threatened to stab the Duke of Hamilton for changing his mind about the marriage. The old ditherer was always opposed to this for it makes his claim more distant and advances Lennox.

Every earl and lord has dined with Darnley and pledged a kingdom in his cups. Was he drunk when he drew his blade?

Seton
I have not seen Lord Darnley in drink.

Beaton
Unlike her Saviour, Seton does not keep company with sinners. Darnley and Rizzio drink deeply every night with whoever else will join them from hall or kitchen. Either Mary does not see, or deliberately turns a blind eye. Maister Knox will sniff them out shortly.

Livingston
I have heard that Darnley and David Rizzio have shared a bed. Are they Greeks?

Beaton
Livingston is listening to servants' gossip. If they collapsed senseless from drink on one couch, what matter that one gawping lassie puts her head round the door?

Livingston
What will Darnley do next? He is like a child who must always be given a new toy lest he breaks out in some fresh mischief.

Beaton
Randolph has received more letters. He says London is buzzing like a hornets' nest. Cecil thinks the English will flock to Mary's support if she gives birth to an heir. The Catholics will try to assassinate Elizabeth. Spies are to be sent to Scotland and the north. Lady Lennox is imprisoned in the Tower. Lord Lennox and Darnley are both ordered south.

Livingston
Beaton as ever has the English news. Mary has it too, and shuts herself up to rage and lament. Will this finish it? Will she give way? If war with England follows, she cannot die in battle like her father and grandfather.

Beaton
Let Darnley do the fighting, if he's fit for anything more than drinking and wenching.

Seton
What does Beaton mean? Has she heard more of Livingston's gossip?

Beaton
He is in Edinburgh nightly and is the talk of the town. Out of spite. Things must be resolved soon.

Livingston
Mary should send him back to England.

Beaton
And what then? Will she beg Moray's forgiveness and marry her own brother?

Fleming
Lennox and Darnley are commanded to stay in Scotland. The banns of marriage are to be read in St Giles Kirk. Darnley is proclaimed Duke of Albany. Randolph is denied Beaton's company unless he attends the marriage.

Beaton
Why should I be sad on my wedding day?
    Darnley insists on being proclaimed King. Maitland and Melville insist Parliament should be consulted. The Council is against it to a man, even with Moray, Hamilton and Argyll absent. But Lennox says his son will not marry to be ruled by his wife, as if he were a mere nobleman his family are of royal descent.
    The heralds waited outside to process to the Mercat Cross. Mary withdrew to speak with Darnley. Returning she said she will submit to her husband's will. They will rule jointly. She commanded the lords' consent. The marriage was proclaimed at the Cross and Darnley is to be crowned after the wedding.
    I am reduced to making daily notes, so much has happened so fast. To what end we know not. God himself abides the outcome.

Seton
Our times are in His hand. Seton will keep vigil in the Chapel with Her Majesty tonight in remembrance of King Francis her former husband.

Beaton
There has been little sleep and much merriment for three nights, but before the day ends, Livingston has promised, with Fleming and I helping, to describe the marriage, for I can write no longer.

Livingston
At five o'clock on the first morning we dressed Mary in her mourning gown with the wide black hood and her white veil. Though we took a

little wine, we abstained from food. When all was ready lords Lennox and
Athol attended at her chambers in full ceremonial costume and led the
Queen to the Chapel Royal.

There we waited with the Dean of Restalrig and other priests until the
Duke of Albany was brought by the same lords. He was arrayed in gold
and silver and bore himself proudly. As the banns were read for the third
time, the lords and Ladies entered behind until the Chapel was almost full.
A notary recorded that none spoke against the banns or gave any cause why
the marriage should not proceed.

The vows were spoken in the Catholic rite. Three rings were placed on
Mary's fingers. They knelt. The musicians sang and many prayers were
spoken. Then Darnley rose and taking a kiss withdrew to her chamber
while the Mass was said.

Coming out from the Chapel into the general apartments, Mary gathered
many round her, and at her invitation, though displaying reluctance, each
drew out a pin from her garments, signifying an end to her mourning. Then
we closed around her and taking her aside robed her anew in blue and gold
with a shining headpiece in silver satin. But she did not go to bed, saying to
us all that she did not marry for lust but for the sake of her kingdom.

Feasting followed with the whole Court in attendance. They went to
the balcony to show themselves to the people. Trumpets were sounded and
largesse scattered to the cheering multitude. The Heralds processed to the
gates and proclaimed their Majesties King Henry and Queen Mary to rule
jointly in both their names. This was heard in silence within the company,
none saying 'Amen', save only my Lord of Lennox who cried 'God Save His
Grace.'

Then the King and Queen were led to table, sitting to left and right at
the head. Each was served by three earls as carver, cupbearer, and taster.
When all was done the tables were taken out and dancing began, followed
by supper and music and dancing, till they went to bed.

And so it continued for two further nights. We saw the new masque
of 'Diana Despoiled', which Maister Buchanan produced in celebration
of Lord Lennox's triumph. There were numerous players with singers,
acrobats and fools, such as we have not seen since leaving France. The
Queen's fool Margritte ran about crying 'give me a bairn', while beating the
men with her wand.

Beaton

But who will call him King Henry, when all can see he is plain Darnley
still? Though mightily pleased and condescending to all, especially the
Marys.

Maister Knox added his own commemoration of the wedding, by
preaching against 'balling, dancing and banqueting' while the things of God
lie barren and neglected. 'Carnal marriages,' he said, 'begin in happiness

but end in tears', though he pretends not to touch on the present case. The Marys would have been disappointed with his approval. But Darnley was muttering in his cups that he would slit that scarecrow's godly windpipe, if he did not give over croaking.

Royal Marriage
Scotland, 1565–1567

Mary

A GREY SUMMER day without diversion. Darnley is asleep after staying up late drinking. I call a groom and ride out of Holyrood on my favourite mare. Along the dykes we go towards the river, when something turns me back in the direction of the Castle. I slip up the hill at a trot and canter through the gatehouse.

There are royal rooms here which I have not used. More secure, I suppose, than the Abbey, but exposed to the east wind even in a milder season. The guards are startled to see their Queen so anonymous, but I pass through the portcullis and up the stony road, leaving my horse outside the inner gate.

My mother sought refuge here, and tried to govern from this ancient fortress. They blockaded her in, and abandoned their Queen even in her illness. My Scottish lords.

She must have walked in this courtyard and along these high ramparts.

Until you could walk no longer.

King David's Tower stands high above me, but spread out all around are the hills, the plain, the river unrolling like a map. If man could fly as a bird this is where he should circle and wheel over the earth. Free, so free and light in the air. Like a winged spirit.

I should come here more often, away from Court, to where I can be alone. But then they would follow me. I am not permitted to be by myself any longer.

He is a handsome gallant. His accomplishments would shine in France. He bore Elizabeth's sword of state. When we dance together, he draws admiring eyes.

When he lies tangled in the sheets, unconscious, he breaks into a sweat and I wonder if he is ill again. Is that a strange odour in the air? He is my husband and comes to my bed when and how he pleases.

We are not able to talk together about what is most important.

The old chapel is neglected. Inside is dusty, with stools and benches stacked as if in store. The Blessed Sacrament is absent yet it is peaceful and sheltered. Queen Margaret knelt before this altar, and prayed for the rough King of Scots whom she had wed. She was a stranger to this land, fleeing from the storm. But her heart was for the poor, the orphaned, and for the children she gave Scotland. So many Kings and Queens came from her womb.

Saint Margaret of Scotland. Her faith gave strength and consolation. She sought solitude. Pray for me, Margaret. Pray for me, Mary. Pray for me, Mother. For you know my hopes and my fear.

Elizabeth will not aid me. She will not recognise my right or take me to her heart. Perhaps she is afraid, alone at the centre of Cecil's web. Yet she is free and unwed. I cannot count on her help, even when that is what she wants to give. She cannot live by her own desires.

Lady Lennox is royal, descended, like me, from Henry Tudor. Does she think kindly of me when my own family leaves me to fend for myself? My own mother lost to me. She is the mother of my husband, a new King Henry. We are all Stewarts and Tudors also, thistles and roses entwined.

She sent me Darnley. My fresh-faced long limbed wooer, determined to please and gain his place. And I was charmed, seduced by his attentions. She is sent to the Tower for her part in my marriage, yet prison is nothing to such a woman if her ambition is finally fulfilled.

What does her jewel mean, her enigmatic gift? I have worn it inside my bodice these last days, and open its encrusted crown when alone or pensive. Two hearts joined by a love knot and pierced by Cupid's arrows. 'What we resolve'. MSL: Matthew and Margaret; Lennox and Stewart. Does love provide the key? Is Darnley my cipher?

Open again, within the winged heart. Beneath are engraved hands and the horn, a skull and crossbones. 'Death shall dissolve'. Only death; though even death may not dissolve the bond of love, if we are faithful beyond the grave.

Close one lid, then the next, all enwrapped in a golden heart inscribed with a Crown, which is borne aloft by Faith, Hope, Truth and Triumph. For surely these shall, no should, overcome. Then at the centre of the labyrinth – 'Who hopes still and endures, shall win the prize of their pretence.'

To what do we pretend, other than the thrones of England and of Scotland joined as one? That is what Lady Lennox wants, and all of Europe supports my cause, except Cecil who would have me Queen of Nowhere. Even the Protestants want our two kingdoms made into one, if I will renounce religion. Randolph boasts openly that one Mass is but a feather in the scale against the wealth of London.

Beaton taunts and teases him, because she knows he will never have her hand. Does Randolph take to her bed? Opposites attract, and sometimes affinities repulse one another. I used to condemn such behaviour.

Is Lady Margaret instructing me to forsake all else for love of her son? Or does she hint at a concealed purpose? No insensate jewel can answer such questions; only the heart against which it leans. And my heart is unknown, though my own.

I cannot stay any longer, confined by this dusty stone. I do not want to be calm or still, when my rule is threatened, my marriage attacked. I must act like a Queen and enforce my will. Those who believe I am supine before their lordly whim will receive a sharp lesson. I am like you, Mother, in self-command, but have also learned that there is a time to strike back and show no weakness. I am born to rule, this nation at the least, and will not deny my birthright for any man. I shall be a Queen first and foremost.

Clerks bring another pile of charters, papers for signature, orders of Council. Yesterday's mountain still towers unfinished. He takes himself off for three days hunting, without a word. Henry and Marie, King and Queen of Scotland; when His Majesty deigns to address state business. Everything is left to me without a thought or backward glance. Refused my bed he goes rooting elsewhere for his pleasures.

Maitland says we should make a stamp of his signature and apply it at our own convenience.

'Is that not forgery?'

'No, for we are reproducing what is authentic.'

'How do I know you are not copying my signature as well?'

'Your Majesty knows that would be impossible, it is so distinctive.'

'I see you have studied the question.'

He examines me with his soulful eyes, gauging my mood. It is lighter since he came to relieve my struggles. I have paid little attention to Maitland in recent months, but his small, bustling figure contains kindness and great insight.

As we are together privately in the charter room, I ask him to weigh the factions, now that Moray is openly defiant. I have done this so many times in my head, but it is reassuring to hear it in another's voice. He reinvents the world in patterns of the mind, making slight precise gestures and taking off his bonnet to show graying hair and a deeply lined brow.

For the Earl of Moray, there is Hamilton, Argyll, Glencairn, Lindsay, Boyd and Ochiltree, father of Knox's new bride. And worst of all Kirkcaldy, whose Protestant allegiance seems to overtop all his gallantry. I thought I knew William Kirkcaldy as a faithful friend.

Yet Hamilton might send men, and waver at home in Lanarkshire. If Argyll is threatened in his homeland, he will withdraw westwards into the mountains and leave Glasgow to my loyal subjects. We reckon like a merchant's tally.

'For Your Majesty, there is Athol, Lennox, Errol, Lindsay, Ruthven, Morton, Seton, Home and countless gentlemen. It is a goodly number, though Hamilton and Argyll can each count on an army.'

My husband brings in the Stewarts by his father, and the Douglas by his mother. But I did not expect Morton himself to join my party. Maitland noted my surprise.

'Lady Douglas has surrendered her claim to the Earldom of Angus to Morton's nephew. Now he can strip the lands and rents for his own profit.'

'That is the key to Morton's support for my marriage. And his Protestant soul,' I reflected bitterly.

'I expect religion plays small part in his case.'

There was humour and a barb in his reply.

'You are right. I apologise, Maitland. The rebels call on Elizabeth to help them. An English army might tip the scales against me.'

'But we shall write and remind Her Majesty of England that all Christian Princes will be ranged against her, if she aids treasonous revolt. She abhors disobedience. And what if Spain or France were to come to your side by attacking England?'

'Will they?'

'No, but thinking they might should be enough to keep the English border secure.'

Again a wry smile played over the Secretary's neat features, which seem somehow compressed within his round face.

'Moray believes Elizabeth will send weapons and money because Cecil and Leicester urge it.'

'Forgive me, Your Majesty, but it is a fault in your brother to presume that others estimate him at his own valuation.'

'Even Knox has tempered his fires this time.'

'He has fallen out of love with Moray, but no one believes that the Protestant faith is threatened by your marriage, not even Master Knox, the fount of every godly fear and suspicion.'

It is a relief to be so frank on this subject, which was impossible when Moray shared our counsels.

'I have promised not to overturn the order of religion, Maitland, and I am sincere.'

'Of course. Yet it might be prudent to reissue your proclamation on religion.'

'Not if I have to sign one more official paper.'

'In this way you will isolate the preachers, and separate the rude propagandists from their patrons. The populace hungers for calumny and filthy imputations.'

'The poor priests have been spattered with eggs, beaten, and worse, in the High Street of my capital. It is vile and disgusting. One day this will have an end.'

'It is Your Majesty's person, not the priests for whom I am anxious. Be politic, Highness, always politic, for we will not fathom the multitude.'

Maitland resumed his bonnet and turned back to the papers.

'What else have I been, Secretary, since the nursery, except politic?'

Walking is the best thing at Holyrood, because the garden is so green. When the sun comes out, my roses and the summer beds show brightly against the foliage. Did you think of that when you planted out these borders? The foliage is never so brilliant in France except in spring.

Darnley came back to me yesterday like a child needing comfort and forgiveness. His bouts of dissipation waste his health, but I can take him in my arms like a nursemaid. He is tender then, happy to rest and be gentle. I took him breakfast in my chamber, so that I could serve him myself and we could gossip as we used to do when he came first to Court. He wants to meet the French ambassador with me today.

Why has the Medici sent her ambassador here? What does she want of me now that my marriage is done? It is good though to have news from France.

We sit together in the garden to enjoy the sun with wine and raisins. France wants me to negotiate with Moray and prevent a war against England. The French care only for what you can smell from Paris. They do not understand our nation. This is not some family falling out, but unlawful rebellion. If Moray and Knox have their way there will be no King or Queen other than a puppet crown. They want power to rule the commonwealth, as they style it, without reference to God's appointed rulers. Every crowned head in Europe is in danger from their heresy.

I shall not compromise but crush them, otherwise there will be no peace in this realm and I will spend every day looking behind me, trembling for an assassin's blow. Let the Medici consider that instead of France's convenience.

Darnley supports me in everything I say but goes further, urging a Catholic league between France and Spain to reassert royal supremacy throughout Christendom.

Between the normal ambassador purrings, I saw Castlenau look shrewdly through Darnley as if to say, 'and I wonder whose supremacy is uppermost in your mind, young man.' Then he turned that keen gaze on me and asked how I would defeat the rebels.

'Will you risk a war?'

This was the moment of error, as in the course of our inconsequential chatter that morning I had not told Darnley of my decision.

'To play for time would be to surrender my queenship. I have freed young Huntly from prison and restored the Earldom to his name. As you know, Ambassador, the Gordon following matches that of either Argyll or the Hamiltons, and they ascribe the downfall of their father, the former Earl, to Moray. I have also recalled the Earl of Bothwell from exile. He will command my army, since he is a valiant and experienced soldier – a match, I believe, for Kirkcaldy.'

'And no lover of my Lord Moray,' murmured the ambassador in appreciation of the hostile forces I was unleashing on my errant brother. He will think differently in the future of this young and untried queen.

'Bothwell,' spat Darnley, 'in command. Over my dead body will that earringed pirate order about a Lennox Stewart.'

The Ambassador looked shocked. I was angry but unmoved, refusing to reply. So he hurled his goblet to the ground and stormed off shouting for a horse. There ends our reconciliation.

'My husband is young, Ambassador, and at times impetuous.'

'Indeed.'

'By combining Huntly and Bothwell, north and south, against the rebels, I believe I can defeat them.'

'Your Majesty should have been born a man. Yet what a loss that would have been to the Pantheon of Beauty.'

Every word of this conversation, amplified and embroidered, will be repeated at the Louvre, to general satisfaction.

Darnley met later with Castlenau, and asked him to request the order of St Michael and an invitation to visit the French Court as King of Scots. He spoils everything with willful pride. Fleming tells me that boasting one night of being King of England, he swore all the Protestants in Scotland were nothing compared to the English Catholics who would support him. Who can restrain or control his foolishness?

He is friendly with Rizzio – perhaps my dear David can temper this rashness. Or James Balfour whose company he also seeks. But I do not trust Balfour: he has already turned his coat against Moray. I must ask Maitland's advice, and not let him drift from my side at any cost. He is shrewd and farseeing in his myriad minded fashion.

Bothwell is back, pacing into the audience room like some animal returned into the wild. There is a spring in his step, only partially curbed. He comes straight forward and kneels, as if the last year in exile had never been. I give him my hand.

'Majesty, I shall be your champion against all.'

'You are most welcome to my Court, my Lord.'

'Those who maligned me were false. I am your loyal servant, just as Earl Patrick, my father, defended your royal mother when she was Queen.'

'The Hepburns are always ready with a sword, but also with their tongue. It is the talk of Europe that from both Elizabeth and my gracious self your lordship could not make one honest woman.'

'Your Highness should not consider such foolish reports. Five hundred moss troopers are at my command and they shall speak for your cause when it matters.'

Still quick and bold, the Bothwell of old. Yet the eyes are more lined, the dark curls a little grizzled at the side. His barely suppressed force is, if anything, more impatient and eager for action.

'I do not doubt your loyal service and I am glad of it at this challenging time. We shall confer later today with all the lords in council to decide our necessities.'

'Be guided by me in these matters, Majesty. I am the one who can aid you in your time of need.'

He bends over my hand and presses his lips again, before turning and striding out. He is certainly the man I need now, but I had forgotten his vivid presence. Cold banishment seems to have stoked not dampened the fires of ambition. My Court must mould itself to this force of nature or divert it elsewhere.

Darnley is petulant and tiresome at Council, and his father will not gainsay him on the smallest matter. So now Lennox must lead the vanguard, while Bothwell and Darnley share command of the main body. If glances could kill, Bothwell's black eyes would skewer Henry on the spot. But he kept silent and smouldered. I would gladly put them all aside and lead myself.

At night Darnley comes in a foul temper and demands I surrender myself instantly to his desires. He expends himself in my body after rough embrace, devoid of tenderness or remorse. I submit to this for my own purpose, but I cannot forget the contempt he displays or the coldness of his averted gaze. Are all men so callous?

Nonetheless, I have seen further into Darnley's mind. He is not so absent on his search for pleasure as might appear. He believes the whole nobility and people are looking to him as their commander, thinking it shameful that any woman should govern a man. The nation breathed relief when I submitted to him and restored nature's proper order. He is like Knox – 'God preserve us from that monster in nature, the rule of women.'

On this, as so much else, my husband is deluded. Any honour and majesty Henry Darnley enjoys comes from me. I chose him out of my own affection, against the will of many of the nobility and of my cousin Elizabeth. Let Darnley remember his dependence on my authority, lest he become a danger to our cause and to himself.

Finally I am quit of all these tiresome protocols and quarrelsome men. I am a man myself in horse and helmet, and shall ride with my troops. We drive Moray and his dwindling band west and east and south, but they will not stand to face my forces.

I can lie out like any trooper, wrapped in my plaid, and mount again with the simplest toilette. I keep pace with any man, and when the enemy runs before us I exult at this defeat like a pagan. Suddenly I realise how much I have wearied of my duties and of these fractious lordlings.

This is more like the hunt. I lose myself in swift pursuit. I urge on the pack as our quarry disappears over yet another hill. I do not care to catch them as long as I can keep up the chase, and forget I was ever born to rule. If only they would break formation, I would become as the wind for speed and perfect freedom.

Day Book of the Marys

Beaton
The rebels are driven from the field. Thanks be to God, we can turn a new chapter in this book. The Queen has gambled and won. Now she can reign like an Elizabeth in her own realm. Scotland is secure and I delight in her triumph.

Fleming
The Queen is shut up in her chambers seeing no one. The triumph has drained her of all energy and good spirits. She is prostrate and our every moment is devoted to her recovery. The strain has been too great for a woman to bear on her own.

Beaton
Fleming is too traditional. She has carried all before her, always in the foremost, driving the rebels like chaff before a storm. She was born for this. Now her brother Moray must kneel before Elizabeth in London. He expects a sympathetic welcome from his patron, and instead must beg forgiveness for the sin of rebellion, which she herself fomented. She sends him to Newcastle like a beaten dog, tail between his legs, so that all Europe can be shown that he is punished and that the Queen of England has not meddled. No one can match the English theatricals.

Even Livingston is giddy with victory because the gentle knight she desires has been bound and taken captive with chains of love. Mary is the undisputed victor.

Fleming
Extravagant talk will bring trouble. The Queen must reunite the country and end faction. There is no glory in a civil war.

Beaton
Fleming is mealy mouthed, like the Secretary whose tongue seems layered with texts. Unalloyed triumph – Mary has conquered by her strength alone, for all to see. It is a new dawn for our kingdom of Scotland. We should be celebrating with a Te Deum and High Mass in every Cathedral that is not ruined.

Fleming
Please, no more. We should be discreet, thankful that danger is past for us all.

Beaton
Our book is secret, unless one named Mary betrays us.

Seton
We shall never betray each other.

   Yet we shall not always remain together. Livingston will wed her true love, Sempill. She goes with joy and our blessings, the first to marry after Mary. That marriage changed everything, for us all. Livingston is first to leave the Queen's service, yet she will not be the last.

Fleming
We cannot know what the future holds. For now we must get Mary well. We shall all dance together at the wedding feast.

Beaton
The Queen has not shown blood for two months. Her great tiredness was also a sign. No one is willing to openly acknowledge what everyone hopes. Mary is with child.

   This makes Her Majesty's victory complete, for she will give two kingdoms an heir. Secure succession by true descent is her holy grail. She has proven herself fruitful unlike Elizabeth's barren stock. Everyone is glad and barely able to repress their joy. Soon she will announce her condition, and the news will resound through Europe.

Livingston
I know someone who will not be glad. He is denied her bed. Even a month ago he could command his times. Now the door is shut against him. May she never again have to submit to such embraces.

Fleming
This is the law of marriage, that wives obey their husbands.

Beaton
And that husbands love their wives. He is a lecher, not a lover. Perhaps she can be quit of him when the child is born.

Fleming
The Queen cannot divorce her husband. That would renew faction and undo our hard won peace. It should not be even murmured.

Beaton
Darnley is the cause of faction. He wants Parliament to give him the Crown Matrimonial and forfeit the rebel lords. He would like to be king in his own right, and act without Mary's authority. He makes enemies with

little effort and even his friends provoke dislike.

Livingston
Suddenly Court is full of life and bustle. Mary blooms, and all the talk is births and weddings, including my own. The great lords are in attendance to congratulate the Queen and join in games and dancing. Old friendships are renewed and Mary is surrounded with a circle of warmth. Her natural kin, Lady Argyll and Lord John Stewart, are present, with her cousin Athol, and the dowager Lady Huntly, old enmities laid aside, and her Secretary Rizzio who guards her time. They protect Mary from the press of government like a family. And dear Fleming watches over all.

Sometimes when it is winter outside no one notices because everything within is warm. Our ears are filled with poetry and music; our eyes with new paintings, the making of bridal gowns, and daily commissions to the goldsmiths. But the wind still blows and hail strikes the windows unheeded. Maitland says the Queen depends too much on too few. He has withdrawn from the Queen's inner counsels to allow Rizzio his place.

Fleming
Does David Rizzio understand the Scottish lords? Can he advise Mary? William should remain close to counsel her. Mary is arranging Bothwell's marriage. She has chosen an alliance with the Gordons – the hand of Lady Jean, Huntly's sister. The bride brings a huge dowry to Hepburn's estates, and the Queen's blessing. It is his reward for loyalty, and, in his own manner, devotion.

This will outshine Livingston's, even Moray's, wedding. The pride and lineage of two great houses will be on display and the wealth of one. Their union confirms the newfound strength of Mary's reign.

Livingston
Does Bothwell love the Lady Jean?

Beaton
Does he know the Lady Jean? I thought she was pledged heart to heart with Ogilvie of Boyne?

Livingston
Lady Huntly has broken their engagement for this marriage. His other women will have to be discarded too. Did the mistress not return to Denmark with her whelps?

Beaton
The Danish one, while the French resides in Paris. But there is some slut in Haddington and new hints.

Livingston
What hints? Beaton must share, not tease.

Beaton
That some young beauty is imprisoned like a princess in the towers of
Hermitage, at Earl Hepburn's pleasure. Only here there is no breath of
scandal.

Livingston
Does the Queen listen to such gossip?

Beaton
Who knows what Mary is told or if she hears about such things? She is not
a Cecil, fed vile rumour by spies and informers – the spider at the centre of
his web, sucking in every kind of poison.

Livingston
Rumour or knowledge. Does Rizzio not tell her? Perhaps the Queen
intends this marriage to confine the Earl.

Seton
Why are we no longer nearest to her thoughts and conversation?

Livingston
We must all plan new dresses and look our best. Who will be next?

Beaton
What is to be done about Darnley? He wants the Crown Matrimonial and
kingly power. He wants it now when Parliament convenes. Mary only asks
for civility, but he drinks and rants. When he saw the new coins with his
portrait moved to one side, he went to the Mint scattering moulds and
dies. He had to be restrained by the Queen's guard. He claims kingship yet
lacks all dignity or self-control. What can Mary do with such a consort?
    When she tried to stop him drinking at the Provost's dinner his abuse
was in full public view. She is bitterly hurt. How could the father of her
child behave so?

Livingston
He is madly jealous of everyone – Mary herself, Rizzio, Bothwell, even his
unborn child. He will not desist till he is elevated by Parliament. He thinks
the lords will be persuaded without the Queen's consent. And what then?

Seton
I pray they may be reunited by their faith, and restore the freedom of the

Mass. The King attended Mass at Christmas with great devotion and that may be a sign of his repentance.

Fleming

Disturbing religion is the worst choice of all, dear Seton, but I gladly kneel beside you to ask that harmony may be recovered between the husband and the wife. Why should this time of happiness for Mary be so marred? She deserves finally some simple gladness.

Seton

Like God's own mother. She will intercede for Mary. Even John Knox cannot stop women seeking the comfort of Our Lady in their hearts.

Beaton

Melville was with the Queen all afternoon. He wants her to be guided by the Council and not to rely on Rizzio. He went around this several times in different words like a horse in exercise, while Mary grew more restive.

'Your Majesty knows how often since returning from France you have tried to bring the kingdom together, yet have been frustrated by factions outwith your control. But now you have the opportunity to influence all parties by pardoning the Earl of Moray and his allies, and bringing them home. Or, at the least, prolonging this Parliament and delaying any forfeiture of estates until you decide whether it would be better to proffer the hope of obtaining your pardon on the basis of conditions you will set forth.'

'When I sought their agreement, as subjects to their natural ruler, they withheld it, so why should I pay attention to their pleas now? That would be to show womanly weakness.'

'It is no little matter, Majesty -you who can choose the best and leave the worst in all that happens – to win the hearts of all your subjects, and also that goodly number in England who follow their religion, and who would admire such princely virtues and, seeing Your Majesty master your own passions, would think you worthy to reign over kingdoms, finding you ready to forgive and loath to use vengeance, especially against subjects who have already been vanquished and are unworthy of your wrath, so that clemency at such a time would prove most convenient, and fairness more profitable than rigour, for extremity often provokes desperate remedies.'

I think this was Melville's longest utterance yet without drawing breath, but I may not have the whole.

'Did Maitland suggest this to you? I defy them. What can they do? What would they dare to do? Are you now Mister Secretary's mouthpiece?'

Mary was angry, and it was a shame to see poor Melville so berated, but he is more supple than at first appears. With head demurely lowered in submission, he worked his way back round to his point.

'Your Majesty must know, by your leave, it is only in obedience to your own command that I show you my opinion for the weal of your person and reign.'

The Queen softened, granting it was good advice but saying she could not find it in her heart to deal with Moray any more. Yet she urged him to go on offering his counsel, as 'she would perhaps do better another time.' Melville saw an opening.

'Many powerful noblemen are banished and lodged as close as Newcastle. At home are more noblemen who are their friends and relations. Regardless of their loyalty, or religion, they are malcontent at suggestions that the exiles may have their estates confiscated at this Parliament, and other grants of land revoked. I myself have heard threatening speeches that we shall see some alteration before Parliament ends.'

'I too have heard these rumours, but our countrymen are talkative even in easier times.'

Mary was resolute, so Melville withdrew scraping and mumbling.

Seton

Livingston normally writes about weddings, but Livingston is not here. But she did attend Earl Bothwell's marriage to Lady Jean. The ceremony was Protestant with vows and an exchange of rings. The Earl was in gold and black with an ermine cape. He looks more like an Italian or Spanish nobleman, and bore himself with the formal manner of Europe rather than our native courtesy. Jean Gordon is a pure born Scots lady in her looks and manner, tall and graceful with slender, finely moulded features and fair skin, She wears her hair tightly drawn back showing some austere hardness in the bone, which is the northern character. She was dressed in blue and silver satin.

I have written this passage after asking Mary how she would describe the bridal couple, for she notices these things. She says that Lady Jean is handsome while James Hepburn has an ugliness which sometimes appears like beauty. She was astonished to know that we still kept our books. So I left this volume free out of the chest in case she might like to glance at these pages. Then we can be intimate, as in former days.

A French artist came to paint the bride and bridegroom as a double portrait. Rizzio was master of ceremonies for the feasts and masquings, which continued for five days. He was in his element. Darnley had been away but came back on the day of the marriage. The music was very fine. Livingston describes dancing better than I. She and Mary have to be careful of their condition. Everyone was exhausted before the end.

Beaton

Castlenau has arrived again from France to make Darnley a Knight of the Order of St Michael. Also an emissary comes with a letter from the Pope.

So nothing does but that Henry, first of that name in Scotland, will be invested at a great ceremony with the nobility in attendance. All to show he should be King in his own right. He wants the royal insignia displayed on his shield but Mary dismisses the request – 'Give him only his due.'

Fleming

Darnley's campaign is dangerous, especially when he embroils the Queen. At Candlemas he and Mary bore tapers at the head of a procession into Mass. If the Court turn Catholic, why not the nation? Darnley has told the French he will restore religion in Scotland. A messenger has been sent to Spain. William fears he may revive Mary's Catholic claim to England and prove Cecil right. It is a madness encouraged by Rizzio and Balfour, who cluster round him like flies to meat. Her Majesty is too withdrawn to direct events, too caught up by her condition. I cannot make her listen to my warnings; I wish that Maitland would stay closer to her affairs and disregard Rizzio. The Italian cannot help her deal with Scottish lords.

Beaton

This book must not be left out but locked away from prying eyes. Randolph will report it all. Yet I do not credit Darnley's theatricals. It is hard to take him seriously, since he is like the cock on a weathervane, crowing in whatever direction the wind turns. This may be some charade, played to win some other prize. Henry Darnley is an unlikely crusader, more at home in a whorehouse than in the cloister.

I have heard that Lord Lennox went into the west to meet with Argyll. Two days running, I saw Archibald Douglas, Darnley's Uncle, coming from the King's apartments. He is Morton's tool and no Catholic.

Fleming

Beaton has sharp eyes and ears. Everyone jostles for position at this Parliament, and Darnley's unstable nature makes him the lodestone of uncertainty. What will Mary decide?

Randolph has been ordered to depart Scotland for aiding Moray's past rebellion with subventions from Elizabeth. It seems old news, but he leaves before Parliament convenes. And Beaton's marriage to Lord Ogilvie of Boyne has been announced. She is to quit Court immediately to prepare for her wedding. He is a fine Catholic gentleman, recently disappointed in his love for Lady Jean Gordon.

There are, of course, long connections between Beaton's family and the Ogilvies. Her affections were engaged when we went north to Aberdeen.

Seton

This wedding is very sudden. Has Beaton been reproved for her fondness with the English Ambassador? She did not share her thoughts, but left in the bustle as everyone arrived for Parliament. We shall not see her again before the marriage. How can we continue writing?

Fleming
The Queen is suddenly astir with much business. I think the marriage was decided some while ago, and then brought forward before Parliament's affairs overtook her. I was present at their parting. Mary and Beaton clung to each other and swore undying friendship. We shall miss Beaton sorely – mistress of humour, lashing everyone with her wicked, satiric tongue. Only a fit of the giggles could subdue her sharp wits. I wish we were not losing her, for we shall be left dull. Beaton was always able to keep her own thoughts private when she wished, even when she was very small. She is the brightest of us all and the best author of this book. She wrote more than anyone else, when you read back. Who will keep the book now that Seton and I are the only two?

Seton
Fleming's heart and mind are already elsewhere. I will never leave Mary's side by my own will or desire. And I shall always keep this book safe and treasure it. All our precious happy days are pressed between its pages.

Mary

STRETCHED AND SMOOTH, further and rounder. So fine under my palm and soft till the bump, the kick, poking through my skin, our skin. Feel it. Touch on the palm. This life is getting stronger, man child or woman. A kicking boy, or a leaping girl like Livingston, living and growing in my body, as I did in yours. You cannot imagine what this is like until it is happening. And then you cannot describe it because you are inside too, enfolded. The mothers, only they can understand.

What do we want for you, my little womb child?

A happy life in your own land. What do we want for you?

A kingdom secure and strong. What do we want for you, my little baby?

Skill, wise learning and courage. What do we want for you, my unborn treasure?

A loving father on earth as well as heaven. Amen. Amen.

He cannot spoil your future. You will be the tie that unites and reconciles. You are the bond of peace between families, queens and nations. And you are child of my own flesh, fruit of my womb.

I shall not allow your father's ambitions to thwart our happiness, or his discordant boasting. He shall not receive the crown until he proves himself worthy to share in government. He will not make free any longer with our body. This is our land, your native place, and you are safe here and protected.

I shall make peace for this kingdom by my own right, and yours that is to come. I shall pardon the rebels in due course, but not yet. Let them wait a while on my good pleasure.

Your uncle Moray is obdurate. He is a Stewart, but must renounce all pretensions before he can return. My own good brother must acknowledge that kingship cannot be usurped. He drinks from Knox's cup when it suits his purpose, unaware that he is spreading poison. Without authority there is only chaos and destruction, which is why God has appointed monarchs to rule and subjects to obey. 'Beware the Bastard,' Rizzio has warned, but this Bastard will remain in exile till his choler is cooled and his lesson learned.

Lady Moray though will have my personal protection and a place at my side. Hamilton was banished to France for his part in the rebellion but is pardoned without confiscations. I show mercy as well as statecraft. The old Duke has suffered enough, and his family is a counterweight to the Lennox claims. We shall always have Hamiltons close to the crown.

As for Argyll, he is loyal at heart, though earnest in religion. He shall be recalled and reconciled to my dear sister Jean. I know what aggravation she has endured amongst these Highlanders. You marry the clan and not the chief alone: we can confide in each other's troubles. However, I shall take Bute from Argyll and give the island to Lennox. That will teach the Chief a lesson that he understands. And sweeten the bitter taste of Hamilton's pardon for Darnley and his besotted father.

Bothwell should be rewarded for his part. He wants the rich acres of Haddington Abbey to join to Hailes and Crichton. But these lands were promised to Maitland and are the cause of some new quarrel. Were ever two men so unlike? Neighbours and rivals, there is no end to the bickering. Fleming will hear nothing said against her William, yet he is in the sulks with Rizzio and keeps his distance, gazing soulfully from afar at his true love. Is he still Moray's man at heart?

When I turn twenty-five, I can revoke all grants of land to replenish the exchequer. That is what my father would have done, which makes these nobles sweat, unmoved by religion and its holy obligations. My Scottish lords, who believe they have the right to share the government and despoil the Church for private gain. With Rizzio and Balfour at my side I shall manage them, despite Cecil and all England's interfering. Let them learn from Randolph's ignominious exit and cease meddling.

I shall make God's peace, my little one, and give the ministers their livings. But let each practice their belief free from persecution. If all faiths in these islands are tolerant, then our kingdoms can unite. Blessed are the peacemakers. This Parliament inaugurates a new age of harmony, heralded by your birth. I shall make the way smooth and glad for you and for our people.

Beaton will be missed. She was our eyes and sharpened wits. When all else failed we could be merry in her jests. Yet it was wise of Fleming to see the danger and avert it through this marriage. Her departure will close the Book of Marys. I can at least depend on Fleming. We shall see Beaton back at court ere long with Lord Ogilvie in attendance.

The poets will write of new dawns, new birth, and I shall be lightened of this blessed cargo. Together we make the age again.

We are here alone. My bedchamber in darkness and the whole palace eerily quiet. Old Lady Huntly has gone with the message, but I have no idea who is still here, who has escaped. All other attendants have been denied me. Calm. I must remain calm till this beating pulse lessens, this thumping of my blood around you.

He strolled in as is his way, coming and going as he pleases. Had he eaten? Will he join our little party – Jean, Rizzio, Erskine – round a supper table, there in the little chamber?

I can never sit in that room again.

When he touched you at my waist I thought he was in a better mood, wanting to come up later to my bed. Everything seemed easy. Even when Ruthven appeared like a gaunt apparition in his grey flesh and armour, I thought he had wandered through illness. But then the nightmare was ours.

'Let that man Davie come out?' croaked Ruthven hoarsely.

'Why? What has he done?'

'He has offended your honour, shut off your husband from the crown, and come between you and the nobility of this realm.'

'Is this your work?'

Darnley looks stupid and avoids my eye.

'If my Secretary has done wrong then he will be tried in Parliament.'

'Let him come out,' Ruthven snarls.

'Justice, Your Majesty, please, justice. Save my life.'

Rizzio is on his knees, clutching my legs. Ruthven starts forward. Erskine tries to stop him, then the furies break. Men crashing in, more crowding at the door. Morton, Lindsay, Kerr, gun in hand, and many more. Over goes the table with a smash of dishes. Jean grabs the candles, darkness sways.

'Sir, take the Queen to you.' I feel his arms hold me from behind. I feel a dagger pass my cheek and strike below. Screams, more blows as he is torn from my flesh. Cold metal on my womb, Kerr's pistol at me. As he is dragged out, they fall on him like animals rending their prey, stabbed, slashed beyond bearing. Darnley keeps by me the whole time but his dagger is left sticking out of Rizzio's bloody corpse.

My poor David. Soul of wit and music, a lifeless heap of rags.

The room empties. Ruthven slumps into a chair ghostly pale. Am I to be next? I shall show them no fear. My weak, stupid, vicious husband has spoiled everything beyond repair.

'These are the wages of tyranny. Depriving the nobility of their rights, exiling some, and treating with foreign Catholic princes without our consent.' Ruthven wheezes through his grey skin.

'Are you not a member of my Council?'

'It is because of this base servant, nestling like an adder in your bosom, that your husband has not been made King in his own right. Now the venom is drawn.'

'I have been denied my rights.' Henry finds his injured voice.

'How can you say so much? I took you from a low estate and made you my consort.'

'But that loathsome toad enjoyed your company. You played cards with him in your bedchamber into the night, while I am shut away without entertainment.'

Resentful jealous child.

'Is this the conversation of a gentleman, of a king before his subjects?'

Ruthven has taken to studying the floor.

'I dare not speak of such matters. I am not so bold.'

'Whenever I come you are sick or unwilling. Is that the entertainment of a gentleman?' Henry has found his usual vein.

'Only when he lacks the loyalty and chastity of a husband.'

'What have I done to disappoint you? Where have I failed in my offices? Are the fruits not plain to see? I am willing to do whatever becomes a good husband. Though I may be of low estate in your haughty eyes, yet I am the husband you promised to obey, and make me equal in all things. But that Italian vermin came between us and stained my honour. See my dagger sticking from his flesh. That wipes all clean.'

Do not weep, do not rage, Mary. Above all, show no hint of weakness.

'My Lord, whatever offence has been done to me, you are the cause. I shall be your wife no longer, nor ever lie with you, nor ever like you more, until I find the way to make your heart as sorrowful as mine is now.'

Ruthven cannot bear this. The old brute is embarrassed.

'Please, Your Majesty, be of good comfort. Receive your husband, and the counsel of your nobility. Then your government will be as prosperous as in the days of any King.'

'Or in the days of the Queen, my mother. You had some hand in that too, Lord Ruthven.'

He claws at his throat. 'Please God, some wine, a cup of wine, for saving of my life.'

'Is that your sickness, to be quaffing wine in full armour?'

'God forbid Your Majesty should ever sicken as I do.'

'If I die through this child, or my kingdom perish, then my friends in France and Spain will take revenge on you and all your kin.'

'Why would great princes meddle with a poor man such as me, a mere subject? As for your child or kingdom, they cannot perish except by your own hand since there is not a man in this palace who would permit harm to come to Your Majesty more than to their own hearts. If anyone is to be blamed for causing harm this night it is the King, your husband.'

Hauling himself painfully to his feet, Ruthven departs without even as a glance at Darnley. Then he follows the old man's clanking footsteps. I sit on alone, frozen as my mind revolves.

Within the hour there is tumult in the palace yards: the Provost and his men are at the gates. Darnley is sent out to quiet them and assure them of my safety. He, not poor bloodied Rizzio, is the viper whose poison must be purged.

Lady Huntly returns unchallenged. Bothwell and her son have escaped by leaping from the rear apartments. They stand ready to aid my flight if it can be contrived. Athol, Maitland, Balfour, Melville, have been let away; they are not needed for Morton's brutal work, nor can they help me here.

I sit here through the hours of night to devise a way. I am on my own, with only wit to shield us from destruction. I am like my mother now, besieged in her own house. How she fought to save me from this. Why did we ever leave our France for these black shores? God preserve me through the dark. I will not lay down my head, lest these black events break back into my mind. I won't go back into the nightmare.

'Are you alright?'

The narrow head peers down over my couch.

'The midwife is attending me.' I thought that face was handsome and alluring once. 'Are my ladies to be allowed through?'

'Yes, it's done, but you're not to try and escape in disguise.'

'How would I escape in this condition? '

'Will the child be alright?'

'I have no idea. If you are so concerned for the child you should have spared me last night's bloodshed. It seems peaceful enough, considering.'

'We can have another. I don't want it to die.'

'Or put my life in danger?'

'No.'

'You've thought better of it then. If I die you're nothing. Just another pretender to the throne of Scotland. You wouldn't last six months.'

'Don't say that.'

'You'd be fleeing back to England with your tail between your legs, begging Elizabeth's forgiveness, like Moray.'

'No, I wouldn't. My father will protect me. And anyway Moray is on his way back to Edinburgh.'

'With all the exiled lords?'

'Yes, to meet with me. And Morton'

This was worse than I had imagined, no casual brutality, but carefully planned, bloody rebellion.

'A Parliament of all the rebels,' I mocked.

'Don't twist everything round. That's what you always do. We're restoring the government. I'm dissolving Parliament.'

'So all their lands are safe. And how will you get your precious Crown without Parliament? Don't you see you're being used?'

'They need me to secure their pardon.'

'And then your part is over. They'll brush you aside if you don't do their will.'

'Shut up, you bitch; stop twisting it all.'

He goes off to the window to sulk. Shouts down for wine. But he's turning it over, beginning to worry.

'What about your religion?'

'What about it?'

'I thought you wanted to impress the world by restoring Scotland's religion?'

'Well I had to promise the Protestants to leave things as they are. What else could I do for now? At least I tried which is more than can be said for you. And don't think that hasn't been noticed by the people who matter, because it has. The Pope's ambassador brought me a personal message.'

'Your faith in exchange for your Crown – there's a bargain. But you're still Catholic. Do you really think they'll let you continue in power? They'll bring in their godly kingdom and make Moray its King.'

'It's Morton that's in command.'

'So why are they bringing back Moray?'

That hits home. He looks uneasy.

'What should we do?'

'Offer them the pardon, and then escape out of their power.'

'How?'

'I can get messages out of here.'

'To Bothwell? I don't trust him, or Huntly.'

'Would you rather stay here with Morton after I've gone?'

'You wouldn't leave me behind.'

'Of course not, Harry. You're my husband and the father of my child. We can reign together as we always planned before these stupid quarrels. When our heir is safely born then we can inherit England's crown as well. Your mother always wanted this.'

'You make it sound so simple. How do I know I can trust you?'

'Come to my bed tonight, my love, and I'll prove my faithfulness But not a word to anyone. They must believe you are still with them, or we will both be ruined. And ask Moray to come and see me.'

'I knew you would come round, when we had got rid of Rizzio.'

Finally I am able to wash and take refreshment. Lady Huntly brings messages urging me to escape over the wall in a chair lowered by ropes. I cannot flee until I have lulled their suspicions. By taking Darnley with me I remove their figurehead and excuse. They will be exposed as traitors without cause.

When Moray comes I throw my arms about his neck and weep. If you had been here, I would not have been treated in this way. He looks uncomfortable. Did he know? Even so I need him now to divide the ranks of my enemies. He retires believing his return is welcome.

We slip out through the wine cellars after curfew and creep past Rizzio's newly dug grave. Their guards have been withdrawn, since the rebel had agreed to my departure tomorrow with their pardon sealed. Due to fatigue and nausea, and being early abed, I delayed signing until the morning. I would like to see their faces when they find the bird has flown with its quill.

And I have Darnley under my wing, for now at least. In his drunken stupor he failed to make his assignation, coming up the private stair instead at first light. It was easy then to fend him off with morning sickness. I will not sleep beside that man again. He makes my skin prickle with disgust and loathing.

Even riding for Dunbar, he could not keep his nerve, whipping the horses beyond endurance, panic stricken that we might be overtaken. 'Come on, come on,' he screeches like one demented, regardless of my pregnant belly or pillion saddle. 'Why don't you ride ahead?' I mock, and without a word he gallops away, leaving us to face pursuers. Must I always take the man's part by myself?

Crossing a sea bridge between the massive towers, we pass into the castle yard. I feel the nightmare begin to fade. But I will not stop. I am lifted bodily from the horse. Bothwell is there. I am in the arms of Lady Hepburn, carried to the hall. Let me stand. I am well, the bairn unhurt. Let us warm ourselves by the kitchen fire; we can make eggs in the French style; let us joke and deride, and plan their demise. Where is Darnley? Good, good, within the walls. Yes, take my arm, yes let me lean, and slide, and fall in safety.

What has to be done is done. Within days it is accomplished. But there is no triumph in this, no satisfaction. I have been imprisoned, pursued in my own kingdom. A loyal servant is violently killed before my eyes, my life threatened. And the root cause is my own husband.

I am reconciled with the exiles. Argyll was first to come in – he is loyal to the crown in everything after religion – then Glencairn and Rothes, and of course Moray. Balfour was my emissary in this business; Maitland is in the north afraid to face me. Was he instrumental in the murder? Balfour is his match though in deceit.

I must endure these men as the price for driving Morton and the assassins out. Eighty conspirators led by the Douglas faction are forfeit and outlawed beyond the kingdom. Let them confer with their ally Cecil in England. Melville bleats on about reconciliation and harmony, but there can be no peace with murderous rebels.

His Majesty King Henry has made a proclamation, affirming his innocence of any part in the foul deed. No sooner issued than Ruthven sends me the conspirators' sworn bond, signed by Darnley. He is a bare faced liar in addition to all else, never to be trusted or believed again. But it does not cancel the guilt of the rest. Ruthven died a few days later in England. They say he saw angels descending around his deathbed; they were coming to take him to hell.

Moray, Argyll, and Glencairn return to Council with Bothwell, Huntly and Athol. How the wheel turns. Only Morton and Ruthven are absent. Maitland will be reappointed. What was the last year for?

In future I will think more of castles and less of councils. Dunbar is granted as a royal fief to Bothwell so that I can count on safe refuge. I have furnished the apartments at Edinburgh Castle since Holyrood cannot be defended. I shall stay there until the child is born. If the baby lives he will go to Stirling. If I live. I have made Erskine Earl of Mar and guardian of my heir.

This swollen burden is my whole life. It has swallowed all else in is weight and pressure. My legs are sore and heavy, and I am breathless on the stair. Beaton has come back as Lady Ogilvie to stay beside me, but Livingston has given birth to her own little baby boy. I find comfort in Seton's prayers.

Fleming looks after everything but is reserved, a little distant. She wants to marry Maitland, a strange match for such beauty. Yet who am I to advise on choosing husbands? Darnley is out of sight, out of mind for me, though carefully watched by Balfour.

I think that I will die in childbed. What is there left to live for? I will bequeath Scotland an infant as my father left me. There will be a Council of Regency once more; the papers are all drafted, excluding Darnley. If it survives this child will finally unite two kingdoms. Elizabeth will ensure my heir's safety and upbringing. She will inherit the fruits of my labour.

What would have been my part had I gone to England as a bairn instead of France? Could we live different lives, or are we destined to one path? Would England have made me someone else, not myself? When Henry Tudor's frail Edward died, I would have been at England's mercy, pawn for a kingdom. One child may not be sufficient.

But I am the child of France. I can be no other. Without her I would have lacked life, joy, love. Every day I picture and long for that country's gardens, rivers, woods. All my family is in France, and my heart aches for each and every one. I have remembered them all in my will. What playmates we were together as children. What young courtiers we became. Anne, little Charles, and poor lost Louis, and of course dear Francis. How pure and true our child love was. How innocent. He is gone but there are other children now, nieces, nephews and cousins. Each of them will have a gift from Mary; to recall her by when they have grown up into this harsh world.

I can still make a kingdom within my mind. I have my unicorn tapestries around me even in this gloomy fortress. Their flowers and fabled creatures recover for me a lost paradise when all was golden bright with promise. Tears come easily, but these are tears of joy not pity. In these rooms my body is confined but not my dreaming spirit.

I cheat long afternoons with the Marys still around me. We read aloud and play at cards, and sometimes Beaton sings. No dancing for me now. We eat early and I take some wine to lull me into fitful sleep. Then I do not think of mother's swollen body laid out in Margaret's Chapel, or of Rizzio clutching at my legs, or of riding frantic through the night. Always riding somewhere in the darkness, whipping on my horse, pursued by faceless fears.

***

Weightless. A cloud in the sky. White floating, unbound. Free from pain, at last, free. Are these gossamer veils the air breathes through? Will an angel part them, or just faithful Seton. It is wonderful without pain.

Did I die? The doctors say I was all but dead, for some minutes at least. What did I experience? Nothing. Then they bound my limbs and bled and purged. And I am unconscious, finally emptied of the fever and the stabbing furies. Peace at the end. Can I begin afresh now, come home to my body? Or shall I just be dead.

It is so different from birth, alive through all the struggling sweating hours, surrounded by anxious faces, the washings, wipings, bathing of my lips and brow. I felt the burden and the pain, till finally the red fires tearing, the unbearable pressure, the voice screaming from my roots. The agony, the joy. I was delivered of a healthy boy. But the pain went on in my wounds, my side, my aching breasts.

I have not been well since then, not my own self. Those weeks and months are like a blur. Was I in my right mind? Shouting and swearing at Darnley, fearing his every conversation. And when he stood by the cradle, I blush at my frankness.

'God has given us a son, begotten by none but you. Let everyone here bear witness. So much is he your son that I fear for him hereafter.'

And why did I let him back to my bed? And when he raged and threatened, say I was with child again?

'We can always get another,' was his curt dismissal.

Get another – he was too soused with whisky to know where he was or what he did. Never again will I let that foul drunkard corrupt my flesh. I am inviolate now. My body is my own again.

I know him so well, his low deceit and baseness. He is bereft of manliness or virtue, a child turned vicious when he cannot have his will in everything.

Yet his pretensions are dangerous. I was right to send my infant to Stirling, where he is well guarded. Darnley wants to treat with Catholic princes and masquerade as the champion of faith. That cannot be for us now, not for Scotland. I need the lords around me, Moray with Bothwell, and Argyll with young Huntly, all Protestants. And Maitland to steer the government. They will not have James to set up against me; he is safe, especially from his own father.

That is what I must live for, to see my child succeed. He is my god-given purpose. Elizabeth sees that. 'The Queen of Scots is lighter of a bonny boy, while I am but a barren stock.'

Yet I nearly died within these floating curtains.

I shall write to Elizabeth and ask her to be my son's guardian in the event of my death. That will seal our bond of kinship and affection. She too will have her share of the bairn. We will deal with each other as mothers and as queens.

He will secure the succession for us both. It is no longer me, but James, that is the fruit and issue. I will withdraw my claim as long as Elizabeth lives and take my place after any child she bears, for she will bear none. So I am no longer a threat and I have provided an heir for England as well as Scotland. Elizabeth understands her duty as a queen. The child changes everything, and can bring us together. Not even Cecil can prevent it. I shall write to her as soon as I am able, and correspond directly without the intermediary of secretaries. Melville will assist me and keep everything discreet in London.

It is a relief to see things clearing. I can begin to leave these obscure months behind. Today in my weakness I feel some stirring. I am not forsaken. Our Lord has restored some part of me to a better prospect.

One cursory visit, through my long days of illness, and then back to Glasgow Darnley goes. Next he appears again unannounced. For a whole day I reason with him in the presence of my counsellors. If he could tell me how I had offended him. But again he recites the same old tale – the nobility show him no respect and I refuse to make him King. Yet all the remedies are in his own hands, and have been from the start. Can his foolish father not put him on the right path?

Finally he departs, saying he will go abroad, I will see his face no more, he will live in exile, and so forth. He could be anywhere, intent on any mischief, but Balfour has cunningly kept in his confidence and informs us of his whereabouts. And of his mad schemes to fortify Scarborough Castle, or invade the Scilly Isles in aid of a Catholic claim to the crown of England. God help him, but is my husband mad? A brain diseased, poisoned by malice and suspicion.

Will anyone attend to such ravings? He has written to the Holy Father complaining of my lack of zeal for true religion. Lennox remains in Glasgow surrounded by a large following. The garrisons at Stirling and at Dumbarton are increased as a precaution. More expense from my own purse, when all my revenues are already stretched by the main business. We have spent three days in Council planning the Prince's baptism at Stirling, between times discussing what to do. In twos and threes, privately. Nothing must be allowed to reflect on James. The talk goes round in circles. Moray, Athol, Bothwell, Huntly, consult by turn.

Coming to Craigmillar usually raises my spirits. It is so lovely here with the wooded slopes, the sweeping view over Edinburgh and out onto the river. Gardens and orchards climb the southern slopes, where some of my own servants have settled. It reminds them of France. October sun has made the colours red and gold. But today these surroundings bring no comfort. This lovely castle seems more prison than pleasure ground.

In every chamber of the great tower they come to and fro with darkening brows. They look at me as if I were an invalid in need of urgent remedy. I wish I were dead, for then I would be quit of them all. Some argue for divorce, but if the marriage is questioned then James' rights are put at jeopardy. Did this island's troubles not flow from Henry's first divorce, and his denial of legitimate succession?

Others say Darnley should be imprisoned or tried for treason. Maitland insinuates it can be done without harm to my honour, or my son's position, and that Moray will look through his fingers at it. What can Maitland contrive? I cannot be compromised when my accord with Elizabeth is so close. Nothing unbecoming to a queen shall besmirch my name. They must understand that, even if their own reputations shrug off such qualms.

What is to be done? Nothing until the baptism is performed and James acknowledged by all the ambassadors. Then we shall see. The baptism will be the most magnificent event in Scotland since my mother's royal entry. I am sparing no expense and it will be by Catholic rite, whatever may follow. This ceremony and its attendant celebrations will resound through Europe, and be remembered as long as the Kingdom of the Scots endures.

I must not give way to melancholy, but play the part for which I was born. 'Be a queen, *ma petite*, and do your duty, then nothing can befall that God does not intend. *Courage, Marie, ma perle, toujours courage*'. And we parted never to meet again in this world. But the mothers do not forget, on earth or in heaven. My hands were inside Grannie's lined palms clasped in her prayers. And today I have a *petit garçon* who will put his hands in mine and pray for me always whatever befalls.

Elizabeth sends a golden font, as godmother. The ambassador brings letters confirming her agreement to my proposals. All that is left is to review her father's will and restore our place in England's royal line, James' and mine. Elizabeth will insist, whatever objection Parliament makes. It is not a matter of religion but of lineage.

Even Cecil, it seems, has agreed, though on condition that Morton and the murderers are recalled from exile. What does that matter now? It can be done after the baptism. All should be united since the crown is firmly established, succession secured, and peace made with our neighbours.

How grown James already is. A lusty child, with the auburn colour of the Stewarts. I have his nursery fitted out with every convenience, a rocking cradle at the centre. I wish my illness had allowed more time to sit and fondly gape and hold him in my arms. He will be shown off to the ambassadors, called one by one into the nursery to hear him bawl and wrastle, proving he will live to reign.

Our little Prince will be carried from the Palace to the Chapel by the Comte de Brienne, on behalf of King Charles of France. He is followed in procession by the Catholic earls bearing the basin, the salt, the laver and holy cross. My courtiers line the way resplendent in full dress beneath the blazing *flambeaux*, some cloth of gold, some in silver according to degree. I have selected the materials for each costume, and each and every one will shine, by royal command.

Archbishop Hamilton will receive us at the door surrounded by the lesser clergy. So even the old Duke is represented on this auspicious day. The Countess of Argyll, my dear Jean, stands in for Elizabeth. She will take the baby in her arms and hold him at the font. In the name of Father, Son and Holy Ghost, a goodly Prince for both our kingdoms. James by the grace of God, King to be of Scotland, and in time of England.

As we process out of the Chapel Royal, the Protestant lords accompany me to the great Hall where the feasting and masquing will begin. Musicians and players are ordered from the three kingdoms, and Maister Buchanan has all in hand for royal tableaux. The final act is a masterstroke – fireworks positioned round the castle and the surrounding hills illuminate the night skies in a myriad of colours, putting Nature herself to shame. I remember such displays in my childhood, but nothing like this has been seen in Scotland. Bastian, my designer, has excelled himself in the art of theatre. This triumph shows a new age of monarchy has dawned, hailed by signs in the heavens. Birth is to women what men gain through war.

Everything goes perfectly. Even the faults turn to advantage. When the stage machine breaks, and French satyrs wag their tails, the English take offence. But they ascribe these insults to England being so favoured. What could mar my triumph? The fireworks provide a matchless finale. I am able to dance once more, feeling strength and pleasure return to my body. Health is reborn with some fragments of my beauty, as everyone remarks. I wear black no longer.

My husband did not attend our son's baptism but sulked in his chamber, because he said the English would not recognise his place. Perhaps they perceived it all too plainly. Still believing in his power to hurt, he creeps off again to his father's house in Glasgow, where he feels safe and cherished. In truth he is ignored by all. I could weep for such a husband, but shall not give way to pensive thoughts or fears. Darnley will be dealt with in my own way soon. For now let him gang his ain gait, and be satisfied with the leavings. He will have nothing more of me.

Bothwell and Moray come together and press for Morton's pardon. It is unusual to see those two united on any matter. At another time it might arouse suspicion, but, after Elizabeth's assurances, I have my own reasons for consenting. This is the first day of Christmas. Let the holy season bring amity and goodwill to our land. Over seventy conspirators will be forgiven though bound by strict condition to maintain the peace.

As I read the papers prepared by Maitland, I see the name Kerr of Fawdonside and for a moment sense cold steel against my stomach.

A shadow passes over and then I sign.

The whole Court is moved again to Holyrood. There we have the first wedding after Christmas. Fleming finally has her Maitland. Morton will be back in Scotland within days and my accord with Elizabeth sealed. So this marriage binds the Court together in one party, and Fleming will remain in my service with her husband. What abundant beauty to rest in the arms of such a learned man. Even beside his father, gallant old Sir Richard, Maitland looks like a schoolmaster. Yet Fleming has always been earnest like the eldest daughter with a gaggle of wayward sisters.

Word comes from Glasgow: Darnley is gravely ill with a fever of the pox. A few days later I set out to visit my ailing husband. The town is packed with Lennoxmen, so Bothwell and Huntly bring me as far as Falkirk where I am given a bodyguard of Hamiltons. The numbers here are proof, were any needed, that despite his illness Darnley intended new harm to James and to my throne. Now any attack on Stirling will be in vain: the chick has flown his coop.

Darnley is lying in the castle, secluded in an upper chamber. I do not fear the pox since I had it as a girl, but this is worse – a putrid fever. The smell is overpowering and I have to force myself to the bedside. His breath stinks but he does not want me close enough to see the sores; his face is covered with taffeta to mask his vanity.

'How are you, Henry?'

'The doctors say it's past the worst. You could have come sooner. I might have died.'

'I came as soon as I could. Have the eruptions ceased?'

'Yes, but they're all over me – foul black things. Will I be left scarred, Mary?'

'Not necessarily; my skin recovered without blemish when I was a girl. How have you been treated?'

'With mercury. Can you not tell? I've lost my sense of smell.'

'It kills the poison.'

'What poison? Who wants me dead?'

'The disease, I mean, the infection,' I reassured.

'They do want me dead though, don't they, plotting at Craigmillar.'

'I will not allow anyone to harm you.' For someone so withdrawn from Court he was still well informed.

'Yes, I heard you put a stop to it. You can't divorce me.'

'I don't want to divorce, for the sake of our son.'

'But you do still love me.'

How strange that sounded from behind his mask; only the eyes seemed alive, glinting with suspicion.

'That is why I am here,' I countered. 'You will see that I still care for you.'

'How long are you staying?'

'For the rest of the week, and as soon as you can be moved I want you to come to Edinburgh, where I can look after you till you are fully recovered.'

'And my powers restored in every way.'

'As you please.'

'I am your husband.'

'That is undeniable, Henry, though it has not always appeared so.'

'I will have my rights.'

'Don't upset yourself. I have come to make sure you will get better. For now you must rest.'

'When will you come again?'

'I will be here tomorrow, after you have had the sulphurs.'

'You must keep your promise.'

So back I go each day, with inconsequential talk, winning back his ever wavering trust, showing him affection and concern. I even touched his hands, and saw the pustules drained and scabbing.

It is the only way to go on. I shall keep him where he can be watched and harm prevented. First I will take him to convalesce at Craigmillar, where we shall see. It can be his home, or a spacious prison if he chooses.

Perhaps if he is pampered and indulged he will settle down to be a dependent child again. Sitting by his side I could be a tender caring mother. Perhaps he has suffered the fantasies of a fevered mind and is now returning to a calmer frame. Was he deluded by this strange disease? Can he find peace in my bed?

The remains of handsome youth. What will come, will come; if that must be the price. I hardly know or care any longer for my flesh. I am a stranger in this body. It seems to be only what other men desire. Or wish to destroy. Is that what it costs to be a Queen? Only my heart is my own. The casket is foreign to the jewel it houses.

After four days he agrees to come with me. He is much better, the doctors say, and after more baths the cure will be complete. I order a horse litter so he can travel with my escort slowly back to Edinburgh.

On the way he announces he will not go to Craigmillar, which rouses his fears. He has taken a house at Kirk o' Field, belonging to the Balfours. I know the place. It is a quiet lodging by the old church, looking south from the town onto gardens and orchards. The priests chose well, for it has a pleasant open air, a short ride from Holyrood along the edge of the royal park. It will do as well as any other.

I send ahead and have the house quickly furnished out of the palace. He can live quietly there and I can visit until he is fit to come to Holyrood. All being well, the worst may be over for us both.

The pustules have cleared. A last round of bathing and he will come back to Holyrood to climb the private stair. The mask is gone. His face is healing.

This is a day of bustle and distraction. We attend the last Mass before Ash Wednesday and, changing quickly, go straight on to Bastian and Christine's wedding. What fun there is when my servants marry within the household and remain part of the family. I wonder if Bastian will wear one of his satyr costumes with the tail, but all his conduct is decent and merry. Christine looks her best in the dress I had made. Her husband may be the best stage designer in two kingdoms, but I am still Queen when it comes to judging a bridal gown.

The party will go on all day and I promise to join the dancing later. 'If Your Majesty do not dance the marriage is nothing,' chides the groom with shoulders raised and hands outspread with Gallic indignation. But I must go on to a banquet receiving a new ambassador. Bothwell, Argyll, and Huntly are there along with the chief courtiers and, after dinner, I take them with me up to Kirk o' Field. Better with company to smooth over any ill-temper. Lady Moray is about to go into labour, so my brother has left already for Fife.

Wine has been sent ahead with a musician to celebrate Darnley's return to health and humour. The lords roll dice at the table while I remain beside the invalid.

'I have written today to my father.'

'He will be very glad of your news.'

'He will be curious as to how I have recovered so quickly.'

'It is because of rest and good treatment. You have been a good patient,' I soothed with half a mind on the clicking dice.

'But I am better through the kindness of those who for a time concealed their goodwill. That is what I said to father. I mean you, my love, the Queen, who has treated me like a natural and loving wife. What do you think of that, Mary Stewart?'

'I am glad of your good opinion.'

'Not everyone loves you, Mary, as I do. There are those who would plot against you even now.'

'I fear that is true. And against our son, Prince James.'

'I know nothing of that. But there are devils who whispered something else in my ear. Shall I tell you what they said?

'If you want to, Henry.' He had my full attention.

'They said that I should kill you and take the throne.'

'Were they wise?'

'They are evil, as devils are.'

'Then you had best ignore them.'

'When you are loving to me, I do not hear those voices. Stay with me tonight.'

'I cannot stay tonight.'

'Why not, you slept downstairs last night.'

'I have to go to Bastian and Christine's wedding party. The horses are waiting in the yard.'

'Send them away. You make too much of base servants. Stay tonight if you value my life.'

'I promised, Henry, and anyway tomorrow you will be at Holyrood.'

'Alright if you must. Maybe it's better that way. I will come up our stair when it is dark. Promise that you will be waiting for me. Promise, Mary, I can be your King again.'

'Till, tomorrow, then. See, take this ring as a pledge of our friendship. Good night, and sleep well.'

I held out the ring, unable to touch his finger, and he snatched it from my hand.

'Tell them to leave the wine.'

'To horse, gentleman, hurry, we must see the new bride to her bed.'

So we go out into the court with grooms milling round and torches lighting our party into the saddles. French Paris is there with a face like a guiser. Hooves clatter out into the night, and down to Holyrood we go to drain the marriage bowl to the lees. And so to bed.

At two o'clock noise like a battery of guns wakes me from deep slumber. I send messengers to find out what has happened. The guards are up and arming. Erskine is by my side. Where is Bothwell?

They return quickly to tell me that the house at Kirk o' Field is reduced to rubble. Darnley, laid out in his nightshirt, is in a field beyond the wall. His manservant stretched beside him. Dead.

They have tried to kill me. And Henry has been murdered.

Everything undone. Ruined. All ruins.

Breaking the Kingdom
Scotland, 1567–1573

Maitland of Lethington

HOW FOOLISH I have been, to miss so much. I waited, and desired. But now my joy is full, here with my own Fleming.

It is beyond the craft of words. We are finally together at Lethington, walking, talking, waking, sleeping, and waking again to love. Now this is my precious Fleming's home. And she is mine, to have and hold forever.

The ways of God are strange beyond our knowing, and deeper than my philosophy.

I see this place afresh as if newly come home. How well the beds and borders look, even in winter. The gardens have mended well since the siege. The orchards are recovering too. And she glides through it all wrapped in the sable hood from Muscovy. I see it through her eyes. Her lips and cheeks shine in the chill, breath white in the air.

A winter angel has roused me from my long winter, consumed by affairs of state, my heart wasted and wearied by calculation. Now I am waking and new life lies ahead. I never knew nor believed in this before. I look back at the man I used to be as if he were some half-formed stranger.

Fleming moves my father to take up his pen and dally with the muses once again. Sir Richard is happy to see me married, and imagining his grandsons running in the garden.

At Lethington, we are on a different planet from the Court, another universe if such a thing exists. Philosophers say there may be infinite worlds beyond our knowing. Yet messages go to and fro. The Marys cannot be separated, and it is the Queen who at last allowed our marriage. She could not resist Fleming any longer. But I must not be the same Maitland as before. I shall live differently, united with my love and faithful to her truth. She holds my conscience in her steady gaze. She has made me single-minded.

Darnley dead, lying naked in an orchard. Kirk o' Field House exploded. I can't grasp it. Some foolish bungling, or Bothwell's work? He has aimed at his own mark.

Balfour assured me it was all in train. I should not concern myself. A plot to kill the Queen would be uncovered, Darnley imprisoned and divorced, without taint on the Queen or Prince James.

But not murdered. This brings ruin. Scotland's disgrace and ruin in its wake. Word will go around Europe like a death knell. No one will credit an accident. The Queen turned assassin, will be the cry on Protestant lips and many Catholic ones beside. Every alliance will be put under question, the English above all, just when it mattered most.

Fleming, Fleming, your Mary is in danger, mortal danger. She will be blamed. Who has contrived this disaster?

I must consider. Keep myself away or return immediately? Surely Mary will recall me. Dispatches must be sent to all Europe, with news of immediate arrests and trials of those responsible. Ambassadors instructed. Only decisive action will save her. I should go to Edinburgh without delay.

Who did this? Not Bothwell alone. It has the Douglas sign – bloody revenge regardless of royal status. They have not forgiven Darnley's betrayal. But who would unleash them? Morton no doubt, but not alone.

Moray. Would James Stewart be so foul? Not unless he wants to crown an infant King and rule in his place. He cannot supplant a legitimate Queen, but a murderess... We are fishing in black depths. One man is usually found in murky places. Somewhere this bears Cecil's hand.

In Edinburgh Bothwell wastes no time. Mary has made him her principal defender and Edinburgh swarms with Borders troopers. What other sword arm could she turn to? But at night placards creep out naming him as murderer.

The Queen promises a reward for information or capture of her husband's assassins, and goes into mourning. The Council deliberates but few wish to enquire too closely into the bloody waters in which so many have paddled. Darnley is buried privately at night in the Abbey tombs, like Rizzio. Ignominious in death, as he was notorious in life.

She seems strangely unaffected as if these dire events had taken place in some foreign land and to another monarch. She knew nothing of it, and believes she was the target.

Moray appears to withdraw from affairs. I fear his cold calculation. And Morton cannot expose Bothwell without betraying his own part. So for now the rash Earl must run his course. No good can come of it. Balfour is named on the placards as co-conspirator, yet rewarded with Governorship of the Castle for revealing the plot. Which plot? Even the street hawkers can see the gutters running foul.

Lennox demands justice for his butchered son, and Cecil divides us from London, urging a trial. How pleased he must be to have destroyed the hard won harmony of sister queens, at the very moment of its consummation. His hatred for the neighbour nation is undiminished, but this time his work has been done by others, leaving him without blot or stain.

Mary is alone as never before. Elizabeth reproaches her while even her own family suspect the worst. The Pope blames all on her failure to restore the Catholic faith as he directed and as Darnley feigned to desire.

I beg Her Majesty to put an end to the rumours of complicity. Bothwell is summoned to answer the accusers, but Lennox declines to attend an assize surrounded by armed men. Morton avoids the jury on the grounds that Darnley was his relation. Moray refuses to serve. The Earl is acquitted, and the whispers become murmuring streams.

Moray requests permission to leave Scotland for Europe. He takes a fond farewell of his sister, and Mary cries on his shoulder, saying he is all the family she has. The man is inscrutable. He anticipates worse to come and will consult with Cecil in England. Does he design destruction while washing his own hands of blood?

I am powerless to influence events. Fleming returns to be with the Queen. My dear love is indisposed today. There may be promise of joyful news to come. In the midst of all this gloom I am surprised by my own good fortune.

Bothwell is proposing himself as the Queen's next husband. He openly courts support. He is preposterous, but in deadly earnest. He commands the government and swaggers around Holyrood as if none dare deny him. Can she not see where this is tending and put an end to it now? God knows what persuasions he is exerting. I cannot speak of it lest I provoke her to vindicate his monstrous claims. Fleming is our only hope.

Placards have begun to name Mary as whore and murderess. She is the mermaid and he the lustful hare. The preachers hint darkly and godly insinuations abound. Propaganda turns on her as the Catholic Jezebel, Bloody Mary reborn. Thank God Knox is still away in England, for he will proclaim the rotten fruit of Queenship. How the zealots have waited their chance to attack her, and now she is giving it to them in willful blindness. Or is it despair?

Fleming says Her Majesty is distressed within herself, despite her public composure. She seems to hope little for her future, and acts only to ensure her son's safety. The old pains in her side are renewed. Fleming and Seton sit all night with her for the Easter vigil, sharing tears and lamentations through the watches. Is the Queen's conscience troubled? Does she know that Bothwell is divorcing his wife?

Bothwell

I SHOULD HAVE smelt the rats right away. God knows, I've lived with plenty ever since. Filthy vermin. Laid out so neatly in the orchard for all to see. I was glad to see him dead and my way clear so I didn't stop to puzzle, thinking he had tried to flee, and Kerr had finished the business. He was suited for such work. I never stopped to think.

But Morton knew from the start. And Moray was behind him, even then, pulling the strings while keeping out of sight. The Bastard wanted her pulled down as well, and I was his dupe. God damn them to a hell of torments worse than mine and never ending. May the rats eat their living flesh. The Bastard behind that smooth mask, always uneasy till all the reins are in his hands. These hands will pull you down. And Morton ready to betray his own mother if it put more gold in his coffers. I was his convenience for a time.

And milksop Maitland – he believed Balfour's fictions, outplayed at his own double game. I should have killed Master Secretary when I had the chance.

They called Darnley down, as if they had come to warn him. I see it now. And the brainless scabbie boy was wetting himself, so he was lowered from the window in a chair, to escape the danger. His own mother's Douglas kin took him in their arms, choked the life out of him and dropped him beneath the trees like a rag doll. They left his limp corpse lying there to cry for revenge. Against me, who laid not one blow on him.

They were cunning, God rot them. If I had them here I'd crush the breath out of them both and break them against that wall till the stones ran with blood and flesh, like piss and shite. Why should I lie alone in this muck?

But I never dishonoured her bed, as I am a knight and gentleman. Lord High Admiral of Scotland, Duke of Orkney, Keeper of Liddesdale. Warden of the Marches. And Her Majesty's Consort. She was my prize and I was eager for the taking. But I stood by her, to save her from the black hounds who would tear her down. I saw the fear in her eyes, knowing she could be next. When the rest deserted I was her rock, as I stood by her mother to the last. She gave herself willingly to my strong arm.

They're liars. I loved Mary Stewart. I will always be loyal to her. I am her rightful husband, not Norfolk or some papist princeling. I did not force her love. She was not made for vicious little cowards like Darnley, but for a real man. An Earl of Scotland fit to be her King.

I am James Hepburn still, for all I have suffered. This arm is hers while there's breath in my body. Just send for me, write, give me a word, a message. Call me back to your side, out of this darkness.

They treated me as if I were some boorish trooper, a Border reiver tolerated amongst the nobles. Maitland, Moray, Athol and their tribe. A duke of the realm, and in command with sufficient force at my disposal. I knew what I wanted and how to get it, which is the first best rule of war. Since Lennox was afraid to show his face, Morton silenced, and Moray standing apart the field was mine.

At Parliament I carried the sceptre and all was disposed according to my will. With lands granted to Argyll, Morton and Huntly, none dare oppose me. That night I hosted the nobility of Scotland at Ainslie's Tavern. Who had more right? Gold flowed like wine and wine like water.

Then I broached the Queen's marriage, her desire for protection, and the advantage of marriage to a native Scot. Now that my innocence of Darnley's death was clear, who better to stand by her side than James Hepburn? That got their attention, even in drink. I had surrounded the Tavern with my guards. To a man they agreed to consider the matter and to sign a bond pledging their support.

Athol, Maitland and Argyll were absent, but I told the rest my proposal had the Queen's support, because it would put an end to insecurity. They could see that for themselves. At last I would get a standing army and defend Scotland's borders against all comers. I already had Dunbar. Once king, everything would be in my grasp. To achieve what none could do before me since the time of Robert Bruce, and make our nation strong, independent of foreign aid or interference.

All that remained was to propose myself to the Queen. She was taking the air at Seton Castle after recent shocks, so I rode to attend on her in private audience. I pledged hand and sword to her service, if she would accept me as her husband. It was the old game we played in the gardens of France, but my turn had come round. I saw plainly she wanted to rest in my strength, yet was afraid of scandal, her former consort being so recently slain. I condoled with her on such inconvenience, but warned her of more trouble to come if she was not hedged about with force.

She protested that Lady Jean was my lawful wife and recently near to death. I assured her that Countess Jean was recovered and that we were divorcing by mutual agreement since our marriage bed had proved fruitless. Moreover her ladyship's conscience was troubled as to whether dispensation had been obtained from the Pope in Rome for our union. Mary professed astonishment that things had come to such a pass, yet I could see this news was not unwelcome.

I said I would wait a while for her answer, but that in the meantime we should fetch Prince James from Stirling, and put him under the same strong protection enjoyed by Her Majesty. She agreed to this and I departed.

The Queen was pale and strained without her usual bloom. It was not a love match I offered, but alliance with a statesman and soldier. She was no longer the girl but a mature woman in need of a husband – a Queen without strength of arms unless some nobleman provide them.

While Mary pondered my plea – not, surely, unexpected as she pretended – events were moving against us. Morton was wavering despite signing the Ainslie bond. Kirkcaldy was openly calling for the Queen to be wrested from the hands of the late King's murderers. William the ever upright, but a man to be reckoned with nonetheless. Could he not have rested content breeding little Granges? Argyll had withdrawn from Court, and Athol too. But I could cow them into submission, once the main thing was grasped.

The time for action had arrived, and I am the man to strike boldly when the time is right. To gamble when the stakes are high. Earl Bothwell always in the foremost. Keep faith.

Maitland of Lethington

I HAVE COME home tonight to Lethington with thankful relief. Today I looked death in the face and lived, but only through Mary's gracious intervention. He would have cut me down like some beggar in his path, or a quivering hind pinioned by hounds. There is no mercy in his nature, and now he has the Queen herself in his power.

Yesterday began normally enough with Her Majesty's visit to Stirling. Melville and I were of the party with Mar and a modest escort. We were hospitably received at the Castle though Mary surprised the company by asking for James to be given over to her care in Edinburgh. Mar's genial face closed at that request, since his mind read this as Bothwell's care, and so did others present. He filled an awkward silence by saying that he would need the full Council's written authorisation, before surrendering his guardianship. Mary reddened but restrained any impulse to anger, seeming to accept this refusal.

We went up to the nursery to find a screaming infant vigorously rocked in a vain attempt at pacification. She had the child onto her knee and danced him out of his fury. You could see the Stewart blood in his colour and his temper. A fine roistering bairn. He was unfamiliar with his mother, and so curious. She patted and petted with a will, till the nurse took him back for feeding. It was affecting to see the reluctance with which she gave the little prince over. When he had gone she sat a while and rocked the empty cradle.

It was time to set off for Edinburgh, but the Queen became indisposed with the old pains in her side, so we stopped for the night at Linlithgow in order that she could rest. Starting off again this morning we approached the Almond Bridge, to find a large body of horsemen gathered there. Bordersmen with Bothwell at their head.

He splashed through the water onto our bank, and warned us of an ambush on the road into town, aiming at Her Majesty's capture or destruction. Dispatching a messenger to the Provost, Mary agreed to go into East Lothian with the Earl's escort. When I questioned the necessity, and the source of this reported ambush, he rode his horse between me and the Queen, took her bridle and led her over the river.

We had no choice but to follow on, riding hard for Dunbar, where the castle was fully garrisoned and clearly ready to receive us. As soon as Mary had dismounted and gone inside, both Melville and I protested at this barefaced abduction of Her Majesty. Contemptuously Bothwell turned Melville's horse at the head and slapping its rear quarters sent it galloping out the gate. Then he pulled me out of the saddle and put his dagger to my neck. He was within an inch of driving it home when Mary herself appeared, hurrying over the yard to interpose herself between the Earl and his murderous intent. Reluctantly he lowered the blade and at her insistence stepped back, leaving me free to mount and ride away after Melville.

Never have I felt death's chill so near. I am expecting Fleming hourly. I need her embrace like a child roused from sleep by bad dreams. But this is no fantasy from which we can suddenly awaken; we are trapped in our own worst fears.

Sister Beth

'SISTER ELIZABETH, BETH.'

'Leave me be.'

'I have a warm posset for you, Sister.'

'God strike me down, your reverence, I just closed my eyes for a moment.'

'It's me, Francesca, your novice once, Sister.'

'Could you not have said before, lassie, and spared me the fright. What is it you want? '

'Look, I have warm milk with spices and a lace of brandy.'

'God bless you, child, for I'm far spent. Are we writing today?'

'We haven't written for weeks, Sister, you've been so poorly.'

'Have I? Well, God knows, I've cause. But we must write. There are things I have to tell before, well before. I can't bear them on my own any longer. It's too hard. Have you got your quill? Sit down beside me and keep an old woman company. Don't leave me till we have it all scribed.'

'Is it about the Queen?'

'Aye, and other things? Where will I start?'

'With Earl Bothwell, after Darnley's murder.'

'There's no play without the Devil, right enough. He was home again, married to Jean Huntly and riding high. I provided for the wedding feast at Crichton. Hundreds of deer were slaughtered; mountains of salmon broiled. Then Darnley was blown up and throttled at the Kirk o' Field. Nothing like making certain, to be sure.'

'Was Bothwell guilty?'

'In it up to his neck, but never alone. They all wanted rid of that pocky lad, including Mary, though she never spoke her mind outright. So our Jamie decided he would speak it for her. It was like cauld kail re-het, for this was Earl Patrick's aim, to marry the widow. Only Jamie was more willing to force his suit. Pat would upend a serving lass though not a Queen; our bold boy had no like scruples. The Edinburgh crowd was already naming him assassin, so he had to get her in his hands before anything was proved against him. He kidnapped her on the road from Stirling and brought her here to Dunbar.'

'We're in Haddington, at the Convent House.'

'I know that, booby, but then I was at Dunbar. They made it a fearful rocky place, safe by sea and land. It was Signor Ubaldino's work, that dear man.'

'Why were you at Dunbar?'

'He had me brought there to manage the household after his sister left. And to prepare for entertainment. Which shows he knew who was coming.'

'The Queen.'

'Aye, Queen Mary herself, the bonnie lass – woman I suppose. And long like her mother with the supple limbs and thick auburn hair when she let it down. She had beauty, that's the plain truth, even in that plight. Widowed,

kidnapped, and denied her own counsellors and servants. That was what he
needed to exercise his wiles. To have her in his power alone. He planned it
all like some thieving raid.'

'Did he, you know, Sister?'

'I'm failing, Francesca, my glass is running out. So I want you to put this
down in words. Not my kind of words, like gossip, but church words, book
words. It's on my conscience and I can't rest easy till I spit it out. Who knows
the next bout might be my last. It's burning in my chest, but I think a sup
of wine might ease me after the posset. Good girl. Are you ready? I need to
remember, and settle my accounts.

'He chased off Melville and then Maitland. They shot out of Dunbar
like ponies on the bolt. I showed the Queen up to her chamber. It was next
to Bothwell's. She had no female attendant apart from me. I was her Mary,
so I made all comfortable and ordered supper to be served for her and his
lordship in private.

'They sat late, Francesca, I swear, arguing and discussing. Those were no
love birds. Then he goes into his chamber. But he went to her in the night
– sheets tell their own tale – and she took him into her bed. Why give way
to him? She a queen and he but a needy earl who had snatched her in the
country like a reiver. Aye but he had something that swerved women into
his arms. There was the Danish woman who lived at Morham believing he
would marry her. There was that wee whore he wynched in Haddington,
when Lady Jean proved cold. And there was some French hussy of high
degree who possessed his body and wanted more. Her letters and poems
were lying in his bedchamber at Dunbar. I only know a few French words
but they were all in those letters. I'm not saying Mary Stewart loved him but
she felt desire, in Dunbar at least. I should know.

'Not that she got much by it, all the same. He was off after two nights in
the love nest to Edinburgh. It was not her body he wanted but her hand in
marriage. He had the first and was impatient to grab the second. Where the
bold Pat had failed he would triumph, the Hepburns would never look back.
It was too valuable a prize to let slip love dallying.

She was weepy when he left, and lay abed. I cosseted her with cordials and
sweetmeats. She lapped up the attention like a child denied affection. She was
a lovely woman, and used to command, but conscience troubled her peace.
Put that down clearly, lass, I know the signs all too well. He was married and
she barely a widow. Most of all she craved rest, and release from fear. She
had enough and more than enough trouble for one lifetime. James Hepburn
seemed safe harbour from a storm of dangers.

'It's a strange thing, Francesca. Women can command better than any
man. And see how things need to be arranged. As I should know as well
as anyone. But times we surrender without reason. She was in that state,
wanting to lose her will, for a while at least. God knows she paid a sore price.

'For twelve days she rested in my care. But then the Earl returned with a great following. He shut himself up in her chamber. But not to woo, not our Jamie; I had my ear to the door. It was all about divorces with legal papers from the Court and from the Church. He said his union to Lady Jean Gordon was banned by the Pope so he had to divorce, which was odd reasoning for a Protestant. But I would swear, Francesca, that they had a dispensation for the marriage. Aye and what about Bothwell himself? Some rumoured he was Marie de Guise's bairn which made Mary half sib. They never asked the Holy Father about that. But folk would smear anything with foul, sticky tongues. Pat got nowhere near the Guise's bed.

'They set out for Edinburgh in state, to enter the capital together. He was already King in his mind's eye and bore himself like the master. He had waited a long time for this moment and nothing would sour it. She looked neither left nor right, like someone whose course had been set by fate.'

'Was that the last you saw of them?'

'Of the Queen, God help her. He came running back later, but I'd gone. Couldn't look at him. Shall never see his devil face again.'

'Are you alright, Sister? Shall I write anything more?'

'I've never spoken about it. There was no one I could tell before.'

'Don't. We'll have some supper. Drink this now, you're white.'

'I need no drink, may it never pass my lips again. Listen to me, lassie. When he had gone off with his new conquest to play the King, they released a woman from the cellars. She had been down there since I arrived to make all ready for the royal arrival. You could see why. She was beautiful beyond describing, with golden hair and a full mature figure. Not young but still in her prime. Yet she had a lost look about her, the empty eye. This was his bed skivvy when nothing else would serve. They said she had been kept at Hermiston, and brought here when Dunbar became his stronghold. They named her Christine Sinclair. Write that clearly.

'She was no Sinclair. I knew her, as God's my witness, the minute I set eyes on her bonny face, for my own child taken so many years before to Hermiston. She was wandering about now like some lost calf bleating for its cow. Where was Earl Jamie? She had few words but repeated them over and again. They told her he had gone to Edinburgh to marry the Queen. I can hear that cry still tearing at my breast. Like she herself had been torn from it so long before.

'They tried restraining her. I watched like one turned to stone. Then she ran out the postern. I had to sit down and force breath back into my body.'

'Did you make yourself known to her, Sister?'

'They brought her body back the next day. She had walked into the sea and lain down beneath the cold salt waves.'

'God be merciful to you and yours.'

'I had her in my arms again. I helped to lay her out. We stripped off the sodden clothes from that smooth white body. Then we saw.'

'What was it, Sister?'

'Tender flesh, my own flesh, cut and scored. Her skin was scarred across the back and shoulders and on the breast, even on the breast. Red angry weals, raised to the touch. Aye, you may stare. His idea of sport, to inflict pain because she was slave to his will, his filthy passions, laid bare for all to see.

'So she was buried fast, with only my prayers to carry her soul over. But our Lady Mother has pity enough for all her daughters. Her heart can heal, though we cannot forget, nor yet forgive. Come to my old weary arms, lassie. Beth Hepburn has room here for a world of sorrows. Mother Mary be my witness, I never delighted in another's pain.

'I crawled back here to our house, the old done woman you've known so long. And she's gone to her rest, poor lamb, where I'll join her shortly. He's dying in some foreign land, tethered to a post. Bound like a dumb beast. I take no pleasure in it, mind, yet I have no pity either. I save that for my lost bairn, and for Mary Stewart. Our troubles have no end. God has questions to answer too, when all's said and done.

'Ach, stop greeting. You've a kind heart. Pass me over that box of scents. Dab this behind your ears, and we'll freshen up. I don't need to be smelly. See that little phial – it's a fragrant balm. Splash some on my bosom. I'm old meat but I'm not rotten yet.'

Kirkcaldy of Grange

THE DARNLEY MARRIAGE was wrong and I opposed it. All I earned for my pains was exile and penury in England with Moray, until Rizzio was dispatched for his trouble and we came home. I kept to Fife and avoided Court. I had good reason to be at home, but equal cause to keep away. Violence breeds more violence; murder begets murder.

But the old cause comes round again. Government thwarted, the kingdom divided, and amity with England threatened. By sword and Book we steadfast stand. I can hear the good Treasurer urging at my shoulder – time for Kirkcaldys to be up and doing.

Who could rest with affairs as they stood? The King of Scots had been killed on his sickbed, or strangled attempting to flee. And Her Majesty, his own wife, made no haste to apprehend the culprits. The people were stirred up by dark suspicion. Placards demanded justice, accusing Bothwell and Mary herself of murder. Worse, of whoring herself to her own husband's killer.

Then Moray left for France, and I decided to follow, not add to Scotland's woes through civil war. I thought that was Moray's motive too, but James Stewart was ever a closed book. How simple I was, content to live secluded on my estates, unaware that half the nobility of Scotland were complicit in the crime. Did Mary know that then? They called no witnesses, for fear their part might be revealed. Even though Lennox demanded justice for his slaughtered son and Elizabeth instructed law from distant London. She should have looked closer to home.

So Moray thought to make a clean pair of heels in expectation, or hope, of worse to come. And I was minded to go as well until things would mend or smash entirely. Then Maitland came between me and my intent. His messenger arrived, as we were packing to depart. The Queen was in great danger. Bothwell had seized her person and would now secure the crown. He must be stopped for sake of everything we held dear and had fought to maintain.

How could I refuse such a plea? I rode immediately to Stirling where some of the nobility were gathering to prevent Bothwell and rescue the Queen. Mar came down from the castle to pledge Prince James' safety. That wee lad was our guarantee now of Scotland's and England's future, two Protestant nations.

Word came that Bothwell had already married the Queen, so we advanced to take Edinburgh. James Balfour was Castle Governor at Bothwell's bidding, but turned his coat again. A secret Council was held declaring Bothwell the late King's murderer, on Balfour's testimony. This was most convenient for them all. Then, pretending still to hold the Castle for Mary, Balfour delayed the advance of her supporters, while urging Bothwell to leave Dunbar as Edinburgh was ready to receive them back.

In truth the Queen was blackened daily by pulpit and placard. But the deceit worked, drawing Mary's forces as far as Seton Castle. Bothwell took position on Carberry Hill while we formed below, joined by Argyll's reinforcements and the Ayrshire earls. Morton was principal, with Argyll heading the Protestant interest, but there were Catholics too, such as Athol, who felt Her Majesty mishandled.

Bothwell came out and rode up and down with his banners defying us to single combat. Young Lindsay began to arm, swearing to avenge his cousin Darnley's death, but Mary forbade the combat.

Further parley followed with messages to and fro while the day grew hot. Fortunately we had streams and a well behind us while they baked on the hilltop. I could see men at their edge and rear beginning to slip away, and sent a company of horse round their flank to block off any retreat to Dunbar. We wanted to settle it there to our advantage.

Concerned for Her Majesty, I offered to go up under a flag of truce. As I approached I saw Bothwell signal to a trooper to shoot, but Mary saw it too and stopped him, reproving the man for bloody treachery. I knew there could be no safety for the kingdom, or for Mary herself, until Hepburn was removed.

The Queen was wildly clad in a short petticoat that showed her bare legs, and a common bonnet. Yet her cheeks were fired, her hair loose and she seemed in command. I bowed and offered her safe conduct back to Edinburgh and restoration of her government, if she renounced Bothwell. But she refused saying he was her lawful husband and not to be cast off like a worn garment.

She charged us as rebels, demanding to know why we had risen against her. I said it was because her new husband was condemned for murder of the late King. She said he had been cleared of the charge by judicial process, and that any further matters should be investigated by Parliament not by armed combats or revolts.

I protested our loyalty and said that we would not depart until she was at liberty from Earl Bothwell's forces and under the protection of the nobility of the realm. She mocked at that, yet even as we spoke her supporters were melting away into late afternoon. She withdrew to consult with Bothwell and then asked if he would be given safe passage from the field. I went back to Morton and Argyll, who reluctantly agreed since Mary would not yield unless this was conceded. He would have to await another day of reckoning.

So I rode back up the hill and, finally, it was concluded. Respective positions were held until Bothwell rode off with a small following. As she bade him be gone she wept, and he protested wanting to stay, fearful he would be taken and killed. But she assured him of the agreement. Still mounted, he took her hand between his, pressed it and then releasing her, he swung round galloping off towards higher ground with all the instincts of a reiver for survival.

She waited an hour to let him away, and then turned to me saying, 'Laird of Grange, I give myself up to you under the terms agreed with the lords.' I led her down under escort to where we were already forming up. Mary Seton, her only attendant, came behind on a pony. I was ashamed to accompany such distress. All men watched in silence as she joined the column still clad in the red petticoat, and some inclined their heads.

But as we moved off there were mutterings of 'whore', 'adulterer' and a few cries of 'burn the murderess.' I kept close by her mount while one by one the lords came to greet her. 'How is this, my Lord Morton?' she demanded. 'I am told all this is done to bring justice on the King's murderers, but that you are chief among them?' He turned away with a black look. Most were respectful but when Lindsay tried to kiss her hand she burst out in a passion, saying she would have his head for what he had done today. She saw herself suddenly as a prisoner under armed guard, and raged that she would turn the tables to hang them all. Better to have kept silent had she known the enemies that surrounded her.

As we approached the men dispersed to camps, leaving only the Queen with the lords and a heavily armed escort. She was expecting to go to Holyrood, but instead we proceeded to the Netherbow Port. Here Her Majesty's travails began in earnest, for warned ahead, the common sort were gathered at the gate, holding a banner of murdered Darnley with Prince James kneeling beside his father's corpse beseeching justice. As we came near a great howling got up with screams of hate and bloody cries for Mary to be hanged or burned. I came level with her horse's head in a vain attempt to screen her person. She kept upright in the saddle, though numbed by shock.

When we turned onto the High Street we could see the passage narrowed on both sides by mobs of folk pressing in and impeding our progress. The escort went in front to clear the path but I felt the spittle of their fury and feared the Queen might be torn from her seat. 'Whore', 'murderer' came at us like roaring waves of sound, and Mary's head bent before the storm. Eventually we reached the Provost's house where she was hurried up into a bedroom and I saw no more of her that night. The lords retired to feast and plan their next steps, but I was not party to their Council.

The next day Mary came to her window dishevelled and weeping, asking the people's help in her distress. They began to gather around the house and to take pity on her state. She was not naked or distraught as some alleged, for I saw her with my own eyes. She was a queen even in her distress, and the mood of the town changed as their old love for her revived. I stood nearby, as did Maitland and others sympathetic to her cause, but when she called out to her good Secretary he pulled down his hat and hurried away.

The lords convened at the Provost's house, and I went in to demand that the promises given to Her Majesty the day before be honoured. They agreed the Queen should go to Holyrood and be freely restored. When this had been publicly proclaimed I left them to their own devices. The crowd was satisfied, though some lingered on the street until she was taken to the palace by Morton and Athol, still half-dressed and under armed escort.

That night the Queen was roused from her sleep and hurried away with a wrap thrown over her nightgown. They rode hard all night to be received in the morning onto Lochleven Island. There Her Majesty was forcibly confined under the guard of Sir William Douglas.

I cannot clear myself of blame for these events. Queen Mary had been falsely handled and my own part appeared treacherous. But it was much later before I understood what had taken place. The depths of their deceit were not yet disclosed.

The Council resumed at Holyrood but without young Huntly, the Hamiltons, or, of course, Bothwell. I went there to protest at what had happened. Their men were all over the palace ransacking the apartments and taking control of government.

I said this was not what had been agreed. When she let Bothwell go, the Queen was to be restored to liberty and government. Then Morton drew out a paper and laid it on the table. It was a letter in the Queen's own hand, written two nights before in the Provost's house. I scanned it quickly before he pulled it back. It swore undying devotion to Bothwell – that she would go the ends of the earth for him in her petticoat if need be. I was shocked. Maitland sat to one side, silent.

Morton pressed his advantage and the others joined in. She was adulterous, passionate and deceitful, unfit to be queen. Lindsay was vehement, swearing she had refused to divorce Bothwell and declared she would not touch food again till reunited with him in the flesh. I asked them what was intended.

Morton pulled out another paper, detailing the charges against her. First that she had behaved tyrannously, breaching the laws of the realm. Second that she had incontinently indulged her passions with Earl Bothwell. Thirdly that she had connived at the murder of her husband the King, and falsely accused others of the deed. It was a sheaf of deadly accusations.

I could not muster my thoughts other than to protest they were threatening the Queen's life. 'No,' said Morton quickly. 'If she resigns her throne in favour of the Prince, not a hair of her head will be harmed.'

'And who is to govern in her place?'

'We have sent for our Lord Moray to come home.'

I should have seen the pieces falling into place. Moray with Cecil at his back. But what else could they do? It seemed better than Morton seizing Scotland by the throat and starting another war.

All I could think of was that Mary must be free of Bothwell, so I asked a commission to hunt him down. And they consented immediately. I continued unwitting, playing the game. Maitland appeared unfathomable neither dissenting nor consenting. He would not meet my eye.

I received a letter from Her Majesty in Lochleven, charging me with breaking her trust, so I replied pledging my opposition to the harsh treatment she had received, and stating my desire for her to divorce Bothwell and recover her honour.

But I was uneasy in my mind and returned to Fife relating everything to Margaret. Word reached us there by reliable testimony that Mary had renounced the Crown in favour of her son and that she had miscarried twins of Bothwell's getting in Lochleven Castle. 'Poor lass,' was all Margaret would say. 'No wonder she would not divorce him.'

I tried to consult with Maitland, but he remained at Court preparing for Moray's government. I spoke to him once in Edinburgh about the commission to pursue Bothwell, when in his oblique way he said, 'Of course anything to which the Queen consented under duress need not be held against her.'

Maitland of Lethington

BOTHWELL HAD TO be stopped; the damage he inflicted ended. He must be pursued and Kirkcaldy is the man to finish it.

But the Queen is in chains. Cruelly imprisoned.

Government must continue. I am indispensable to the conduct of business in the kingdom, as Secretary Cecil is in his of England. I cannot desert my post. Though it pains my heart to hear of Mary's plight, prostrated by sickness and miscarrying in the womb.

Fleming is exchanging notes, and the Queen may be moved out of Lochleven Keep to the round tower where she will have her own rooms. Some of the Douglas household are loyal.

I must be discreet and silent. Her Majesty's friends outnumber her enemies and Mary may soon be freed from her pit. Fleming has sent her an enamelled ring. The emblem is a mouse who frees the lion by gnawing patiently at his royal master's bonds. Patience and time. We must thole and await events.

Moray knows the ways of government and moves the levers of power. So the young Prince is crowned at Stirling and Parliament convened. Most of the nobility do not attend this coronation fearing the taint of treason, but many come to parliament to avert confiscations.

The ministers are triumphant, blowing the Lord's trumpet with puffed out cheeks. Knox himself preaches the righteous overthrow of an evil tyrant. He sees the chance to impose his own tyranny of faith. Moray's Parliament puts their demands into law; his falling out with Master Knox patched up. We are now truly the Protestant nation. None may hold office in Church or State that does not subscribe their creed to the Calvinist letter. And so they gain reward on earth as well as heaven. Had Knox his way, women too would be excluded. The Mass is banned on penalty of death, as if that ancient rite were some foul contagion.

The deposition of the Queen, the coronation of the King in her place, and Moray's Regency: all ratified in due order. She is condemned for complicity in the former King's murder without right of reply or appeal. The grounds – some private and unshown letters, sent by her to Bothwell, are alleged to prove her guilt. Any punishment deemed appropriate is authorised. The preachers bay for her blood with Knox in the van. He sees his quarry stumble and closes in without mercy or compassion. God protect us from such religion.

Elizabeth rails at her Council in London, demanding action on behalf of her sister Queen. She is the only thing that stays their hand from bloody regicide, since they cannot act without her approval. Cecil temporises, qualifies and redrafts in his usual fashion, buying time. He is of a mind with Knox in wanting Mary dead, most conveniently in Scotland. So he joins discreetly in the chorus of condemnation, led by those who themselves contrived the deed of which she stands accused.

Yet England must not intervene by force. Then this country would turn again to France and all the labour of these years be lost. The interests of the kingdom must be foremost, not the power of faction.

But Mary Stewart gave up her crown under threat of execution. Lindsay urged violence on her person and in her presence. What would good Sir David have said to that? The Queen told Fleming that on his return Moray left her one whole night expecting death. He revealed his nature in the end.

Are the Scots a cruel and barbarous people, bereft of civilised manners? Our most Christian nation – the more Christian the crueller. I feel shame to see a reigning monarch abused in such a fashion, yet it happened before, and with fatal consequence.

She can by law renounce what was given up under duress. She is our Queen by right of blood and birth.

I am like a tumbler on his tightrope, balancing perilously between two falls. On one side I read distrust in Moray's eyes, and see his intent that I should be dispensable. On the other, the Queen's true friends accuse me of betrayal. But Fleming knows my truth.

Maitland. Only that name, skill and foreknowledge can guide me safely over. My beloved wife is with child, and another generation will inhabit Lethington. Bothwell's fall secures the Abbey lands of Haddington to our estate. I must not slip now the stakes are set so high.

Moray has the means to reward his friends and allies and buy support. He and Morton have pillaged the Queen's household at Holyrood. Her jewellery is broken up to be sold and her papers set aside for future use. The country is uneasy under such harsh subjection.

Kirkcaldy of Grange

HE MUST BE hunted down. Ever the source of hurt and mischief, he escapes north and, going to his mother's country in Orkney, gathers a small fleet. Lord High Admiral and Duke of Orkney, the outlaw turns pirate.

Despite making good headway we missed him at Orkney, where the Sinclairs gave us a cold welcome. But we learned at the quayside that Bothwell's fleet was a ragtag collection of small boats with one two-master, the Pelican, a flagship for the Admiral.

We took on what provisions we could and sailed on after him to the Shetlands. A land made of moor and rock, roofs tied against the wind, and squat stone towers. I thought of the Queen looking out of her tower at the lapping waters of Loch Leven.

What did Moray intend? To keep her imprisoned? That could not be; no such thing had ever been. She was a queen in her own country. A return to France could not be allowed, for then the Catholic powers would use her to threaten Scotland and England. Could Moray be trusted any longer to shield her from harm? With Bothwell gone, an accommodation should be reached, restoring some position and dignity.

We had to make good speed, but we were at the mercy of wind, tide and this waste of sea. As usual Bothwell gave a good account. His stragglers went down but exchange of fire continued for three hours, moving steadily out to sea. The Pelican's mainmast was broken and the engagement near conclusion, when a fierce squall blew in. Unfortunately our ships were still in full sail which had to be lowered before we were blown back onto rocks. In the meantime Bothwell ran before the wind with his remaining canvas. We followed after but he had disappeared into the mists.

He was lamed, and at peril on rough seas, but he had escaped. At least we had driven him out of Scotland. Yet, as Moray said, we could not deal in the bear's hide till we had the bear.

Having returned my ships to port, I was barely home when it was Mary's turn. She had escaped in a small boat from Lochleven, and had been taken by the Hamiltons to Glasgow where the west was rallying to her cause. This was a new twist. The old Duke was home from exile and his younger sons assumed the ambitions of their house, aiming once more at the crown, through Mary's hand or leastways the regency.

I hesitated, but only for a moment. This could solve nothing and threatened civil war in Scotland as well as rupture with England. Yet Moray read my mind. A messenger came to Hallyards having ridden hard to deliver his personal letter, begging me in the name of our old comradeship to come immediately, for Christ's sake, to his aid. Moray was always a step ahead of me, one at least.

But this time he was in trouble, cut off in Glasgow by superior forces that were growing by the day. Moray had gained power and government, but he had not won over the nation. I took my best horsemen and rode cross country by Stirling to join him. At least we could count on the Lennoxmen for support.

The Queen's sights were set on Dumbarton where she could establish communication with Europe. She had the Hamilton forces, most of the southwest and Borders, and Argyll's hosting. The deposing of a reigning monarch was too much for his royalist stomach. On our side was Morton with most of the Douglas faction, Moray's personal following, my Fifers and Mar's contingent. It was essential that even with our lesser numbers we blocked the route to Dumbarton. So we moved south of Glasgow, near Langside village.

Maitland was of our number and, as ever, trying negotiation. Moray and Morton had command but gave me the overall direction. In the event we had no time to plan since they advanced on us the next day, determined to press home their advantage and destroy Moray.

I mounted one musketeer behind each of the light horse and spread them through the gardens and orchards and behind field walls above. The Hamiltons came into Langside with gallant style. At the same time, skirting the houses, their vanguard set on us from the flank and forced Moray and Morton back. We lacked sufficient horse to hold them and those we had were overpowered.

This was the point of danger, but by now the Hamiltons were suffering damage from the crossfire of my musketeers. So I threw forward the main body of our foot, pikes to the fore, into the village. The enemy began to fall back in confusion. Yet this was also our last throw, since Argyll's men were ranged behind ready to sweep down on us, and we would have to stand our ground and fight for every bloody inch. Instead the Highlanders turned and ran.

Later we learned that Argyll himself had suffered some fit and his Highlanders were unwilling to bear the brunt without their chief. The Lord of Hosts must have been our friend that day for truly we were facing defeat. But our discipline held, and though Hamilton losses were severe in the village, Moray called off the pursuit, and insisted on prisoners taken, and quarter given.

Mary herself had gone. Later it appeared she had not risked a race to Dumbarton, but rode hard instead to the southwest where she knew the country was friendly to her cause. We rarely see an outcome beyond the next throw.

Langside was a victory based on lessons learned long ago in France and luck. At the summit of my skill and strength, I inflicted defeat on my true queen. And saved the skin of two of the blackest falsest scoundrels my nation has ever known. All that is left to me is to try and amend my fault.

Bothwell

I HAD THE right. They agreed. They signed the bond. They wanted me to marry her. The lying two-faced scum.

I am the King of Scots. Bring me more wine. Come out of the shadows. Show yourselves in the light. Call me a murderer and you'll answer with your life. Single combat – swords and dirks on foot, or lances mounted and armoured. Or I'll tear you apart with my bare hands. Not a man among you has the birth and breeding, or the bloody guts, to fight.

They left us to fry on that hillside. Bring me more wine, you stingy bastards.

I let her go, for her own safety. Under pledge of protection and honorable treatment. She is your queen. Honoured with a prison cell. Treacherous bastards every one, even Kirkcaldy. Aye, William, and you need to learn how to steer a ship.

God but I'm parched, burning.

Keep faith. Hold fast. I'm not finished. I can spring the trap and win. Only her word is enough to free me. Before vile, smooth-faced Moray has me killed. Venomous toad – crush him and piss would squirt out instead of blood.

They would have rallied to my side – Flemings, Hamiltons, Huntly – till they called me murderer and outlaw. Then it began – they had to pull me down, and they took my men one by one and broke them on the wheel, extracting false confessions before stopping their mouths for good.

It was thorough, planned, driven home. First they had to suppress the truth, then cause a lie to flourish. Morton, Lindsay, Maitland and Balfour were all involved – but Moray pulled the strings and looked aslant.

I have written it for all to see. My confession will convince the world by laying bare the face beneath the mask.

Which is why I shall never see daylight again, except through a noose.

And the English were in it too, Cecil's spies and assassins. They tried to kill me in the north but I left their blood on the steps and the old Bishop weeping for my fate. It was his idea to go to Orkney and my Shetland, where I could start another Viking kingdom.

North they came to hunt their quarry down, but I outgunned, outsailed, outwitted plodding Kirkcaldy and sped to Norway's fjords, where I could ally myself with Swedes or Danes and bring an expedition back to free my wife and restore our rule. I was received by Eric Rosencrantz, the Governor of Bergen, establishing my credentials beyond suspicion. I knew the Governor's name from my embassy to Denmark, and he recognised in me a nobleman of true stature.

My ships were being cleared at the Merchants Court for through passage, when in filed a troop of claimants against me. What claim could there be in a town where I knew no one?

Anna the Dane. Anna Thorondsen was in Bergen, living as a merchant.

Hell has no fury like a woman scorned. She lodged a claim for breach of promise and return of her money given years ago in France, with interest and damages. As if the favours I conferred were not royal recompense for such a lowborn bitch. She never even showed her face in court, she was so ashamed and aged. All her relations and connections came instead, relishing the scandal.

'Lord Hepburn has three wives living from which you can judge the value he places on promise of marriage.'

Now I was stuck in Bergen negotiating annual payments and a pension to this grasping fishwife. I should have stuffed her full of salted herrings, which is the currency she understands. The whole place stank of fish. I drank by night and wandered round the booths by day gaping at their glassy eyes.

I could have stayed in France. I had my chance that second time when Moray had me exiled. Taken a noblewoman to wife and lived easy, and God knows I had offers. But France is not Scotland. My curse has been love of my own country and her queen. No second chances, no turning back.

So I gave Rosencrantz my papers which were hidden in the ballast. My whole fortune was laid bare for all to see. The Dukedom in recognition of my marriage, proclamation of outlawry, and a handwritten letter from Mary still in her captivity. They took notice then and had me ferried to Copenhagen on a warship, to await King Frederick's pleasure, or leisure as it proves.

Your Highness' fat pig pleasure. I'm still waiting for you to release the consort of the Queen of Scots, and send me to France. Or to Scotland with a navy at my back. You have no right to hold me here. Bargain if you want, like the fishwife. I'll give you Orkney and Shetland back for my freedom. Read my bloody confession, swine, and you'll see I'm innocent. Be bloody King only this once, instead of a cheating innkeeper. Just decide anyway what to do with me, for I'm rotting in this hole.

Copenhagen Palace. Malmo Castle. Then what? Ask the rats. They're the only ones that know my plight.

Where's my pissing wine! Get it in here or I'll rip your throats. With my bare fangs.

Kirkcaldy of Grange

I THOUGHT THIS castle my surety. It has become a trap. We are hemmed in and blasted by their firepower. This happened at St Andrews so long ago, but I never thought to see the Maiden Fortress breached.

The wells are dry, or foully poisoned. Our throats are dust and ashes.

When Moray granted me the Castle, it seemed that nothing could upset the new dispensation, so firm was its grip on power. I did not consider why Balfour's resignation was so amply compensated. When did I begin to doubt?

Was it the arrest of old Hamilton newly returned from France? Or the attacks on Huntly? Or the bloody suppression of the Borders? It started with the torture and execution of anyone close to Bothwell. French Paris was swiftly and brutally silenced. Something in it bespoke the tyranny I rose against when young. Yet I complied with all their instructions. What I could not understand was the failure in England to openly declare the Queen's guilt.

No one foresaw the Queen's flight one hundred miles cross-country. Nor her decision to seek refuge in England rather than France. Yet Elizabeth was her cousin, and it was always Mary's way to trust her friends or seeming friends.

When Maitland returned from London, out of favour with the Regent, I wondered. But then he was arrested and accused, with Balfour. Moray had presented evidence in England to prove that Bothwell and Mary herself had murdered Darnley. Now suddenly Maitland and Balfour were the instruments of assassination. How many murderers could one King have?

To ensure fair trial I persuaded the guard to release Maitland into my custody and I took him into the castle for safekeeping. That night Moray hurried up with honeyed word to reassure us he would see justice done and that the accusations were the work of Lennox. He is, was, the most plausible of men and I have been moulded by his persuasions. But his eyes are cold. I was disconcerted by their unblinking gaze, even as his blandishments were applied.

Maitland nodded suavely to Moray's tune, but when the Regent had departed, he challenged my acquiescence, and demanded to know on what grounds I held Mary guilty of adultery and murder. I cited her letter to Bothwell on the night of Carberry, when she had pledged her undying love in defiance of our agreement.

Forged. Maitland was adamant. I had been gulled by black hearted falsehood. Mary's only concern had been the baby in her womb. She could not honourably disown the fruit of Hepburn's opportunings.

Forged? Surely Moray had not stooped so low. His own sister, with whose childhood and youth his years were intertwined in France and Scotland. But Morton was a different matter. And Balfour, who had been so suspiciously rewarded.

But the Queen's letters on which Parliament had based the abdication? By what due process? Maitland's logic was unbending, and that chimed with my long harboured doubt. Why had Parliament not investigated the accusations but taken them on trust? Condemning their own queen without a hearing or right of reply. Was this Scots justice?

Forged letters: a tissue of deceit composed from private correspondence of the Queen to various parties, mixed in with love letters and poems sent to Bothwell by some paramour. Maitland had seen them all in England, where even Cecil had declined to publish them or pronounce the case against her proven.

I was reeling but unable to deny Maitland's superior knowledge. He had been accused in order to smother his as yet unspoken disbelief.

I did not know what to do or say, so I maintained a neutral silence. But I refused to surrender the loyal Secretary into Moray's grasp. Meanwhile Balfour was released, either through bribery or because the accusation against him was a cover for the assault on Maitland. Balfour is Scotland's most accomplished double dealer – a strange distinction. In recent months he has joined our party then once more deserted. Beware when Balfour leaves; it marks you as the losing side.

The days of simple truth and upright action have departed. I wish I had the Treasurer at my shoulder but those were simpler times. Pharisees and Sadducees rule the land.

Then Moray was slain in his turn, without forewarning or mercy. The greatest captain in Israel laid low by an assassin's shot. It was a Hamilton conspiracy to strike back for Langside and the old Duke's imprisonment. The tool was a man driven to revenge by some harsh decree that turned his wife out of their home into the snows to die. Such deeds sow whirlwinds of hate that eventually destroy everyone in their path. Hamilton of Bothwellhaugh, primed and positioned, shot Moray in Linlithgow High Street and laid the Regent low. Killing begat killing, and it continues to this day.

I cannot abide foul murder. I thought of all that Moray had achieved, our long association, and comradeship in field of battle. The struggle we had wrought for Scotland's weal. I could not see his honour stained in death, so I carried the lion standard before his coffin, up the High Street from Holyrood into St Giles Kirk. It was lowered before the pulpit, and all Knox's spiritual power, his torrent of words swept across the multitude of bowed heads. 'Blessed are they that die in the Lord. Their earthly labour is ended; their victory ensured'.

This for a forger and deceiver.

My mind and heart were strangers to one another.

English incursions on the Borders; the French mustering an expedition. Scotland once more divided. Have I not lived and fought to end all this? Now it will finish me instead.

Perhaps the Queen could be restored and right order with her? Maitland and I had Edinburgh, with Huntly to the north, Argyll and Hamilton to the west, and half the Borders. They had the Prince, or King as they insist, and Stirling as their capital. They dithered till Elizabeth proposed Lennox for Regent and a parliament was called. I refused them the crown and sceptre from my keeping so it was a poor affair, though attended by all the chief men of their party.

I struck then and could have had the winning stroke. Feinting southwards first, I sent four hundred horse and to break in by night and take all the nobility hostage from their houses. Only Morton kept his head and resisted, giving time for Mar to bring men from the castle and force our attackers to take cover. They panicked. I should have been there to lead. Some rushed their captives off; others stopped to exchange fire and try to hold the street, which raised more confusion. Most of the hostages escaped, except for Lennox. Someone shot him in the back.

Whether one of our fools did it or a pursuer who saw a chance to dispose of his puny leader, I know not. Lennox, unpopular and unlucky to the last, was carried back to expire before his infant grandson, unlamented except by Lady Margaret in London.

We had made things worse, since Mar now succeeded as Regent closely shadowed by the ever ready Morton. The Douglas is our enemy, the one who needs to see us both securely silenced. A siege and blockade began in earnest, and one by one our supporters in the country fell away.

We were still strong, well supplied and holding all of Scotland's cannon. I fortified St Giles to command the town, and put guns on the tower. Now it was cat and mouse, tit for tat, skirmish, raid, reprisal. Morton went off to burn my house and crops in Fife so I went down to Dalkeith and burnt his. He began to hang prisoners without quarter so in the end I replied in kind. My Margaret took refuge in the castle, but Mary Fleming was pregnant again and remained at Lethington with her little boy while Morton's troopers wasted the estate.

Knox raged against me from the pulpit, claiming I had threatened his life. So I offered him a guard and my personal guarantee of safety. He refused both and demanded to continue preaching against the Queen and our cause. Eventually he was persuaded by his young wife to depart to St Andrews. Once, in another age, we were comrades there, besieged together by the French. I feel the loss of that great man's prophetic spirit, yet he is blinded by his hatred of the Queen and fears her restoration like a plague of devils. When did she deny his right to faith in our Lord Jesus?

Maitland is determined to secure a diplomatic triumph. But while his mind continues agile as before his body is giving up the struggle. First his legs and then his belly refused to do their part. Though eating little, his frame began to swell. He had to be carried everywhere in a litter by four men, his resolve undying.

It seemed we could hold out, relying on Elizabeth's refusal to release the Queen or fund an army to put us down. But then I made my second error, agreeing to a truce. The town was weary and disaffected, with more houses damaged by the day. The Netherbow Port was hard to hold, and we had to pull down more houses and build a second gatehouse.

The fighting ceased, and Edinburgh was reopened to trade and movement. But they tricked us and reoccupied the town by force. As negotiation dragged on for months our kingdom shrank to a single fortress. But we would not surrender Mary's right or betray the lords who remained loyal allies. So Morton went instead to buy off Huntly and the Hamiltons.

Now we are alone. While Maitland talks of French or even Spanish aid, we look out at hostile territory on every side.

Mar died still desiring peace, though he could not have it, and Morton finally stepped into the place he coveted so long. He is our greatest foe, since only our deaths fit his purpose. They trench and tighten a ring round the castle rock. I begin to weary.

English cannon are brought north. Siegeworks are laid, gun embrasures mounted, the town walled off and the blockade made secure. Nothing like it has been seen since the siege of Haddington. The jaws are cunningly positioned to close on us from each side with crossfire. We have neither range nor shot to reply in kind. I set the town alight to try and drive them back, but fail to burn the besiegers out, and only draw the hatred of the people on my head.

This struggle has consumed my better self. I have only my will to sustain me, my refusal to deny Her Majesty a second, or a third time. I cannot surrender my honour as it is all that remains.

Every muscle drained and rarely out of armour.

Margaret is gaunt and white, doling out the rations with an iron hand. As the weeks and months drag out I watch her lose faith in my cause. Now she is loyal only out of duty, and shows no inclination towards love. But a young lass comes to my bed and warms my limbs. They used to say I was a lamb at home and like a lion in the field, but even in these wasting days a fire can stir. Life has ground us down till only such wanton acts restore us to ourselves.

Was Bothwell right in this if nothing else? I should have had more women to indulge my manhood. When death stares you in the face, it helps to forget mortality for a moment.

The towers came down today. Yesterday the curtain wall collapsed onto the gatehouse, taking our remaining guns along with it. Their aim is deadly. Maitland is in the cellars day and night, as he cannot bear the noise. The Maiden Castle has crumbled round us.

When the spur was overrun three days since, many of our men took the chance to slip away. We have barely a hundred fit to fight and even they are thirsty, hungry, worn. Margaret stands like a wraith between scant rations and their rage.

They cannot go on and are ready to turn on me unless I end their ordeal. Dust is in our mouths and nostrils. It fills the air like smoke. The wells have been stopped for weeks and we hold out our tongues for rain.

Today I will have myself lowered from the upper wall onto the ruins and surrender under terms. I must give the Castle into Scottish hands, never English. But I cannot entrust myself or Maitland into Morton's keeping. I have ever been a friend to England and though Edinburgh cries for blood, the English army will protect us from their vengeance.

The time has come to finish. Raise a white flag. Let's be done.

Sister Beth

'NOT THE RATS. Please, take them away. I'll eat anything else.'

'Sister, Sister, you're alright.'

'Stop the cannon. I can't bear it. Not another siege. God spare me, I cannot live on vermin. My flesh is parched already.'

'Drink this, Beth. Sit up and lean on my arm. See, smell it.'

'Is it you, Francesca? Wet my lips. That's better, Christ and his Holy Mother be praised.'

'Again, Sister. That's good. It'll calm you.'

'Was I raving?'

'About the siege.'

'I thought I heard the guns.'

'We're too far away to hear them. Maybe just a slight rumble now and then. If it's not thunder.'

'Poor souls, they might starve shut up in that castle. Once I would have smuggled in supplies.'

'No one's starving, Sister. When your fever lowers you'll eat plenty, believe me.'

'Have I finished the writing?'

'We haven't touched it for ages. Would you like to do anymore? I'll fetch my things.'

'No, Francesca. I've done with all the memories, or they've done with me. Bundle it all up.'

'And bury it, Sister?'

'No, lass, I'm no that gyte yet. I want to give it all up.'

'To whom, Sister? There are some delicate...'

'Aye, I ken it's no saintly tale. But Bothwell won't have it.'

'He's still in prison, so they say.'

'May he stay there and rot for what he did to my bonny daughter. My lovely wee lamb, fouled and raped and God knows what else. May the rats eat his flesh.'

'Shall I take it to Hailes?'

'Don't be stupid, girl. I'm done with the Hepburns and all their works. I'll be their woman no longer.'

'Well what do you want me to do, Sister?'

'I'm not long for breathing, that's for sure. Bundle the pages up, every last one, and take them to Lady Maitland.'

'Mary Fleming.'

'Aye the Queen's Mary. I was her Mary once too. Poor woman. She's in prison again and without a good Scots lady to tend her this time.'

'Shall I go to Lethington then?'

'Aye and put it into her own hands. She'll know, or her man will know, what to do, if he ever gets out of that castle alive. Morton wants his head.'

'You're very clear today, Sister. You must be better.'

'Dinnae haver, lass. I'm a done old wandering woman, and you've been a comfort to me. I've left it all to you, Francesca, and the convent. You'll not want while Beth Hepburn has a guinea to her name. Everything except the bundle. I can't find peace of mind till that's laid somewhere to rest.'

'Don't talk that way, Sister, I'll deliver the writings, and come back to tell you what happened. And you can tell me again about the Queen and Earl Bothwell, over a warming supper.'

'I'll not tarnish my lips with his name. Say a rosary with me, and then I'll put my head down to rest. There's a good girl. I can sleep now at last.'

John Knox

An account of the prophet's last days by his Secretary, Bannatyne

WE RETURNED TO Edinburgh in August after a truce was signed between the King's lords and the Queen's party in the castle. As we were not able to go to our former house we were given the goldsmith's mansion in the Netherbow. Its owner was in the castle and had been outlawed for coining. On the first Sunday I helped Master Knox up to St Giles and into the pulpit, but his voice was so feeble that none could hear, and many wept to see the great prophet so decayed and broken.

Most of the time Master Knox remained in bed dictating his 'History' and sometimes writing, rising perhaps once or twice to meet with a visitor or take some nourishment. A small hall was fitted out in the aisles of the church so that he could address the congregation, and many crowded in to hear his words, expounding still the Word of God.

When news came of the terrible massacre of Protestants in Paris his wonted fire and pronounced the judgment of God on the persecutors of His chosen servants. Then he called for Edinburgh Castle to be pulled down on the heads of the ungodly. He warned that if Mary was not silenced her siren voice would once again woo our nation from the path of righteousness, and worked to such a pitch of fury that those who heard him trembled for their lives. He called for the Queen to die that justice might finally be done for her apostasy, adultery, murder and deceit. Neither Scotland nor England could be secure while she remained alive. He swayed the minds and hearts of all the people against her cause, and even her life.

That was his last Sunday sermon. He seemed to sense that time was short. He wrote to Secretary Cecil thanking him for his support, and saying that, while he would have liked to serve the Lord in England, his calling had lain here in Scotland where the labour, though hard, had been fruitful in this miserable wilderness.

He wrote to James Lawson, his chosen successor, urging him to come quickly before it was too late. The day after he attended Lawson's induction he was unable to rise. His breathing was troubled and terrible coughing racked his chest. Master Knox never left the house again.

After the doctor prescribed cordials and some wine, the Master improved and was able to sit up in bed and listen to Mistress Margaret or myself reading from the scriptures. Many friends and public men came to pay their respects and wish him farewell. One evening he was able to get up for supper with some guests, and ordered a new barrel of wine to be broached. Jesting, he ordered everyone to drink their fill since he would not live to drain the cask.

The next morning, however, his fever rose again and he tried to get up to preach thinking it was Sunday. I called the Mistress and she soothed him back to rest.

That evening the Earl of Morton came and sat on the bed. I was at a distance but heard the Master ask if Morton had foreknowledge of Darnley's death. He denied it, and then my Master looked earnestly at him saying that since he was Regent he must mend his ways and serve the Lord in righteousness all his days. Then he gave the Douglas a benediction. As he left the chamber there were tears in Morton's eyes and he took brusque leave of our house.

When James Lawson came the Master could barely speak, but he urged him to go with the Minister of Leith one last time to try and win back Kirkcaldy's soul from the brink.

'Tell him, my once dear William,' he whispered, drawing painful breath, 'that he will miserably perish, since neither the craggy rock in which he trusts, nor the carnal prudence of that godless Maitland he considers like a god, nor the aid of foreigners, will deliver him. Instead he will be disgracefully dragged from his nest and hung on the gallows in the face of the sun. How near his soul is to me, if only I could save him from the fires of punishment.'

He fell back exhausted and did not speak again that night.

The next morning, which was his last, he rose and after sitting awhile in his chair returned to bed, commending his young family to the care of friends. At midday the young Mistress read to him the fifteenth chapter of Corinthians, 'O Death where is thy sting; O grave where is thy victory.' In a voice barely audible he commended his own soul and body to the Lord.

But at five o'clock after sleeping through the afternoon, he suddenly spoke out in a strong voice. 'Go read where I first cast my anchor.' Margaret Stewart knew what he meant and turned to the seventeenth chapter of John.

'I have glorified thee on the earth; I have finished the work thou gavest me to do. And now, O Father, glorify me with thine own self, with the glory which I had with thee before the world was. I have manifested thy name unto the men thou gavest me out of the world... O righteous Father the world has not known thee: but I have known thee, and they have known that you sent me.'

From time to time he was able to take a sip of weak ale held to his lips, and at seven o'clock he fell asleep. At ten o'clock when he was accustomed to say evening prayers he stirred. The doctor lent over to ask if he could hear the prayers being said.

'I would to God that you and all men could hear them as I have. I praise God for that heavenly sound.'

An hour later he died with the Mistress at his bedside.

The funeral was in St Giles, and Regent Morton gave the oration. 'There lies one who neither feared nor flattered any flesh. He has gone to his reward.'

Maitland of Lethington

THIS ROOM IS my world. First I was reduced to a castle and now a prison chamber, while my limbs swell and sweat. So it was for the Queen's mother before she yielded her life. Yet in death she eluded captive bands. The enemy has overrun my body but my spirit is untaken.

My mind is still in my own keeping. Even while they fetch away the issue of my flesh.

I refuse defeat because our cause is right. Only confinement such as this puts Her Majesty at the mercy of Catholic plots and English malice. This is her kingdom and I will die within it in earnest of my loyalty, my conviction of her just cause and unblemished name.

But not at their hands. Maitland will not be handled by usurpers. By my couch I have a balm for all my woes. I can die like an ancient Roman.

Will that give the godly satisfaction? To say I departed as a pagan stoic?

I pull the stopper and pour out a little on the ground. Then place the phial back in my satchel. If death comes to me unsummoned, they can never tell the manner or the form of Maitland's passing. I defy their shitting prophets and all the mean foolishness of men. I have ensured these words will outlast my mortal frame.

Let the garments wither. Maitland will endure uncorrupted. My love is beyond any taint. God preserve you, Fleming. And may Kirkcaldy rest in peace.

I am resolute and composed. I regard these strange sensations with disdain. I am, yet awhile, Maitland. *Maître. Magus.*

Bothwell

FUCKING WHORE. I'LL stake you here and now. And whip your skin to red ribbons.

No, I don't want to sniff your tail. Get out of here you foul lying bitch. And take your scales and stinking fish.

I am the King. Everybody feeds on me. Gnaw. Gnaw. Bloody gnaw.

If I catch just one of you fat little bastards I'll crunch your bones and chew off your head. I am a mountain, a citadel, flesh. This is my body that cannot be broken. Tough, yet it can be chewed.

Here is the last King of Scots. Eat me now, and let me rule the dark.

One day I'll run along the riverbed and feel the water flowing on my bones.

Christ, how I long for my own land. In that other country.

Final Reckonings
England and France, 1586–1597

James Maitland

HOW VIVID THOSE last fatal months become across the gap of years. Only William Maitland's resolve to steer events, with Kirkcaldy's determination to purge the stain on his honour, could have continued the hopeless defence of Edinburgh Castle. The St Bartholomew's Day atrocity in France swung opinion in England and then Scotland away from Queen Mary. Events had moved far beyond the control of her last loyal allies.

The vindictiveness of the Scottish lords after the castle's ruin was beyond reason or measure. Morton was merciless. My mother, Mary Fleming, pleaded for the return of my father's body. But Regent Morton commanded that the corpse be tried for treason and then brutally dissolved. Only a direct appeal to Queen Elizabeth averted this outrage. Nonetheless Morton kept the body in Leith until rats ran freely in and out beneath the door. Finally William Maitland was sealed in lead and laid to rest in Haddington.

Lady Margaret Kirkcaldy was even less fortunate. One hundred gentlemen of Scotland, from all parties, pledged five thousand crowns for her husband's security. This was an exceptional tribute in a time of civil war. But, unusually for Morton, he desired Kirkcaldy's lasting silence at any price. Sir William was hung, drawn and quartered and months later his broken remnants were cast into an unmarked pit in Greyfriars. Only recently have his mortal remains been returned to the family vault in Fife.

They died brave and unyielding. Yet I can see their cause was lost long before these days of desperate courage. It died at Kirk o' Field.

Who killed Henry Darnley, and why? Many have ceased to ask the question, which was then on every lip, because they believe that Mary caused his death. And that is why she was overthrown. So history is read in reverse.

Like a puzzle master I must lay out all the pieces and order them afresh. When assembled I believe that they will reveal a picture very different from the one that has become so popular. For what can compete with the allure of an adulteress and seducer who incites her lover to murder her own husband and then marries him? Especially when the principal actors are kings and queens.

Who killed Henry Darnley? The main instruments were James Balfour and Morton's cousin, Archibald Douglas. It was Douglas, along with Kerr of Fawdonside and other ruffians, who strangled Darnley in the orchard. So Morton was avenged for the Rizzio betrayal and his exile.

But it was Balfour who devised a double plot with Bothwell as its seeming instrument; Morton and Moray were behind him in the shadows. Weak minded Darnley was convinced by Balfour that the Queen's assassination was the only way to preserve his own life and moreover gain the crown. So Darnley agreed to come to Balfour's house at Kirk o' Field where a large quantity of gunpowder would be stored in the cellars.

When the torchlit escort from Holyrood signalled Mary's return from

Holyrood, the fuse would be fired and Darnley make his escape. Bothwell would delay the Queen's arrival to prevent any danger. On the night this plan nearly unravelled when Mary changed her mind about staying at Kirk o' Field. However Bothwell set out regardless, torches ablaze, knowing Mary to be completely out of harm's way. Taken by surprise Darnley gave the hurried order and had himself lowered in a chair from the window as intended, but in his nightshirt.

The supposed purpose was to expose Darnley as a traitor so that he could be imprisoned and divorced, not slain. Bothwell was party to this design as was my father. But Morton and Moray, in league with Cecil, had decided to go further and kill the King. Unlike Maitland, Bothwell was content to see Darnley dead and his path to Mary cleared. But the others had a longer, deeper aim. They wanted Darnley silenced and Bothwell blamed. They knew that his involvement would taint Mary by association and rock the throne. So Bothwell was duped and for a moment my father's attention had fatally strayed.

That was dark diplomacy, but Cecil's hand reached far into our affairs. He constantly primed Moray to believe that he should reign in Scotland, by right of religion, in his sister's place. When Moray's rebellion against the Darnley marriage failed and Elizabeth disowned him, Cecil covertly encouraged Rizzio's slaughter, which threatened Mary's own life. And conveniently restored Moray.

But the master stroke was the return of Morton from exile, engineered by Cecil in exchange for Elizabeth's agreement to become Prince James' guardian. Rather than see two Queens united against him, he prompted Morton's hand. There was no accident in that sequence, no chaos of events, but cunning design. Even Knox was used as a channel to the zealots, so that the campaign of placards denouncing Bothwell, and then Mary, was begun before Darnley's corpse was in its grave.

The escape from Lochleven upset his calculations. Even Morton had baulked at judicial murder of the Queen, allowing a reverse. Only Kirkcaldy's generalship at Langside saved the day and drove the butterfly back into Cecil's sticky web. Elizabeth's own reluctance to condone judicial murder dragged out the drama, but its final act had always been foreseen.

What did my father know of this? Cecil's remorseless enmity he understood. He was party to the plot to remove Darnley from the scene but did he guess at worse and avert his gaze? If there was one man that Maitland wholeheartedly despised it was Bothwell. Did his mind divide into two compartments, each denying knowledge of the other? In one he saw the consequences for Mary of Darnley's assassination. But in the other, with a gambler's calculation, he allowed things to proceed to the chance of Bothwell's fall. In Scotland old enmities are like rocks beneath the heather.

When events spun out of control, Maitland was feverishly driven to action. Perhaps on this wider stage he could devise a solution. His diplomatic and legal mind perceived an opportunity where others saw only disaster. He relished the chance to show his paces in this crisis. The fatal error might yet be retrieved.

Her Majesty of Scotland was now to be accused in England but not tried, since one Queen cannot sit in judgment on another. So a joint Commission was established between England and Scotland to consider the circumstances of Darnley's murder and Mary's supposed abdication.

George Buchanan compiled the evidence against the Queen, for whom he had played both poet and playwright. But Buchanan was Protestant and republican, while his family owed allegiance to the Earls of Lennox. None could have been more vindictive or inventive in his lurid inventions of adultery, begun with Bothwell mere weeks after Prince James' birth, and followed by deceit and entrapment of poor Darnley, rightful King of Scots. His 'Detection' is notorious, but remains the contagious source of Mary's blackened name.

But Mary had strong support amongst English lords, not least the Catholic sympathisers, and Elizabeth rigidly upheld her royal prerogatives. Buchanan's fiction needed proofs. Now Moray and Morton had to produce evidence against her for examination. The private letters, so far unshown to any but themselves, must justify the overthrow of one rightful Queen to another. So work began sifting the papers seized at Holyrood and Dunbar.

These papers are separately bound and wrapped. They are not in my father's hand but copies of other letters, or at least extracts from them. The letters are annotated but the identity writer is unclear. The letters purport to be written by Queen Mary and implicate her in the murder. Either my father was party to the falsehoods, in form at least, or he discovered the mechanism of the plot from an inside source, Scottish or English.

As for myself, if I hear nothing from you to the contrary, I will bring the man to Craigmillar on Monday. And I will go to Edinburgh to be bled.

He is the merriest that you ever saw, and shows me by every means he can that he loves me. You would think he is making love to me, which gives me so much joy that the pain in my side starts up. It is sore today but when Paris brings me his commission it will make amends.

Please send me your news in general, and what I should do if you have not returned when I arrive. For if you are not wise, I can see the whole burden falling on my shoulders. Provide for all and consider well.

Beneath this letter is subscribed, 'A short letter from Glasgow to the Earl Bothwell. Proves her disdain against her husband.' This is crossed out and replaced with 'written by Her Majesty to her husband Lord Darnley concerning her 'man', the infant Prince James. And a commission for medicines.' A longer letter follows.

He prayed me to come again, which I did, and told me his grief, and that I was the cause of his sickness because I was estranged from him, in these words.

'You ask what I meant in my letters by your cruelty. I mean your refusal to accept my repentance. I have done amiss, but so have many of your subjects and you pardoned them. I am young. You'll say you have forgiven me many times but I return to my faults. But may someone of my age for lack of counsel fail sometimes and miss the mark, yet in the end repent and rebuke himself from his own experience? If I get your pardon I will never fall short again, and plead nothing except we be at bed and table again as husband and wife. And if I don't I will never rise from this bed. Tell me your resolution, for God knows I am punished for making you my God and having no other mind but of you. When we are separated anything I hear about you stays in my brain and incites my troubled wits to anger.'

He wanted me to stay with him in his lodging, but I refused saying he had to be purged and that could not be done here. I told him I would take him myself to Craigmillar so that the physicians and I could cure him away from my son. He said he was ready to go with me as soon as I decided to leave.

He would not let me go, but wanted me to watch with him. I made out as if I believed it all, though I had heard it so many times before, and that I would think upon it. I excused myself from sitting with him due to his lack of sleep. You never heard someone speak so humbly and contritely, and were it not I know his heart to be of wax and mine of diamond, no stroke except one from your pen, could prevent me pitying him. But fear not, this fortress will endure till death.

I am weary and asleep, yet I cannot stop scribbling as long as there is paper. Cursed be this pocky fellow that gives me so much grief, for I have much pleasanter things to write were it not for him. He is not much deformed in face but socially repulsive. I was nearly killed with his breath, though I sat no closer than the bolster and he was on the far side of his bed.

He has great suspicion, yet trusts in my word, but not so far as to tell me all he is devising. However if you want me to disclose to him then I will draw all out, though I will never be willing to deceive someone who puts his trust in me. He will not come unless I am with him at bed and board as before. Nevertheless you may command me in all things, and do not think less of me for it, since you are the cause. I would not do this for my own revenge.

This letter, without address or signature like the first, is subscribed, 'the long letter written from Glasgow by the Queen of Scots to the Earl of Bothwell'. Once more the subscription is crossed out and replaced by 'a composite letter composed from correspondence to the Earl of Moray from Glasgow, and letters to the Earl of Bothwell after he was married to the Queen.' One further paragraph is appended by itself.

The bearer of this will tell you much more on my authority. It is late and I have many things to write, so you can trust his word. He will go anywhere on my instruction. Alas, I never deceived anyone, but I submit entirely to your will. Send me your will and I will obey you in all things. Take counsel with yourself if you cannot find some secret medicine, for he will take physic and the baths at Craigmillar. He may be there for a long time.

Below this is written, 'Of the Earl Bothwell, and of the lodging in Edinburgh.' Beside this is scribbled in an uncertain hand, 'Not Craigmillar, Kirk o' Field. Manifest falsehood.'

There is a short account of the supposed trial written by my father, but much later. By this time he was already besieged in Edinburgh Castle, and looking back in justification. He refers to the letters but does not quote from them or acknowledge the existence of these copies, if that is what they are.

Their side pressed for written proof or evidence. Moray protests reluctance, unwilling to blacken his sister's name, or be the means to incriminate her. Yet at the same time he was seeking a secret guarantee before he showed his hand – that Mary would not be restored whatever the outcome.

Morton set a silver casket on the table, the one reputedly secured from Bothwell's servants. And piece by piece, despite Moray's feigned protests, Secretary Wood snatches out the letters to be displayed. They were copied by Cecil's clerks and then returned.

George Buchanan and Wood worked the deceit together, but Buchanan authored the story. A beautiful but adulterous queen plots with her lover to secretly kill her husband the King. Then the murderer joins his paramour on the throne, threatening the welfare of her young son, the prince and heir. Tyranny reigns triumphant and true religion is set at naught.

Together these two learned scholars tortured French Paris, extracted a false confession, and had him hanged in St Andrews. Yet as the noose tightened his last words were 'I took no letters to Lord Bothwell from the Queen in Glasgow.' He proclaims their lie even on the scaffold, and is silenced.

The final work is artful since nothing has been entirely forged, merely altered by date, time or recipient. So letters to Darnley pretend to be written to Bothwell, while letters and love poems sent by one of Bothwell's many women are passed off as Mary's.

It seems persuasive, not least to those who already want to believe the worst. Until fabrication is matched against known facts. Why should the Queen write from Glasgow to Bothwell in Edinburgh, on the eve of Darnley's return? He had just left Her Majesty to attend to matters in the Borders, as she knew. Why accuse her of plotting Darnley's death at Kirk o' Field, while publishing her intention to seclude him at Craigmillar Castle?

Not even Cecil could swallow such a confection whole. So proceedings must be suspended, moved to London with the membership widened or watered down, Elizabeth consulted, and so forth. The blunt truth is it would not hold up, so things must be fudged; conclusions were no longer palatable. Mary could not be condemned; nor could she be restored without damning Moray and the Protestant lords.

I proposed the Queen should marry Norfolk, England's premier peer, and share the sovereignty in Scotland with her son. Or live honourably in England as Queen Dowager, protecting James' inheritance and the union of the two crowns in due season. This was statesmanlike compromise with an end to war, murder, and calumny.

But Moray could not abide her freedom. He feared any challenge to his version of events. He has become trapped within his own falsehoods. To defend the lie of Mary's guilt, many men have been ruthlessly destroyed. No other version of events can be allowed. All is justified by religion and the security of England, even deceiving its Queen.

I marvel how the godly can convince themselves that foul means are justified by pious ends. They believe so firmly in their righteousness that any contrary evidence can be excluded. The Good Regent betrayed Norfolk's correspondence to Elizabeth before she had been consulted. His actions take Norfolk to the Tower and eventually the scaffold. His own sister he condemns to imprisonment in England. She is too dangerous to release, but risky to confine. Our Queen has the worst of both worlds, while Moray was left to rule in Scotland for a time.

I came back to Lethington. Not even my infant son, nor Fleming's pregnancy, could raise my spirits from the slough. I was ignored at Court and Council while, bit by bit, Moray tamed dissent and brought the land to heel by force of arms, judicial execution, and the bribery of office. The Prince remained at Stirling guarded by Mar and tutored by Buchanan, the man who named his mother whore and murderess.

My father's arrest and rescue by Kirkcaldy followed, along with their seclusion in the castle. For them the final act had commenced.

Cecil's hatred though was still unslaked. He was determined on Mary's death, nothing less sufficing. He feared that in her confinement the Catholic Queen became an even greater threat to England than she had been reigning in Scotland. In pursuit of his master's goal, Walsingham directed a constant flow of provocation towards Mary's inner circle to lure her into treasonable communication. Most English Catholics dwell in dread and caution, so these pledges of imminent restoration appeared from associates of Spain or the Papacy, at several removes. Yet Cecil magnified the dangers, painted rebellion in apocalyptic hues, and prevented Elizabeth at any cost from helping her royal cousin.

Everything returns to Mary. She is the force of attraction and repulsion that moved events. She is the creature at the centre of the labyrinth, the monstrous woman as Knox would have it, born to rule. But in her we find a source of truth, and beauty – a legitimate Queen whose faithfulness upheld the rights of our ancient nation.

All along she has tried to tell her story but few have listened. We prefer the mermaid whore or a martyr sealed in holy silence. It has been my privilege to go beyond the veil.

Amidst the papers I received at Rheims is a brief note written by Mary Seton, when still confined in England.

'Though all the world stand against us, my trust in Mary remains steadfast. In love that surrenders life itself, we find our purpose and our deepest joy. I thank God for what I have known and would not have chosen any other path than to serve Her Majesty.'

This is the authentic voice of the shadow who shelters in the Abbey St Pierre. She left it for us to find before age and time could silence her. I thank her for allowing me to tell this story, and gain my release. At last I am free to find my own way of love, unhindered by the shackles of the past.

Mary

SETON LEAVES ME tomorrow, early in the morning. She is worn down by our hardships and seems twice her age. All of her youth was devoted to my service and now she has been sacrificed to our misfortune. I remember her coming to my side even at Carberry Hill. Now I must let her depart, though it tears my own heart.

Imprisonment wastes and wears. That, at least, I have learned in England. My household shrinks as we are confined to smaller and stonier quarters. Damp runs down these walls till each month and year is imprinted in my flesh, my aching bones.

The dignity of my Court is lost. I cannot get my rents from France so everyone must make do and mend. Fortunately I can sew and embroider. I owe that to Grannie Bourbon, who has not written to me for many years.

I commend Seton to my aunt at Rheims. She will care for her bodily needs and comfort her soul. To all who love me I am faithful and generous. Through my intercession Lady Margaret Kirkcaldy is also at Rheims. They can pray at my mother's grave while I remain entombed in England.

I can see no hope of release. Failing an invasion, my days are prescribed. They are at Elizabeth's disposal, the cousin who cannot look me in the face, far less treat me as sisters should. I am at her mercy without hope of alteration. She cannot see me alive nor bear to have me dead. Her features are closed to me; she has become more mask than woman

So I have gathered up my papers, letters and journals, to send away to Rheims. Seton will hide them in her person and keep them secure till need arises. I have always depended on Seton, more than all my other Marys, who left me one by one to marry. Perhaps I have presumed on her devotion.

Now I place my reputation in her trustworthy hands. Who will dress my hair? From this time forwards I may have to wear my wig. Whatsoever, Seton must go, before English servitude stops her breath for ever. She is the last, sorely missed by me above all others.

Grannie Bourbon said I married beneath me and so brought disaster on my own head. None is left to intercede on my behalf. The Medici always despised and envied me. When *Maman* was in Scotland, and the snake glowered on my charms, Annette de Bourbon was my mainstay and consolation. Now I am bereft of family. I am finally alone.

Beside my bed I have the double portrait of my infant son and of his father. Framed in gold they are always before my eyes, the altarpiece of my devotion.

They say I connived to murder Darnley. False; all lies and treachery. God knows he repaid my love in bitter coin, but I never sought his death. He was the father of my child, our heir and successor, pledge of the double crown. Despite his cruelty, the violence of his assault on Rizzio and on my person, I needed Henry Stewart to live. I was the greatest loser by his annihilation. Those who slaughtered Darnley aimed at my destruction first, and when that failed, they used his death to pull me down into the mire. We were both victims of their dark devising – to besmirch my name and defile my crown. Filth was their natural element.

Morton, Balfour, Bothwell, aye Bothwell, were the guilty ones. Even Maitland looked aside and pretended to some deeper scheme. So many nobles gave assent, but Moray's was the guiding hand. And, behind him, hateful Cecil. Could they not see the price Scotland would pay for such royal assassination? Most were blinded by lusts for land and revenge.

Yet my brother, the good Lord James, aimed at my downfall from the start. I see that now. I was innocent of his resentment and his craving for power. Even wealth was just the means to a long harboured end. I did not understand the Bastard's need, burning beneath that impassive brow. It was not just that he desired my place; he wove a net of calumny and falsehood in which to trap me. I was innocent, uncomprehending of such malign intent. He wore a mask of reason, and wrapped himself in the guise of piety. But he became the direst traitor, a tool of English policy and cunning.

Yesterday I had word from Prince James in Scotland. It is the first time he has written to me, despite all my presents, notes and anxious solicitations through the long years of captivity. My child, my grown up boy whom I have not seen or touched since they took him from my arms as a baby. He was not allowed to write nor ever shown my letters. But now he has come of age. My royal son.

James utterly repudiates my claim to restoration. He will countenance neither the compromise of shared rule, nor my return to Scotland. Subservient to Elizabeth's desires, he has set me aside in favour of his own succession to the English throne. He wants to call me Queen Mother. Words cold and sharp as a blade.

False, ungrateful child. Have I endured so long to be spurned by my own son? What unnatural offspring could deny his own birth in such callous fashion? Like me he was divided from his parents in infancy, yet dearly loved, never abandoned. What have they done to him? Moray, Morton and Buchanan – the teacher who calls me 'whore' to his face. They have frozen his heart and turned his love to iron disdain.

Merciful Lord, grant me strength in my weakness. Supplant my will with thine and help me to submit. Drive out unruly desires, and be thou only Master of my passion. Make me alone your dwelling place, your cell, your desert and retreat. Sole spouse of Christ.

It is not my first captivity. As the world knows I was imprisoned in Lochleven Castle. Long before I was given refuge on an island; then I was confined on one, in breach of every guarantee and promise. In defiance of my rights and status. My life hung by a thread. Like the Princes in the Tower my death would be convenient and unseen.

I was not able to defend myself, or even to understand my situation. They demanded I repudiate Earl Bothwell, but I carried his bairn in my womb. Bairns, as it turned out. He was my lawful husband, not paramour or illicit lover. I lay numbed by pain and shock till in a bloody flux I lost the tiny babes.

To this infirm state, weak from loss of blood, fevered and inflamed in all my lower parts, came Lord Lindsay threatening death unless I signed their abdication. Not mine. Never mine. Even in my extremity I am the Queen; I do not renounce my crown. Only God's decree can remove what has been ordained for me. I signed their papers under duress, knowing that my brother Moray was hastening to Lochleven to relieve my oppression and distress.

Then finally I knew James for what he is, or was. God does not forget; his judgments are sure and just. The smouldering fire of his resentment, the determination to rule in my place, the cold anger. He harangued me like some canting preacher. The muscles worked beneath his impassive mask.

John Knox had more fellow feeling than my own brother. He called me murderer and adulterer and left me a whole night trembling in expectation of a violent end. He proved what I had known but not experienced directly for myself – how religion could be an instrument of hate and fear. So I named him Regent in my place and prepared for long imprisonment or early death.

He did not live long to enjoy his mean triumph. Shot down in his prime by a Hamilton bullet. Even tenacious Morton is deposed and brought to trial in Scotland. The mills grind slow but sure. God pulls the tyrants from their throne and raises the oppressed. They deserved their end.

How things come round. A wheel without remorse or remedy.

I still have the ring that Fleming sent me on the island. The lion is bound while a faithful mouse gnawsthenet. Time and patience, Maitland was trying to tell me. So many years ago. I maun thole.

Now I embroider the cat and the mouse. A big striped ugly ginger cat, playing with its prey. Who does that remind us of? What truths there are in simple creatures. Where would I be without my little darling dogs? They know their mother and run to my hand to nuzzle and pet. We spoil each other with our titbits and chatter. Such pleasures are a comfort for creatures made to give and receive love.

My supposed letters have been published for all to gloat over. Discovered by Morton like long lost treasure in a casket, they are Moray's artifice. Now Cecil spreads them about, though covertly for fear of Elizabeth's disapproval. Am I not still Queen? Perhaps even the hate filled Secretary is shamed to openly put his name to such blatant fabrication. Having presumed to try a reigning monarch like some common criminal, he then resorts to blackening me in the court of opinion. And those who want to believe give eager credence.

Yet their story bears scant examination. It is a tissue of half-truths, sleights of hand and brazen forgery. All mixed with a dramatist's most tempting devices – secret passion, adultery, treason, murder. Seneca would be proud. It should be made a stage play for the multitude. How could Buchanan, scholar of truth, my royal poet, stoop so low as to become Moray's crooked scalpel?

In my lifetime, I have been garlanded by two great poets, Master Ronsard and Maister Buchanan. The first has proved true gold, the second base metal. Given my teachers in the Muse, how could anyone think I penned such dreadful poems as the woman in those letters? That I, a queen, should write like some abandoned mistress would be laughable, if not beneath contempt. Bothwell was well supplied with discarded paramours, so they had a choice of falsehoods.

It was Ronsard who first praised me to the Muse, and my honour is still protected by his art. Faithful Ronsard, when others fall away, you remember me in sickness and in trouble.

I did not conspire with Bothwell. Is that not clear for all to see? Yes, when Darnley abused me and when he died, I leaned on Hepburn's strong arm for my defence. What else could I do, surrounded as I was by divisive faction, disloyal magnates, and greedy lords. They had tried to kill me and my infant in the womb. They lured me to Kirk o' Field intending my destruction. No woman could resist such an attack alone. Bothwell was my protector and I had every right to depend on his loyal service and to reward him. My hardy Border Earl.

But he was not satisfied with being my chief support and counsellor. He seized me at Almond Brig and carried me away to Dunbar Castle. Like Darnley he wanted to be King of Scotland; to possess Scotland he needed to secure my person. I was in a daze or sleep, numbed by the fear of all that had passed and might still come. I gave way, surrendering myself to his strong embrace and so to marriage. What else was left me, alone and threatened on all sides?

Did something in Hepburn stir and excite? He was a man of action and of danger, no politic courtier. A hairy Esau to Maitland's smooth Jacob. I had not been intimate with such a man. Yet, if I were attracted, the allure was soon proved false. He was unfeeling in his relations, callous and domineering.

If, for a passing moment, I thought I could return to my first gallant knight, I was cruelly deceived. When Bothwell had an equal share in my body and in the offices of state, then he told me of his part in Darnley's death. I was no murderer but I had married one.

He had allowed Balfour to lead Darnley on with his crazy Catholic plot, while coldly planning with the other lords to have him killed. Now I was in Bothwell's power, as later I would be in Moray's prison. The protector was in truth a predator. So I simply exchanged one captivity for another. And this is now my third, in England.

I am no longer able to ride. My gaolers do not want me out and about in the country, even under armed escort. So much they fear England's Catholic queen. Sadly my limbs are no longer fit to guide that supple lovely creature beneath my flesh. I must be carried in a litter like some aged invalid.

Those last days of freedom seem like a dream. The escape by boat in disguise, the ride to Hamilton. How glad the people were to receive me. Then, after Langside, the desperate flight by day and night through the hills and down the valley of the Ken to Dundrennan. I could have lived wild in that country and endured all hardships. I should have been a soldier, not a queen.

Langside was my undoing. Brave Kirkcaldy, I salute you. If only you had drawn the sword for me when victory could still have been wrested from misfortune. Now you are gone into the dark as well, my own dear love, my gallant knight. Proud as a Scot you bore French arms, and we rode out together on the meadows as dew sparkled in the rising sun. I do not forget. I should have married for the heart and not the head; that is my one true loss amidst all the baubles. I have been too politic. I have been a queen first before all else. But I am womanly by nature.

Elizabeth tried to save me from Lochleven. She knew my life was endangered and sent Throckmorton to intervene and demand my release. So when the dream crumbled at Langside, I came to England, riding south by day and night with eight or nine men around me. They told me not to cross the border since an English refuge could only be false comfort to a Scottish queen.

But Elizabeth was my cousin, a sister queen, no hateful Medici. I knew that meeting face to face we would fall into each other's arms, as family should, and be firm, loving friends for life. That is why she will not see me, until one of us is dead.

I sat in the bows of a fishing boat, huddled in my cloak, as they rowed me over grey Solway. A sudden dread gripped me. Should I turn for France? The moment passed. I had struggled enough and could do no more. Bear no more violence, flights, alarms. Even prison would be more welcome than this constant fear. So I resigned myself to what might come.

The Marys were my best part. Fleming played mother, sometimes in earnest when I was bereft. Beaton was my foil, Livingston my freer self, and Seton my conscience. We were raised together and did not realise what we had. What is life without fun and mischief to leaven the duties of the day? We had our joys pressed down and running over. I should have kept the Marys' love closer round me in Scotland. I let other loyalties and cares intrude. Our ring was broken. They are all mature women now and lost to me, even Seton at the last.

But I can summon those memories and laugh aloud, even in this prison. I name each one of you for luck, and call a blessing on your heads. Fleming, Beaton, Livingston, Seton, and Mary Stewart. We are Five Marys, like a snatch or song from old forgotten times.

Small comforts cheer. Food and wine. My little dogs and turtle doves love me. Some new satins and a silver headdress. Silken threads for the embroideries run smooth between my still slender fingers. For the most part, resignation, prayer, repentance. It is not easy when feelings overwhelm and cruel neglect stares me in the face. Harsh pettifogging rules or worse, much worse. Outright rejection by those from whom love might be expected.

God does not fail me if I surrender to his holy will. Sweet Jesus, I have your thorn still. Help me in my hour of need.

I had thought to marry Norfolk and restore my fortunes. Bothwell was far away, like a forgotten season, his pleas unanswered. I am told he is turned lunatic, raving like a beast in chains. He was ever the bear ready for a fight, till biting on its own caged flesh he tears himself to death. I had severed all connection with that rash man, from the time his seed miscarried in my womb. So I divorced him who had been my undoing. Marriage to Norfolk might repair the damage. Maitland said it could be done.

But for some there could be no accommodation. Moray, Morton, Knox, and Cecil above all. With Walsingham his ruthless instrument of deceit and torture. They brought gallant Norfolk down and cut off all my hopes in England, and in Scotland. They could not abide any restoration lest their falsehood be exposed. I scorn their souls.

So I am Queen without a throne, but Queen regardless by birth and blood. I am Mary Queen of Scots, and heir to England. I cannot be divided from my legitimate line even in death. From my veins the blood of future kings will flow.

My claim is vested in the one true Catholic Faith. So I must look to Spain and Rome for succour. If Elizabeth will not help me, then her faithful Catholic subjects will. I shall live to see Cecil go to the block and suffer what he has contrived for others. So many loyal, devoted, broken and offered on the altar.

Seton will take my portrait with her in a roll of cloth. Full length in formal dress, you cannot see my swollen legs or thickened waist. I am myself in height, elegance, command. I wear the crucifix about my neck, a veil of mourning on my auburn locks. I own this image. The Catholic Queen. A Mary in devotion, sacrifice and faith. This is my body.

I was born to govern, but suffered tumult and revolt. I was raised beloved, and expected love, but have received harsh blows, hate, malign deceit. My passion longed for life, but man's cold indifference drove me back upon myself. Yet I remain every inch a Queen. My heart is my own. I stand unbowed.

The theatre of this world is wider than the realm of England. Other eyes will meet my gaze in places far beyond this island prison, in other times. So my days are swallowed up. Death itself may be the perfect art, if hand and eye keep steady.

Everything I am, and have been, was given to me by my mother. Birth, affection, honour, courage. So I take her own emblem to myself. The Phoenix who dies but is reborn. And I have sown her motto here below the sign. 'In my end is my beginning.'

Seton, please dear Seton, don't leave me now alone. God give me strength. I must let her go. Let all go. Subdue unruly heart and will.

This too will pass. Leave only my obedient self to stand. The earthly body spent, surrendered to decay.

Jesu, I put my hope in Thee
Dear Lord of mine, now set me free.
In cruel chains, in miserable pain I long –
In weakness and sighing, kneeling and crying –
To see Thee, freedom I implore.

Mary Stewart has written this by her own hand.

Questions for Discussion

In what ways does *Ballad of the Five Marys* match what you know about Mary Queen of Scots? In what ways does it contradict your expectations?

Which narrators do you trust in the story and which do you distrust? And why?

Is the Mary depicted in the novel a queen first and a woman second, or the other way round?

What does *Ballad of the Five Marys* tell us about the position of women in society, then and now?

Was Mary guilty, partly guilty, or wholly innocent of Darnley's murder? What are the reasons for your view?

Does James Maitland come to know his father better through the novel? What does he discover through his search and how is he left at the end?

Was Mary's judgement of men flawed, or were her choices just limited? What is your assessment of the men who mattered most in her life?

How do you see the characters of the Four Marys and the choices they make?

Is this just a historical story or does it tell us anything about Scottish society today?

Does the novel comment directly or indirectly on the question of Scottish Independence? And in what way?

Luath Press Limited

committed to publishing well written books worth reading

LUATH PRESS takes its name from Robert Burns, whose little collie Luath (*Gael.*, swift or nimble) tripped up Jean Armour at a wedding and gave him the chance to speak to the woman who was to be his wife and the abiding love of his life. Burns called one of the 'Twa Dogs' Luath after Cuchullin's hunting dog in Ossian's *Fingal*.
Luath Press was established in 1981 in the heart of Burns country, and is now based a few steps up the road from Burns' first lodgings on Edinburgh's Royal Mile. Luath offers you distinctive writing with a hint of unexpected pleasures.
Most bookshops in the UK, the US, Canada, Australia, New Zealand and parts of Europe, either carry our books in stock or can order them for you. To order direct from us, please send a £sterling cheque, postal order, international money order or your credit card details (number, address of cardholder and expiry date) to us at the address below. Please add post and packing as follows: UK – £1.00 per delivery address; overseas surface mail – £2.50 per delivery address; overseas airmail – £3.50 for the first book to each delivery address, plus £1.00 for each additional book by airmail to the same address. If your order is a gift, we will happily enclose your card or message at no extra charge.

Luath Press Limited
543/2 Castlehill
The Royal Mile
Edinburgh EH1 2ND
Scotland
Telephone: +44 (0)131 225 4326 (24 hours)
Fax: +44 (0)131 225 4324
email: sales@luath. co.uk
Website: www. luath.co.uk